The Apocalypse Exile

The Undead World Novel 6

By Peter Meredith

Fictional works by Peter Meredith:

A Perfect America
The Sacrificial Daughter
The Apocalypse Crusade War of the Undead: Day One
The Apocalypse Crusade War of the Undead: Day Two
The Apocalypse Crusade War of the Undead Day Three
The Horror of the Shade: Trilogy of the Void 1
An Illusion of Hell: Trilogy of the Void 2
Hell Blade: Trilogy of the Void 3
The Punished
Sprite
The Blood Lure The Hidden Land Novel 1
The King's Trap The Hidden Land Novel 2
To Ensnare a Queen The Hidden Land Novel 3
The Apocalypse: The Undead World Novel 1
The Apocalypse Survivors: The Undead World Novel 2
The Apocalypse Outcasts: The Undead World Novel 3
The Apocalypse Fugitives: The Undead World Novel 4
The Apocalypse Renegades: The Undead World Novel 5
The Apocalypse Exile: The Undead World Novel 6
The Apocalypse War: The Undead World Novel 7
The Apocalypse Executioner: The Undead World Novel 8
The Apocalypse Revenge: The Undead World Novel 9
The Edge of Hell: Gods of the Undead Book One
The Edge of Temptation: Gods of the Undead Book Two
Pen(Novella)
A Sliver of Perfection (Novella)
The Haunting At Red Feathers(Short Story)
The Haunting On Colonel's Row(Short Story)
The Drawer(Short Story)
The Eyes in the Storm(Short Story)
The Witch: Jillybean in the Undead World

Chapter 1

The Night Before

Jillybean/Eve

In the dead of night, the barn was worked over in shadows and even with her night eyes as tuned as they could be, the little girl could not make out the gun. It sat where the shadows pooled deeply and because it was the color of pitch itself, she had to find it by feel alone. She wished she could've plucked it up from memory, however that memory was being withheld from her. All she knew was that *he* carried one, somewhere.

When they had been waiting for the River King to deliver the renegades and the payment that he had promised in exchange for his pontoon bridge, she had seen *him* with the gun in his hands. Even the memory sent a shiver of hate down her back. She couldn't stand him with his stupid sweater vests and his gruesome face and his high and mighty attitude. He was as small and weak as a woman, and he was also bossy and mean and ugly, and by golly, he would pay.

First Neil would pay and then that stupid baby would get what was coming to her.

The baby would pay because she hated it, pure and simple, but with Neil, she had actual reasons to kill him. For one, he had taken her guns. They were hers by all rights. She had won them in combat...at least she had won the .22 in combat. She couldn't remember where she had picked up the .25 caliber handgun. It was sometime in the long ago. Her memory was like that. Things either happened yesterday or the day before or in the long ago when everything was hazy and all she saw in her mind were incomplete and blurry images. All that mattered was that she remembered the gun.

She also remembered the second bounty hunter they had sent to kill her...Earl? Ernie? Harold? His name was something like that, but it hardly mattered what it was, because he was dead. Earl or Ernie, or Harold had tried to kill her, only she had been quicker and smarter and he had been dumb and slow. He had thought that she was weak. But she wasn't. Jillybean was weak for sure. When Eve had shot the bounty hunter, Jillybean had been in tears over a stupid stuffed animal of all things.

Eve had shot Earl or Ernie, or Harold like a dog, just like she had shot the first bounty hunter—though in truth she liked dogs, except for the bitey-ones of course, and she wouldn't really shoot a dog, not unless she had to. And especially she wouldn't shoot a puppy. She loved puppies. They were always so soft and cute and they had such big paws for their size. She liked how they would trip over those paws when they were playing...

"Stop it, Jillybean!" Eve hissed under her breath. "I know what you're doing."

Jillybean was trying to distract her, trying to stop her, trying to keep her from doing what was right. It was right and good that Neil be made to pay. He had unfairly taken her guns and he also looked at her funny all the time and he always told her what to do and where to sit and when to eat. And worst of all, he kept saying: *I'm so sorry, Jillybean*, which was just bullshit.

Inside her, Jillybean was mad at the swear word. She made a noise like a marble falling on a dinner plate. It was an annoying sound and it kept going: *clack, clack, clack*. "Stop it," Eve hissed. "So what if it's a bad word? Everybody else says it. Everyone says all sorts of..."

Just then Neil rolled over.

Eve went stock-still, not daring to move. She'd been too loud and that was Jillybean's fault as well. Everything was Jillybean's fault. It was she who had saved Neil from the monsters when she was only supposed to have saved Captain Grey. Captain Grey was strong. Eve didn't need anyone but him. The rest could all die and she would be perfectly happy and that went doubly for Neil. That Neil was still alive was just wrong. He had taken her guns. He had mocked her with his eyes. And he kept calling her "Jillybean" and that was also stupid and wrong and she hated it so much!

Neil smacked his lips as if he were dreaming of something tasty. Eve knew it meant he was asleep because there was never anything tasty any more. It was always canned beans or canned corn or canned crap. Eve was just about sick to death of it and that was Neil's doing, too. He always made her eat stupid vegetables which tasted icky and gross. She hadn't had anything good to eat since her mom had died. Her mom used to make all sorts of yummy treats.

An image of an apple pie with a wedge missing came to mind. It was golden brown and the edges bubbled as if it were still piping hot. Then came an image of a slice of pie on a plate. There was vanilla ice cream on top, just starting to melt. And now came an image of lasagna with cheese oozing down the sides. She loved her mom's lasagna.

Eve's stomach growled, loudly. It was as loud as a lion's roar in the little girl's ears, but Neil didn't budge. The barn was a shade of black that made normally straight lines twist and it made static shapes contort into amorphous blobs, but it wasn't exactly a quiet place. Many of the stupid renegades snored and others talked in their sleep and still others thrashed about or even yelled. In all that, the growl of Eve's stomach went unnoticed and her earlier whispering probably hadn't been heard by anyone, even on a subconscious level.

Jillybean tried to distract her some more, sending memories and images through her head, but when she pictured a juicy watermelon, Eve remembered about the black seeds and how once when she was very little she had choked on one. Just like that, Jillybean was thrust back deep into the subconscious of her mind where everything was echoey and vague and hard to grasp. Jillybean felt tiny in there, just a mote of dust floating around in a chasm.

"Finally," Eve whispered when Jillybean was gone. She bent, feeling for the gun, her small hands touching the lump of darkness immediately in front of her. It was Neil's back. Then she felt his belt and then a shoe, and then the floor of the barn. She reached over him and felt part of a blanket and then vinyl and buckles. His backpack—this was it!

Ever so slowly, she crept her fingers around it until she found the open zipper of the main pouch and then she dug into it with greedy hands. The gun was right on top. Its grip was very big compared to her tiny fingers.

She could've searched further and perhaps found the smaller pistols that Neil had stolen from her, but it was the big gun she wanted. She was going to suicide Neil. Eve knew all about suicide. The renegades had frequently talked about killing themselves: when they would do it and why and most importantly, how. A lot of them liked the idea of shooting themselves in the brain and that's what Eve planned on doing to Neil. One shot, bam right to the head and then she would scamper back to where she had laid out her bedroll. Once there she would pretend to be frightened by the noise and she would act like everything was so alarming and scary—she might even pretend to be Jillybean because everyone loved Jillybean and wouldn't blame her for a second because she was so pure and sweet.

Eve liked the idea of using her hated rival in order to cover up a...was this murder? Murder was wrong and bad and Eve was never either of those two things. She couldn't remember a single instance of her ever being bad or wrong. And killing Neil wasn't murder if it was *justified*. That was a word she had plucked from Jillybean's mind and neither of them was sure exactly what it meant. As far as she could tell, the word made seemingly bad things okay to do. And this really wasn't all that bad since Neil had been mean first.

With her moral compass adequately centered on the grey area between right and wrong, Eve bent to the task of ridding herself of Neil. In order for her to orient herself properly, she leaned over him, looking like an eager night creature.

His breath was a soft whistle. Oh, so gently, she reached out and touched his hair so she knew where to shoot. Next she checked the safety on the gun—she knew all about safeties and guns in general; she was very smart when it came to simple methods of killing. The gun made a little *click* noise as she set it to fire. Now it was just a matter of pulling the trigger, dropping the gun and running for her bed of blankets.

She shook in excitement as she brought the gun up. Since it was so big, she held it two-handed and used both thumbs to draw the hammer back. To Eve the sound of the springs working inside the heavy metal gun was very loud in her ears and she was sure everyone had to have heard. The baby heard them, at least.

Just as the hammer came all the way back, the baby made a noise of anger. It was a tiny little cry that had Eve's heart in her throat.

That sound is the real Eve, a voice in her head said. *You're not the real Eve*. It was that danged Jillybean talking again. She was always nagging about something. A part of Eve wanted to use the gun to silence that voice forever. A hot bullet would stop its hated sound in a heartbeat. *It would also stop you*, Jillybean said.

"Just shut up," hissed the little girl. She pointed the gun at her own head, digging it into her temple, threatening Jillybean. Finally, she was quiet, but the baby wasn't. She was making a soft whining sound and it was only a matter of time before someone would flick on a flashlight. When that happened, Eve would be caught for certain. *You better do something*. She didn't know if the thought had originated with her or with Jillybean, but it didn't matter, because it was correct.

Leaving Neil, the little girl slipped over to where the baby was lying, bundled in a soft quilt that had stupid yellow ducks stitched all over it. Eve hated the baby as much as she did Neil. She hated that everyone loved the baby and thought she was so perfect. But she wasn't. She was disgusting and smelled like old poop, but for some reason, the entire group was straight up stupid over her. If she smiled they made such a fuss and if she pouted they all bent over backwards to stick something in her mouth.

"I've got something I can stick in its mouth," Eve snarled. Just then she wanted to stick the pistol in the baby's mouth and pull the trigger. It would be wholly *justified*, because if she didn't kill it someone would wake up and catch her with the gun and then Neil would still be alive and he would sit her down and subject her to one of his useless "talks." She hated the talks, they were so boring and pointless.

Eve stuck the gun in the baby's face and her moral compass didn't flick out of the grey area, it didn't even budge, and the only bit of "bad feelings" she had over the coming murder was that it would be too dark to see the baby's pink brains blast across the barn. She would like to see that.

The barrel was an inch away from the perfect little lips when Jillybean spoke into her mind: *They'll know it was you. Babies don't suicide themselves.*

This stopped Eve. Yes, she wanted to kill the hated little thing, but she couldn't be caught doing it. That would mean more than just a talking to. The group didn't understand about the real truth, and they didn't understand her higher moral view which was stated simply: if Eve thought something was good then it *was* good even if everyone else thought it was bad.

If she got caught, they'd kick her out of the group. Eve didn't want to be alone. She hated Neil and the baby and thought the rest were pathetic, but they were better than being alone. Being alone was bad.

Just then, the baby made another sound and Eve's rage kicked up a notch until it was nearly overpowering. Somehow a nasty idea made it through: *Strangle the baby tonight. Shut its stupid mouth forever. No one will know it was you. Maybe you could even stick a magic marble in its mouth. They will think it was an accident. And then tomorrow kill Neil. Suicide him. People will understand. They'll think he was all sad. People suicide themselves over being sad. Stupid people that is.*

"Yes," Eve whispered, putting the gun down on the edge of the quilt. "And Neil is real stupid. Everyone knows that." There was a magic marble in her pocket, only she didn't want to use it. She wanted to *feel* the death. She laid a hand on the baby's mouth and clamped it down firmly. The baby tried to move its stupid head but Eve was strong. When she wanted to be, she could be much stronger than people would ever give her credit for.

She was strong, but also gentle. It wouldn't do for her to leave red finger marks on the baby's ugly face. That wouldn't be right or smart.

The baby's dimpled little hands came up and grabbed Eve's thumb; her eyes were huge and staring and her face was changing colors. Eve couldn't see the color change, but she could imagine it: pink then red, then blue, then purple, then...dead. Eve was grinning wickedly. Her lips pulled back showing off her little kid teeth as if she were just on the verge of taking a bite from the squirming baby.

Inside her, Jillybean was frantic, trapped in her own body, forced to watch from the grinning squints of Eve's eyes as her baby sister made feeble gestures toward living. The baby wriggled and kicked, but her muscles were growing weaker with every passing second.

Though Jillybean was denied the use of her body, she still had the full ability of her mind. It was an immature mind with wide gaps in knowledge and yet it was still a powerful mind. She knew what she knew and she could still think with the perfect clarity that astounded those of a middling intelligence. She understood that she had lost the battle for control of her body, but she had not lost the battle of her mind—that was still up for grabs. However it could not be won through debate or in the arena of ideas. Eve's emotional state was too powerful for logic—her hate was so immense that it wouldn't even wilt before Jillybean's reasoning.

There was only one way to win the battle of her mind and that was to shut it down.

Jillybean let out a scream that trembled her eardrums and caused her eyes to bug out. Inside the silken cavern walls of her soul it rang, while outside her body, the barn and the people in it went on with their night undisturbed—

the scream was entirely internal. It was a psychic storm that only affected Jillybean and Eve; it was silent but still tremendous in its scope.

Eve knelt over the baby, stunned by the explosion of "noise" within her and, as Jillybean had hoped, it practically paralyzed Eve. Gasping, she fell forward, her hands leaving the baby to break her fall.

The baby, the real Eve, filled her lungs to their fullest, but she did not scream. She needed air too badly to scream just yet. The scream came four seconds later and it was loud enough to bring on the dead, and to finally stop Jillybean's psychic blast. Jillybean slumped forward, feeling as though a bomb had gone off inside her skull. Eve was still there inside her, sharing control of her body but Sadie woke and started to scramble around for the baby. Eve pushed Neil's gun under the ducky quilt. She then vanished into one of the crevices of Jillybean's mind to escape any blame.

"It's ok, Evie," Sadie mumbled, slowly coming awake. The girl put out a hand and the first thing she felt was Jillybean's skinny arm. "Huh?"

At the touch, guilt rushed over Jillybean, engulfing her, swamping her, so that she was drowning in it. She grabbed the crying baby and stood, holding her to her chest. It wasn't easy. Her legs wobbled and her hands shook; even her lips jabbered up and down as she whispered: "It's ok. It's ok. I'm sorry. I'm so sorry."

Suddenly a beam of light, an accusing white eye blared into her face, blinding her. "Jillybean?" Sadie asked in confusion.

The single word was filled with such a sensation of blame that it seemed as though that even in sleep, Sadie knew everything about the gun and how it had been Jillybean's tiny hands that had been smothering the baby. Jillybean felt the guilt to such a degree that she wanted to die. She wanted to suicide herself. Tears streamed down her face, dropping delicate, clear flowers onto the baby's forehead...no, not 'the baby.'

"Her name is Eve," Jillybean said and louder she added: "You are the real Eve, not her."

All of this only made Sadie screw up her face to a greater degree than it had been. "What did you do, Jillybean?"

The question was a bullet to the seven-year-old's heart and she nearly spilled everything pent up inside of her, only others were coming awake, now. Neil was one of them. Jillybean couldn't look in his direction. The guilt over wanting to kill him was another anchor on her soul. *Not kill, suicide him*—the words came trickling up from some black part of her.

"I-I was j-just going to the bathroom and I-I tripped on Eve," Jillybean lied. The lie came so easy to her that it was horrible. When had she become so comfortable with lying? Her daddy had taught her that lying was bad, that it was just wrong. That meant she wasn't just bad, she was wrong too.

Wrong was a good word for how she felt—she was just wrong.

"Be careful next time," Sadie said, taking the crying infant. "Go back to bed."

The barn quieted once more, but it was a long time before Jillybean got up. She went to where she had left the gun beneath the ducky blanket. The other girl inside her grew like a summoned demon at the sight of it, however Jillybean was too quick. She grabbed it, leapt three different people as though she were playing an advanced form of hopscotch, and shoved the gun back into Neil's pack before *she* could take over.

"Too slow," Jillybean hissed in angry triumph.

A voice came floating up out of the inky depths of her mind: *This time*, it said. It was angry too; angry at everything: angry at the death of her parents, and it was angry that Ram had been turned into a zombie and that Sarah had been tortured with fire and then shot for no reason. It was angry that Nico was murdered and that Big Jim had been killed for nothing. It was angry that Neil had tried to give her to Abraham, and it was angry that people hunted them endlessly. It was angry that she wasn't able to be a right, proper little girl and go to school. Instead she had to kill people with bullets and bombs and flaming ships.

She was in a rage that Eve got to be a baby, but Jillybean couldn't be a normal girl...and it made something inside her furious and hateful and...evil.

While everyone else slept in the barn, Jillybean cried.

Chapter 2

Brad Crane

The horseman in his bright armor and his tall wings, edged the stallion closer to the little man in the sweater vest, enjoying the way he leaned back away from horse, intimidated by the raw power of the beast. Brad Crane also liked what he saw behind the man: an entire barn full of cowering people thrown into fear by the appearance of one person...and a few thousand zombies.

He also liked what he saw outside the barn: four large five-ton trucks and a pick-up sitting side by side. They were likely jammed with supplies and they were practically his for the taking. He kept the smile from his lips, however. Now was not the time to gloat, now was the time to overawe the weaklings.

"We fight," the little man in front said. He had his jaw set and his eyes were as squinting and as steely as he could make them, which, considering the ruined nature of his face was considerable. In Brad's opinion, he was one of the most gruesome people he had ever looked upon. Every inch of his face was swollen and scabbed and his skin ranged from yellow to purple, with many unpleasant colors in between. There were zombies that were better looking. The man's outfit did not match the face. It was an outfit straight out of suburbia: the checkered sweater vest was awful, but he also wore "Mom" jeans and ridiculous purple crocs on his feet.

His entire aspect was both confusing and pathetic. He looked like a nerd who had, for once, decided against giving over his lunch money. He was tense and nervous. His body was a quivering spring and his untrained finger was already on the trigger of his M4. He stood, poised for action but he was practically the only one.

Almost all of the sixty three people in the large barn had taken a collective step back at Brad's approach. They

14

stared at him as if he was greater than all of them combined. On his black horse, with his wings tall and stiff in the morning breeze he seemed a giant. There was silence after the little man's grand proclamation; the hodge-podge group cowered.

Brad made sure to hold the contemptuous sneer on his lips.

It was obvious the little man with purple shoes was unimpressed with Brad. He ran his eyes over the wings on Brad's back and saw they were only made of white silk, pulled tight over a wire frame, and his armor, which had been so dazzling before, was simply worked aluminum plating. It would repel teeth and the scabby claws of the zombies, but even a small caliber bullet would pierce it. He also took in the spear, seeing that it was more of a herding tool rather than a weapon of war. Lastly, the little man raised what was left of his right eyebrow as he glanced at Brad's bolt action rifle strapped to his saddle—it wasn't a good weapon for close action.

"We fight!" the little man cried again, louder. Had there been crickets in the barn they would have been heard to chirp. Confused, he looked back to see only three of his friends ready to go and one was a little girl! A deep-chested soldier and a striking blonde woman were the other two; the rest looked to be hiding behind their weapons instead of presenting them in a warlike manner.

Brad chuckled, gazing at them as they shook with fear. "If you fight, then you die," he said. "It's as simple as that."

The tall blonde woman calmly took the binoculars from a skinny punk of a girl and gave another glance at the horde of zombies behind Brad. "There's not many of the humans, Neil. I can only see three of them from this doorway. I'd bet there aren't more than twenty of the riders all told."

"Only twenty?" Brad scoffed. "I have more men than that surrounding you. And besides, we have enough grey meat to tear this barn down and kill the lot of you. Your name is Neil? Well, Neil, you have only two choices in the matter. Submit or die."

"We will not submit and nor will we allow our belongings to be plundered," Neil replied, stepping forward aggressively, only to step back again as the horse swung its large head around towards him. "We are all armed and you can rest assured that we will give a fine account of ourselves. If you think you have encountered a weak group, you are mistaken, sir. So go back to your friends and let them know that we plan on fighting to the death."

This did not sit well with the rest of the group. There were whisperings and a general murmur of negativity sprang up. "We should bargain with them," a man with slicked hair and a pinched, nervous face, said.

Neil looked to be thinking this over when the little girl standing at his side said: "No, that's wrong, Fred." She wore a yellow sundress which was wrinkled to such a degree that it might have been made out of paper fetched from a trash can and unballed before being cut to fit a little girl. On her feet were ancient Keds; they had been white at one time. Now they were dingy with river water, mud, and yesterday's Oklahoma dust. Her fly-away brown hair was lightened by the first rays of the sun and strewn with the hay she had picked up in sleep. The rider and horse seemed not to have affected her at all.

At her words, the whisperings and the general murmur died away. "We should not bargain with him," she continued in her little girl voice. "We should kill him, quickly." She turned to Neil and whispered: "If I kill him can I have the horse?" Her eyes were greedy, whether for the horse or the chance to kill, it was hard to tell. Brad stared at her with his lip twisted in disgust and she glared right back.

"You would listen to a girl?" Brad demanded. "A crazy girl?"

"I would sooner listen to her than to you." Neil shot back. "You come here demanding our surrender. The answer is: hell no! We have done nothing wrong. We are just passing through, so take your threats elsewhere, because we will fight you. Some of us are highly trained marksmen." Neil inclined his head to the soldier and asked him: "Would you have trouble knocking some of those men out of their saddles at this distance, Grey?"

Grey took his eyes off the man for a second to look out at the horde. "With those wings they make excellent targets," Grey said. "I couldn't miss."

Brad glanced back, squinting at the distant figures of his men. He had to laugh; a short barking sound of derision. He swung his shoulder length blonde hair away from his face and said: "I've heard my share of big talk since the apocalypse, but that's some bullshit. I'm betting you couldn't hit dick from this distance. And even if you could, how do you plan on dealing with two thousand stiffs? Really, Neil, your only choice is to surrender now and save your worthless skins."

"That won't happen," Neil snarled.

"I told you we should kill him," the little girl said. "It'll be easy and there'll be one less of them to fight. He might even be their leader and if he dies, maybe the others won't know what to do. They'll be…what's the word, Jillybean? Right, confused. They'll be confused and stupid and easier to kill. And we can have their horses for ourselves."

"Jillybean! That's enough" Grey admonished. He glared her into silence and then turned to Neil. "She has a point. We can use horses where we're going. We should make sure not to kill them."

Brad felt his smirk begin to draw down. The group wasn't knuckling under as he had expected. They were certainly an odd bunch. Neil appeared to be the classic wimp and yet he had more backbone than any of them. And there was something definitely wrong with the little girl. Her eyes weren't right and she had a sick manner about her—sick in the head, that is. And Brad certainly didn't care for Grey's icy stare or for the tall woman's calm demeanor. The rest didn't look like much, but these four were trouble.

Despite his smirk and his confidence, Brad couldn't afford trouble. The truth was he only had eighteen men with him, and five weren't men at all. Two were middling teens and three were women; they weren't much in the way of fighters, meaning he would have to play this smart if he was going to gain substantially. "And where are you supposedly going?" he asked.

"Back to Colorado," Grey replied, lifting an eyebrow.

"Colorado?" he asked nonchalantly. The one word had sent his hopes crashing. Men from Colorado had a reputation: they excelled at violence. Brad looked Grey over with a discriminating eye. He took in the soldier's rough appearance and his cold hazel eyes and the way his weapon was as immaculate as his attire was purposely grungy. He looked as though he could blend in with any patch of dirt and, once invisible, kill with impunity.

Grey stared right back and there was nothing nonchalant about him. He was all business and there was no lie in the way he seemed completely prepared to take the little girl's suggestion and shoot Brad on the spot. "Yes, Colorado," Grey replied. "I am Captain James Grey of the 3rd Battalion. I am escorting these people by order of General Johnston."

Fuuuck! Brad cursed, inwardly. This man wouldn't be bullied and neither would Neil, regardless of his geeky nature. Brad certainly didn't have the means to fight them. Yes, he could have sicced his horde on the renegades and probably killed them all, but where was the profit in that? Half of them were women and they were a bunch of ripe tomatoes in his eyes. They would fetch a pretty penny at the slave markets. It was even possible that the women were worth much more than what was in their trucks. The men and boys would be sold to the arena masters or, if they had that mercenary gleam, they would be asked to join the ranks of the Azael. Too bad the soldier would never sign up. The men from Colorado also had the reputation of being goody-two-shoes.

Brad looked at his options: he couldn't bully them, and a fight would be a waste, so that only left trickery.

Suddenly, he brightened and smiled, showing even teeth. "Hells bells, why didn't you say you were from Colorado in the first place. That changes everything. Put up your guns, you are among friends. We know of the mountain people, in fact we trade with them regularly."

The people in the barn let out a collective breath. It was such a unified chorus that it sounded like choreographed wind. They then began whispering to each other, excitedly and there were smiles where fear had been a second before. Only the little girl still glared with the same intensity as she had. Her disappointment was obvious. Whether at losing the opportunity to kill or at gaining the rider's horse, or both, Brad couldn't tell. Either way, she was freaky.

"I'm so relieved," Neil said and then shaped his wounded face into something that could only be called a smile simply because teeth showed. Despite the "smile" he hadn't dropped his gun by an inch.

"As am I," Brad answered, releasing the bridle so the horse could pick at the hay, lying underfoot. "I thought you were part of one of the bandit groups operating around these parts. Very dangerous men they are. Murderers and slavers, the lot of them. But you're from Colorado! How lucky. If you'd like, we can escort you to the border. Oklahoma isn't far. Just a few miles back the way you came."

"But we're going to Colorado," the Goth girl said, speaking up for the first time. She held a baby in her arms and had seemed halfway between the sheep of the larger group and the shepherds of the smaller group led by Grey and Neil. "You heard us say we're going to Colorado not Oklahoma."

Brad gave her a very slow and deliberate once over, liking what he saw and thinking she would go for a thousand easily in the markets. Many men liked them young. "Yes, but I didn't know you'd be traveling through our lands. That changes things. Everyone traveling through our lands needs an escort." He smiled down on the teen. "...for their own protection, of course." He pointed with his spear out at the circling zombies. "The plains are home to millions of them. Sometimes in herds as far as the eye can see. You can't get through without protection."

Neil's gun was still up and his baby-blue eyes were at squints. "I'm sure I must be misunderstanding you. What you just said has the ring of the Jersey mafia behind it— you know, providing the threat that people pay to be protected against. Is that what I'm hearing?"

It was exactly that. "No, of course not," Brad lied. "The danger is very real."

"And you say you're with the Azael?" Grey asked. "I didn't realize you were operating so far south. The last I heard you were only operating in Nebraska."

"Then you've been out of the loop for quite some time. We've been expanding, franchising you might say. Ever since the king came up with the new look, we've been growing, taking over more and more land. Really, business is thriving."

Just then, the horse swung his head and made a snuffling sort of noise in the direction of Neil's purple crocs, causing the small man to take a step back, as if afraid the horse would take a bite of the rubber footwear. As he did, he asked: "Your new look? You mean the fake wings and the spear helps you in some way?"

Before the rider could answer, Jillybean snorted, "Sheesh, what a moron…no, I won't shut up! It's not my fault he's a moron." She seemed to be talking to someone just off her left shoulder, only there was no one standing there.

Those around the little girl glanced away from her, embarrassed. Brad gave her a queer look before answering Neil's question. "Yeah, they keep the stiffs from hurting us. Because of the wings, they don't see us as human, but just in case, we're armored." He smacked his mailed thigh as emphasis.

"It's an improvement, I guess," Grey said. "They used to dress like transsexual gypsies. No offense, but those outfits were lame."

"What's a transsexual gypsy look like?" the Goth girl with the baby asked with a laugh. "Did you guys wear pantyhose or something?"

Brad grinned, liking her white teeth and flawless, pale skin. "No, not pantyhose. We wear all these different colored scarves and shawls when we need to. It confused the stiffs and they rarely attacked. But, I would agree with you, Grey, those outfits aren't in the least bit manly. I like the new ones better, especially the spear. It's very handy. You'd be surprised to learn how easy it is to herd the stiffs."

"That's because they were people and people are like fucking sheep," Jillybean said, in a soft, hating voice. Again, the little group around her shared embarrassed looks.

The grin on Brad's face faded. The little girl was crazy. There was no questioning that now. And that was really too bad, a cute little thing like that would fetch two thousand in the market with no problem, otherwise. Brad didn't want to know what a man would see in a skinny little runt like Jillybean, he only knew some would pay for her. Even warped in the head they would pay, they just wouldn't pay as much.

Neil pretended Jillybean hadn't said anything. He straightened his checkered sweater vest by pulling down on its lower hem, cleared his throat importantly and asked: "So, how much to be escorted through your lands?"

"Two hundred a head," Brad answered, without hesitation.

Just as quickly, Neil replied: "Too high."

Damn, that geek is tough, Brad thought. Aloud he shot back: "One-eighty. It's really the lowest I can go. I hope you understand."

Jillybean had been watching intently, an ugly look on her soft features. "That's a lie," she said. When she spoke she had everyone's attention. The little group looked nervous as though she was about to spew more crazy. "He could do it for free if he wanted to or at the least he could do it for just the cost of the gas, but he wants more. He wants whatever you'll pay him. If I had to guess, I'd say he's just making numbers up."

She was exactly right. There wasn't a fixed sum since the Azael charged the various people looking to cross their territory whatever could be extorted from them. Brad grunted, then leaned over the pommel of his saddle and stared down at the girl. She stared right back, not blinking an eye. "Hey kid," he said to her in a low growl. "Why don't you go play? The grownups are trying to talk."

"And why don't you go fu…"

Jillybean was cut off as Neil slapped a hand over her mouth. "I'm so sorry about that. She hasn't been feeling quite herself lately." He turned to the Goth girl. "Sadie, can you take her somewhere, please?"

Sadie took the little girl's hand. "Come along Jilly…I mean Eve. Come on. Neil's got this."

"No he doesn't. Neil is weak," Jillybean said, as she was dragged away. "He'll give everything away."

Everything? Brad liked the sound of that. It made it seem that one-eighty a head was very doable. He caught himself grinning and quickly looked away, back to where his drovers were circling the zombies just beyond the reach of their eyesight. From this distance, the zombies could only make out the barn and even that just barely. He lifted his spear straight up and then brought it down straight in front of him three times so that the flag on it snapped lightly—the signal for *stand down*.

When he glanced back, Neil had a finger in the air. "Can you give us a second?" he asked. "I would like to confer with my friends concerning the affordability of your services and whether we feel they are necessary or not."

"Oh, they are very necessary," Brad said, easily. "You see I know which wells are poisoned and which are not. I know where the mega-herds are currently roaming. Some of these herds take up land equal in size to Rhode Island. And I know what bridges are out, which are guarded by bandits, which charge a toll. Trust me, I'll save you money and I might even save your lives though that's not a guarantee."

Neil went a little green. "Poisoned wells? That's not so good. We're just going to, uh, confer, like I said." The three of them, Grey, Neil, and the woman, stepped away to talk while Brad watched the woman's backside in her tight jeans.

He guessed they would come back with an offer around one-thirty to try to get him to come down. To that he would reply: *Forget everything else, the rivers are undrinkable and the wells are poisoned. You need me...one-seventy eight.* Eventually they would settle somewhere around one-sixty three a head, but Brad would get at least one-eighty by the end of the trip. He'd recoup his costs in a number of ways. There'd be the repair charges when their trucks would "run over" the nails set deliberately in their treads. Then there would be the water fees, as Brad intended to steer the group into the driest regions where water was strictly guarded. And there would be whatever his boys could win at gambling using marked decks, loaded dice and secret hand codes. And of course, there would be whatever could be stolen when heads were turned.

Brad had a hundred ways to turn heads: easy women, spiked alcohol, a sudden truck fire—theirs of course, but the simplest method of misdirection would be the "sudden" appearance of a zombie horde, one just large enough to drain the group of their ammo which could only be restocked by Brad, obviously at a price...a very high price.

Brad would get his pay. The trip wasn't going to be a good one for these renegades. All sorts of accidents were going to befall them and with each incident they would come to need him more and more. He would bleed them dry.

Chapter 3

Neil Martin

"So what do we do?" Neil asked. He had his ass on a bale of hay or wheat or some such long, yellowish grass. When it came to farming, he was generally clueless beyond the fact that seeds went into the ground and then you watered them. All he knew was that there was something poking him where it shouldn't. He gave his rear a shimmy to the left and said: "Do we try to skirt the land of the Azael or do we go with Brad? I, for one, don't trust him."

"Neither do I," Deanna agreed. "First, he wants to take us prisoner and, then we're supposed to be all chummy with him? That's the most ridiculous thing I've ever heard. I say we go around."

Captain Grey slid a creased map from his cargo pocket and opened it up. He tapped the town of Battleboro. "We are just north of here and we need to get here, Estes Park. That's a thousand miles on a straight line. If we go around, we add another thousand to our trip, give or take. A lot of that land will be hot and very dry, but water won't be our biggest problem. It's the lack of fuel. We have maybe six hundred miles worth in our tanks, and that means we're going to have to scrounge, which means fighting the stiffs. The longer route might be more dangerous and it will definitely mean we'll burn through our supplies as fast as if we traded them to cross."

"So you're saying you think we should cross with Brad?" Neil asked.

"No," Grey answered. "I'm just giving you the facts so you can make up your mind. You're the leader here, not me." He suddenly smiled and then chuckled as if the idea of Neil being leader was humorous. Neil glared and Grey laughed harder for a moment before saying: "It's not you, Neil...ok, it's a little you. I was just picturing when you said: *We fight!* It got all quiet and you should have seen

Fred Trigg. He was ducking behind Mike Gates like a kid hiding behind his mother's skirt."

Deanna didn't share in the laughter. "They were all like that," she groused. "I was embarrassed for you, Neil. After all you've done for them, they cowered and let you hang out to dry. Jillybean was right, they're like sheep."

They were like sheep in a way, Neil had to admit. After so many days of being hounded and persecuted, the renegades had a haunted look about them, as if they were on the verge of giving up and accepting whatever crap that came their way without a fight. Neil wasn't close to giving up, and couldn't understand why any of them would want to. So, things hadn't gone according to plan and perhaps their lives hadn't been a picnic, but what had they really lost? To Neil, the damage to Jillybean's mind was the biggest loss the group had sustained while escaping from the River King. Strangely, the injuries to his face didn't concern him, while the deaths of Big Jim and the cage fighters registered only a passing sadness. Constant death had inured him and had turned him cold.

But they all needed Jillybean. She squatted next to the back door of the barn, her knees jutting, frog-like from beneath her yellow sundress. Without Ipes clutched in the crook of her arm, there was an air of loneliness about her. Sadie stood near, rocking Eve who was going through a bottle with her usual quiet concentration, but no one else got too close.

Neil had made sure to keep Jillybean away from the others as much as possible. Few knew that Ipes was gone and that there was something evil taking up residence in her mind. She was hard to put up with, changing personalities in a blink, or more often than not, living with both going at the same time.

There were times when he would look at her and see plots and schemes bubbling up behind her blue eyes. In the three days since she lost Ipes, her eyes had changed. Gone was the innocence. Now, they were devoid of emotion, except hate, that is. *If looks could kill…*how many times had he heard that old cliché? With Jillybean, it seemed true. Half the time she looked his way, Neil was sure she was actually contemplating his murder. He tried to laugh it off when it happened, and yet, at the same time his balls would try to crawl up into his body.

The group didn't need to know any of this, although Neil wondered whether it would really matter. They were all very pro Jillybean now. Regardless of the fact that it had been Neil and Deanna who had freed Captain Grey and the cage-fighters and it had been Sadie who had found the secret pontoon bridge that had been instrumental in gaining the release of the renegades, their rescue from the hands of the River King had been chalked up totally to Jillybean. The thinking went: if the rescuers needed rescuing, then the ultimate rescuer was to be given credit. And this hadn't been the first time she had rescued them. Strictly speaking, they held her in awe and, if she had been only a little older, she could have been queen of the little group.

It was a scary thought to Neil.

"Sheep or not, I still have to figure a way to get them to safety," he said. "So, I have one vote for going the long way and one for the short. That's just great. I was secretly hoping to just go along with whatever you two wanted."

"It's not easy being the leader," Grey said. Suddenly he clapped Neil on the back and added: "I'll be honest with you, when you were first elected, I figured I'd be running the group, using you as a figure head, but I underestimated you. So far you've proven more capable than I gave you credit for."

Neil went a shade of...the color was indescribable except to say his disfigured face wasn't helped by the blush of red beneath the yellowed purple. "Thanks...uh, that's nice and all, but that doesn't help me decide which way to go. The wrong choice could mean we're screwed."

"We might be screwed with either choice," Deanna said, trying to be helpful.

It wasn't helpful. Neil wished he had more time to think through the situation, however, the horseman was getting impatient, sighing loudly, and the renegades kept looking at Neil, expectantly. All of them, except for Jillybean. Gently, she reached out and picked something up and brought it to eye level. It was a butterfly with wings of orange and black. It flapped its wings in an easy, lazy manner but did not fly away. It sat on the fairway of the little girl's palm, looking contented.

Out of the blue, Jillybean slapped her other hand down on the insect, crushing it. She then peeked her hand back so she could see the destruction she had caused. There was a smudge of orange and black on one hand and in the other was the crushed butterfly. It lifted one of its once beautiful wings slowly and then died.

Neil had seen his share of senseless killings since the coming of the apocalypse but this was one of the worst. It seemed to him that two innocent creatures were killed by the single blow.

"If I were leader, we'd take the shorter path," Grey said. "So far, I've found that the further we go the more crap and the more evil we have to deal with. I don't trust Brad, but I think the most he will do is screw us on the cost. He's not going to ruin his ability to trade with the people of Colorado."

Deanna raised an eyebrow at this. "Do I need to remind you that we thought the same thing about the River King?"

"That was different," Grey answered her. "The River King knew who we were. This guy doesn't. As far as he knows we're just travelers heading to Colorado. As long as that's all he knows, he has no reason to try anything untoward."

"Maybe," Deanna said.

Grey gave her a shrug. "Yes, there's always a "maybe," or a "perhaps," but we can't live like that or we'll get nowhere. If we go with Brad, what sort of bargain can we strike?"

Neil watched the two, quietly. Their conversation had as much to do with the obvious vibe between them as it did the question of the route. Both were almost formal in the way they spoke to each other, as if they were afraid of hurting the others feelings by disagreeing with them. From

Neil's perspective their courtship, which neither would ever admit was actually happening, was comically sad. Grey was so chivalrous and deferential concerning what Deanna had done to survive, that he was nearly robotic around her, while she wrapped herself in such a stiff, crooked form of feminism that her tone of voice practically screamed: *Don't touch me!* to any man who came near. Yet neither could hide the look in their eyes.

They both so clearly wanted to give up the charade, that there was a sort of office pool going on among the renegades. The first public display of affection won the prize: the last can of Dinty Moore soup. Neil had 7pm, five days from then and he liked his chances.

Neil considered the likelihood of a good bargain with Brad and said: "We're not in a good position to bargain. We have slightly more than two-thousand rounds of ammo and slightly fewer than nineteen hundred cans of food, and not enough fuel to get to Colorado going straight through. It would help if we lost two of the trucks. It'll be pretty cramped, but if we take all the diesel from one of the five tons and the Dodge pick-up, that'll extend our range by about twenty-five percent."

"That just might be enough to get us to Colorado if we go straight through," Grey said.

"But it won't help us with food or ammo," Deanna said. "If we figure we'll go through three cans of food per person per day, a three day trip will cost us about five hundred and seventy cans, leaving us with only thirteen hundred to bargain with. Add that to our entire load of ammo and that only comes up to about fifty-five per person. Brad won't go for that. There's no way."

"Which brings us to our main sticking point: how would we pay for the trip with Brad? Given enough time we might be able to scrounge for the fee, but that could take weeks or even months. What about your general?" Neil asked Grey. "Would he help us? Would he cover what we're short by?"

28

A pained expression crossed Grey's face. "He's pretty old school and thinks people ought to take responsibility for their own lives."

"We would pay him back, of course" Neil said. "If we have to borrow anything, I would take the debt on, personally."

Grey shook his head. "No. It'll have to be on me. Brad won't believe that we're good for it unless I put my honor on the bargain."

What about my honor? Neil wanted to ask. He didn't; he only sighed and took a long weary look outside. Which way to turn? The short and, hopefully, quicker route with a man that none of them trusted or the longer, possibly more dangerous route around the southern border of Kansas and then along the spine of the Rockies where who knew what awaited them?

Brad watched the deliberation, leaning on his pommel; he spat in the dust of the barn when he saw Neil looking at him. It was a calculated move: a show of nonchalance coupled with intimidation.

Neil was no longer so easily intimidated. He turned away as though he found the move without interest and found his eyes immediately drawn to Jillybean; there was still the smear of orange from the dead butterfly on her palm. She was staring slack-jawed at a barn post, seemingly in a trance. There was no way of knowing if she was locked in a mental battle with the evil thing within her or just drooling like an idiot. He suspected the mental battle as the most probable. Idiot was not a word suited for Jillybean.

"We go around," Neil said, the decision coming to him in a flash of intuition. The danger of going with Brad was clear and obvious. They'd be sticking their heads in the lion's mouth once more where a slip of the tongue would doom them. By all appearances the Azael were thieving gypsies at best and bloodthirsty pirates at worst. In this case the unknowns were not nearly as bad. After all, the renegades knew how to take care of themselves around zombies and they knew how to scrounge for supplies better than anyone.

Deanna looked relieved, while Grey only nodded, his feelings, as always, carefully hidden. Brad could not hide his disappointment. "Damn it, Neil. You're being an idiot. The way around is far more dangerous than you can imagine. The Texans…you don't want to deal with them and the bandits in New Mexico won't just rob you blind, they'll rape the women in front of you. I've heard stories."

"Regardless, we go around," Neil replied. "So, if you'd move your little ring of zombies, that would be great." Brad tried once more to change Neil's mind, but the smaller man could not be moved. Only after Neil said: "I have spoken," and then made a show of leisurely re-buttoning his brown checkered sweater vest. Only then did Brad kick his horse off in an angry canter.

The moment he was gone, Neil turned to Grey. "We need to consolidate everything into the three best trucks. Transfer the fuel and food and anything else you think we might need. Get a crew together to help. Deanna, spread the word that we're safe, at least for the moment, and that we're going to be taking a slightly longer route."

In twenty minutes, the food and fuel were transferred and the renegades briefed. They were ready to go, but it took much longer for Brad's people to nudge the zombies off the main road. The zombies milled around like the mindless beasts they were and it was an hour before Neil thought it was safe to go. During that time, Brad came back and kept up an insistent chatter about how foolish he was being.

"We will see," Neil said.

"Yes, you will," Brad replied.

The three five-tons were now crammed with people, food, water and ammo. There was little room for anything else. Grey drove the first truck and next to him sat Deanna. She was somewhat of a permanent fixture at his side now. Next to her was Jillybean, her feet resting on a box of 9mm NATO rounds, her eyes watching the running scenery as though she were committing it to memory, and Neil guessed that she was.

Neil was at the window, enjoying the cool breeze of the morning. It was the finest morning that he could remember and he realized he hadn't been so relaxed in ages. They drove west for an hour, speedily at first, but gradually going slower and slower. In many places the highway was blocked by sudden and inexplicable jams of old and lifeless cars. Time and again they were forced to turn around and reroute themselves. During these times the zombie menace grew, especially if they were near the many rinky-dink towns that crouched along the frontage roads.

"I'm glad we got rid of the Dodge," he said, rolling up the window and shutting out the fine morning. Thankfully, there were few of the quasi-dead creatures in the middle of the road. Most came out from beneath the trees that were gradually growing more and more sparse the further they traveled west, or out from beneath the eaves of buildings: the Jiffy Lubes, the 7-11s, and the McDonalds, which seemed mandatory structures in every town. Grey did his best to speed past the throngs, which reached out and clawed long lines into the green-painted sides of the truck, but when he couldn't get past, they were forced to go through them.

Neil's stomach went wacky as they bounced over the vile bodies and the sound of their innards rupturing reached his delicate ears.

So many roads were blocked that to leave the lands of the Azael, they were gradually turned from their route. They had initially struck out southwest, but soon they were pushed west and that lasted only a few miles before they were forced back north again.

"This is wrong," Jillybean said, sitting up to see over the bulky dash of the five-ton. "Do you know you're heading back to the horse person? I really am sure he's this way. Will we get to see his horse, do you think? I wasn't allowed to see the horse, before. *She* wouldn't let me. All I got to do was smell him, which was only ok. It reminded me of when I got to ride a pony when we went to the state fair back when I was little and my daddy was still not a monster."

"We're not going back, Jillybean," Grey said. "And don't worry, I bet there will be more horses to see along the way." His eyes, always scanning ahead, went to slits; there was a sign coming up and a dusty road cutting across their front. "Is that road on the map?"

As Neil would get car-sick if he took his eyes off the road for more than a few seconds, Deanna was the navigator. The map lay open on her knees, pinned down by her finger as she traced the small secondary road they were on. "No, but it's heading west, and the next one going in that direction won't be for another twelve miles. That will put us right back in Azael lands. So…" She looked to Neil for a decision.

The little green sign said *CO 33.D*. It was weathered and faded, looking older than the dirt road it marked. The road itself consisted of little more than ruts in the dirt. It seemed to go nowhere. On one side of it were rolling hills that looked to have been used to graze cattle, on the other was a low fence, holding in the tired remains of a farm.

"Take it," he ordered, quietly. There wasn't a single zombie in evidence, the deciding factor.

At first, the decision seemed to be the right one. The brown dirt road went on for two miles seeming to point at a lonely homestead which came into focus as they closed on it. It started as a smudge on the horizon but firmed up slowly until it was recognizable as a two-story home with a detached shed and an old and shabby barn. It looked as desolate as could be and yet it sat off an actual paved road that crossed the dirt trail at right angles. Grey didn't need to be told to turn south.

They began to relax when they saw the sign for I-166, the east-west highway they had been on forty minutes before. "That took us a little out of our way," Neil said. "But no great loss, except for some gas."

Grey only grunted in his throat. On the left was a local airport, its single runway already starting to crack and heave. There was only one plane on the tarmac. Sitting in the sun was a small, white Cessna with improbable red racing stripes that ran up its aging fuselage. It wasn't going anywhere; one of its wings was broken square in two.

Further down the road, they could see the beginnings of a town. As an archway of sorts, they crossed beneath a train trestle with a train still on it. It had been a cargo train, and as far as the eye could see in either direction, which wasn't very far because the tracks curved to run around a series of hills, were the train's many freight cars, laid out end-to-end with their doors flung wide. There was no sense stopping. It had to have been plundered long before.

On the other side of the trestle was an ugly, semi-industrialized area. Along with lines of monotonous, concrete warehouses and five-story high, joined mega-silos there was a factory that produced corn oil. A sign on the side of the main building read *APC Corn Oil*. Across the street was a dairy and if the smiling cow on its sign were discounted, it was an equally dismal-looking building. Neil found it hard to believe that food of any sort was processed there.

Not only was the area depressing, it also stank of ancient spoilt milk and zombies.

Many hundreds of zombies came charging out at the trucks from both of the industrial buildings. Many hundreds more came out from the warehouses that lined the road, turning it into something of a man-made canyon of cement. Grey floored the gas pedal and the truck picked up speed. The sounds of their huge engines echoed loudly and reached out to announce their presence. The echoes summoned every creature for miles.

The five-tons weren't fast trucks, topping out at just over sixty, but they were quick enough to out-pace the zombies. Neil was just pulling the side mirror around so that he could see them dwindling in size when Grey slammed on the brakes. The street in front was flooding with the undead. It was an amazing and horrifying sight. In seconds, there was a solid wall of them, thousands deep.

Charging, they were like ants boiling out of a kicked-over hill.

"Turn!" Neil yelled. He pointed to the right where a road ran between more grey cement buildings. Grey stomped the gas and heeled the five-ton over. Everyone slid along the bench seat into the captain, Neil included. He clawed back to the window in time to catch a glimpse of a sign that read *Cousins Industrial Park*. Beneath the name was a map. It went by in a blink.

"What did that say?" he asked with a sinking feeling.

Deanna answered: "I think it said *Cousins Industrial Park*."

The sinking feeling bottomed out in the empty pit of his stomach as he saw that the road was short, lined on both sides by more warehouses. There were zombies here, as well. They were awful things, dragging limbs and sometimes lines of intestines behind them, but they weren't the reason for the fear mounting in Neil. Abruptly, Grey came to the end of the road. It ended at another warehouse, this one a city block in size. In the front was a wide open lot, ready to receive twenty semi-trucks at a time. It was surrounded by high fencing beyond which lay a dense forest and more zombies.

"What do we do?" Neil asked, forgetting that he was the leader.

"We'll try around back," Grey said and then chugged the truck around the near side of the warehouse. It turned out that there wasn't any 'around back.' The fencing came right up to the edge of the building. Their options were now even fewer. The warehouse had too many gaping doors to be held against the onrushing zombies and the fence and the trees were too much of a barrier for the five-tons to surmount. They could probably hide in some of the warehouses, but for how long? There were so many zombies that there was no knowing when or even if they'd move on. They seemed to be congregating in the area and their numbers were beyond anything Neil had ever seen before.

34

"We have to go back the way we came," Neil said. "Turn us around."

Grey swept them in a wide circle. Neil was able to see the panic and the puzzlement on Michael Gates and Sadie's faces as they, too, turned in a sharp circle. He could hear his daughter yell: "We can't go back!" She was right. The short road back was thronged, while in the parking lot before the larger warehouse, the faster zombies streamed toward them.

"Go to the right," Neil said pointing toward the far end of the warehouse. "We'll lure as many as we can down there so that hopefully there will be fewer on the road. Unless someone has a better plan?" Both he and Deanna looked at Jillybean. When she only shrugged, Grey turned the truck to the right. Behind them, the other two trucks kept so close, a person could jump from one to the other.

"Not too fast," Neil said. "We want as many as we can in this open area." The captain slowed the truck to that of a fast walk and now they could hear the panic in the covered bed of the truck. Neil rolled down the window and yelled: "Tighten the covering! Cinch it down tight." Even with the green canvas pulled taut there would still be the rear opening to worry about. There was nothing anyone could do about that and Neil told himself that the truck was tall and the bed was high off the ground.

"They should be fine," he whispered.

The lead truck reached the end of the warehouse's receiving area and Grey turned it in a wide arc. "Wow," Deanna said. In front of them were a couple of thousand zombies. They were of every type: old, young, tall, short, with skin and without, limbed and unlimbed. It looked like hell had cracked open.

Grey's hands were tight on the steering wheel; they were the only indication that he might have been nervous. "Guns at the ready," he said in a calm voice as he gradually picked up speed and aimed the truck where the zombies were fewest in number. "Safeties on until they're needed."

The next few minutes were an absolute horror and it was a wonder Neil kept his breakfast down. Grey drove with steady determination into the horde and at first it was 'just' terrible as they were still in the open. It was when they were in the man-made canyon of the smaller warehouses that things became nearly too much to bear.

The beasts threw themselves in front of the trucks and those in the cab jounced up and down as black blood flew and fanned out from the tires. There were so many of the zombies that the truck's momentum diminished. It was like plowing through a bog and, at one point, the entire back end of the truck slewed to the right as if it were sliding down hill.

"Steer into the skid," Grey said, reminding himself. He turned the wheel to the right, but still the truck slid and still the zombies turned to black scum under the grinding tires.

Their speed had dropped to almost zero when Neil, who was staring out the window with eyes that were almost popping out of his head, saw something that resembled a tattered grey and black flag fly up in the air and then slap wetly against one of the smaller warehouses that lined the road. It had been the skin of one of *them*.

Next, the front of the warehouse was rattled by a spray of bones that tinkled and bounced off the glass doors. The vomit was close to the top of Neil's throat, now, however he was able to put it aside as the truck's wheels finally dug their way through the undead and found purchase on the concrete. They immediately lurched forward and Grey gunned the engine which roared as it plowed furiously through the horde, going faster and faster until they were on the street that cut through the town.

There were only slightly fewer zombies here, however after what they had just gone through it was like splashing through a rain puddle and after only a minute they were free and racing back toward the trestle and the train as the last of the clinging zombies fell away. Smiling, Neil glanced in the side mirror and saw something that made his face freeze in place.

The other two trucks were not behind them.

When Deanna saw, she asked: "What do we do?"

Grey was already slowing down. There was an intersection just ahead and Neil knew what the captain would
do when he reached it. "We go back for them," Neil said.

Chapter 4

Sadie Walcott

Because of the baby, Sadie was always allotted a seat in the front. Without fail, she chose to ride in the second truck with Michael Gates, who had become its permanent driver. He was a sweet man and seemed to have a hundred different stories to tell every day. His one downfall: he was frequently flatulent. Sometimes it was bad enough to wake Eve.

When they had passed the trestle and train and slowed near the dairy processing plant where thousands of gallons of milk had curdled and had become some sort of crusted bacterial flan, Sadie thought it was one of those times Michael had cut loose. "This is a pretty stinky little town," Michael had said.

"Yeah, the 'town' is pretty stinky," Sadie answered.

Next to her, Joslyn Reynolds snorted as if the comment was funnier than it was. She had whined her way to the front seat, kicking Michael's wife, Marybeth to the back. "It's only fair," she had said when they had left Brad behind. "The front isn't just for Neil's friends."

At the window was Lindsey Caro. She had been rescued from Gunner's encampment at the Piggly Wiggly. The chains that had held her to the stained mattress had been unlocked by 'Jillybean herself,' something Lindsey was oddly proud of and had mentioned to Sadie more than once. At Sadie's comment, Lindsey gave her a dirty look. Lindsey was a dour girl and hadn't laughed at any of Michael's stories—not that Sadie had either. The black cloud in her mind was as dark as the clothes she wrapped herself in.

Luckily, Sadie had Eve to take care of. Anything was better than facing the depression growing inside of her—almost anything. When the lead truck took a sudden turn to the right, Sadie couldn't believe her eyes. Sure, she had seen the growing numbers of zombies around them, however her view out front had been blocked by Grey's five-ton.

"Holy shit!" Joslyn cried upon seeing the thousands of zombies. "Turn! Turn!"

Michael was already turning into the industrial park. None of them noticed the map of the different businesses housed there, so they didn't notice the fact that there was only one way out of the complex and that was the way they had come in. Michael, driving as though he thought he'd be left behind if he didn't keep up, was again so close that it was a shock to him when Grey took a wide turn at the far end of the building.

"What's he doing?" Michael asked.

It became obvious seconds later when they saw the chain-link fence and the thick trees. They had trapped themselves. Joslyn began to curse, Lindsey began to moan, and Michael suddenly sprouted rows of deep, worry lines across his forehead.

"Trust Neil," Sadie said. "He'll know what to do." Despite her confidence, she unzipped Eve's diaper bag and brought out the earmuffs she had fashioned for the infant. She had found child-sized ear protection at a sporting goods store where Neil had stopped at two days before in Arkansas. To convert them to infant size took only the removal of a heavy spring that clamped the earpieces down too hard. They were big, but they would protect Eve's hearing. In the same bag were her own muffs. She fitted them on her head and then took out her Glock and checked the load.

Joslyn watched her as if guns were altogether foreign to her. Only when Sadie slapped the clip back into place did Joslyn dig in her pack for her own gun. She had the .25 caliber pistol that Neil had taken from Jillybean. She also checked her clip. "Eight bullets. All I've got is eight bullets!"

"That's more than I got," Lindsey said, her voice was harsh and close to hysterics. "I don't have anything."

"It'll be ok. Trust Neil," Sadie said again. They were driving slowly toward the end of a large open lot. There was nothing beyond it but more fencing and trees and zombies. She almost lost faith in Neil when the lead truck turned slowly as if Grey was uncertain what he was doing. He then aimed back the way they came, moving at a deliberate pace. Michael kept right on his tail and Ricky, driving the third truck was right on theirs; they were as close as railroad cars.

Then they were among the zombies and gaps appeared between the three trucks. The lead truck, smashing into the face of the horde, bounced up and down. It bucked and jerked and shuddered, its rear sometimes swinging out or in. Its speed was erratic causing Michael to slow down to a dangerous degree. The five-ton was a tall vehicle and had to be climbed to be accessed—the zombies were doing just that.

Lindsey began screaming and pointing out the window. She kicked back from the door, forcing Joslyn into Sadie and Sadie into Michael. "Get off!" Michael yelled. "I can't drive." Ahead of them, the lead truck suddenly began slewing to the right and was within a second of becoming bogged down in the mass of squirming, flailing creatures.

Michael was forced to stop.

The view out the front window was appalling. Uncountable numbers of zombies surged up to them like a slow-motion grey wave that crested higher and higher as the beasts shoved their kindred beneath them to get at the humans trapped in the truck. Their piled bodies were as high as the hood and up to the doors when Grey finally got his truck moving again.

Michael was already stomping the gas as Joslyn reached across Sadie to hammer on his forearm, screaming: "Go! Go! Go!" at the top of her lungs.

The five-ton bellowed and snorted like a beast as its six wheels dug in and drove up the piled zombies in front of them. The nose of the truck went up as they mounted the writhing mound and then, like a ship in a storm, they pitched downward only to have their momentum stall completely. It felt as though they were high-centered, however it was simply the weight of the truck crushing and collapsing the mound.

The engine roared as Michael kept the gas pedal pegged. At first, the wheels spun uselessly, then the mound of bodies seemed to shift and undulate. The right side of the truck suddenly pitched down and to the side. The angle was so severe that Lindsey slid to the door and Joslyn slid into her. Sadie stuck her black sneakered foot out and held her and Eve back. The baby was clinging like a monkey with both her arms and legs wrapped tight against Sadie's slim body. She was surprisingly strong for a nine-month old and she needed all that strength when the passenger side door suddenly opened.

With the truck canted, the zombies were at door level and an unfortunate, scabbed-over grey hand had gotten to the handle by accident. Since they were without locks, army truck doors were a simple matter to open; a yank was all it took.

Lindsey's screaming reached a glass-shattering pitch as the zombies fought each other to get at her. She kicked backwards and flailed in a panic similar to that of a person drowning. Joslyn was affected in the same manner and she scrambled over Sadie and Eve, clawing and kicking.

"Stop!" Sadie screamed, trying to protect Eve. Joslyn continued to fight to get further from the door. In essence, she trampled right over them both. Sadie was forced to twist around to keep Eve from being used as a foothold. Joslyn dug a boot into Sadie's back, scraping skin back, uncaringly. Joslyn was so far gone in fear she even grabbed the steering wheel to keep from sliding to where the hungry zombies waited. The extra weight on the steering wheel kept Michael from being able to right the truck. They were on a huge pile of zombies with the engine roaring and the wheels skidding and slipping in the horrible mud and mulch created from the blood and tissue of ground up zombies.

The sound of the truck, the incessant moans of the zombies and the howling screams of Lindsey as she was pulled down into the arms of the zombies, penetrated right through the earmuffs on Sadie's head. It was so loud she could barely hear Michael when he shouted: "They're leaving us!"

Sure enough, as Sadie struggled up to see out the front window she saw the lead truck had freed itself from the densest part of the horde and was escaping, black smoke shooting into the air from its exhaust pipes. Sadie had one thought: *What about me?* She couldn't believe Neil was leaving her behind to be overwhelmed and eaten by the thousands of undead. The idea left her breathless and the sight of the truck vanishing plus all the mayhem around her, left Sadie physically numb.

She was jarred back to her awful reality when the truck lurched again. With three different forces acting on her body, she slid closer to the open door. The first force was simple gravity sucking her down, the next was Joslyn kicking her in the back, using her to plug the opening, and the third was Lindsey who had a hold of one of her Converse sneakers and was using it to keep from being dragged out of the truck.

With one hand clutching the baby and the other on the grip of her Glock, Sadie could only stop her slide by again sticking her foot out to the dash.

Lindsey's screams took on a new note of pain to go with her panic. The endlessly grasping hands of the zombies had pulled off her shoes and now her lower legs and feet were being chewed upon. "Help me!" she screamed at the top of her lungs in desperation.

"Pull yourself up," Sadie yelled back. She could do nothing for the woman except hold on for as long as she could. Lindsey tried with all her might to get away, however the zombies were limitless in number and too many of them had a grip of her lower body either with their hands or with their teeth and she was slowly pulled out of the truck.

And with her went Sadie.

"Let go!" Sadie cried. "You're going to kill me, too!" Lindsey's terror was too great and her mind too far gone for her to realize that she was dooming Sadie. This left Sadie without a choice. She could see that Lindsey was already bitten in a number of places. Sadie wasn't going to drop what she had in her hands—her only weapon and the precious baby—to try to pull an infected woman into the truck.

"Help me," Lindsey begged. Her eyes were pleading and desperate. She was so pitiful that it was physically painful for Sadie when she pointed the Glock and shot Lindsey in her pleading face.

That second seemed to extend and elongate as if emotional pain could affect time. It drew out cruelly so that Sadie could savor every horrible detail of it. Lindsey's fear-stricken face contorted one muscle at a time, until she had switched out fear for utter shock. Slowly her head went back—likely it snapped back, however for Sadie it was glacial in its speed and the blood that sprayed in the air lingered like a sun-shower on a July day.

Sadie got to see it all: the grey porridge of brain that slapped against the lower edge of the door. The 'O' of puzzlement Lindsey's mouth made, the hands that came up out of the mass of undead, engulfing her, the lustful teeth rearing up and then chomping down, biting through the thin cotton of her clothing.

Lindsey lost her grip on Sadie's foot, and she was carried out into the sea of zombies. She was like a sinking ship. In that slow-motion view of Sadie's, the girl was slowly engulfed, slipping beneath the grey waves until she was gone.

From behind Sadie, Joslyn accused: "What did you just do?"

Sadie couldn't answer. Guilt had her by the throat. A million excuses ran through her mind: Lindsey had been bitten! She was going to die anyway! She shouldn't have been trying to pull Sadie down with her! None of that mattered. Once again, Sadie had killed without a second's hesitation. Once again, she had put her needs ahead of any consideration…not that she had taken even a moment to consider anything at all. She had taken an innocent life to save her own.

The thought fed the black cloud in her mind. It churned, an evil tempest, brooding, reeking, foul, however there was no time for Sadie to breathe in that self-hate. The truck was still canted and bucking and her pathetic, greedy life was still in danger. The cloud would wait. It was patient. *If* Sadie lived it would be there, waiting.

Somewhere in those endless seconds, she blinked and time snapped back into place. It was with surprise that she felt herself still sliding toward the grey horde. With one hand around the baby and the other holding the Glock, she had to rely on her feet. She braced her left foot on the dash and the right—the one that still felt Lindsey's ghostly fingers on them—on the door frame. She was splayed and open and, beneath her exposed undercarriage, was the horde, surging and moaning in hunger, clawing over each other to get at her.

Time seemed to speed up more and more quickly as hands took the door and pulled it back and others grabbed the frame and mouths with broken teeth breathed their horrid breath up at her.

"Drive!" yelled Sadie and then fired the Glock. Her hand thrummed at the violence of the weapon. A beastly thing with dangling lips and only a single ear fell away with what was left of its brain adding to the mess on the door.

Michael had been attempting to drive them out, but had only succeeded in spinning his wheels as he tried to force his way into the teeth of a veritable grey wave. So many of the undead surged toward the truck that the mound became a hill and their shredded bodies acted almost like a treadmill. The tires went round and round and the beasts were turned to grey, creamed corn mush that shot out the back.

Still, it was an all-wheel drive vehicle and, gradually, the truck conquered the hill of bodies, only to sink down into the trough where it bogged down in exactly the same spot as Grey's truck had, only now the bog of shredded skin, and ruptured intestines and the foul soup of black blood was deeper. To make matters worse, Michael also had to contend with the drag of the fifty or so zombies clinging to the sides of the truck.

Michael hit the gas for all he was worth and, just as Grey's truck had done, Michael's truck slewed to the right. As a good 'ole boy from Alabama, he had never driven in snow or even ice and when the truck began to skid, he didn't turn into it as he should have done and thus he continued to slide until his rear wheel went into the gutter and the truck's momentum ceased. Out of ideas, he gunned the Cummins 240 horsepower engine until it screamed as if in pain. A shudder racked the truck. It shimmied and shook as if it was coming apart. Confused, Michael stared down at the dash, perhaps thinking that the dials would tell him what he was doing wrong. When an explanation didn't present itself, he decided to put the truck in reverse. Before he could do so, his door was pulled open and he was confronted with the same horror Sadie was dealing with. The zombies were mounded as high as the doors.

Sadie cleared her door with two quick shots and then leaned dangerously out over the reaching hands of the zombies to shut it—all the while clutching Eve to her breast. The door was shut for barely a second before she saw the handle turn. Shoving the gun under her leg, she reached out and grabbed the handle. There was a shot behind her. It was a tinny sound and she guessed that Joslyn had used the .25.

There were more gunshots cracking the air outside. As Sadie strained one-handed to hold the door closed she had a perfect view of the side mirror. In it, she could see the last truck reversing down the road, heading toward the large warehouse. Veronica Hennesy was in the passenger seat, blasting back the beasts with a shotgun. She looked desperate and afraid, but all Sadie could think was that they were abandoning her as well. Just as Neil had.

But did it matter whether or not they left? The side mirror also showed her that the zombies were piled so high they were at the height of the tailgate and were climbing up into the bed. There was a fierce battle going on back there to keep them at bay, while upfront, both doors were being assaulted. Sadie glanced back at Michael. He should've been doing something about getting the truck freed but he was red in the face, straining to keep his door from being pulled open.

The only person who seemed to be doing nothing was Joslyn. She sat between Michael and Sadie completely useless. "Take... the...baby," Sadie gasped.

At first Joslyn appeared shocked and slightly appalled at the idea of handling Eve, but when Sadie added: "Now, you stupid cow!" she put down her little gun and took the infant, holding her like a man might.

"We're fucked," Joslyn said.

It appeared so, Sadie thought, as she witnessed the first of the zombies climb onto the hood of the five-ton. It didn't hesitate. It threw itself at the windshield, thumping the glass with it fists and snarling like a rabid dog. A second zombie joined it a few moments later and the glass shook under their blows.

Sadie's hands began to ache with the strain of pulling on the door handle for so long. She wouldn't be able to last. *If only Neil and Grey and Jilly were here*, she thought. Neil wasn't the smartest, or the toughest, or even the bravest, but he always came through, somehow. And Grey would've been able to fight off the zombies and drive the truck at the same time. And Jillybean would've been able to figure out a way to lock doors that had no locks and she would've been able to fulcrum the truck right off the pile of undead.

Sadie couldn't do anything of those things. All she had was her guts and her quickness.

Her hand tired and the door handle slipped out of her sweaty grip. The door flung wide. Dozens of clawed and diseased hands reached for her, but she was too fast. Sadie grabbed up her Glock in a blur and fired five-six-seven times. She could've fired a hundred times and it wouldn't have made all that much difference, but seven was enough to clear the door. Before the beasts could recover, she leaned out over them and pulled the door inward.

An arm was in the way, keeping the door from closing. Sadie kicked at it, however more hands and fingers reached up under the edge and began to pry the door back open again. "Son of a bitch!" she hissed and then let the door open a little more and fired through the crack. Four bullets were enough to clear the door. Those were four bullets that she desperately needed. The Glock had started with a load of fifteen; she had four shots left and another fourteen in a spare clip in her back pocket—that was it. Nineteen rounds. It wasn't nearly enough.

Fearing she wouldn't have time later, she dug out the full spare and switched out clips. She had just slapped the spare clip in place when there was a renewed scrabbling of claws on the door and she saw the handle begin to turn once more. She grabbed it with both hands.

Now, a crack appeared on the corner of the windshield. The beasts there were pounding with hate-driven strength. Gradually the crack started questing upwards.

In the bed, there were screams of terror and gunshots that sounded with a constant rhythm. Joslyn made a whining noise in her throat. "Someone do something," she said. The only one who could do anything beyond what it took for personal survival was Michael.

Keeping one hand on his door handle, he reached over and, with much grinding of gears, he struggled the long-handled stick into reverse. He then fed it gas and the machine shuddered and shook as the wheels spun. The truck pressed against the hundreds of straining bodies and it didn't move more than three feet. He then ground the transmission into first gear and the truck bounced back to where it had been. He revved the engine, but after a few useless seconds of this, he let off the gas and once again grabbed the door handle with his other hand. He had done everything he could within his limited ability.

The hood was covered in the undead now. Michael's door started to open and he was forced to use all his strength to keep it closed. The gunfire from the bed reached a fevered pitch; they had no door to hold the beasts back. Sadie began thinking about the end. Should she pray? Would it matter if she did? The black cloud in her mind, the one that whispered 'murderer,' suggested that it wouldn't. The black cloud knew how many people she had killed. It knew how many she had murdered. It knew she deserved the death that was coming.

"But I still have nineteen bullets," she said, gripping the gun. There were seventeen for 'them,' one for Eve and one for herself. She decided that Joslyn and Michael would have to fend for themselves. They had guns and they were adults. Sadie took a breath and released the door handle, letting in the great stink of the zombies. She felt amazingly calm.

"What are you doing?" Joslyn asked, her eyes were huge in fear.

Before Sadie answered, she fired three times to clear the door. "My hands are too tired and too slippery with sweat. I can't hold the door and..." Sadie paused to fire again, enjoying the hot gunpowder smell that wafted from out of the barrel of the gun. "And we're stuck. I'm going to end it right. You two should consider doing the same." She shot once more. From this range she couldn't miss. "Eleven," she said, keeping track. Another shot: "Ten."

Joslyn gaped for a second and then as understanding struck her, she beat on Michael's arm and cried out: "Drive or do something." He tried, however the truck only rocked and shuddered and roared. It was hopelessly stuck, three quarters of it buried in the undulating mound of the dead. It started pitching side to side under the power of the zombie horde.

"Seven...six...five..." Sadie counted down. A sense of relief, of letting go, swept her. It was a pleasant feeling, but a sad one. She felt unfinished. She felt as though there were a thousand things she had left undone or unsaid and a thousand places she hadn't been, and a thousand sights she hadn't seen.

When Sadie's gun ran dry, she paused to switch out the clips. Now there were only two rounds for the undead, one for Eve and one last to send her to hell. "I hope you're ready," she said to Michael. She didn't care for or about Joslyn but she knew Michael to be a nice man.

He licked his lips and then jerked as the cracks in the windshield began to star. The panel of glass was beginning to bow inwards. He nodded. Their time was done.

Sadie turned back to the door, stuck her arm out so that the barrel of the Glock was an inch from the hungry mouth of a zombie. With part of a blouse hanging from its putrid body, Sadie saw it had been a human woman at one time. Perhaps it used to have a family and a job and a nice house. Maybe it once had a life worth living. Sadie shot it and felt a moment of jealousy.

"Three left," she said. There were four or five zombies in the lower part of the doorway. She kicked the closest one in the face and then turned to Joslyn. "Let me have Eve." Even though it was obvious what Sadie was about to do, Joslyn didn't hesitate. She gave up the baby and then pointed her little .25 in Sadie's direction. "Don't be stupid," Sadie said. "I'm not going to waste a bullet on you. You're safe from me, but not from them."

The Goth girl turned back to the door with the gun pointed out at the sea of zombies that were swamping the truck. Sadie then forgot about Joslyn, her mind was on the now heavy gun and the little bundle in her arms. "Make it quick," she said to herself. "One for them, one for Eve, one for me. Make it quick." She had to be quick; three zombies had fought to the top of the heap and were in the lower part of the doorway struggling to climb up into the cab.

She had to be quick, but she hesitated—Eve had reached out and took hold of her black t-shirt. That little, soft hand with its tiny fingers had such a grip. It clung with the desperation of life. Still with the ear protection clamped on her round head, she was pouting and afraid. She saw the monsters coming for her and held desperately to the girl who had called her sister for the last seven months.

The gun shook and Sadie was never further from pulling the trigger than just then. However a slime-covered hand fell on her leg, the long, broken nails making a whisker sound on her black jeans. "One for them," Sadie said and killed the undead beast. "One for Eve." She pointed the still smoking barrel Eve's way. Suddenly, the world drew away and became so silent that Sadie could hear the hissing of the gun barrel as it cooled and she could hear Eve's breath coming in and out of her pert little nose, and she could hear the springs working in the Glock as she drew back the trigger.

The trigger went back as far as it could, releasing the coiled spring and sending the firing pin flashing forward.

In that split second, another foul hand took hold of her jeans at the cuff just above her right Converse and pulled, jerking Sadie around just as the gun barked and flashed and Eve flinched, as her head whipped back. Instantaneously, the impact of taking yet another innocent life struck Sadie like a sledge between the eyes. Regret over shooting the gun stabbed her in the heart and she silently begged for the bullet to come back, to undo the damage it had done.

There was no undoing the act. There was now only her own death to accomplish and that was happening quickly. Even then, she was being pulled around and then down toward the mob of undead and all she could think about was the terrible thing she had done. Hands tore at her and teeth gnawed on the tough hide of her black jeans.

Slowly, almost casually, Sadie brought the gun to her temple. The muzzle burned her flesh, marking her with a small, red circle. She squirreled her right eye shut from the pain and from the imminent blast of the gun, and started to pull the trigger one last time—but then a new sound came to her, breaking through the cacophony of the moans and guns blasting.

Meep! Meep! Meep!

It was the sound of a horn. Captain Grey's truck was returning! It was plowing through the wash of undead and as she watched, Captain Grey climbed out to stand on the fender as Neil took the wheel. Grey's M4 carbine was aimed straight at her and for a heartbeat she was sure he was going to shoot her. He would be within his rights considering what she had done. In fact, the idea of rescue suddenly made her sick. What would they say about Eve? What would they do when they found out that Sadie had killed the baby? It would be better for everyone if he killed her right then.

His gun flashed a number of times and the hands holding her fell away. She was half in and half out of the truck and she could have, if she wanted to, climb back in, only she didn't want to. Guilt held her back. With tears streaming down her face Sadie put the gun back to her temple.

She brought the baby up one last time to kiss her goodbye...and nearly dropped her. Eve was crying, howling like a banshee. Her earmuffs sat cockeyed on her head and there was a wicked dent on the metal band that held the muffs in place. Sadie's bullet had missed!

Sudden feeling swept over the numbness that had gripped her and she could see and hear and breathe again. She was still alive and everything was still good. She fought and clawed back into the truck as Grey fired all around her. Then, miraculously, she was inside again, live and whole, as was Eve.

Grinning, she shut the door. When she turned, she saw Joslyn staring at her in disbelief. Michael hadn't seen anything. He was too busy fighting with all his strength to keep his door from being yanked out of his hands. He weakened a second later and the door was pulled halfway open. Desperately he tried to get his M16 from the floorboard before he could be pulled out of the truck by the zombies.

Sadie saw he'd be too slow by half. She leaned across Joslyn and fired over Michael's back, killing a single zombie who fell back into the crowd. There were others but she was out of ammo. Still with the screaming baby clutched to her side she tossed the Glock on the seat and grabbed the .25 from Joslyn's useless hands.

"Hey!" Joslyn cried.

"Lean back or I'll shoot you," Sadie said. Her voice was deadly cold. Joslyn flattened herself and Sadie shot across her breasts, clearing the door long enough for Michael to shut it again. There wasn't time to celebrate this minor victory. Captain Grey was yelling and pointing at them but they couldn't hear what he was saying. "Try the truck again," Sadie suggested as she attempted to calm the baby down. Putting the earmuffs back in place helped and corking her mouth with a pacifier reduced her cry to a chest-hitching sniffle.

Michael tried to move the truck again, but it was still just as stuck. Eventually, Grey stopped yelling and with a scowl, he climbed back into his truck before the zombies could swamp them as well. Then he left, heading back to the large warehouse in their rear.

"Hey, where are they going?" Joslyn demanded, angrily.

"Oh, just relax," Sadie snapped. "I told you we could trust Neil."

Joslyn eyed her while wearing a sneer and said: "I trust Neil. It's you I don't trust."

Guilt gripped Sadie from within making it feel like someone was squeezing her heart with icy fingers. She rallied, saying: "The baby is fine. There's not a scratch on her."

"What about Lindsey?" Joslyn shot back. "She's got more than a scratch on her."

Sadie couldn't say anything to that. The guilt was back, stronger than before, and had her by the throat, closing off her airway. In all the chaos, she had forgotten about Lindsey. She wouldn't forget now. The picture of Lindsey the moment before Sadie shot her, appeared in her mind. It spread itself out filling her consciousness and Sadie knew it would never go away.

Chapter 5

Captain Grey

"Move over, Neil," Grey said, climbing practically on top of the smaller man. He dropped the hot M4 into Neil's lap and said: "Reload this will you? My God, where did Michael learn to drive?" He had meant it as something of a joke, however no one responded with even a glimmer of a grin.

Neil was staring at the fearful scene around the other truck in a state of shock. Grey didn't blame him as it was simply awful, he had never seen such a grisly, bloody sight. The mound of ground-up and shredded human meat was amazing in size and utterly disgusting. Neil started to turn green.

To get him refocused, Grey reached over and tapped the M4. "Come on, Neil. I'm going to need it here pretty quickly." The soldier then stuck the old M809 five-ton into gear, fed it gas and slowly released the clutch, gaining traction over the bodies in front of them and picking up speed.

As Grey plowed through the horde, Neil reloaded the gun. Jillybean knelt on the bench and stared all around. Her lips were so puckered that they had disappeared from her face. Deanna was grim and beautiful. There wasn't any fear about her whatsoever and that was beautiful as well. Grey caught himself staring at her. When she glanced toward him, he quickly looked away, turning his eyes to the ugly task at hand.

It was three minutes of gruesome driving to reach the open area in front of the largest warehouse. No one knew what to expect when they got there. Grey feared that the people in the other truck had tried to get to the warehouse in order to make a stand. He knew that if they had it would be their final stand. Almost as a rule, warehouses were wide open places with nowhere to hide except perched on whatever merchandise was being stored there. Sometimes there were offices, but usually they were thrown in as an afterthought and had cheap doors, thin walls, and little in the way of protection.

He didn't think Ricky and the others would go for that. He figured they would make a dash for whatever area of fencing was most clear of the stiffs and attempt to climb their way to freedom—another bad move. Grey didn't think much of their chances. Trying to escape this cauldron of undead on foot would take a mental toughness that few of them possessed.

The group hadn't chosen either of these two dubious options. For whatever reason, Ricky was driving the truck in slow circles, crushing the undead beneath the worn and aging tires of the M809. If he thought that attrition would allow them a chance at freedom, he was very much mistaken. For every one of the zombies that went down, two more took its place.

The truck resembled a mastodon, surrounded by countless wolves. Zombies clung all over it. They were on the doors and gas tanks, on the fenders, the hood, and even on the canvas covering the bed. They were slowing it down and when it finally came to a standstill, it would be mobbed and overwhelmed.

Grey charged up, flattening everything in his path. He took a curving course so that he chugged along thirty yards to the side of Ricky's truck and running parallel. "Let me have the weapon, and prepare to take the wheel," he ordered. Neil handed over the gun and slid over in a seamless transition as Grey stepped out onto the fender. As the truck rattled over the bodies, he clung to the side mirror with his left hand, the muscles of his arm bulged and the veins showed like snakes riding beneath his skin. One handed, he shouldered the M4 and fired, killing those zombies who were dragging open Veronica's door in the other truck.

When it was clear, he shouted: "Roll down your window!"

Veronica rolled it part way down and screamed across the gulf that separated them: "What are we going to do? There's too many of them!"

Grey pointed back the way he had come. "Go back! It's not that bad. Just stay to the left. Tell Ricky not to stop or slow down, no matter what. We'll meet past the trestle bridge where it's clear." She gave a thumbs up and Grey climbed back in, again taking the wheel.

"How are going to free Michael's truck?" Neil asked. He had begun topping off the magazines as soon as he had slid over. It wasn't an easy thing to do as the truck bounced over body after body and as many bullets went bouncing away as went into the magazine.

"We'll push them out. It'll be no problem." He had all the confidence in the world, not only in his ability as a driver, but also in the Army trucks—they just had to be handled with a steady hand and a judicious use of the gas pedal.

For a few seconds Grey kept his truck back, allowing Ricky some room to make his run down the zombie-clogged street. With so much of the attention on Michael's truck, the left side of the street wasn't as densely packed and Ricky managed to blast a path through. A few times he started to bog down or slide in the remains of dead or crippled zombies, however he kept the engine pounding. Once he got past the tremendous mound, he was able to pick up speed and he quickly turned onto the main road and was gone from sight.

"Now it's our turn," Grey said, moving the stick through the gears. He knew he would need all the momentum he could get. Not only did he have to climb the mound, he had to have enough oomph to get Michael moving as well.

The mound proved to be a speed-sapping obstacle. The truck went slower and slower as it crawled upward over the undead. Still, it reached Michael's truck with enough of a surge that it should have sent it onward, but there was only a tremendous crash and then both trucks settled deeper into the mound of flesh.

"Son of a bitch!" Grey cursed. "He never turned his wheel! Wait here."

Almost hidden by the swelling and the bruising was Neil's look of confusion. "Wait here? Where would I go? Where do you think you're going?"

"Out for a stroll," Grey said. It sounded sarcastic but Neil's jaw dropped when Grey took the M4 from his hand and opened the door. Neil started to say something, only Grey had shut the door and was climbing onto the hood of the great truck. He took three steps and leapt across to the bed of Michael's truck—the back gate was slick with blood, thankfully all of it was black.

The renegades reached out for him, some to steady him, others to pull him into the bed. There were eighteen people in the cramped bed and they all began babbling and pointing at once. "Let go!" he demanded, slapping at the hands on him. "I have to get up front."

"You can't," one of them said. Compared to the bright sky, it was dim in the back of the truck and Grey couldn't make out who was talking. The person went on: "There's no access door to the front."

He wanted to say: *No shit*, but he held back. "I know. I'm going up top." He slung his rifle on his back, got a good grip of the bed frame and heaved himself up. Because Michael was still battling in vain to free his truck, Grey had to crawl to keep from pitching over the side. Seconds later he was at the front where the hood was covered in the undead pounding on the windshield or tearing at the metal of the truck

The M4 was off his back in a flash and he swept them aside with blazing hot lead. He then leaned over the passenger side door and shot four of the beasts who were slowly dragging it open. He did the same with the driver's side. He then knocked on the glass.

"Hey," Michael gushed as he rolled down his window. He was red in the face and there might have been tears in his eyes. Grey pretended not to notice as Michael started jabbering: "I'm so glad to see you. We're just about as stuck as can get and there were these..."

Angrily, Grey interrupted him. "Turn your damned wheels! They're pointed right at the curb."

"Oh! I didn't know. You can't tell from up here, not with all the zombies. All I can see are..."

There was no time for wasted words or wasted seconds and so Grey interrupted him once more: "I'm going to tap you again with my truck. Give it all the gas you got and then meet us up passed the trestle bridge." Michael was saying something but Grey was already crawling back the way he had come. For him, it was just a hop, skip and a jump back to his truck, and after shooting a couple stiffs that had struggled up to the level of the door he climbed in and handed Neil the M4.

"Hold on, it's going to get bumpy," he said, and then gave Deanna a wink. He couldn't say why he had winked. He had meant for it to come across as light-hearted, but he was instantly sure it looked cocky instead. Embarrassed, he regretted it immediately. She only gave him a small and unreadable smile in return.

Stifling another curse at his stupidity, he worked the truck into first gear and slid and skidded his way forward until the grill of his truck clubbed into the back bumper of Michael's truck, crushing a number of zombies who were attempting to get at the renegades.

Both machines roared and belched smoke into the sky as they ground slowly forward. Zombies surged at them with even more hungry desperation. Suddenly, Deanna's door was pulled open and she reached out with both hands to shut it. She was red in the face and breathless from the struggle by the time she was able to close it again. "You better hurry," she said. "I won't be able to hold on for long."

"I can hold it for you," Jillybean said. For the moment, at least, her eyes were the clear blue that marked her as free of the evil creature inside her.

"No, honey," Deanna said, grunting with the effort of holding the door closed. "It's a lot harder than it looks."

Jillybean shook her head. "No, I don't think so. Watch." The little girl leaned across Deanna's struggling body, took hold of her seat belt, wrapped it once around the door handle and then looped it behind the passenger side head rest. "You can let go now."

Tentatively, Deanna released her grip. The door creaked open about three inches and wouldn't go any further. The seat belt was tight as a bowstring. Deanna made a noise that suggested: *Why didn't I think of that?* Jillybean then pointed at the gap and the claws reaching up through it and said: "If that opening makes you nervous, you can roll the window down part way and shoot the monster, that way you don't have to open the door if you don't wanna."

The hands could only reach so far, only half a foot or so. She was safely out of their reach. "I think it's good the way it is, thanks," Deanna said. "No need to waste bullets."

During this, Grey was bull-dogging his truck, mashing it against Michael's without regard to the damage he was doing to the rear of the vehicle. The tail gate was crumpled and probably useless. Still, Grey pounded the truck, until it started moving on its own.

When they had both slogged clear of the main throng of zombies and had turned back toward the trestle bridge and the zombies had lost their grip and fallen from the trucks, one by one, Grey broke out a rare smile and exclaimed: "And that is how it's done!" Deanna gave him a grin while Jillybean leaned back onto the bench—she didn't smile. She was jittery, her eyes flicking everywhere and her hands touching the dash as if the feeling was new. This was sadly normal for Jillybean, now; joy was infrequent and anger a constant backdrop. She was drifting between mental states now that the danger was over.

Neil wasn't smiling either. "If we got through that unscathed, I'd be very surprised, and, of course, we have another decision in front of us: do we go on the way we had planned? That might have been just a taste of what could be waiting for us and it was a fiasco. How much ammo did we just burn through? Five hundred rounds? A thousand?"

Deanna shook her head. "No way it was that much. I'd say two-hundred, tops."

"No, Neil is right on this," Grey said. "Ammo goes faster than you can imagine in battle, and I heard at least two guns going full auto there for a while. But...but we should get an actual count before making any decision about changing course." He had added this last point, quickly. Deanna's face had begun to set in something that was close to a frown and he hated the idea of being the person who had caused that.

It turned out Neil was right, and not just about the numbers of bullets used—all together they had fired over eight-hundred rounds—he was also right about the human cost. Joslyn stunned everyone with an accusation of murder. Sadie hung her head as Joslyn started bleating about what had happened in the cab of the second truck. "Instead of helping Lindsey, Sadie shot her like a dog." Everyone stared at the Goth girl. In the silence she had caused, Joslyn added: "And then she wanted to kill Eve!"

Michael immediately shouted Joslyn down: "It wasn't anything like that! Lindsey had been bitten and was being dragged out into the horde. There was no saving her and Sadie did what she had to do, which is more than you did. It was a mercy killing, for Pete's sake!" Michael was in a rage at the stupidity of the accusation, however Grey noted he hadn't mentioned anything about Eve. That point was glossed right over.

With one drama seemingly ended, Fred Trigg suddenly pointed a finger to begin another. "She got bit." He had singled out a woman named Arlene, one of the ex-whores. At one time she had been pretty, however the apocalypse had worn away that layer and underneath was a pinched, nervous woman.

Deanna stepped between Arlene and Fred so that the finger was pointing at her. She glared until Fred put his hand down. When she continued to glare, he stuck the offending hand in his pocket. Arlene hid behind Deanna. "It wasn't my fault," she said. She was alabaster in color and expression, and, at the confession, the other renegades began to move slowly away from her, most with either nervous looks or disgusted ones.

"Of course it's not your fault," Neil said to her in a kind voice. He then turned to Grey. "Get your med kit, quick. There may still be time to wash out the wound."

"It's too late," Arlene mumbled. Her arms were crossed and each hand had a grip on her bare flesh, making indented half-moon nail marks. There was blood on her left calf where the BDUs she had picked up at Fort Campbell were torn. The blood was already a dark maroon and sticky to the touch.

Neil shook his head. "It's never too late, Arlene. You never know."

Grey knew that this time Neil was wrong. He had heard of only two instances that a person was blooded by a stiff and lived. One being Neil's friend Ram and the other had been a private under his command the year before during their long retreat north from Santa Fe. That had been a hellacious three weeks of no sleep and running battles, desperately trying to keep their dwindling brigade between the stiffs and the fleeing civilians. The private, a mere boy in Grey's eyes, had been trapped along with his entire squad in the basement of a suburban tract house in some dusty, desert town. With supplies being rationed down to a few hundred calories a day, they were as famished as wolves and had gone scavenging, only to be separated from the main force and trapped.

The boy was the only one to return. When he did, his eyes were empty, his cheeks hollow. There was no more fight left in him. He hobbled everywhere because he had cut all the toes off his left foot with his Ka-bar. As his story went, the squad had fought to the last bullet in the dim and cramped basement. When the zombies had broken through the door, the other men had started swinging their M16s like they were clubs in order to allow the private, Yeager was his name, an opportunity to escape. He had wriggled part-way through a squat little box of a window when a stiff had caught him by the foot as he had struggled out into the daylight. The beast had ripped off his boot and had bitten his toes down to the bone.

Grey didn't buy the story. He was sure they'd been trapped and he was sure that Yeager's toes had been bitten, but there was a lie somewhere in the tale. For one, properly laced combat boots couldn't be simply 'ripped' off, no matter how strong the zombie was. For two, Yeager hadn't been so well-liked that the other men in his squad would lay down their lives for him. What was for sure was that his toes had been chopped clean off and he had come back without a single bullet on his person.

Arlene wasn't going to be as lucky; she was going to lose a lot more than a few toes. As the others milled and talked about the battle, Grey took Arlene to the driver's side of his five-ton; he kept his med-bag stuffed in the small space behind the seat. Quickly, he pulled out scissors, rubbing alcohol and a roll of gauze bandages. Had this been any other injury he would've dug out more: bacitracin, a scalpel, a suture kit, sterile gloves, and antibiotics—all that would have been a waste with Arlene.

The second he cut away the lower leg of her BDUs he saw the bite was raggedly deep and the edges looked like hamburger. Equally dire was that at least fifteen minutes had passed since she'd been bitten. The virus had to be in her system.

"It's bad, isn't it," she said, her voice cracking. "I'm going to die, aren't I?"

He couldn't lie to her. "I think so, but that doesn't mean we can't try. This may sting a little." He had a large supply of rubbing alcohol and so he didn't hold back; he poured it generously into the wound. She didn't gasp in pain as he had expected not even when he worked the alcohol into her raw flesh. She only stared out at the ugly scrub-like landscape.

"Hey! Arlene!" he barked, trying to bring her around. If there was one thing he knew, attitude played a huge role in any healing process. He needed her alert, talking and hoping for the best. "Look at me. You can't give up."

"I think I want to," she answered in a ghost of a voice. "I'm tired of all of this...and there are so many of them. From the back of the truck we saw all those thousands of zombies and at first we thought it'd be ok since we were driving away from them, but then we went in that circle. We knew we were going back into the horde. We tried to keep quiet and those near the gate scrunched down, but it didn't matter. They piled up and up and up and up. We prayed and hoped that they wouldn't see us, but someone panicked, Jackie, I think. She started yelling for Michael to do something. He had been just sitting there for the longest time and we were stuck, defenseless."

She grabbed his arm and squeezed, hard. It was an urgent, pleading squeeze. "It didn't make any sense to just sit there with all those zombies climbing over each other to get at us."

"Yes, I agree it didn't make..."

As though his voice was only a passing wind, Arlene spoke over him: "They kept getting higher and so the people with the biggest guns went to the gate and started shooting. It was so loud and the guns were bright; me and some of the other girls just huddled in the back with our hands clamped over our ears and we would've been safe for a while but then one of *them* stuck an arm under the canvas and grabbed Fred. He screamed and started shooting the canvas.

"We all fell to the other side of the truck, but the people there pushed us off and there was all this shoving. I don't know what happened next. All I knew was that the canvas was being shredded by the bullets and the zombies were ripping at the holes, making them bigger. Then everyone was shooting and people were knocking each other about...and that's when I got bit. I was on the bench trying not to get shot or knocked over, only something tripped me and, and, and I lost my balance, and they had me by the foot and they bit me...and...and..."

Her chest was heaving and her heart rate was skyrocketing, spreading the virus further into her system. He took both of her hands into his and said: "Shush now. You have to try to relax." Like a dishtowel, she went instantly limp and would only a mumble 'yes' or 'no' from then on.

He bandaged her leg and then went to look for someone to watch over her. No one would except, Sadie, who looked just as friendless as the doomed woman. The Goth girl wasn't well liked among the Renegades. They blamed her, at least partially, for her father's evil, and it didn't help that in the previous couple of days since her daring escape, she had been quiet and aloof. Some thought of her as stuck up. And now she had killed Lindsey. Although no one saw her as criminally guilty they were still swayed by the descriptions of the killing spread by Joslyn.

"Thanks," Grey said as Sadie came up, still holding Eve. "Try not to get her too riled, but don't let her sink into a depression either."

"Keep her luke-warm?" Sadie asked, listlessly. "I can do that. We'll talk about the weather."

Grey thanked her again and went to find Neil who was attempting to get a bullet count from the crowd of renegades. Deanna stood next to him with a pen in one hand and a scrap of paper in the other. When the last bullet had been accounted for she summed up the numbers, and all the while, the tip of her tongue, pretty and pink, stuck out between her lips.

"We have 1,276 rounds that fit into six different types of guns," she said, adding lamely: "It's not much."

"We need to take the short route," Neil stated at once. "One more attack like this and we're done."

Deanna didn't like the idea, her deep frown said as much, but she didn't fight it. "What are we going to do about Arlene? She's a good person."

"That was never in question," Grey said. "Right now, Neil has to think about the safety of the group. No one knows when her viral load will hit critical mass. Even before she turns into one of them, she'll be able to spread the virus. An accidental scratch could be a death sentence for somebody." They both turned to look at Neil.

He made calipers out of his fingers and touched the bridge of his nose as a pained expression swept across his features. "Critical mass or not, we don't shoot her until she goes into the delirium phase, unless she asks to be shot, that is. Then we do it quickly and humanely. That begs another question of who is going to…but I suppose, I mean, I guess I should, uh, be the one who does it. Pull the trigger, I mean."

If it wasn't such a sad subject, the idea of Neil as executioner would've had Grey chuckling, but just then with Arlene sitting in the grass and staring out, unblinking, and looking somewhat zombiefied already, a laugh was the furthest thing from his throat. "No, Neil. You're the leader here. You can't also be the executioner. It'll undermine your credibility. I'll do it. I've done it before. You get the people ready to go. I'll go talk to her."

It was a subject that wasn't easily broached. Sadie and Arlene were sitting in silence. Arlene had the thousand yard stare of a man pulled out of the line after a month of straight combat. Sadie matched the stare with one of her own. Perhaps because of all the excitement, or perhaps because she'd been ignored, Eve was fast asleep in Sadie's arms. There was a small red mark on the top of her head that Grey noticed only in passing.

"Sadie, I got this," he told her.

"She wouldn't talk," Sadie said as she struggled up without waking the baby. "I tried."

Keeping his voice pitched low and somber, he told her: "Thanks. I'm sure you did your best."

Arlene heard the change in his tone and though her eyes remained diffused and locked on something miles away that no one else could see, her right eyebrow went up ever so slightly. "What happened to keeping a positive attitude?" she asked. "Did you finally figure out that you're going to have to kill me?"

"It's a conversation that we should…" His voice caught as a tear, fat as a raindrop slid out of her eye and laid a track down her cheek to her chin where it hung for a moment until a second and a third joined it. It then slipped off and splashed onto her shirt. Possibly, in the most cowardly moment of his life, Grey said: "No, I mean, it's too early. It's a conversation for down the road."

She sniffled and nodded and then kept sniffling and nodding until he added: "Would you like to ride up front with me and Neil?" Her next nod was of greater depth and the sniffle louder.

Chapter 6

Neil Martin

Arlene asked for the window seat. It was a request that couldn't be refused even if it meant Neil got carsick. He kept a plastic bag open on his lap and he frequently had to take large steadying breaths to keep his breakfast in place. Arlene didn't speak. She only stared out the window as her time among the living counted down.

Size played a role in the progression of the *Super Soldier Virus*; the smaller the person, the quicker they succumbed. She was small and slim to the point of being frail —her time wouldn't be very long in coming.

Not only was Arlene quiet, so too, were Neil and Captain Grey. It was just the three of them up front. Because Jillybean could be unexpectedly nasty, Deanna volunteered to ride in the back with her. Although there was room, no one else jumped at the chance to sit in the front; Arlene was already dead to most of them.

"Sure is a pretty day," Captain Grey said. It was. Nothing else needed to be said on the matter. Neil, who was normally the resident optimist, saw the perfect blue and felt a wisp of cool, morning air and all he could think about was that he had lost two people and it wasn't even ten—he too was counting Arlene among the dead. It made it hard to strike up a conversation.

The silence drew out as they retraced their route. The quiet was only broken when they finally saw the barn they had slept in the night before and Brad's herd of zombies which was no longer arrayed in great circle. It was more of an amorphous blob. They knew it was Brad's because of the riders among them with their tall wings and shining armor. Arlene started weeping again at the sight of the blob and for one moment, Neil wondered if he would have to pay Brad for her.

The thought by itself made him a horrible person. Again, he pinched the bridge of his nose. He didn't have a migraine, it just helped calm him for some reason.

Grey stopped the truck a good quarter mile back from the mob of zombies. "He's going to be an ass, you know it."

"Yep," said Neil. "But I should be able to handle him. You forget, I was the original corporate raider back in the day."

The soldier raised an eyebrow as Brad came galloping up wearing a huge grin. "You think that'll help you in some way?" Grey asked.

"Not in the least," Neil replied with a grin. "We both know he's got me by the short and curlies here. I should get going to talk to him and uh…Arlene? I need to…" He faltered when Arlene didn't budge or act in any way as if she had heard him. Grey opened his door and slid out.

"You want me to go with you?" Grey asked.

Neil cast a glance at Brad. The horseman was running his fingers through his long blonde hair; he was so high up he seemed like a giant. Amazingly, Neil felt a stab of jealousy. He hadn't felt jealous since the old time in the old world. Since then he had been either too busy to even consider jealousy as an emotion or he'd been with Sarah and jealousy was what everyone else was feeling. She had been that beautiful.

He sighed, picturing her when he had first met her in the Illinois River; she'd been streaming water from her torso while only wearing a white shirt…with nothing underneath. Another sigh, and then he said: "No, I got this. How do I look?"

"Well, you've looked worse."

"Yeah," Neil replied. The day they had escaped from the River King he had looked more like a zombie than most zombies. Those injuries were mending, slowly, but he was beginning to see himself beneath the swelling and bruising. In preparation for his meeting with Brad, he tucked his shirt into his pants, adjusted his sweater vest and then marched forward, mentally readying himself. He was going to be screwed in the negotiations, there was no getting around that. His one job was to minimize the damage.

"So, you're back?" Brad asked, rhetorically. He leaned over his saddle and smirked in the direction of the three trucks. Neil glanced back; the trucks were splashed all over with black blood and there were ugly rags of flesh hanging from the axles. "Looks like you guys ran into a little trouble right off the bat."

"That?" Neil pretended to be a little shocked. "Please, that was nothing. Just a few stiffs; nothing we haven't seen a hundred times. No, we simply had a change of mind. We took a vote and more of us have decided that the shorter route might be better. So we'll accept the one-eighty a head."

Brad looked confused as if they hadn't agreed on the number three hours before. "Huh? One-eighty? No, that was the old amount. You got to realize that these sorts of things change, depending on need and availability. I had something come up. Some of my men are otherwise engaged. I'm sure you understand how these things go. I'm sorry, but I'm going to have to charge two-fifty a head."

Neil blew out a long breath. "And that's as low as you can go?"

"Yep."

That's some hardball, he's playing, Neil thought. "Then I suppose Captain Grey will take it. I will let him know." Neil walked away without glancing back. He was playing his one card: the walk away.

"Hey, Neil," Brad called after him. "What are you talking about? Hey…hey…what do you mean Captain Grey? Is he in charge, or what?"

Behind him, Neil could hear the clop of the horse, following after—a good sign. He stopped; it wouldn't do to lead Brad all the way back to the trucks where Fred would undoubtedly say something to ruin any chance at haggling Brad down. "Captain Grey will continue on with you, the rest of us are heading south east. We're thinking Louisiana. I'm not a fan of the bugs and snakes, but the shrimp should be plentiful and there are many islands in the Mississippi that we can fortify. Best of all, we won't have to worry about winter. I've always hated winter."

He turned to leave and Brad spurred his horse around to cut Neil off. "You're not going to haggle? That's short-sighted as a leader, don't you think? And Louisiana? You must be crazy. Where do you think all those stiffs in the Mississippi go? You couldn't pay me to go to New Orleans. I bet there are a few million zombies roaming that city."

"Hmm, I never thought about that," Neil replied. "Well then, maybe Pensacola, Florida. My parents took me there once as a kid. It was beautiful. Thanks for the advice, Brad." Neil gave him a smile and a wave and went back to walking.

"Hold on," Brad said in a hissing whisper. "If it's the money...I can do two-thirty."

A thrill like Neil hadn't felt since his business days went through him. He had always loved playing *The Game*. "It is the money, Brad but it's also about saving face. Two-thirty is as bad as two-fifty. How am I going to look going back to them saying that I just got fucked in the ass?" Neil never cursed unless it was for effect during negotiations. For some reason men admired other men who sprinkled vulgarity lightly in their conversations. Too much and you were without class, too little and you were a wimpy prude.

"Two hundred then," Brad said. "Even they have to realize things have changed."

Brad's horse was way too close to Neil and seemed very curious. It was snuffling its big nose along Neil's sweater vest. Neil took a step back—usually a bad sign in negotiations, but he was already at such a distinct disadvantage, being in such a low and submissive position, that it didn't matter all that much.

"If I bring back any offer above one-eighty then the only thing that will have changed in their eyes is that they'll realize that you can't be trusted. That you will take advantage of people and will likely cheat them every step of the way to Colorado. So if you can't come down, then I think this is goodbye."

The horse swung its head as Brad clutched the reins tight—a show of irritation on Brad's part. This was unbelievable. Neil could actually feel Brad begin to cave. As a further way to cement his 'walking away from the table' bid, Neil stuck out his hand to Brad. "Thanks anyways and no hard feeling."

The big man clucked his tongue at the hand and said: "Well, fuck. I guess we could do one-eighty, but I'm really getting screwed on the deal. You know that."

Neil knew the exact opposite was true but he went along. "Yeah, but sometimes that's how business works." The two men stared at each other and there was no love to be lost between them. There wasn't even a smidge of 'like' and Neil felt that he had won only the first battle in a long war between them.

Once the price was settled, there came a long interval as Brad rode away to make arrangements for the crossing. His horsemen broke up the mob of zombies and set them to walking across the plain. Then in a long line, they sat on their steeds staring at the renegades and whispering to themselves. Sometimes they would point or laugh.

This didn't bother the renegades who had been in a jolly mood ever since Neil explained they were being given safe passage to Colorado. They had cheered loudly at that. The idea of being safe in any regard very much appealed to them and no one grumbled over the price, especially since they had figured it would be so much more.

The sun was straight above their heads before Brad rode up in a Toyota Camry the color of road dust. He was no longer dressed in armor and his wings were gone. As a replacement to the fantastic outfit, he wore a mad swirling of colorful scarves as did the three women in the car with him. The outfits, especially on the women, were beguiling. They flowed and shimmered so that the bodies beneath were only hinted at and yet those hints were tremendously alluring. Even to Neil, who had assumed he was beyond such things since he was still feeling the sting of Sarah's passing.

Two of the women had hair that had been teased into a 1980's mass that made their heads look overly large. The third was bosomy in a manner that wasn't likely ever going to be replicated now that every plastic surgeon in the country was dead. Her chest pushed out the scarves to a ridiculous degree and yet Neil found her the least attractive. Her face was washed out and plain, while her hair hung limp and plastered wetly to her head as if a cube of lard had melted on her crown.

The women mingled with the renegades smiling and chatting as if they were old friends. They were very curious over everything and everyone, especially Eve and Jillybean. "There are no children among the Azael," Brad explained.

"It's not allowed?" Deanna demanded to know, her arms folded in front of her. She appeared strangely angry to Neil.

"It's not illegal," Brad explained. "It's more uh, frowned upon. The King and pretty much everyone else feels it's too early to take a chance on getting pregnant. You know, for the woman's sake." Deanna didn't look mollified by the answer and so Brad glossed over the entire subject. "But that isn't something we have to worry about. Right now, we are coming to a great adventure. The plains can be dangerous. We'll see zombies in the millions. If you fall into one of those herds they'll tear you apart and strip the flesh off of you in seconds, just like a school of piranha. But it's not just the mega-hordes you have to be careful of. The land is utterly barren. There isn't a drop of gas between here and the Rockies. As well, practically every well and every river is poisoned with the decaying bodies of the undead. And to make matters worse, there are bloodthirsty bandits who won't think twice about killing you. Lucky for you, I will be your guide. Only I can keep you safe."

This last brought cheers from the renegades.

Brad was all smiles, warm assurances and glib talk of an easy trip across the plains under his guiding hand and to the renegades, whose reality had been constant strife and storms, his words were all sunshine and rainbows. They were happy at their sudden good fortune and, as they climbed up into the baking hot five-ton trucks, they were giddy and laughed. Even Deanna, who looked upon Brad with all the suspicion a sparrow has for a cat, managed to smile in hope.

They plowed down the road, the Camry leading the three trucks, and Neil was just starting to think that this time everything was going to be all right when he glanced in the side mirror and saw the second truck in the line flashing its lights.

"Oh, boy," he whispered. Louder he said: "Grey, you better stop. Something's wrong."

There were four of them in the cab. Sitting next to Grey was Jillybean, who had been on her best behavior—meaning she was acting like her old self. Neil was next to her and then came Arlene staring lifelessly out the window; she was even whiter than ever and there was perspiration in her lank hair. She had to be feeling the virus start to kick in.

Out of habit, Neil supposed, Captain Grey pulled over to the side of the road. It wasn't at all necessary, there wasn't any other traffic on the road besides the usual scattering of stalled-out cars that sat low and hunched on flat tires. From a distance, they had a predatory look, like lions on the verge of pouncing. Up close, the illusion gave way to reality. Invariably, the cars were littered all around with brilliant shards of glass and, most of the time, the ground was strewn with the possessions of the one-time owners. This never failed to depress Neil. Though what was worse was when the road was stained black with old blood or when there were bones bleaching in the sun on its hot surface or when they came across ragged sheets of discarded skin looking like rat-chewed piles of dusty clothes.

Grey stopped just opposite one of these metaled corpses. It had been someone's baby. A four-door Mercedes which, at one time, had the same value as the average three-bedroom house. Now it sat covered in dust, its tires flat and the trunk popped open. Lying on the hood was the half-consumed corpse of a baby boy. From one of the windows, a torn, blue blanket flapped in the breeze. The captain didn't give it a second glance as he leapt down out of the cab.

When his door slammed, Arlene jumped a little and then looked around as if just coming awake. "I have to go to the bathroom," she said, dully, and opened her door. She eyed the dead car on a "just in case" level and then climbed out, favoring her wounded leg.

As leader, Neil couldn't just sit there, worrying, he had to go and actively worry. "Stay here," he said to Jillybean, though he didn't know why. The land was parade ground flat. The road had been cut between two immense farms and, as far as the eye could see, there was nothing but fields. These were in that halfway stage in their reversion back to nature: stalks of corn sat in clumps here and there, but they were wild grown and stunted from lack of proper watering. Between the clumps was waist-high prairie grass: bull grass and poke mixed with windblown wheat and barley. There were no zombies in sight.

The honest truth was that Jillybean was likely the most dangerous thing within ten miles.

Jillybean didn't answer Neil or even acknowledge he had said a thing. She simply stared at the baby on the Mercedes. The staring was another side effect of the Post-Traumatic Stress Disorder that she suffered from. It was seemingly harmless, but Neil liked it less than the plotting looks she would give him. What would happen if the staring became permanent? What would happen if that big brain of hers just shut down forever? Death, obviously.

"Hey, Jillybean, look at me." He gave her a gentle tap on the shoulder. Anything more would have had her leaping out of her trance with her claws raking at his eyes.

Slowly she turned her head and began blinking. "Do you think Mister Brad will let me ride his horse?" she asked.

"I don't know, sweetheart. He's not riding his horse anymore. He's in that Camry." Neil pointed at the car. Very slowly, as if the girl was drugged, she turned to look out the front window. "I think one of his men back at the barn has the horse."

"The horse was better," she whispered. There was a pause and then she said in a deeper voice: "I agree."

Neil kept the smile glued in place. "Wait here. I'll be right back." Her eyes clicked over from the tired look to the plotting one in a blink, but she tried to hide it by giving Neil what she thought was a smile. It was really a combination of a sneer and a look of disgust. It wasn't pleasant. "Ok, then," he said when he couldn't think of anything better, and then left her.

Fred Trigg, hanging out of the back of the five-ton asked Neil as he hurried by: "What's wrong?"

"I can't tell from here, now can I?" Neil answered, just managing to hold in his irritation. "Do me a favor and keep everyone in the truck. I know it's hot, but if this is nothing, we'll want to get moving right away and rounding everyone up is like herding cats."

Someone said: "That's not fair. They get to get out." People from the other trucks were climbing down to stand around the back of the middle truck. Neil didn't like the look of it. The way the men stood and pointed and the way women held themselves anxiously, meant it was undoubtedly a mechanical issue.

Grey came trotting back to the first truck. "Flat tire," he announced to everyone. "Michael doesn't have a spare and…crap, neither do we. Let's hope Ricky's got one or it's going to get cramped." Thankfully, the last truck in line had a spare. It was unslung from beneath the undercarriage and rolled to the middle one. Soon Captain Grey was sweating with the rising heat of the day, and cursing as he tried to loosen the dozen lug nuts off the shredded up original. They seemed welded in place.

"Is there an issue?" Brad asked, jovially. Wearing his strange shift of scarves, he came strolling up, drinking from a water bottle, the sides of which were damp with condensation as if it had just been pulled from an ice chest. Neil stared at it in open desire; he couldn't remember the last time he had a cold drink. Just looking at it, made him suddenly parched and he swallowed what felt like equal parts sand and sweat.

"Just a flat," Grey answered. He looked up to see the water bottle. His eyes narrowed before he went back to the lug nuts. "It's nothing we can't handle."

Brad chugged the last of the water, ran a multi-hued sleeve across his mouth and then casually chucked the plastic into the ditch beside the road. "Good. We have a long way to go before we can get to the first safe zone in Stafford. You don't want to get caught out on the prairie when the sun goes down. There's no telling what may happen."

In spite of the warning, he didn't seem worried. For a good part of the time they were stranded there, he sipped his cold drinks or snoozed in the shade of the truck while the three very friendly women who had accompanied him in the Camry went among the renegades with smiles and pleasantries. They were very charming and chatted harmlessly about supposedly inconsequential things. Neil watched nervously, afraid that someone would let slip where they'd been and who they were; there were times when the renegades had all the innate sense of a flight of pigeons.

Surreptitiously, Neil gathered a member of each of the different factions: the Gates family, the prisoners freed from Gunner's prison, and the women who had escaped from The Island. They stood behind the last truck looking confused about Neil's nervous behavior.

"I know I've said this before, but we need to tell everyone not to talk to Brad or his women about anything more serious than the weather. If it gets out who we are and where we just came from, we'll be screwed."

"We're not idiots," Ricky answered. "Everyone knows what's at stake."

When they slipped back to join the others, Ricky was proved, at least partially incorrect. Twenty three of the renegades were chugging from cold water bottles and exclaiming that they had never tasted such refreshing water in their lives.

"Tell me those are free," Neil hissed in a whisper to Sadie who was sitting in the shade, fanning Eve with a shirt.

Her Goth look appeared to be wilting with the July heat. "I wish. They're asking ten per bottle." She shook her head as Neil blanched at the waste. "Why do we bother with them, Neil? Sometimes it just doesn't seem worth it to me."

It was a good question and one that Neil had asked himself a number of times. All of the fighting and the scrambling and the constant hurt had taken a toll on them. Neil was battered physically, Jillybean was cracking mentally, and Sadie was starting to break emotionally. She had kept a stiff upper lip when Ram had died, and, when Nico and Sarah were murdered, she had managed to keep up a façade of toughness, but now that she had killed in cold blood, she walked around in somewhat of a fog. The only thing that seemed to keep her sane was Eve, whom she kept within arm's reach day and night.

"I don't know why we bother," Neil admitted. "Maybe it's because we're supposed to be the good guys."

Sadie dropped her chin at the idea of being a *good guy*. "Good guys don't murder unarmed prisoners," she said in a whisper.

"It wasn't murder, Sadie. You know that. What happened might lie in a grey area, I don't know, but it wasn't murder. You were being held against your will in an armed camp. Legally speaking, nothing you did was wrong."

"I killed Lindsey and I k-killed strangers, Neil. I killed people who were just in the wrong place at the wrong time and I killed...I killed a man when he was on his knees. He had given up, Neil." She began fanning Eve faster, blowing the wisps of her hair back and forth. "He said he wouldn't tell. He said I could go and no one would know, but I couldn't trust him, so I killed him. I shot him in the back of the head, execution style. Neil, do you know what that makes me?"

"Human?" Neil said as quickly as he could before she could spit out the words: *an executioner*. "You did what you had to in order to save me and to save Eve and Captain Grey. I think we both know what would've happened if you had let that man live."

"What about the guard at the front door? Or what about the man I ran into out in the parking lot? Or the guy on the stairs? What about them? I killed them all. I didn't even say a word. I didn't ask them their names or if they were nice or anything. I just killed them one after another. Bang, bang, bang! At first, I was ok with it. You know I was like you. I made excuses and pretended that it was ok. Now I dream about it. In the dreams, I just kill *people*. They're not even bad guys. Sometimes they're not guys at all." Her eyes flicked to the baby.

She was whipping the shirt over Eve now and the baby girl was blinking in confusion. "Hey! Slow down there," Neil said putting out a hand to slow the shirt. He tried to smile with his warped and butchered face; Sadie glanced at him once and then pressed the shirt to her eyes.

"In my dreams, I'm like Jillybean. I just a…." She choked, a muffled sound through the shirt.

"How are you like Jillybean?" a woman's voice asked. Both Sadie and Neil jerked and glanced up to see one of Brad's women standing above them. It was one of the bushy brunettes. She had a knapsack filled with cold water bottles. She held one out to Neil. "Please take one. Brad says they're free for you."

"No," Neil said. "Thank you, but no. We can't afford…I mean they can't afford it and I don't want to set a bad example."

The woman seemed pleasantly perplexed by his answer. "I could hide it for you and they'll never know. Here, I'll put it in this scarf." She took a scarf from her chest, revealing a surprising amount of cleavage. Neil's eyes slipped down to take in the supple curves, but only for a second and then he shook his head and acted as though the baby was of greatest interest. "Suit yourself," the woman said. She too looked down on the baby and broke into a wide smile. "Is this Jillybean's sister?"

Neil kept quiet, letting Sadie answer, hoping she would find some ray of happiness in talking about the baby. She was slow to answer, and spoke only a single word: "No."

The brunette cast a quick look back to where Brad was sitting, surrounded by the renegades. They had roused him and now he was laughing and smiling and was quite the contrast to dour Captain Grey who worked nearby with a snarl on his lips. "Can I hold her, please?" the woman asked. There was a note of honest desperation to her and after only the slightest hesitation, Sadie held up Eve like an offering. "She is precious," the woman said, speaking almost to herself.

For just that moment, the woman was herself. Her guard came down and Neil saw her perhaps as she had been before the apocalypse: pretty, sweet, motherly. By her look and the ease with which she had taken Eve, he guessed that she had been a young mother. This begged the dreadful question: where was her child? He didn't want to know the answer.

"How did she manage to live, I wonder?" the woman asked. "And Jillybean…are her parents alive? Are they among you?"

"No," Neil answered, reaching for the baby. "And if you don't mind that's a touchy subject. I would prefer not to talk about it."

The woman's false exterior sprang back into being. "I will not pry then, but what about you? Neil, is it? Those look like bite marks on your face. Were they from a zombie? Does that mean you're immune? News of a vaccine has reached our ears, but there are so many rumors that we don't know what's true."

Neil didn't know how to answer that without giving away the fact that he had been to New York recently. That could lead to many questions that he shouldn't answer. "Car accident actually. If you'll excuse me, I have to get this show on the road." As he handed Eve back to Sadie, he gave her a covert, warning look not to say too much. He then went to where Grey was straining at the rusted-over lug nuts. "What can I do to help?"

"With your hand and your arm, I doubt there's anything."

With barely a grimace of pain, Neil lifted the arm that had been dislocated, not quite a week before. It was stiff but useable. The hand where his left ring finger had been bitten off was another story; it was a constant nagging pain that never left him, even in sleep. "I'm doing better. I can get you some water at least."

He retrieved the water from the truck and, though it was hot as piss, it seemed to help Grey's mood. Nothing helped the lug nuts, however. Brad offered the use of another truck—at a ridiculous price, of course. Grey turned him down. Brad then offered to bring out his personal mechanic, again at a hefty cost. Grey just shook his head and went back to work. Finally, after a delay of nearly two hours, the last of the lug nuts came loose. Quickly, the spare was hefted into place and the old shredded up tire pushed to the side of the road.

Then Grey was barking orders, yelling the renegades into their trucks. Hot and tired, Neil, Deanna and Grey climbed up into the cab. They were about to leave when Neil realized he hadn't seen Jillybean in all the time they had been pulled over and she wasn't in the cab. "Stop! Where's Jillybean? And where's Arlene?" A shiver ran up his back as he pictured what Jillybean could be doing to Arlene even then.

Grey let out a groan over the further delay. He had worked the hardest and his BDUs were sponge-like with sweat. Deanna patted him on the thigh. "Me and Neil will take care of this," she said and then, much to the surprise of both Grey and Neil, she climbed over the soldier, her full breasts practically in his face, and hopped out through the driver's door.

"Well, ok," Grey said.

Neil went out the easy way, muttering: "Lucky bastard." He expected Jillybean to be quickly found: she was likely in the same truck with Sadie and Eve, or perhaps playing a game with ten-year-old Joe Gates with whom she had an uneasy friendship.

She was in neither spot and Arlene was nowhere in sight. Deanna and Neil checked beneath the trucks and in their hot and crowded beds, asking the sweating and annoyed renegades if they had seen either. No one had and when they reached the back of the third truck, Deanna was panicking. She started to run to the nearest stand of corn when Joslyn, who was in the last truck and standing high up on its back gate, cried: "There she is." Joslyn pointed back the way they had come and far down the road, Neil could just make out a little lump of yellow.

Both Neil and Deanna took off at a run, though with the heat baking up off the black top, they were quickly exhausted and staggering. Neil felt near to passing out by the time they came up on the little girl. Strangely, she was carrying a piece of black rubber from a tire in the crook of her arm where Ipes had used to sit. When Neil turned her around, he saw that her eyes were vacant and unfocused.

"Hi," he said gently. "Where are you off to? Just taking a stroll?"

She blinked slowly as though just waking up. She looked around without recognition as to where she was. "I don't know. *She* had an idea about wheels and…and that's all I remember."

"Do you mean Arlene?"

"Who…oh, no, not her. I mean the other girl. You know."

The mention of the other *girl* within Jillybean never failed to elicit a painfully fake smile from Neil. He was at a loss about what to do with this other person. He hoped that by doing nothing and ignoring the problem it would just go away. So far, that hadn't been working, but Neil wasn't going to give up. They were still on the road. They were still fleeing from danger and there was no way of knowing what danger was still before them. When they got to Colorado, things would be different and he would reevaluate her situation and perhaps his plan to deal with it.

"That's ok," Neil said, soothingly. He reached out and brushed a stray strand of her fly-away brown hair from her eyes and added, "No harm, no foul."

Jillybean shook her head. "But I think there will be harm," she whispered as though disgorging a vital secret. "*She* wants to hurt people."

"And *she* hasn't seen Arlene?"

Jillybean shook her head. This was both good and bad. They were still missing one renegade.

With much grumbling the renegades were shooed out of the trucks and back into the raging sun. Before Arlene had been bitten, the renegades would have killed for her, now they were trying their best to forget her. In groups of three, they spread out, but didn't have to go past the second stand of corn stalks to find her body lying in a pool of blood. Sixty feet from the trucks she had slit her own throat without a sound.

Chapter 7

Jillybean/Eve

They did not make it to the safe zone in Stafford, Kansas. Much to everyone's annoyance, Brad took them on a winding path that led them all over south-eastern Kansas. The tall, blonde man claimed he was avoiding the mega-hordes, but there was no way to be sure. Neil and Grey could do nothing but gripe and worry over their rapidly diminishing fuel reserves.

Jillybean doubted everything Brad said. Then again, she had taken to doubting everything that entered her ears. The other girl inside of her, the false Eve, was constantly talking or making noise like radio static. It was enough to go crazy over and the seven-year-old was sure she was crazy.

Talking to Ipes hadn't been crazy because he was real. He had a real body that people could see. Jillybean could remember all of him: the stripes of black and white, his big nose which he didn't like when she made fun of it, his round belly where the cookies went, his hands which were supposed to be hooves but they were not, and yet they weren't exactly hands either. They were flat and he used to say he could flip pancakes with them. She missed him terribly.

There was an actual pain in her chest that hadn't gone away or diminished since he had been thrown over the bridge railing by Ernest. Killing the bounty hunter was the only thing the other girl inside her had ever done right.

"My name is Eve," *she* said.

Jillybean glanced around furtively at the others. She could only tell if the voice had been "real" if they looked over at her, or if they stopped talking all at once, or if they pretended not to have heard but twitched all the same. Neil's hand with a fork full of beans, stopped just an inch from his lips. He pretended to blow on the beans as if they were hot before making a resumption of eating.

"He heard you," Jillybean said, so low under her breath that no one could possibly hear but Eve. "You have to be quieter."

No I don't, Eve spat. *Who cares if he heard me? I don't care. Neil is a shit-fuck-fart.*

The pain in her chest spiked and her face contorted. She hated it when Eve called people names, especially bad names like *shit-fuck-fart*. It was bad, though she didn't understand exactly how. "Neil is good to us. Look at what he gave us to eat, spaghetti and meatballs, our favorite. He's eating beans so we don't have to. That's what means he's nice."

Neil's fork stopped again and his eyes were tucked to the corner of his face so that he could look at her in a sneaky way. That's how Eve put it: *sneaky.* The word echoed through the static making Jillybean put a finger in her ear and twist it about.

"You ok?" Neil asked.

The renegades sat in small groups in the back room of a post office. There was mail everywhere, mostly "junk" mail as her daddy would've called it, but there was also normal mail, like letters and post cards. Some people were reading the normal mail but why, Jillybean couldn't fathom. The letters seemed to make them sad. Some were even crying. Sadie was one of these. The real Eve was lying next to Sadie, grabbing her own toes and making raspberry noises, but Sadie wasn't even paying attention.

Why isn't he asking Sadie if she's ok? the other girl asked. *Cuz she isn't ok.*

"That's none of our beeswax," Jillybean hissed under her breath. She forced a smile where it didn't belong and said to Neil: "I'm ok. I'm just tired, maybe. So…where are we?"

Neil shrugged and Grey muttered: "Nowhere…but at least we made crappy time. Whose idea was it to come with these freaking gypsies?"

Next to him, Deanna was leaning against her pack and looking at the stark-white ceiling, which, because of the dark, was a dull grey color. She nudged the soldier with her elbow and laughed. "I believe that was a certain Captain Grey. You and Neil ganged up on me like boys always do, and overruled me. I was the one who wanted to take the long way. We still can, you know."

"No," Neil said. "We've thrown in our lot with them for good or bad. Perhaps it'll get better."

"It won't, idiot," Jillybean, or rather Eve, snarled. The little girl gasped at what Eve had said and lowered her eyes thinking that a punishment was coming, only the grown-ups pretended they hadn't heard.

It's because they're stupid. We both know what daddy would've done. Probably washed our mouth out with soap, I bet.

"He would never have done that to me," Jillybean said under her breath once again. "Maybe he would've done it to you, but not to me, because I know how to behave!" Her voice had crept up and Neil heard. He suggested that it was time for sleep even though it wasn't much past nine. Jillybean was very tired but also nervous. *She* was waiting for the adults to go to sleep. When they did, *she* would walk among them like a ghost, creating mischief or spinning evil, as she had the night before.

She was stronger than Ipes had been and Jillybean was afraid what night would bring. She was afraid that she wouldn't be able stop *her* this time.

Around her, the grownups were settling down; conversations died or drifted into quiet whispers and their eyes were closing or blinking slowly. With every second that passed they were closer to sleep and to death. Jillybean felt it as a certainty. *She* would not be stopped. *She* was evil. *She* hated with a feeling like a rotten tooth. It throbbed in Jillybean's mind. *She* hated Neil. *She* hated the way he stared at her and pretended to care when all he really cared about were the stupid sheep preparing for bed in the back storeroom of the post office.

And *she* was jealous. The feeling made Jillybean sick; it made her want to puke up bile and the ugly, mottled green grease from the root of her body. *She* was jealous of the real Eve with such a passion that it hurt Jillybean's heart.

The little girl knew she couldn't be left alone that night. She knew that she had to be watched at all times or something bad would happen. She wanted to warn the others, only the other girl in her wouldn't allow it. *Don't do it*, she cautioned. *You won't like what I'll do.*

Jillybean tried not to let her fear show. "Whatever you do to me, you'll be doing to yourself also. I'm not ascared."

We'll see, was all *she* said in answer, which only made Jillybean that much more frightened. But afraid or not Jillybean would not be intimidated. She had to let the others know that she had to be watched over as though she were a criminal, one of the bad guys. She raised her hand and the other girl growled in her mind: *Don't do it, I swear!*

"Excuse me?" Jillybean said, speaking rapidly. "Would it be ok if I slept with the guar..." In the middle of the word: 'guard,' Jillybean's throat clamped shut as if a giant had seized her by the throat and was squeezing the air out of her.

"You want to sleep where?" Neil asked. He was right next to the little girl and he jerked when her hand shot out and began slapping his shoulder. "You ok, Jillybean?"

The storage room of the post office had nothing to illuminate it save for the pale beams from a quarter-moon filtering in through windows covered in old dust. The fact that Jillybean's face was blossoming into red went unseen.

"What's wrong?" Grey asked, sitting up. Jillybean could only shake her head. She had been caught with a lung-full of air and now it felt like her body was swelling and that her chest was a balloon about to pop. She fell back onto her blanket, hoping to relieve the pressure swelling her. When she looked down the length of her body, she looked normal, but that couldn't be, she could hear her ribs expanding with tiny cracking noises, as though hairline fractures were worming outward through the bone.

"She might be having a fit," Neil said. He knelt over her, peering into her face. With his injuries and the dark, he looked like a monster, but one with kind eyes. "Jillybean! What's wrong? Can you talk?" The little girl couldn't talk; *she* wouldn't allow it. Neil took her by the shoulders and gave her a short, violent shake, and yelled: "Jillybean!"

Then he was shoved out of the way by Captain Grey. "I need light," he barked. Sadie kept one nearby so she could attend to the baby at night. She slapped it into Grey's outstretched hand. Then Jillybean was blinded as the light struck her wide-flung eyes. Grey loomed over her, a strange dark-shadowed giant with a single blaring white eye.

There was a chorused gasp at what the light displayed. "She's choking," Deanna cried. Grey handed her the light and then bent over Jillybean. Her jaw had been locked in a half-state of openness and now she felt Grey's fingers on her teeth as he pried her mouth to its widest. Next she felt a heavy finger smush her tongue down. He took the light back and turned it this way and that. Beyond the light, Jillybean could see his concern growing. "There's nothing there."

Jillybean was beyond frantic; she was even beyond panic. She was in a stage of fear that was utterly mindless. Her eyes were beginning to dim and her heart, which had been going a mile a minute, was slowing and now each beat was accompanied by a stab of pain. She was going to die. The other girl was going to kill her to keep her from talking.

Do you understand now? the voice said into her head —it seemed awfully far away and so too, did Captain Grey. He had shrunk and the edges of his face were soft and fading. He was yelling something about a scalpel, only Jillybean didn't know what that was and Ipes wasn't around to pull the word from her subconscious. Her hands had been on the olive drab t-shirt he always wore under his BDUs, and now her fingers lost all their strength and slid down his chest with a whisper of cotton. *You see what I can do?* the voice said. *You see that I can kill you whenever I want? You will listen to me or I will walk you off a cliff or have you eaten by the monsters. Do you want me to do that?*

Suddenly, the giant hand that had been crushing her throat pulled away and air rushed into her lungs. She gasped once and then immediately cried out: "No, I'll be good, I promise, I'll be good."

In surprise, Grey swung back to her and she threw herself into him and sobbed in misery. "Hey, it's ok," he said, stroking her hair. "You are good, ok? Ok? Can you tell me what happened just now?"

In Jillybean's head the other girl, said, *No, you won't tell.*

Even if she had been allowed to, Jillybean couldn't have spoken a single word just then. She crushed her face to his chest and cried like she hadn't since the day she had found her mom dead in her bed with her skin stretched drum-tight over the bones of her face. That was also the day that Ipes had first spoken to her.

Don't be afraid of her, the stuffed animal that she carried in the crook of her arm had said. *You should hug her and tell her that you love her. She won't hurt you, I promise.*

Jillybean hadn't reacted in fear to the voice. For one it had seemed like the most natural thing in the world for the zebra to speak, and for two she was too...numb wasn't the right word, though it was close. She was too broken. Her father had left her to die and her mother had given up on life. Outside her home she saw the world she had known crumble away—her friends from the neighborhood: Janice and Becky and Paula and even Billy from across the street, had all been eaten or had run away until it was just Jillybean and her mommy who never said anything and only stared at the ceiling and who daily grew less.

When she was nearly dead, about a week away, Jilly-bean couldn't stay in the same room with her for very long. Her mommy started to look like she was becoming a scary skeleton. The bones of her face began to protrude, becoming more and more obvious, and her eyes sunk to become twin caves. Jillybean feared that when her mommy died her bones would leap out of her spit skin and start dancing around the room with a clinking sound. In her mind, her mom's skeleton would be very, very hungry since she had not eaten anything in so long. The skeleton would want to eat Jillybean, even though she was also mostly just skin and bones.

All that wintry day, Jillybean had kept away from the room with her mommy's nearly dead body in it. That was wrong because at that point her mommy wasn't dead and she needed water to live, but Jillybean was afraid, and her fear escalated as the day passed over into the gloom of evening. Then she heard a voice in her head: *She needs you. She'll die without you.* The voice had been calm and confident. It was the voice of Ipes, though she wouldn't know that until her mommy actually died a week later.

In that week, the skeleton of her mommy had become ever more pronounced as though it couldn't wait for her mommy to die so that it could get out, but still, Jillybean had trudged up the stairs performing her duty as a daughter. Even at six years old, she knew what was expected of her. It was almost the same as it was for an infant. Her mom needed to be changed and washed and then Jillybean would dribble water into her mouth. It would take an hour for her to finish a cup.

It was never just pure melted ice. At that time she still had a few crackers left and a little meat and a package of mixed vegetables that she took from the freezer and let sit to thaw. The freezer had lost all its power long before, just like the rest of the house, but Jillybean kept it packed with ice or snow from the yard, though at that time, the freezer was almost all ice with very little food and the cabinet next to the oven where her mommy kept the cans properly faced and in alphabetized order was empty, save for the dust that always crept over everything.

She had eaten the last of the mustard the week before, holding the spoon before her with a shaking hand. When nothing but air came when she squeezed the bottle, she had taken a knife to it, cutting it down the middle, before licking its innards until the flavor was gone and only yellow plastic was left.

Then her mom had died.

Death held a particular fear for the little girl. In her extensive experience with death, it wasn't as permanent as she wished. And it was evil. It made dead people evil. Her friend Becky was always very nice but then she had died and took to walking around the neighborhood wearing the same dress every day. Jillybean saw her eat a man. She had been with a bunch of other evil dead people and they had eaten a man who had been running down the road screaming like a girl. He screamed when Becky ate him, too.

That was why she was so afraid that week before her mommy died. Her mommy had lain in bed with her cheeks sunken and her skin like a layer of paint on her skeleton, especially around the deep, dark hollows of her eyes. Her lips were no longer full, but reed thin and always peeled back so that her teeth showed. With her gums receding, her teeth looked very long.

On the day her mommy died, Jillybean stood in the bedroom doorway just as she always did, watching to make sure that her mommy's chest rose and fell, because that's what meant being alive. Only, her chest didn't move that day. For five long minutes, Jillybean stared. She stared and stared and didn't notice the tears running down her face or the pain that grew inside of her until Ipes spoke from the crook of her arm.

The pain started as a noise in her mind. It was white noise that slowly deafened her with its silence, until it filled her head completely that she couldn't bear it, and when she finally "broke," she didn't even notice.

Her mind broke from the fear. She had been, for some time, so dreadfully afraid that it couldn't be put into words. Now, she was broken and she was alone. The little girl was alone in a way few people had ever known. Even prisoners locked away in solitary confinement saw their jailers at feeding times and they heard the whispers and moans of the other inmates, but Jillybean was utterly alone. She was alone in a dead house, on a dead street, in a dead neighborhood, in a city filled with dead neighborhoods.

Just then, standing in her mother's doorway, she knew she would be alone forever. Alone, except for the undead. They would always be there outside her window, waiting to eat her.

Those were the last thoughts she had before she broke.

The pain and the sorrow and the damage of that break went unfelt and unremarked and the only sign of it was when the zebra in the little blue shirt with the words: *Too Cute!* on the front suddenly spoke: *Don't be afraid to hug her. She's still your mother and she would never hurt you. Even now.*

Jillybean heard and obeyed. She walked on spider-thin legs to the bed and performed her final duty. She cried at her mother's passing and cried nearly ceaselessly during the days that followed. Having Ipes around made it tolerable and she grew and she healed but the scar of her break was ever on her mind. There had been no way to know how weak that scar actually was because she always had Ipes.

She had relied on him, even when she had Ram; and she had been smart, too. As proof of her wisdom, the strong Ram had died and Ipes was still there. When Sarah had been murdered, putting her body in front of Jillybean, protecting her, Ipes was still there. And when Jillybean had shot the bounty hunter, and when she had blown up the bridge, and sunk the barge and the ferry boats, he was there.

Ipes was always supposed to be there, but then Ernest had pitched him into the river. Just like that, her friend was gone. In that moment, her mind cracked wide open and hate came pouring out in the form of Eve.

Gone was the kind and wise-cracking zebra. Gone was the part of her that kept the silence and the loneliness at bay. Gone was the part of her that taught her patience and respect and caution and love. In its place was this low creature that knew only want and lust and need and fury. It was everything Ipes wasn't. And it was stronger than Ipes. It was stronger even than Jillybean, as it had just proved.

As Jillybean sobbed in Captain Grey's chest, it was *She* who whispered into Jillybean's ear:

YOU CAN'T TOUCH ME.
YOU CAN'T HURT ME.
YOU CAN ONLY SUBMIT AND
BECOME ME.

Chapter 8

Captain Grey

Grey slept, if "slept" was indeed the proper verb for what consisted of little more than lying in a stuporous heat with his eyes mostly closed, with Jillybean just inches away.

He slept as he had in Iraq during those times when making it back to base wasn't an option, and the desert, or the back streets of Fallujah was his nest for the night. He slept with a literal eye half-cracked and his mind in a state of "pause."

When, at two in the morning, Jillybean suddenly stood up, moving with the grace and silence of a stalking jungle cat, Grey's dark eyes opened a hair wider. He watched her as she stopped over Neil and stared down at him, a sneer on her face. Her eyes were pale zeros in the night, devoid of thought beyond the unpleasant. With a derisive snort at Neil, she left him and went to Sadie and snorted again. When the Goth girl rolled over, Grey saw that it was the baby who was being glared at.

This had Grey on edge, ready to leap up to protect the infant from the disturbed girl. There was no need. Jillybean blinked hard, shook her head once and then moved on, like the specter of death in a wrinkled yellow dress. Where her shadow, inky black, fell across the sleeping renegades, they stirred uneasily, something that seemed to please her and he saw her teeth gleam.

Grey watched her through slitted eyes as she moved about them, pausing over some, ignoring others. She stood a long time over the still form of Joe Gates and then she knelt. When she straightened, a line of silver in her hand caught the weak light in a brief flash.

She then crept to the doorway that led to the front where the now-dead postmen would receive mail and sell stamps and where the Christmas lines would snake and

92

squiggle around the room, held in place by shabby velvet ropes.

The captain stood, following after the little girl, and she was clueless to his presence. She was a genius in her way, mostly on a physical level where she understood the workings and mechanics of both nature and man on a level few adults were cognizant of; however, she was still just a child and her hearing and vision weren't anything but average, while Grey could be slick as oil when he wished. Soundlessly, he followed her through the front room and lurked in the deeper shadows as she went to the building's front door, which was propped open by a brick.

Jillybean glanced out at the guard on duty. From his vantage, Grey couldn't see who it was, but he knew nonetheless it was Veronica, one of the women from the Island. She had never shared her last name with Grey and he had never asked. This was true with most of the women, Deanna included. They acted as though, by being anonymous in this minor way, they could begin anew and that their pasts could be forgotten or ascribed to someone else. He was fine by that.

Grey watched the little girl for some time and, at first, he assumed that she was about to make an attempt at running away. It wouldn't be difficult for someone as smart as Jillybean. Even in the daytime it wouldn't be all that hard, but at night it would be a cinch to slip out into the shadows and disappear forever. However, she didn't make the attempt. After what looked like a whispered conversation with herself that involved very little sound but much moving of lips and gesturing of her hands, she turned back the way she had come.

Instead of retreating further into the shadows, Grey stepped forward. To her, he must have appeared monstrous, dark and of course scary, and so, her reaction was amazing. She dropped into a crouch and within a blink she had the stolen knife out and held at the ready, looking like a trained knife fighter.

Impressed, Grey stepped forward slowly with his hand out. "I'll take that."

When she saw who it was, the signs of a quick mental calculation crossed her face and then she stepped back, putting her hand out to find the cracked door, just in case she wanted to run was his guess. "I don't have to," she said in a childish voice. Her voice was always childish in its way, young-sounding, but now it had a smarmy, know-it-all quality as well. "It's my knife and I have the right to have it because...because of the monsters and such."

"It's not your knife," he answered, easing forward. "We both know that you stole it from Joe Gates. Thievery is a crime, Jillybean. We don't allow thieves in this group. Now, give it to me. I won't ask again."

More calculations made her eyes dart and her brow crinkle. Quickly, she came to realize that no amount of genius would allow her to keep the knife. "Ok, here." The knife was out, extended. In the dark, it was pale, its edges blurry, its point *seemingly* dull. She stood relaxed and yet Grey had seen how fast she had stepped into a natural fighting stance. He didn't and couldn't trust her.

He had seen too many soldiers with Post-Traumatic Stress Disorder. Most of these men had the form of PTSD called *Play The System Disorder*. It was the version which every serving soldier had seen a hundred times, but never talked about. This version involved a lifetime of receiving "disability" pay from the army for a diagnosis that couldn't be seen, and as long as the money kept flowing, was practically impossible to cure. Grey was embarrassed to be associated with a person with that form of PTSD.

Then there was the true version, the very sad, real version. It was unpredictable and frequently led to deeper issues, although he had never heard of it deteriorating in the way it was happening to Jillybean.

There was definitely something more serious going on with her than PTSD, which usually presented with headaches, night terrors, depression and anxiety. Jillybean's mental state was worlds beyond that. Before he had met Jillybean, he never believed for a second in multiple personalities. Truly, he thought it was all a load of psychiatric bullshit, but Ipes had been an eye-opener. The stuffed animal had been completely real in Jillybean's mind. For her, it was a distinct and separate individual, complete with its own personality, its own manner of speaking, and in many cases, its own memories.

Having the stuffed animal speak through the little girl had been definitely strange to the arrow-straight and rational thinking army captain and at first he thought it had been nothing but a bid for attention, only the zebra and the little girl didn't seem to care about attention. They cared and feared for their lives and the lives of their friends. That's what had driven them to step boldly into one dangerous situation after another and, with each intense adult step, the damage to the little girl's mind had grown.

Grey had worried over her, fretting that she was taking on more than she could handle. He had watched Neil drive her and, perhaps use her, especially when he became leader of the renegades. Neil was determined to see them safely through to Colorado, but at a cost that Grey didn't agree with. These were adults relying on a seven-year-old who had already been through way more than any child should. It wasn't right and, for his part, he wanted to keep her far away from the least hint of danger…unfortunately that would mean locking her away in a windowless room.

Even in Colorado, where the mountains held back the larger zombie hordes, there was still danger. Raiders were constantly nibbling on their borders and stray zombies made hunting as dangerous for the hunters as the deer they stalked. And then there was General Johnston's insistence of carrying on a knightly and Christian image.

Grey agreed that if mankind had a chance of rising above anarchy and the inevitable return to the dark ages where might made right and evil flourished, then "goodness" had to triumph. For it to do so meant someone had to stand up to the worst of mankind, it meant fighting, it meant death.

It meant that Jillybean would always be one step from bloodshed but, if he could keep her that step away, Grey would do it. The Estes valley, thirty miles into the Colorado Rockies was the best chance she had. There was danger, yes, but there were also soft green fields she could run in, and icy cold lakes stocked with bass and rainbow trout where she could paddle little boats, and the air there was as clean as when God first breathed it onto the earth. She could fly a kite there and be nothing but a kid once more. There she could be happy. There she could grow and heal. There she could be whole in body and mind again.

But to get there they had nine hundred miles of danger to traverse, starting with the two feet that separated them and the six inches of razor-sharp metal at the end of her hand. Joe Gates was always sharpening his knife in an attempt to demonstrate to everyone that he wasn't a boy, but rather he was *a man in training*.

Jillybean had an adverse effect on him. Here was a tiny, strip of a girl who could blow up bridges and boats, and break people out of jails and to whom everyone looked the second things got sticky. Yes, she was clearly crazy, but she was also a genius and dangerous. She was a powerful force, not just in the group, but to the peoples of New York, and New Eden, and to the River King, and if the people of the Azael weren't careful, to them as well. Jillybean's very presence had made Joe bold and reckless and yet these traits went mostly unrecognized because Jillybean was always center-stage.

Even there, in the dead of night, Jillybean held the group's fate in her hand. Had Grey not been so vigilant, who knows where she would be now and what she would be doing? The knife had been stolen for a purpose. A gun could've been just as easily picked up, but guns were loud killers, while knives were quiet ones. Guns were for defense from the zombies or the wild men of the world, but a knife was for slitting throats in the dead of night or gutting a man in his sleep.

With the night throwing its dark arms over their shoulders, and wrapping them in shadow, the two stood closer than fencers. Grey could see her sizing him up, judging the distance between them, considering, perhaps, the ramifications of not handing him the knife but instead driving it into his guts and giving it a quick twist.

He saw her lethality, knowing that, had it been Neil standing here, she would have lunged into him, piercing his flesh with the metal thorn and laughing at him as his blood crowded out of him. Grey saw this, but stepped forward anyway; her crazy was no match for his size, speed and skill. She saw his eyes and the fact that he stood ready to snatch the knife. She was too smart to make the attempt and her hand opened so the blade sat on her palm.

Still, he didn't trust her and took her wrist first.

"I was just borrowing it," she lied, as he whipped the blade away out of sight. "I had to go to the bathroom and I don't like the ones in here. They're very, extra stinky. Even Jil…I mean everyone thinks so."

"How about I escort you somewhere outside then? I'll keep you safe."

"Sure." Her smile was another of her bad lies.

He led her to the front door and cleared his throat, so as not to startle Veronica. The woman jumped anyway. "You're early Jos, but if…" She choked on her words as she saw Grey, but rallied with a smile. "Are you checking up on me or looking for an excuse to get me alone and chat me…" Again her words faltered. This time because she saw Jillybean. The girl might have been considered a good luck charm and a genius, but she was also strange and off-putting. When she looked at a person with her sharp eyes, few of the renegades could stand before her. They joked, when she wasn't around, that it felt like they were bugs beneath an alien microscope when she looked at them. They felt naked and their secrets laid bare.

"She has to use the bathroom is all," Grey said. "Is it clear?"

"It's hard to tell. There's a herd nearby," she answered, keeping her voice low. "When I came on shift, William said a herd of zombies was moving through, but I don't know. By the sounds of it, they stopped moving. Listen." The three of them held their breath and the night became alive with sound: cicadas mostly, but there was also the distant moan of zombies as pervasive as the dark.

"Probably a mile off," Grey said. "Anything closer?"

"A gang of them tromped right in front of me a half hour ago. They went that way." She pointed across the highway where more derelict farmland sat. It was practically all they had seen during their long day of driving.

Grey thanked her and then he and Jillybean walked off in the opposite direction she had pointed. The little girl was uneasy with him so close and snuck her eyes up at him every few steps. He directed her to a field of winter wheat that had gone unharvested and was grown tall, but was now browned from the endless sun. "In there." He gave her back a nudge and considered giving her a warning against running away but decided against it. She knew as well as he did they were in the middle of nowhere and that running meant death from starvation or thirst or the zombies.

At one point in the endless turnings that Brad had led them on, they crossed high over a wide, shit-brown river that had been chugged full of stiffs. There were more of them on either bank, thousands more, maybe even tens of thousands more. Brad had stopped the Toyota midway on the bridge, went to the edge and hooked a shoe on the lower bar of the guard railing. He had waved an arm in a grand gesture and said: "That's why you hired me. That horde there is just a small one. Some go for miles in every direction. And look at that water. The waters are spoilt like that all over the prairie."

It had been an impressive display of propaganda that had quieted some of the talk that had been going around during that long hot day.

It had been oppressively hot in the trucks, and the shut up post office had been little better, though it was as safe as Brad said it would be. Despite its supposed safety, Brad hadn't slept there. He had claimed a need for gas and had driven off at sunset.

Thankfully, it was cool under the stars. As he waited on Jillybean, Grey limboed a snap and crackle out of his back with the help of his knuckles and then stopped to listen. Sounds in the night carry easily through the dark. Far away the zombies moaned or growled and seemed nearer that they were. Closer at hand there was a whispered conversation in the dried-out wheat stalks where Jillybean had disappeared.

The little girl was quiet and he only caught segments of what was being said: "That's not true…They'll never know…Do you think they'll blame….Oh, please…have jails, if everyone is good?"

Grey could make nothing from the snatches of words and he was just creeping forward so he could hear better, when Jillybean addressed him: "Mister Captain Grey, sir? Are all the people in Colorado good? Like you I mean?"

"Yes, for the most part," he answered, hedging slightly. No group was comprised solely of good or bad people. There was always a mix of the ambitious, the driven, the greedy and the conniving, though in this case they were what he would call good. "Why do you ask? Are you worried about fitting in? Because you shouldn't. You're a good person. Deep down you are sweet, and caring. You just have to remember that."

She giggled, an evil sound that sent a shiver down his back. Before he could recover from this, she began hissing at herself to be quiet. If he hadn't known better, he would've bet good money that there were two girls hiding in the bush.

"What if I do something bad?" she asked. "You'll punish me, right? You just don't let bad people walk around like everyone else, right? You have jails, right?"

"Not for people like you, Jillybean. No matter what you think, you are a good person. Jail is for evil people, murderers and rapists, people like that. So please, don't think you'll ever go to jail."

More whispering from the brush. "You see, it's going to be like…you don't know…seen it myself. They banished her…what's that mean? …you out of the group… and we'll be alone." From what Grey could tell, the Jillybean voice was trying to get the other side of her, the evil Eve side, to be good so they wouldn't be kicked out or banished.

Grey was leaning in to hear more when Jillybean suddenly appeared. Her yellow dress, muted by the dark, had blended in with the wheat and only her pale white face stood out. He felt a moment of shock, realizing that if she had another knife she could have gutted him. "Whoa, you scared me," he said.

She grinned and it was the grin of a hungry skeleton; for a second, she was unrecognizable. "I should scare you," she hissed. "I...I...I..." Her words ground to a halt and there was a confusion of lines on her little girl face, which she forced carefully back into place so that she looked again like Jillybean. "I mean, uh, that I didn't mean that. I meant that because it's dark I should scare you."

"You shouldn't lie, Jillybean," Grey warned her. "Tell me what the other person in you wants to do."

"Hurt people," she said in a rush and then stood looking about as if expecting something bad to happen. When whatever it was didn't happen, she let out a breath and went on: "But I told her she'd go to jail or be banished, like that one woman. Won't that happen?" She asked this as if pleading with Grey to agree. She had her small hand on his hip, her nails, quick-bit near to nothing, made scritching noises on his BDUs.

"Yeah, that's what will happen," Grey lied, thinking, incorrectly, that he was helping Jillybean control the evil side of her.

Chapter 9

Melanie Hewitt

Twenty minutes before the sun broke the horizon, the brick post office had finally reached a point that could be called comfortably cool. By twenty minutes after dawn, the sun was once again pounding down. The rays baked the red bricks and, with the dusty windows capturing the heat, the post office was as hot as a green house.

Grey and Jillybean were the last to stir. The rest sat up, smacking cotton-dry lips and began to scramble for water bottles and warm canteens. A number of the renegades, twenty three to be precise, felt an urgency and began scrambling for the bathrooms. The twenty three, as Neil was able to deduce later, had two things in common: explosive diarrhea and they were the only ones who had bought Brad's cold water on credit.

Soon the six stalls, evenly divided between the men's and lady's rooms were brimming with foulness causing the last woman in line, the sad and disfigured Melanie, to figure something else out before her bowels let go in a rush.

Melanie had been a slave in the River King's kitchens; it was hot work and sometimes dangerous. The women were weighed every morning with any increase in weight three days running being considered *prima facie* evidence of theft of food. Beatings were frequent and she generally worked from before sun up until just after ten at night; it was bad, but at least she wasn't being raped.

She had been released by the River King in the trade that freed the renegades. Because she hadn't been with the others, she had almost been forgotten and only at the last minute did Deanna remember her. She had good reason to be happy with her new-found freedom, right up until that morning.

The pain in her gut was horrendous, but one look at the mess in the commodes had her spinning away with sweat across her forehead. She turned to the ancient sinks, which were supported by metaled alphabets of exposed plumbing, and considered using the basins to evacuate the steaming mess in her bowels.

The thought lasted no more than a second. The sinks were no use since the smell had her stomach heaving and she knew she was going to explode both fore and aft.

Melanie ran from the room and out the front door, hurrying past a startled Joslyn Reynolds who was yawning away the final few minutes of her two-hour guard shift. In front of Melanie was the dinky two-lane highway they had been traveling on and beyond that a tall growth of winter wheat that stood higher than her head.

"Where are you going?" Joslyn hissed, as Melanie started for the wheat. Melanie did not answer; she had one hand across her mouth and another clenching her bottom. Before the black top was a drainage ditch which she leapt. Then she was on the asphalt and for just a moment, she stopped in the middle of the road where all the world could see her.

She had forgotten to grab toilet paper and she knew she was going to need an entire roll. The pause was for seconds only. It was obvious she wouldn't be able make it back before her bowels let go. She wondered if she could even make it across the street, and yet the pause drew out for a second longer.

At one end of that endless road, was the sun blasting into her face, turning the world gold. At the other end was the moon. It was resting on the horizon, looking to have landed somewhere at the very far end of Kansas. All around it, the air was a soft, cool denim blue.

Melanie was standing, seemingly right between these two celestial opposites.

It was marvelous, perhaps the most perfect moment in her otherwise dismal life. She wished she could stay and see the pendulum of God swinging around her but her intestines spasmed, reminding her how insignificant she really was.

With a grunt and an: "Oh, my God!" she leapt the drainage ditch on the far side of the road and then she was among the tall grasses of the plains. "Keep going. Just keep going!" She was too close. When she looked back, she could still see Joslyn too clearly and she wanted to put a little distance between them. So she hurried another twenty yards, yanked down her pants, squatted and let go. Despite the pain knifing through her guts, she felt the most immense sense of relief—she *hadn't* crapped her pants. In her book, and it was the saddest book ever written, not crapping her pants was a win.

Now came the acute issue of cleaning herself up. She didn't relish the idea of running her bottom along the ground after the manner of a dog on shag carpet, however there was precious little in the way of green leafy foliage around her. The closest bit of green to her was a glossy plant with a few wide sprigs. These plants numbered only five or six and they were far enough from each other and from her to warrant her working herself about in a squat-waddle that was as unbecoming as it sounded.

As she came up to the third of these, all hunched over and, for the most part unseen, she heard running steps and a whisper that carried: "Melanie!"

Embarrassed at her predicament she said nothing, silently wishing that whoever was out there would go away and leave her in peace. The footsteps whickered through the tall wheat to her right. Her name was whispered again and was answered this time by a low groan. More moans followed the first and then the sound of the running steps retreated quickly.

Groans were all around her now and her heart was pounding out discordant notes that made her breathing erratic and shrill. She was caught in mid-squat by a host of zombies. Almost all of them were shadowy figures moving through the wheat. Only the ones that passed within a few feet were clear to her: they had sunken, dead eyes that were so emotionless that they looked like they belonged more in a fish's head than in a person's. Their mottled and ugly grey skin was covered in sores and scars, dirt and feces. They sometimes wore the tattered remains of dresses and suits, pajamas or attire that was no longer discernible beyond the fact that it had been fabric of some sort at one time, however, for the most part, they were hideously naked.

A dozen passed within feet of the girl squatting in the wheat, while a hundred dozen pressed forward heading for the lonely post office. Melanie would've stayed, hunkered down, but there was the sudden *blat* of engines starting up.

They're leaving me! The thought struck her like a slap, galvanizing her into action. She leapt to her feet, hoisting her jeans into place and, without giving a second thought to her state of partial cleanliness, she ran. She didn't run directly to the post office—that would've been stupid even by her standards.

The post office sat at a crossroads which had been laid out with a compass in mind. Some altogether useless road ran north-south and another, the one she had paused on not ten minutes earlier, went precisely east to west. She chose this second one and ran parallel to it, hoping to avoid the zombies and at the same time get ahead of the slow rumbling trucks. Never in her life had she run so fast…and all for nothing.

Fifty yards behind her the five-ton trucks crossed the drainage ditches and drove out into the wheat with their horns tooting and guns blasting any zombie that managed to gain a handhold somewhere on the trucks. Immediately, Melanie stopped and, while the wind ran in and out of her, she waved her arms and jumped up and down. She didn't dare scream, but she did cry, silent, miserable tears.

The three trucks had spread out, though only so much. Like the tines of a fork, they plowed three grooves into the wheat heading north. They were looking for her, but in the wrong place.

Weeping in fright over the idea of being left behind, she ran north waving her hands, praying to be seen. After another fifty yard dash, Melanie was staggering and her chest was heaving. She couldn't have screamed for help if she wanted to; the tears had never stopped.

Then by some miracle, hands were pointing her way and the truck on the far left heeled far over as it turned as sharply as it could. In the front seat, she could see Neil pointing at her as Captain Grey drove. She waved and for some reason Neil jabbed his finger angrily in her direction.

Was he mad that she had a case of diarrhea? That was ridiculous! As if to give credence to the wild thought that they were angry with her, the five-ton turned slightly, chugging on a course that would cross her front thirty yards ahead of her. She was so surprised that she didn't move, not even when Neil swung an M4 up to his shoulder and pointed it right at her.

Her eyes bugged and she stared unblinking until Neil started to shoot right at her! She could hear the bullets crease the air as they zipped by, some of them so close she swore they passed through her hair. With a scream, she broke in stark terror away from the truck with more bullets chasing after. She didn't make it more than thirty yards before exhaustion caught up with her and she staggered, tripping in a chuck-hole and going face first into the dirt.

There was more shooting from all over the field. Alarmed and puzzled, she glanced over her shoulder and saw the truth: Neil hadn't been shooting at her. There were zombies all over the place; some were charging right down on her, the lead ones falling at her feet and at first she assumed they were stepping in chuck-holes as well, but then she saw the blood. It was skipping off the zombies, hanging like a mist, dimming the morning.

Melanie's body reacted while she was still cringing and screaming. Her feet dug at the dirt and her legs pistoned; she was up and running. At first she ran for the safety of Neil's truck, however every zombie within reach was converging on it, making it seem like some great green beast. It shuddered over the zombies, its engine roaring and sparks of fire coming from its windows and out the back. She shied away from it, her mind swept by fear and confusion. Nowhere seemed safe to run but just standing there was worse.

More zombies were breaking through the wheat and suddenly Neil's gun was quiet; he was going through the motions of reloading. She broke to her right. It was no more safe than anywhere else. Zombies charged her and she ran in an arc and always more were in front and the ones behind got closer and closer.

Closer, closer; right behind her. She could hear them moaning excitedly; she could smell the rot and decay wafting from their hungry mouths; she could feel their fingers reaching for her, tangling in her hair. "Neil!" she screeched at the top of her lungs.

The field was all mayhem and death. The three trucks were turning ponderously towards her, but the undead were closer, so close that her shirt was being pulled back, stretching across her throat, slowing her as if she were running in a nightmare.

"Neil!!!!" The scream rose above the chaos in the field. It was everywhere and heard by everyone. Its terror-filled sound engulfed Melanie's mind as she was dragged down and teeth tore into her flesh. She didn't fight back. There was no point. She was too weak and there were too many of them. Her only hope was that Neil would rescue her.

He came charging up, half his small body hanging out the square of a window on the passenger side of the truck, a black rifle in his hands.

"Save me," Melanie begged, one arm outstretched to him, the other was having the long muscle of the bicep being torn off and fought over.

Grimly, Neil saved her. He shot her; her brains blasted out of her head like a stick of butter being struck by a mallet. "Let's get out of here," he said.

Chapter 10

Neil Martin

"I need a drink," Grey said, gripping the steering wheel with white-knuckled fury.

Neil's eyes were on the gun he had used to kill Melanie. He was a little surprised to see that the safety was on. Normally, Grey or Sadie had to remind him. "I need to get drunk," he replied, uncaring that far to their right the sun had barely risen above the edge of the earth. He hadn't eaten breakfast yet and all he could think was that would make getting drunk easier.

"That doesn't sound half bad," Deanna murmured. Her face was red and misty with tears. She sat so close to Grey that no light shone through along the line where their arms and legs warmed each other.

Getting drunk wasn't just a desire for Neil, it was a need. Just then he needed to turn off his mind and not think about Melanie and how she had screamed his name. Even with the loud rumble of the five-ton's engine, he could still hear that scream over and over.

But he couldn't get drunk. People depended on him, people like Melanie.

"Did everyone make it to the trucks?" he asked. "Please tell me that we got everyone out of that damned post office."

"I was the last out," Grey assured, but then his brows came down. "Jillybean is the only one I worry about. She was right next to me, but I went on one side of the truck and she went on the other. I called for her, but then you were there and the damned stiffs were everywhere. I'm sure she got in the back."

"Stop the truck," Neil ordered, quietly. They were two minutes from the field where he had shot Melanie. The three trucks had left her corpse to be eaten and had driven slowly away with a sudden lack of urgency. "Stop and let's do a count."

Again, Grey pulled to the shoulder of the road as he stopped. Neil stood in the door and looked out at the fields before stepping down. The zombies back at the post office had come out of nowhere. The little group had been just waking up when there had been a cry from the guard on duty that someone was in trouble. Unthinkingly, and definitely foolishly, Neil had run out into the field of wheat with the wave of zombies heading right for him.

The fields near them now were empty, save for a few unlimbed stragglers who crawled or pulled themselves along with the use of their arms if they happened to have any, or like inchworms if they didn't; their desperation to kill was unsettling and Neil's face took on a sour look.

Fred Trigg had climbed onto the back gate when they stopped. He, too, wore a sour look, though his was of a perpetual nature. "What's going on? Why'd we stop?"

"Because," Neil answered, unhelpfully. "Climb up on the canvas and keep watch. Everyone else," he announced loudly, "get out of the vehicles and line up on the road. I need to get a count." They did so, barely breaking the natural quiet of the morning. No one spoke, they stood on the side of the road looking glum, all save Jillybean who had struck a pose that suggested she was annoyed with having to stand among the commoners.

Neil was glad she had made it onto the trucks and, at the same time, he wasn't. It seemed to him that her heart was wicker and all the goodness that had been in her had strained out of it over time, leaving only the sludge of madness and the gristle of hate. He was beginning to feel the same way.

After walking up the line and counting each person with a tap on the head, he stood in the road and stared down at his purple crocs, deciding they would have to go. They were utterly ridiculous. They were comfy and whimsical and showed his good natured side. With a cry of frustration, he pulled the right one off and flung it into the field to their front.

"What the hell happened back there?" he demanded, marching with a quirky limp, managing to appear even more ridiculous with only the one croc on his left foot. His anger was such that no one even cracked a smile. "Who was on watch?"

The renegades refused to look up from the yellow stripe beneath their feet and it was Grey who answered: "Joslyn."

Immediately, her pert features spun up a look of innocence. "I didn't do anything wrong. She just came barreling out of the post office and ran across the street. What was I supposed to do? Tackle her?"

"At a minimum, you should've alerted someone that there was a problem. What did you do instead?" The spun look of innocence came unwound and she didn't need to answer for Neil to know she hadn't done anything. He stood before her and glared, barely able to deal with Joslyn. She was the very picture of laziness; unwilling or unable to move and think on her own initiative. So much like an insolent and spoiled teenager.

Playing the role of disappointed parent, he turned from her and addressed the long line of people. "Does anyone know what was going on with Melanie? Why did she run out of a perfectly safe building?"

He was expecting to hear, as way of rationale, something along the lines of a lover's quarrel or an argument between friends. Ricky Lewis, who usually spoke for the prisoners that Jillybean and Captain Grey had rescued from Gunner, said: "My guess is she had the shits." A number of the renegades bobbed their heads in agreement and Ricky added, "I think we ate something bad and it messed with our system, if you know what I mean."

Three people up from Rick, Jillybean rolled her blue eyes and shook her head with exaggerated sweeps. She acted put out over having to deal with lesser minds. "Wrong," she said, "We've been eating out of cans and unless you shared your can of corn with twenty other people, which you didn't, then there is clearly something else affecting you."

She was right. The renegades would usually sit in groups of three or four, each sharing from their individual cans; there was no way twenty people would be simultaneously affected. But if it wasn't the food...suddenly it clicked in his mind. "It was the water that Brad gave us," Neil realized. "Damn it!" A second purple croc sailed out into the field leaving him in the pair of clean, white socks he had picked up two day before when the renegades had raided a derelict Walmart. Almost immediately, the bottom of his foot found a sharp rock and he cursed again.

"I don't get it," Jillybean said to herself. "Tell me again why you think he's smart?"

With an effort, given the mood he was in, Neil ignored the little girl. "Everyone back in the trucks!"

Since the trucks would become blazing hot, getting the renegades into them was a process. There were discussions and sometimes arguments over who sat where the day before, and whose turn it was to be near the back where the wind was coolest, and thus, before half of them had seated themselves, fifteen minutes had gone by. Fred, who was still on top of the canvas of the first truck pointed south. "There's a car. It's red. I think it's Brad."

"Keep your gun ready," Neil said to Grey. Again, a rock bit his foot and he hopped and cursed. If he'd had a third shoe, he would've thrown it as well.

"Maybe you should let me do the talking," Grey said. "You're pretty riled up."

"Good! I want to be riled up. I'm tired of being pushed around and I'm tired of my people dying."

Grey eyed him evenly, looking the small man up and down. "Do you know what you're going to say to him?"

Neil squinted at the car kicking up dust in its wake as it blazed its way up to them. High above, a sky loom threaded together white strands of cirrus in long lines. It was pretty and interesting, but the only thing Neil could see was blackness. "I don't know," was all he answered.

Brad arrived all smiles over a quizzical countenance. "Where are you going? This isn't the way. We need to

110

backtrack a bit…because…" The M4 rifle Neil pointed at Brad's face caused his words to dry up.

"I feel like killing you," he said, simply. He hadn't been lying to Grey. He had no idea what he was going to say, but this seemed as appropriate as anything he could think of. "You are my enemy, after all, and what do we do to our enemies but shoot them?"

"Sometimes we blow them up," Jillybean said.

Neil smirked. "That is very true and if I had a grenade right now, I'd…let's just say it wouldn't be pretty."

Another laugh, this one forced, escaped Brad. "Why don't you tell me what's going on. Was it those zombies? They weren't mine, I can assure you. Do you see any of my herders?"

"We lost one of our people this morning," Neil told him. "She was one of those who drank your dirty water yesterday. Oh, I'm sure you didn't mean for her to die, but you did mean to make her sick. How much do you want to bet that I will find a case of Pepto-Bismol in your car?"

Without asking, Neil stalked to the Camry. The three silk clad women were standing nearby, looking nervous and, in one case, dangerous. The straggly-haired blonde had a hand hidden beneath the overlapping scarves at her hips. Neil turned on her. "Get your hand where I can see it," he snapped. "Or else."

She had him by a head and could look over the top of him easily, still she slid her hands up to shoulder height. She saw the crazy in his eyes.

In the trunk was more water in a cooler, a number of weapons and radios, food, blankets, and yes, thirty bottles of Pepto-Bismol in a cardboard box. He heaved the box out. "Raise your hands if you need some. Brad has very nicely donated some medicine to make amends for giving all of you tainted water. Michael, pass it out."

As Michael Gates took the box and began to go among the renegades, Brad glared at Neil. "You are playing a dangerous game."

"I'm playing a dangerous game? Protecting my people is dangerous to you? Wrong, Brad. It's you who's playing a dangerous game. Do you think we're so weak that we will roll over and take it when you poison us?"

Brad threw his hands in the air and cried: "You weren't poisoned! That was just plain water, the same as what we all drink on the plains. Yes, sometimes it's not the cleanest, but it's not like we have water treatment plants working anymore."

"And yet you conveniently have a box full of Pepto in your car," Neil replied, heatedly. The M4 was up and pointed again. "And all this driving around in circles, are you going to still claim that it's for our own good? Because no one here believes it. Just like with the water and the Pepto, you're creating a problem where none was before and who is the only person we can turn to? You."

"Perhaps it looks that way," Brad answered, standing stiff and angry. "But it is what it is. There are mega-herds. You saw one yesterday for goodness sakes! That was far larger and far more dangerous than what you left back at the post office. I am the one keeping you out of harm's way. Hell, you can't even afford the bridge fees to cross over the Platte…"

Neil held up a hand. "There will be no bridge fees whatsoever. It's preposterous. It's preposterous for someone to charge a fee to cross a bridge he didn't build and can't maintain. It's highway robbery, pure and simple, and if the Azael partake in such shenanigans then, by definition, they are nothing but a bunch of two-bit bandits themselves."

Neil was sure he had crossed a line, but he didn't care. Bullies had to be stood up to.

Brad's blue eyes narrowed. "Bandits? These are our lands you are crossing! I don't know who you think you are, Neil, but you are weak. This entire group is weak. If you weren't, you would've gone around the long way where water is scarce as teats on a bull. Down there the people are crazy. The sun has baked their brains and the lack of food has made them into cannibals. But if you're so tough, go on. I won't stop you. However, if you stay in the land of the Azael, you will do what I tell you, and go where I tell you, and you will thank me and kiss my ass because I'm the only one who can get you through."

For a second they locked eyes, neither backing down an inch, and then Neil threw his head back and laughed. "Cannibals! That's a nice touch. Very scary, but I highly doubt it. It sounds like an old wives tale to me."

"Sounds like bullshit to me, too," Grey said, coming to stand next to Neil. "Are you sure you want to go down this road, Brad? I can assure you that you don't want to mess with the people of Colorado. We won't take it lying down."

"Now I get it," Brad said with a little chuckle. "Now I understand why you talk so tough, Neil. You think soldier-boy here has your back. And you, Grey, you still think the soldiers have the upper hand out here in the west, don't you? Well, you couldn't be more wrong. King Augustus has united all the separate bands on the prairie. We have ten times your numbers and, oh yes, we have weapons now too. Nice ones, good ones. And the king has been looking for an excuse."

Grey was quick to reply: "What do you mean by that?"

"I think you know," Brad answered. "You know these 'great' types. They're never satisfied with what they have. We've heard about how nice your valley is and I'm sure he's thinking to add it to his domain. If I were you, I wouldn't want to be the excuse that starts a war."

Chapter 11

Jillybean/Eve

Just like the day before, they sat four abreast, Grey, Deanna, Jillybean, and Neil. The air in the cab was stuporous and as still and hot as a swamp. They weren't moving. Perhaps as revenge for Neil's uppity mouth, Brad had steered them right into the middle of one of the megaherds and now they were forced to wait until the edges of it washed over them.

Jillybean had never traveled in the west and had never been in a similar situation back in the days before the apocalypse when cars would sometimes get trapped among a herd of cattle being driven from one pasture to another. It was analogous to the pace but not to the stench. The earthy-manure stink of cows could be eye-watering. The rotting acid wafting up from the undead was overpowering. Jillybean had her shirt up over her face.

This helped to muffle her conversation, though with the others dozing fitfully, it didn't matter. "I knew Neil would cave," Eve said. She was picking at her bellybutton and wondering what would happen if it ever unraveled. Would her insides just come gushing out?

He didn't cave, Jillybean replied like an echo in her own head.

"Ok, he knuckled under. Either way, he's soft as that baby's head. Do you remember when you touched her head and it was smushy?"

Jillybean had a sudden flash of unwanted imagination: her finger stabbing into the soft spot on Eve...the real Eve's, head. She could feel warm blood gurgle up as the baby's arms and legs shot straight out. There was laughter in her head, again like an echo bouncing all around so that her blue eyes traced a zigzag pattern in her sockets.

We never touched her like that, so stop. And Neil did what he had to. You heard what would've happened if we had gone around. Cannon-balls! That's what means they eat people.

"Captain Grey didn't believe it, so why should we?"

So you like Captain Grey now? Last night you were vowing to kill him. In an attempt to try to control the other girl inside her, Jillybean had tried to use the threat of imprisonment or banishment. It had worked to a degree. For a time her hate had slithered into the background.

Jillybean couldn't understand the girl at all. She was jealous of everything and everyone. She stole constantly and ate like a pig. At meal times, she went from one little group of people to the next, complaining that Neil was practically starving her. The story she told was that Neil would only give her a few spoonfuls on account that she was so small.

She hated Neil to no end and actively plotted the murder of the baby. But for some reason she liked Fred Trigg who Jillybean thought was a jerk—'jerk' was just about the biggest putdown in her arsenal. The other girl also hated Sadie, which again was a mystery. Sadie had been the quietest person in camp since the renegades had been freed. It was as though she had retreated into herself, a little every day, until only her big dark eyes stuck out. Sadie seemed to care for the baby and nothing else. Sadly, Neil didn't seem to notice. He was focused full square on saving the group. Deanna didn't seem to notice either; she only had eyes for Captain Grey. Wherever he went, she was sure to follow.

"Like that nursery rhyme mommy used to tell us," the other girl said. "The one about the sheep. How did it go again?"

Jillybean didn't know. Ever since Ipes had been…she didn't know if he had been killed or not. He tended to float after all…but ever since he was gone, she had trouble remembering things like she used to. Gone were nursery rhymes and the name of the street she used to live on, and she couldn't remember what her daddy looked like or what he did for a job. She should've known these things.

"It doesn't matter," the other girl said. "Daddy is dead. Just like mommy and stupid old Ipes. And like Eve, too, soon enough."

Do you want to go to jail? Jillybean asked. *That's where they'll put you and they'll lock the door and throw away the key.*

"Not if I do it right," *She* said. "It'll be an accident. Remember the marble from last night…or whenever that was, it's hard to keep track. But whatever; a marble will do it. All I have to do is poke it down her little throat. She doesn't even have teeth to bite me!"

A cascade of black laughter fell through Jillybean's mind, burying her under what felt like an avalanche of bats. Compared to the sound, Jillybean was small and skinny and so very weak. Weak as a shadow and, like one, she matched the color of the strange laughing bats that threatened to bury her. Their laughter wouldn't stop. It went on and on. It was insane laughter, Jillybean realized, and that's what meant crazy, cuckoo for coconuts.

Jillybean knew insanity on an intimate level. When she thought about it, she fooled herself with cartoon images of people bonking themselves on the head with a frying pan as little blue birds revolved around their heads. That was the thin illusion that she justified as understanding so that she was never forced into delving deeper on the subject. Deeper would've had her envisioning her mommy lying in bed, staring at the ceiling as she wasted into nothing, or seeing the cold look in the bounty hunter's eye when she had shot him. There had been no humanity left in him. He liked killing. He 'got off' on it. 'Getting off' was also a subject that she left purposely vague in her mind. Its implications, that all of mankind was so very disgusting and disturbed, was something she felt she had to come to grips with gradually.

If she had delved to the very core of the concept of insanity, she would've seen herself with Ipes, harmlessly talking. Harmless, yes, but also insane.

Ipes wasn't real. He couldn't talk. He wasn't her best friend. He wasn't even an imaginary friend. He was a symptom of her mental disorder. Had she delved deep she would've understood these things and she would've been forced to admit that she was broken and perhaps unfixable. But she wasn't ready to admit the truth, mainly because as one who was insane, the truth of the world could never be perceived fully or properly. It was a vicious and infinite circle.

Just then, sitting in the cab of the five-ton, she saw neither the truck nor the blazing hot July day outside it. She was in the dark of her mind with a crazed laughter taking the form of strange flapping things that resembled ebony books opening and closing on their inky bindings or uneven bats made from a blackness that was deeper than true black—they were shadows of a shadow. They fell on her softly, but thick, like night snow. She couldn't see or think straight with it covering over her and only her fingers stuck out stretching for air or thought.

The strange, black webbiness was a mass that gave under her feet, so that any pushing resulted in maintaining the status quo of her being nearly buried. She panicked, afraid of being swallowed up for all time in the darkening depths of her own mind, where thoughts and memories faded over time, becoming thin, transparent and then, patchy and partial, until they disappeared altogether.

She didn't want to disappear. There were things she had to do—though what, she didn't know. And there were people she had to save—although who was lost on her. And there were battles still to be fought—although against whom she was afraid to know. And she had a life still to live, but she didn't struggle for her life, it was her fear that caused her to spaz, uselessly. But then a voice spoke: *You've tried pushing up, have you tried the opposite?*

The voice was calm and came from the blackness where her thoughts went to die, and that was strange. Jillybean stopped struggling and looked down into the black and saw that she was wrong; it was not altogether black. There were silver lines as thin as a spider's silk descending downward. She had no clue what they were and she really didn't want to find out. This dark, more than any other dark scared her. There were whispers down there. Haunting sounds just on the verge of being understood.

They were puzzles to her, fear-filled ones, because they weren't just puzzles, they were the flagstones of a path and although she didn't know where that path led, she knew it would lead to bad stuff. Hard stuff. Stuff she couldn't handle. Stuff that could turn her catatonic—that could turn her into a useless vegetable. Stuff that would make her like her mother: dead before she died.

But there was also that voice in the dark which upset the teetering deck of cards. The voice had been pleasant. Did that mean there were also pleasant things down there? Or was it all more shadow and fakery? Was the voice fake? Was it a lie? The problem with being insane, even just a little insane, was that nothing could be studied and known for fact because there were no facts that the mind couldn't warp for its own good or its own destruction.

Still the voice was warm and reminded her of someone. And it caused her to think beyond her panic. *Have I tried the opposite?* she asked herself. She had kicked out with her feet but that had been like trying to gain purchase on a cloud. The opposite of push was pull, she decided, and so she began pulling the black webby stuff down. It came down in sticky strings like damp cotton candy and soon her face was out of the black and into the void of her mind.

"Why would pulling work when pushing didn't?" she asked aloud. The words stopped the echoing, flat. Excited she looked up and saw twin lamps of a pale hue. They were the color of bluebells on the first of May. This thought sprung another and soft words floated up from beneath her: *I'm a May Flower.*

She had said that to Ram before he died, when they were in the cleaning store where a heavy black smoke was billowing from the fire, making the room blistering hot. They thought they were going to die but they hadn't. The memory was just as clear and crisp in her mind as an autumn leaf fresh from a leap off a branch.

Jillybean smiled and felt her face work. Above, the twin lamps crinkled. Those were her eyes! Eyes ready to see and a mouth ready to work. How strange. She had never seen herself from the inside before. Normally, when she was taken over by Ipes or this new, nasty girl, she was just a vague notion in her own mind that would come and go, sometimes running the body and sometime riding along as if in the back seat of a car. This was different and somewhat exciting. It was like putting on a turtleneck sweater. There was endless cloth and tunnels going off at angles for the arms to poke through and then there was the long passage for the head and the odd fear of suffocating that always came with it and there was…

"No!" the mouth spoke with sudden, angry authority. "No, you stay in there," the other girl said. *She* was suddenly there in the construct of Jillybean's perceived reality. *She* was a giant with a giant's hand. *She* took a train-sized finger and poked Jillybean down back into the black just like *she* would poke the marble down Eve's throat.

Jillybean tried to fight. Mindlessly, she battled in the inky black nothing, straining against nothing, and receiving nothing as a result. As before she tried pulling but it was only panic, not thought, that drove her limbs. She only sank lower and lower, until she was too afraid to move anymore and there Jillybean waited, held in place, not by the strange cottony blackness, but by that which created it. It was the same force that had created Ipes and the nasty girl running her body. It was the insanity of fear.

Chapter 12

Deanna Russell

The mega-horde finally broke up around them, wandering off in a westerly direction. Brad, who had somehow managed to slip the Camry away when the beasts first appeared, came tooling back. As usual, he was all smiles. He also seemed refreshed and perky. The renegades were haggard in comparison. The heat in the trucks had been stifling and now they began to clamor for water.

Gritting his teeth and biting back a menu of curse words, Neil said: "Well, you got your wish," he said to Brad. "We're at your mercy. We need water, badly. Please show us to the nearest clean stream." The 'please' had been barely civil.

"Careful," Deanna said, under her breath. In her opinion, Neil was being unnecessarily belligerent, antagonizing the one man who could get them to Colorado safely.

Brad shook his head at the angry little man and then seemed to voice Deanna's thoughts aloud: "Gonna fight me tooth and nail? Not the smartest move, Neil. I'm sure your people won't appreciate it if I get angry and leave you bone dry in the middle of Kansas without gas or water."

"You wouldn't," Neil reply. "There's no profit in ditching us. You're here to make money. We both know it so please stop with the savior routine. Just tell me how much it will cost to refill our water supply." In the back of each of the three trucks was a large plastic container that held twenty gallons. Along with their numerous water bottles they had about ninety gallons left, enough to last them a day and a half.

A shrug, a tiny lift of Brad's shoulders was followed by: "Well now, that depends on which of the water stations we go to. Some are more and some are less, but they're all very expensive. It's a resource after all. If we can make it to the North Platte, you'll get the best price. The King is very fair. He only charges market price without adding any fees."

Deanna was confused since the two terms: 'very fair' and 'very expensive,' didn't seem to go either with one another or with the words 'market price.' She stepped forward and demanded: "What do you mean by market prices? We're talking water, not lobsters."

Neil made a sound that was part laugh, part derisive snort. "He means he's going to charge us whatever he can squeeze out of us."

By the shark-like look in Brad's eyes, Deanna saw that he meant to do exactly as Neil said. There was an angry murmur from the renegades who, as usual whenever they stopped, had come gasping out of the trucks. They were beginning to understand that they were getting screwed and that unless the blue sky flipped to black and the heavens opened up, they'd be forced to accept whatever despicable terms were offered by the king of the Azael.

Brad saw their agitation and heard the anger in the voices and yet his grin was undimmed. "Now, now," he said, playing the benevolent father. "Do not fret. My king offers fairly lenient credit terms and…" he paused when the whispering of the renegades increased, "…and is not the 'great' General Johnston of Colorado known for his generosity and kindness? You'll get your water, don't worry."

"That is not the point," Grey said, when all eyes centered on him; he was the General's man after all. "The point is that you are colluding to gouge innocent and destitute travelers. It's neither ethical nor Christian."

Again the lift of the shoulders. "We never said we were Christian, so there goes that point. And yes, you are beggars and not choosers, which really makes things easier on everyone. You'll pay whatever the king says you'll pay. Now, since that's settled, we should get going."

As everyone else started heading back to the trucks wearing hound-dog expressions, Grey stood glaring at Brad's back. Next to him, as always, was Deanna. Hanging around him had become a habit, or a need, or a strong desire she couldn't help…it was one of those and she didn't think too hard on which, afraid to find out it might be something more.

He grunted to her: "I should have listened to you. We should have gone around the long way."

"No duh, you should've listened to me. But who knows?" Deanna said, cheerily. "What if there really are cannibals in Texas? Or vampires in New Mexico?" She laughed a little too loud and then spun Grey around and took him by the arm as if they had just stepped out of some late-night club and onto the curb with a fine, three in the morning mist running on their faces. They started strolling and the conversation that should have been as simple as breathing stalled into a bit of loud clicks as Deanna grew tongue tied and she had trouble even swallowing.

It was the arm, she knew. Taking his arm, in this odd new era where rapes were common place and gentlemen rare, had been extremely forward especially when the latter was involved. There would have been the same uncomfortable reaction if she had taken Neil by the arm or Michael Gates. Had it been the River King, he likely would have grabbed her ass, but Grey was very aware of her past and clearly it affected the way he viewed her and, thus, how he reacted to her.

Because of his gallant nature, she knew he would be afraid to make any sexual move toward her, even if she really, really wanted him to. Ever since that awkward moment in the lake when they were both dripping wet and smiling under a beautifully warm sky, she had known that she was falling for him. Clearly, at least it was clear to Deanna, he was falling for her as well, but that same chivalrous attitude precluded him from making any move.

He likely viewed her as damaged from her experience, both mentally and emotionally.

An ugly thought slipped unwanted into her mind: what if he thought she was damaged physically? Maybe that was why he had kept his guard up around her.

She gave him a quick look and saw the rugged, bristled jaw and the hard eyes. Unexpectedly, he turned and caught her staring. Their eyes locked and there was a moment in which everything in their hard lives fell away, the harsh land, the tired and sweat-smelling renegades, the distant but ever present moan of the zombies, and it was just the two of them, simply a boy and a girl and the wonderful bridge between them. It was a conduit, of expectation, of excitement, of destiny, of souls. It was a conduit of love, and her fear of what he thought of her fell away.

He didn't question it, either.

It was too perfect, perhaps the most perfect moment in her life. There was no need to question the feeling and the thought of what had happened to Neil's perfect love, or Sadie's or Ram's, or even of little Jillybean's, never entered her mind.

She smiled and then he flashed his white teeth and she was happy, so happy that the fact that they seemed unable to talk to each other didn't matter.

"Uh, here we are," Grey said, a very quick moment later. He had, as any gentlemen would, escorted her to the passenger side of the truck where Neil was standing on the fender, looking at them with a raised eyebrow. Neil looked as though he was on the verge of saying something, perhaps a warning about the danger of love in this new undead world, or perhaps a joke to break the silence, or perhaps a word of congratulations. He held his tongue, so Deanna never knew. Higher up in the truck, perched in the middle of the bench, Jillybean was looking at them with an undisguised look of frank disgust.

Deanna suddenly didn't like the little girl anymore, psychosis, or no psychosis. There simply wasn't enough of the old, sweet Jillybean left. "I'm going to go see whether Sadie needs a break from taking care of Eve," Deanna said, giving Grey's arm a last squeeze and letting go. Again, she didn't know why she had. The squeeze had just happened. It was strange, as though her body was giving hints to both of them that there was no need to be as shy as they were.

Grey looked down at the squeezed arm before glancing again into her eyes. Again that connection was there. It was brief, not even a second, but it still conveyed everything the first had. He blinked the moment away and said: "Sure."

Sadie was in the front of the next truck in line. Eve was lolling back, her eyes blissfully closed, her little pink lips parted and a thin arm thrown out. "Are you ready for a break?" Deanna whispered. "I can take over if you want. I know how tiring a baby can be."

The young woman opened her mouth, but then shut it again before shaking her head, letting her short hair hang over her eyes. It was only then that Deanna realized that Sadie hadn't spiked her hair that day or the last. In fact, she couldn't remember the last time she had. And gone, too, was the black eyeliner that she usually gooped on thick. She looked washed out and used up.

"Are you sure? Neil would love for you to ride with him, He doesn't say it, but I think the stress of being the leader is getting to him. He could use you."

"I think he's doing fine," Sadie said, showing some life by giving Deanna a sharp eye. "Neil is stronger than most people think. Didn't you see the way he handled Brad? He didn't take any of his..." she paused and glanced down at the baby, before spelling out: "S.h.i.t."

"Sure. I didn't mean anything except I thought he could use a friend and that you could use a break."

The girl's sharp look dimmed along with her anger, leaving only the same faded look on her face as if age were actively conspiring against her. "Thanks, but I'm good and Eve needs me and...I just don't want to. Jillybean is...I just don't want to."

Deanna told her she understood and, after a last grin that was all muscle and no emotion, she left to hurry back to the lead truck that was sitting, dribbling out a grey smoke from its exhaust. "No luck?" Grey asked, as she climbed up into the cab. He had a smile for her, Neil looked worried and slightly disappointed, and Jillybean gave her a snort that was impossible to read and then faced forward, ignoring her as if she didn't exist.

"The baby was sleeping on her arm," Deanna said as answer, settling herself down close to Grey. So close that again their arms touched. "She didn't want to disturb her." Neil relaxed at this and Grey only shrugged before glancing once at the gas gauge that was on the wrong side of the halfway mark. He muttered a curse and hit the gas, chugging the truck forward. It was after noon and the sun was canted at an angle above them.

For the next hour they drove through sixty miles of sameness. The land, once the breadbasket of the world, looked to have been struck by the same dread disease affecting the human population. Where once everything was lush and green, it was now patchy and ugly, mottled, dry and dying. In direct contradiction, above them was a vast sameness. The sky was a simmering steel blue, marked only by the disc of the sun as it, ever so slowly, moved across the sky.

Brad took them on another convoluted trail where there was a curious lack of signage. They had no idea what roads they were on or what the names were of the dinky little towns they passed. Even Captain Grey grumbled about being "lost."

Two hours into the trip they had a repeat of the day before as trouble struck. The truck beneath them started to vibrate and buck. It shimmied to the right and Neil, master of the obvious, said: "Something's wrong It's another blowout, I bet." He had his feet up on the dash. Once again they were snug in his purple crocs; knowing he would regret not having them, Deanna had fetched the crocs from the field he had thrown them in earlier that morning.

"You think?" Grey snarled as he fought the wheel back to center and slowly hit the brake. He cut the engine and then glanced around at the unruly farmland. Far out among the fields, there were a few ugly beings standing like scarecrows here and there. As they watched, the zombies began heading toward them. Five went for the Camry, which was a few hundred yards ahead, another six, in a jagged line, came for the trucks.

On the floor at Neil's feet was an axe, its steel head was notched and had a case of rust, though it wasn't serious enough to keep it from being used. "I'll take care of them," he said. "You fix the truck."

"Take Deanna as back up," Grey said.

Neil jumped down and held his hand out for Deanna. After her time on the Island where she had been treated like dirt, these little displays of manners had her smiling in spite of their situation. "Thank you, kindly," she said with an exaggerated southern accent.

With a flourish, Neil made a bow, also smiling. His smile didn't last as he saw the blown tire. The back end of what looked like a five inch slag bolt was sticking out of the treads. "Son of a gun!" he swore. "Do you think that's fixable?"

Grey walked around to squat next to the truck, resting his forearms on his thighs. He gave the bolt a wiggle. "Probably not. We don't have tools or anything to patch it with. I swear you're jinxed, Neil. I've never had such a string of bad luck."

"That's not luck, good or bad," Jillybean stated. "That was human done."

"How do you know?" Deanna asked. "Tires pick up nails all the time."

The little girl squinted up, her face once again unpleasant. "I just know. That should be good enough for you." The word 'you' came out in sneer.

Deanna rounded on the little girl with her fists balled and planted on the points of her thin hips. She glared and thought seriously about telling the seven-year-old to 'fuck off.' Instead, she said: "You need to curb your tongue, young lady, or you'll be riding in the back. Is that what you want?" Jillybean puffed up as if she had a thousand words worth of air in her lungs. Deanna only raised an imperious eyebrow, letting the little girl know that she was ready to back up her words with actions.

Jillybean backed down, sulking.

"Good," Deanna said. Inside she felt an odd touch of motherly pride and she thought: *That's how you deal with a head-strong child*. Without realizing it, she rubbed her belly which was no longer as flat as it had once been. "Now, what if this was an act of sabotage? What do we do?"

"It was sabotage," Jillybean told them, in a quieter voice. "*She* said so."

"She who?" Neil asked. "Did Jillybean say that?"

The little girl nodded, her face suddenly vacant. "Yes, Jillybean said to expect this. She said that we shou…" In mid-sentence the girl just trailed off, her eyes staring at the tire.

Neil took her by the shoulders and shook her so that her head jerked back and forth. "Jillybean! Hey, talk to me. What were we supposed to do?" He shook her roughly and none of the renegades said anything. They had come up in dribs and drabs until there were twenty of them watching Neil shout into her face. "Hey! Answer me. What did Jillybean say we…"

She suddenly blinked and stared into Neil's eyes. "Oh, hey, Mister Neil." She gazed around at the others as if the cock had just crowed and she had awakened to find them gathered around her bed. "What's going on?"

"We, uh. We, uh, just wanted to ask you about this tire," he said, gently prying his hands from her shoulders and bringing them to his chest where they opened and closed like a pair of dying spiders. She looked at the tire as if seeing it for the first time in her life. Just as Grey had, she gave the bolt a wiggle before looking back up at Neil.

"It's got a nail sticking out of it," she said, after a moment of consideration. She then squinted up and asked: "What day is it? Is it still today?" This perplexed everyone in earshot. No one knew either the date or what she was talking about.

More gently than he had before, Neil took her, once again, by the shoulders. "You said something about the tires?"

"Oh them. Yeah, they are going to put nails in them just like they did the last one. We should check them before we leave. There'll be more like this one. At least I think so. *She* was aposed to tell you that."

"Ok, thanks, Jilly," Neil said. He stood and looked down the line of trucks. A tired sigh escaped him. He opened his mouth to say something but before he could a gunshot split the air. Brad was shooting the zombies as they came stumping up to the Camry. Neil cast a quick glance over at the ones he had been going to kill—the nearest was fifty yards away. "All right. I need Veronica and Joslyn to check all the remaining tires for more nails. Fred, Michael, William and Grey will change out this tire and I will kill those zombies. Marybeth, climb up on the second truck and take the first watch. We'll switch every twenty minutes. Any questions?"

"Just one," Michael Gates said. "We don't have any more spares and I'm scared to ask how much Brad will charge."

Brad was just coming up to the trucks, a shotgun slung on his shoulder, clothed as he was in his garish silks, the machismo of the long gun clashed. "Charge for what? You guys have another flat? That is some bad luck."

The renegades began muttering to themselves and again, just as earlier, he didn't seem concerned. Casually, he put the gun across his back like a yoke and hung his hands off either end. He breathed out a loud sigh, as though he were filled with sadness over the loss of the tire. "A new tire is pricey, specially one this big. We have to haul it all the way from Topeka and that's a drive both ways. I'd say it would run you over a thousand."

This caused the muttering to step up in tempo. Deanna was among the mutterers. She was so angry that if she had been a man, she likely would have taken a poke at Brad. That's why she was surprised to see Grey was smirking.

"Lucky for us, we don't need a spare. We have six already." He pointed at the undercarriage of the truck. It was ten-wheeled on three axles. "We aren't carrying enough weight that we really need all the wheels. We could lose the middle two and the truck will run just fine."

At the realization, a few of the renegades laughed and all of them grinned. Brad wore a tight smile as he said: "Well that's great, just great. In fact, that's super. I didn't want to go to Topeka anyway."

"No one in their right mind would," Neil said. His was the largest smile of any of them. He clapped Brad on the back, leaving his hand there as if they were good friends. He then addressed the renegades: "Ok people, we all have work to do. Let's get going."

The group broke up. Most of them hurrying to find shade against the trucks. Neil went out into the field and, with Deanna backing him, he struck down the zombies as they came straggling up. It was ugly work and hot. Sweat gathered in his hair and what was left of his baby face glowed red. None of the zombies were particularly large or fast, in fact two had 'turned' as children and were missing significant portions of their anatomy. Together they only had the sum of three arms, two hands, eight fingers and a single set of lips. Even as un-whole as they were, they were still dangerous because of the disease they carried.

Neil muttered: "Just chopping wood, just chopping wood," each time he swung the axe over his head to bring it around in a looping arc. Black blood flew. It was like sludge and Neil was speckled like a gecko when the last zombie came hobbling on one foot through the field. This one had been a woman. She wore a silver cross that glinted like white fire, and one sneaker on her remaining foot. She was otherwise naked and unappealing in every way.

As her disfigured leg ended mid-tibia, she moved at a list of some thirty degrees which, combined with her bobbing up-down, caused Neil to misjudge his swing. The axe cleaved off an ear before burying itself in the side of her neck. She didn't even blink.

She kept coming with hands outstretched, managing to snag his sweater vest. He squawked in typical Neil fashion and leapt back causing the women, whose grip was like iron, to fall forward. She nearly dragged him down and, bent well over at the waist, he was forced to shimmy out of the vest to free himself.

"Jeeze!" he exclaimed and then stomped around the woman to get at the handle of his axe. A tug freed it and then he planted his foot on her back to force her down. "If I live to a hundred, I'll never get used to this," he said before looping the axe around a final time. The strike made a wet sound, like a melon being split. It had Deanna's stomach turning over and, when Neil had to work the axe back and forth in order to free it from the zombie's head, she turned around to find Jillybean right there.

"Hi," the little girl said, brightly, as though there wasn't a pile of bodies in front of her. "I missed you."

"You missed me?" Deanna asked. "What do you mean?"

Jillybean's little face scrunched in as if she was under the effects of a lemon. "I guess I don't know, but it feels like we haven't talked for a long time. Has it been a long time, do you think? Was it a long time since we blew up the bridge?"

"Four or five days," Deanna said, trying to remember. She had always been time conscious before the apocalypse. Ever since, she didn't know one day from another, but at least she was aware of time passing. Jillybean's mental disorder seemed to be causing hiccups in her memory.

"Forget the bridge," Neil whined. "Look at me! It's on me! I think I'm about to puke." He stood with his arms out and his face stricken and wrinkled in disgust. There was a constellation of bloody, diseased freckles across his cheeks and nose. "Is it in my eyes?"

Deanna shook her head. "It's close." She pointed beneath his right eyelid at the drop nearest.

He developed a sudden jittery tic where her finger had indicated. "Oh, jeeze! What the heck am I going to do? I got to get this stuff off of me, but we're out of water." He swallowed, making sure to keep his lips slightly parted and his tongue retracted—all in all looking like a dog retching.

"We're out of water?" Jillybean asked, perplexed at the idea. "That's not good because I'm thirsty real bad and you gots all that blood on you, which is real gross and all. You know what you can do? You could use dirt to clean up. You know, like a bird. Birds take dirt baths sometimes and have you ever seen a dirty bird? It doesn't make any sense really, dirt to clean dirt, but they do it."

Neil looked down at the ground with a hound dog expression. "Dirt? Oh jeeze," he said, before grabbing a handful of dirt. Deanna was skeptical over the idea and yet she wasn't the one with zombie blood all over her. Neil started with his hands and wrists. The dirt was abrasive and it was only a minute before his hands were "clean" meaning free of blood, but otherwise filthy. He moved on to his cheeks and neck where the dirt and sweat mingled to make mud.

Jillybean watched Neil with an amused expression as she pointed out each speckle. Deanna had to concentrate on not cracking up and this was not easy, especially when Jillybean suddenly said: "You know what might also work? Mister Ricky's whiskey drink. He's always taking secret sips, but he's not all that secret, if you ask me."

Neil spat out little flecks of dirt from the end of his tongue. He seemed to have trouble thinking and spitting at the same time. When his mouth was clear, he said in an outraged rush: "He's got alcohol?" Deanna understood this to mean: *He's got alcohol and you didn't tell me?*

Innocently, Jillybean answered: "Yep. And you know what also might work? Eve's baby wipes. If they can clean up poop I bet they'd work on those icky speckles. Hey, Mister Neil? Why do you look like that? You look angry."

He looked almost crazed with the smears of mud and his face red beneath and his eyes blue but wild. A strangled sound escaped him and his hands shook and were spaced as if there was an invisible neck about the size of Jillybean's between them. It was at that moment that Brad sauntered up. His smile was back in place, only now it was wider than ever.

"Giving yourself a facial, Neil?"

The strangling hands bunched and, with some effort, Neil managed to force a hint of politeness into his voice. "What can I do for you?"

"I just wanted to give you a heads up. Me and the girls are leaving for a few hours, while you fix your flat. It's just too hot and we're also running low on water. Would you like for me to pick some up for you? Just fifty rounds a gallon."

"Fifty rounds?" Neil asked, aghast. Deanna was stunned at the amount he was asking. At that rate it would cost them five thousand rounds just to fill their containers, and that would only last a day!

In desperation, Neil looked up at the sky which was as blue and empty as it could be. Brad laughed and said: "Sorry my friend, there's no rain in the forecast, just more sun and more heat. So what's it going to be? I think fifty rounds is fair, especially since you guys aren't nearly as thirsty as you will be in a couple more hours when the price will jump to sixty."

"Sixty?" Jillybean asked with an incredulous laugh. It was an odd sound from a little girl. All three looked down at her and Deanna saw that she had changed. She had gone flinty and cold. There was a brittle edge to her that was sharp and dangerous. "You take that sixty and shove it up your ass."

Chapter 13

Jillybean/Eve

Brad hadn't been mad at Jillybean's swearing at all; it seemed to stiffen him. He had only said: "We'll see if you change your mind when it hits a hundred degrees out here," and then walked away. Neil had stood there hot and tired, with the mud on his face, stunned at first and then angry. Deanna looked nervous and agitated, though Jillybean was only guessing that they were feeling any of these emotions. The world around her was ghost-like and intangible; not quite fully formed. Physical beings were ethereal at best, ghosts that ate and spoke and pissed behind the trucks in steaming arcs, and their emotions were not just hard to fathom, but also difficult to register on her meter of sympathies. They had the feel of actors going through the motions of a performance gone stale through endless repetition.

The other girl in Jillybean had swallowed her up in the black once again, though this time it wasn't nearly so all-encompassing as it had been. Compared to before, there was a lot more light in her prison of bone. It came in spurts, like novas or speeding meteors, or a flicking of a bulb by a naughty child. This light was accompanied by strange utterances. Sometimes sentences, sometimes questions, sometimes the garbled reflection of messages off an aged transom. They zipped in a bat-like echo through the ether of her mind: *Are we going to die of thirst? No, she won't let us. Can't we just get water anywhere? They poisoned it. Why can't we leave the others? They are useless and stupid and I hate them. They will die soon and that's good. What about Captain Grey? He can live. What about water?*

Jillybean realize that her other self was actually trying to think. It was laughable, as it had to filter though a mesh of hate. Even at the best of times, *she* wasn't good at it.

She had too much anger and fear, too much emotion to be good at thinking. *She* could plot, however. *We have to get away from all of them before they all die. Now, before Brad gets back. How? Tell them we have an idea. Tell them we have a secret. Tell them we can find water, but no one can know where we got it.*

"I can get us water," Eve said, the words spitting out of her mouth with no ideas behind them.

Neil, who had been, staring after the Camry as it sped away, turned so fast that he almost fell over. "Where?"

Tell him, you can't tell just yet. Tell him he has to trust you. Tell him you want a gun. "No, I can't do that," Eve hissed aloud, mixing her thoughts with her spoken words. "That has to be secret."

Jillybean was near the surface of her mind and she guessed it was because there was thinking to be done. Jillybean was good at thinking. The other girl wasn't. *She* was good at hating. When *she* hated, Jillybean tended to drown down where there was nothing and the world above was tiny and odd appearing, as though she were looking through a coke bottle—things were warped and blurry, untouchable.

Neil asked again: "Where, Jillybean. Where can we get water?"

The bat-like echo again in Jillybean's mind: "It's a secret that no one can tell in words out loud. But I can show you and one other per…" She paused as another face flashed like a billboard in her mind. The mental picture was of Sadie. *No! Not Sadie,* Eve thought. *She's fast and she's a killer now. She killed all those men and that's what means she's dangerous. We can't trust her.*

Another picture flashed and with it came a wordless echo*: Say, Deanna then.* The picture of Deanna in her mind started bright and white hot, but it quickly began to erode. There was a thought that came with the picture: *We could kill her easy.*

"Deanna can come," the other girl said, out loud, using Jillybean's lips. "I can show her, too, but no one else.

All those others will blab and that poop-face, Brad can't know where we got it from."

Neil embraced the lie and ran back to the trucks yelling: "I want the water carriers and everyone's canteens and bottles in the second truck, right now!"

People were slow to act. Most of them stared in varying degrees of amusement at the little man until Joslyn asked: "Is that dog crap on your face?"

"No, damn it!" Neil snapped. "It's…it's never mind. Where is Ricky?"

Ricky was barked at for holding back the whiskey from the group; however, it was only a light dressing down. Neil was in too much of a rush to be properly angry. He ignored the excited questions from the renegades and pulled Grey to the side and spoke in whispers, pointing once at Jillybean.

She and Deanna hadn't moved, they were still only a few feet from the jumbled pile of dead zombie bodies. "So where are we going?" Deanna asked. They weren't near enough to anyone to be overheard; *she* didn't have an excuse not to answer.

The other girl could think of nothing except hurting Deanna. She had no plan beyond murdering her and Neil, and she didn't even have much of a plan for that. *Their guns*, she thought. *Take one and kill them when they don't expect it.* A picture accompanied this thought: blood splashed on brown dirt, zombies feasting on warm flesh as crows jumped about in the background cawing and waiting their turn impatiently. The air hummed with flies.

Then what? a voice asked.

I'll be free.

I mean, how will you get away? Jillybean was surprised that the voice associated with the question was her own.

A pause in her thinking and then another picture: *Jillybean with sticks tied to her legs and Ipes sliding around on the dash. She was driving a truck that wished to be unbound from the road. It kept surging toward the curbs that held in the street and kept the asphalt from flowing away. It was a chugging and spitting sort of truck and could be described as unruly and ill-tempered, but Jillybean was more than a match for it and aimed it at the front of a building—a Piggly Wiggly where Neil was being held prisoner. Its doors were barred with wood and came up very fast and grew big in her eyes and then the crash and the glass flew and metal screamed as if in agony...*

"I'll need sticks," *She* said, instead of answering Deanna's question. "Sticks or a…a handle from a rake or shovel."

After a look that held a great deal of suspicion, Deanna left to talk to Neil. This was all Jillybean knew for some time. There was a flash of hate as Deanna took a peek back at the little girl and then utter blackness that enveloped her to such an extent she couldn't feel her heart in her chest or the air around her.

Eventually, what felt like days later, Jillybean heard her name and felt a hand shaking her shoulder. She crawled out of a state of consciousness so thick it might as well have been tar.

"Huh?" she said, her eyes blinking, slowly as she looked around, confused.

"Where to now?" Neil asked, again. Jillybean thought it was an 'again' kind of question because it sure did have a familiar ring to it. Like one of those echoes in her mind that kept going and going…only this was real and that meant she was she.

"Hey, I'm me," she said, as the realization struck her. She was in charge of her own body again. She gave Neil a grin and Deanna one, as well, but when Deanna only gave her a narrow look, Jillybean heard the other girl in her mind: *she doesn't trust us. Figure out how to kill her.*

Jillybean saw in her mind why she had been allowed to come back. Neil didn't have a weapon that the other girl could use. He had his axe and it was heavy. Deanna had a pistol in a holster strapped to her side. She kept her right hand very close to it as if she was ready to draw quick like a gun fighter. "But we need water," Jilly whispered. "Even

136

you need water, or you'll die." She was parched; her little tongue was dry as an old sock.

Above, the sun was a silver-blue glare, while around them was more farmland cut up in lines. To their right, the corn formed a green wall. To their left were little, green, shrubby plants that made food of a sort, this Jillybean was sure of, however the plants had no name in her mind.

As Deanna and Neil shared a look over her head, the other girl spoke in a ghostly voice in her head: *Find the water for us and then kill them both or else I will.*

"You don't know how to kill them," Jillybean said in a hissing whisper, casting a furtive look up at Deanna, whose hand had slipped closer to the pistol at her hip. It made Jillybean wonder what the other girl had been doing or saying when she was gone. She was unable to connect the suspicious movement with her own mutterings. "You need me," she added to the other girl.

Although Deanna's brows furrowed, Neil thought she was talking to him and so he answered: "Yes. We need a water source, remember?"

"The waters are zombie soup and the wells are poisoned," Jillybean said. A vivid picture leapt into her mind: they were high above a river that was simply clogged with a gazillion zombies. No one but Neil, who had been vaccinated against the zombie disease, could drink from it, and he looked as though he would rather die of dehydration than take a sip.

But what about the wells?

"Can you, uh, let me by, Miss Deanna? I need to check something out."

Grudgingly, Deanna opened the door and slid out. She kept her eyes full on the little girl as she did. Jillybean went to the open door but did not climb down; she climbed up onto the top of the truck's cab where the heat radiated upwards. It had to be over a hundred and ten degrees and her head swam. She squinted into the shimmering glare in all directions. There were farms and more farms. Some were cut up in squares, some in circles. The idea of a circular farm made no sense to her unless they grew pumpkins, which she knew to be round.

The farmland went further than she could see. They had been passing nothing but farmland for the last three days. If she had to guess, she would've thought they had driven by ten thousand of fields.

There was a farm not far away. From atop the cab she could see a silo and the tip-top of a white building, which she guessed either to be a farmhouse or a barn. "We need to go that way," she said pointing at the building. She knew about farms. Since she had met up with Neil and Ram, they had stayed in barns overnight on several different occasions, though they never got to do much in the way of exploring, which she had always considered "cheap."

But that wasn't the only way she was acquainted with farms. She used to have a picture book called: *Sissy and Me on the Farm*. It was full of all sorts of information about the entire farming experience, as long as one was observant that is, and Jillybean was very observant.

They climbed into the truck and Neil guided the beastly vehicle down to the first turn-off and then down the gravel road, until they pulled into the farm proper. There was the white house with its shutters sitting at diagonals and the roof beginning to peel back. And there was the silo standing as an imposing sentry, and a low slung barn with the carcass of some great beast lying in front of its doors. It had been a bull, or a buffalo, or a wooly mammoth or some such, Jillybean didn't know which.

In the yard of the house Jillybean saw half of what she was looking for. The other half was something she had never seen in real life; only in books such as *Sissy and Me on the Farm*. "Can you drive around a bit, Mister Neil? Like around the barn and the silo and the house and such?"

Neil gave her a skeptical look, but said nothing as he put the truck in gear. He wasn't nearly as smooth as Captain Grey, who could walk the truck around as if it were sliding on ice. Neil somehow bounced the ten-thousand pounds of metal, rubber, and glass, as if he could only make it go by hopping it forward. In that bone-rattling fashion, they turned the curves of an "eight" around the building until Jillybean said: "Nope, it's not here."

With a sigh, Neil said: "Maybe it would help if you told me what you're looking for."

"Oh, that's ok," Jillybean said. "It's not here and that's ok. I was hoping not to see what we didn't see."

This caused both Neil and Deanna to look around, both wearing matching crease lines cutting up their foreheads. "Ok," Deanna said. "What aren't we supposed to see?"

"A well," Jillybean said, happily. She couldn't be happier by not seeing one. The truth was she had never seen a real well. She had only seen them in books, but she had seen the metal contraptions that reminded her of stick-horses she used to gallop behind back when her mommy and daddy had been alive.

"I don't get it," Neil said. "The wells are all poisoned. We can't take the chance of drinking the water from one. Knowing Brad, he had set it up so that we broke down with a poisoned well sitting right down the road."

"Yes," Jillybean said, smiling. "There's no well. But there is one of those hickey-doos."

Neil was clearly flummoxed by the word "hickey-doos", and the concept of a pump not in conjunction with a well had his face all scrunched, making his scars and the primitive stitching around them turn his face nearly as ugly as a zombie's. "But…" was all he could say in his confusion.

Deanna seemed to be mired in the same sort of puzzled quagmire. She was staring at the pump with its long thoracic pipe and its horsey nose and the mane of a pump. "Won't it be…"

"No," Jillybean answered the partial questions, grinning. "Brad *says* he poisoned the wells but there's no well here. That goes down to the water underground and it's very deep. He'd have to drill down pretty deep to poison it and would he really? I don't think so. We've passed a thousand farms and each has a well or one of these pump things. Did these Azael people really go to each one with a vial of poison, or did he just *say* they did?"

"Son of a bitch!" Neil cried, happily. "Why am I so blind?"

"You're not blind," Deanna told him. "You're just too trusting." With a quick look around for zombies, she climbed down from the truck, followed by Neil and Jillybean. "Someone's got to test the water. Jillybean could be wrong."

There was a moment of hesitation and then Neil stepped forward. "I'll do it. Jillybean has my full confidence. Now, how do you get this thing to go? Is there an *on* switch or a button?" He poked around before actually trying to work the pump's handle. It didn't take much more than that to get the water flowing and when it did, it gushed out in a rush, quickly filling a rusty old trough that sat beneath the pump's nose. Neil cupped a hand beneath the flow, brought a small handful to his nose and sniffed.

"Seems ok," he said. A first tentative taste on Neil's part was followed up by the three of them standing stock-still, waiting in silence for something bad to begin happening to him.

If he doesn't die, you'll have to kill him, the other girl within Jillybean said. *We have to find a way to escape.*

"Why?" Jillybean whispered.

You were right, before. We can't go to Colorado. They won't like us in Colorado. They'll put us in jail, so we have to kill these two and escape.

Neil had been standing still, wearing an odd expression; he now shrugged his shoulders and said: "I think the water is good. I feel perfectly fine. It's actually quite tasty."

Kill him, damn it! His back is turned.

"I didn't think water had a taste," Deanna said, making no move toward the water, despite Neil's declaration and the oppressive heat.

Steal the truck and leave them!

"Shut up!" Jillybean suddenly screamed. In frustration she picked up a rock and threw it at the house. More

140

by luck than skill, she struck one of the rectangular panes in the window. The music of glass crashing down filled the still air and over it, Jillybean yelled: "Just shut up and listen to me. We do this my way, ok?"

Once again, as had happened frequently that day, there was an uncomfortable silence—though it wasn't uncomfortable for Jillybean. The other girl was quiet, brooding angrily like a stony malignant tumor. "Good," Jillybean said. Without hesitation, she kinked at the waist and put her mouth to the water gushing out of the rusty spigot.

Neil put a hand between her lips and the water. "Whoa. We don't know if this is poisoned. It could be slow acting."

Jillybean pulled his hand away. "I hope it is poisoned," she said, in a seething rage, speaking to the other girl. "I hope you die. I hope you rot in hell."

Again the silence and again Jillybean was glad for it. At the moment it represented that she had the upper hand. She drank the water and it was cool and wonderful and good.

Chapter 14

Captain Grey

When he had finally gotten off the twelfth lug nut, he rolled the two-hundred and fifty pound tire away to the side of the road to rot forever—forever in a human sense—the sprung tire would still be sitting there, a tree growing from its trough, long after the asphalt of the road had been eroded into nothing by the sun and the wind, and the voracious appetite of time. It would be there, but not for all that much longer. The rubber would split eventually and then the roots of nature would show that the workings of man, despite his conceit, are not forever. Sooner than anyone could expect, once man's time is done he will quickly be forgotten. His landfills will become meccas of life, his bridges will be cast down and the concrete jungles of his cities will be swept away, becoming dust once again.

But before all that, Grey, sweating through his camouflage clothing, grunted as he heaved the tire down into a ditch. He allowed himself just a moment of rest, pausing to push his knuckles into the small of his back. The vertebrae cracked in an uneven wave, like a bone xylophone. The sound and the pain in his back had him feeling every one of thirty-five years.

A long sigh, an old man's sigh, Grey thought, escaped him as he looked far down the road where dust hung in the still air. A car was coming; it was Brad or Neil, heading back. He hoped it was Neil with the water. The last of it had gone to make Eve a distastefully warm bottle of formula and everyone was lying about panting like dogs.

There was another reason why Grey hoped it was Neil: Deanna was with him. When they had left, Grey had been surprised by the sudden feeling of loss and the insane touch of jealousy that had gripped him. It was insane, not because of any out of control rage, but because this was *Neil* he was feeling jealous of!

It took all of two seconds for Grey to analyze the teenage foolishness inside him: somehow, somewhere, and at some time, he had begun to look on Deanna, not as just another woman in need of being rescued, or another of the renegades in need of being shepherded across the country, but as a real woman. A real, available, in his face, constantly near, and sometimes a pain in the butt, woman.

This completely normal observation struck him as odd and it ran a tinny chord within him, like a warning. It didn't make much sense if the warning was taken in the context of the old world, which, more often than not, Grey still did as a matter of habit. In the new undead world, where little things were big and big things gigantic, and, where many things that people had taken for great importance didn't matter a hill of beans, the idea that Deanna could be into him was dangerous.

They lived, essentially without laws and their old mores were near on useless. Jealousies could be deadly and love, as he had already seen, could be a death sentence more often than not. He told himself he had to tread extremely carefully, but when she climbed down from the cab of the five-ton he caught himself staring. There was a moment when she had one long leg extended, reaching for the ground, while the other was canted, on the fender. Her pelvis was open in greeting and he swallowed like a school boy. His eyes quickly glanced to check to see if she had seen him staring. Her face was cast toward the ground, her long hair, the color of honeyed wheat, collected on one side while the other was free, showing off the smooth muscles and tight tendons of her neck.

In comparison, he knew he looked like a grease monkey. His hands were black, and grime streaked him past his elbows. Around his neck and chest was a horse-collar of sweat and there were disgusting, dark crescent moons beneath his arm pits. His hair was unwashed and long, for him at least, and went in all directions except the one that might have been considered stylish.

Her step was light as she dropped to the road. She was fresh-faced and smiling. Unbelievably, she smelled of lilac.

"You're clean," he said. "How?"

"We found water," she whispered. "Jillybean found it, really."

Neil came hurrying around the truck. He too was clean, though in his case it did nothing to help his looks. His many injuries were slow to mend and Grey figured that when they did, he would still be without the boyish good looks he'd had before he had tried to sacrifice himself. "Don't say where we got it from," he hissed at Deanna. "You too, Jillybean. We keep it a secret. I hope you don't take offense, Grey but you know better than anyone that loose lips sink big ships...or something like that."

"I wasn't going to say anything," Jillybean said. "Promise. But lips can't sink a ship, especially not a big one. Icebergs can. That's what I heard. There was this one ship called The Gigantic and this iceberg ate it and all these people got killed-ed. There was also this..."

Just then, Fred Trigg came rushing up. Behind him were the other renegades, their faces eager for water. They crowded so close that Jillybean slid back, next to Grey, using his large body to shield herself. "I don't care if we don't like him," Grey heard the little girl whisper: "We can't kill him."

"Did you get the water?" Fred demanded. It was almost an accusation. He seemed angry that Neil, Deanna and Jillybean had taken the time to bathe.

Neil nodded. "Yes, but..." The renegades pressed forward, en masse, seeming like a mob bent on looting. Neil thrust his hands to the hard blue oval of the sky and put himself between them and the tailgate. "Stop!" He glared. When Grey had first met Neil, a glare from him couldn't wilt lettuce on a hot summer day. Now the look stopped them and kept them from piling over him on their way into the back of the truck. "Hold on! Form a line. All of you from Michael on move back. Don't worry we have plenty of water. Everyone will get some."

In spite of Neil's best efforts the line formed was more of a shifting blob. Grey watched for a moment, and despite his thirst, which was greater than any, seeing as he had done the most and the hardest work, he left and went back to where he was working on the tire. The axle was jacked up, putting the truck on a slight angle. Thankfully, he'd had help from Michael and his brother getting the good middle tire off and then re-positioned in front. He only had to cinch the lugs down and release the jack.

As Neil yelled and pushed and cursed the renegades into line, Grey picked up the wrench and went to work on the nuts. He had only just tightened the third of the twelve, when Deanna came up with two full water bottles. "You should've been in the front of the line. You deserve it more than they do."

"Deserve is probably the worst word in the English language," he said and then took one of the offered bottles and drank deeply. It was refreshingly cool. "Very few people ever get what they deserve. Look at Fred. He deserves a punch in the mouth, and Neil deserves to be treated like a hero and you…" He bit back his words. He had been about to say: *you deserve to be treated like a queen.* That would've been awkward.

"What about me?" She seemed cautiously optimistic at what he might say. "What do I deserve?"

"You deserve better," he replied. It was an honest answer. He was in a squat, again so much like some ignorant grease monkey, while she stood tall and trim above him. She was beautiful while he was grim at the best of times.

Yet his answer was not based on appearances at all. Of all the renegades, she was the only one who had grown as a person in the time he had known her. Neil might have become a stronger leader, but he was also beaten down, his innocence degraded and his cheery outlook replaced by suspicion. Jillybean was damaged goods. Where there had been fine cracks in her psyche there was now a deep gorge of crazy. Michael Gates had gone from a not so great leader of his people to a quiet worker bee who never contributed the least idea to the group. And Sadie looked to have practically given up. Her innocence and her zest for life had been washed away by all the blood she had spilt.

Only Deanna had grown. She had gone from being a cringing whore to one of the most valuable members of the group. She was smart, engaging and protective. In Grey's eyes, she practically glowed—this thought set off another warning bell within him; this one making even less sense than any other.

"I don't think I will get better," she said, a little sadly. His mind had been wandering and at first he thought she meant that she was sick, but that clearly wasn't the case. *Then what did she mean?* he wondered. Was it her life in general that she was talking about getting better, or was it something more specific? Something closer. Something that had to do with the way she was looking at him steadily with her even blue eyes...

"Uh, Mister Captain Grey sir?" Jillybean was suddenly right beside him. He had been staring so intently up at Deanna that his vision had tunneled and he hadn't seen her walking up.

He tried to grin his way past his embarrassment, only at the sight of the little girl, his grin faded away. Her face was pinched and her eyes were narrowed in a look that was curdled hate. "Yes?" he asked, cautiously. She seemed on the edge again, where she could suddenly turn 'evil' for want of a better word—no other word fit so well.

"The people are being real stupid. No one is acting as lookout. They're all just drinking. That's not right. I would tell Neil, only he's already busy trying to keep them from drinking all the water before they waste it." This was spoken in a rush. She had barely paused for a breath and each word had been neatly clipped so that the next could begin as quickly as she could manage to form her lips.

Grey sighed and was about to heave himself up when Deanna put a hand on his shoulder and gave it a squeeze. "No, you've got work to do here. I'll take care of this."

"Thanks. I shouldn't be much long..."

Jillybean interrupted him: "Not her. She's weak and stupid...no she's not. You're stupid!" Jillybean shouted.

146

She stuck her balled fists on her hips and glared off to her right. After a moment, she grunted as if to say: you better not say anything more. She then said to the two adults. "I'm sorry about her. She's very mean and bad, and I hate her very much."

"It's ok, Jillybean," Deanna said. "We understand. I'll take care of this."

Grey watched as Deanna started directing people away from the water. She set watchers at the front and rear of the three trucks and Grey thought she was doing a fine job, but Jillybean only glared and muttered, alternating between strident anger and an evil hissing: "She's doing it wrong! She's a stupid bitch is why. You have to let me kill her. No, never, but she is doing it wrong. You're right about that. They're just sitting there, which is a real waste. It's because they're as stupid as she is."

"Jillybean?" Grey asked in a gentle voice.

She didn't hear. She was in too deep in conversation with herself. As Deanna finished directing the group away from the truck with the water, the little girl walked right past her and to the other renegades.

"Wrong!" she cried. "Why are you all just sitting there?" Her voice carried off into the corn and maybe for miles on the still air. She seemed to be in a volcanic fury over the apparent laziness of the renegades. "Are you waiting for someone else to do your thinking and your work for you? Look at those fields of corn! There's enough food to last us months and you're just sitting there like morons! Get up! You small ones," she said, pointing at Joslyn, Anne and Joe Gates, "carry the guns and guard the others. You big ones, take off your shirts tie the ends and fill them with the corns. When you have enough, there is a fence that's wooden right down the road. Break it up and bring it here. There isn't a lot of firewood for cooking on the prairie. When you're done with that come see me for more instructions."

The little girl, just a tad over forty three inches in height and thin as a reed, astounded the renegades, Captain Grey among them. Her voice was that of a cockatrice, shrill and angry, piping out of her thin body like steam from a kettle, however it was her anger that had them staring in amazement. Her blue eyes popped out of her head and her fly away brown hair was so unbound by normal convention that it gave her the appearance of a tiny budding witch.

The renegades were so surprised that, instead of jumping to her demands, they simply stared. All save for Fred Trigg, that is. As usual, he looked as though something had soured his liver. "Who do you think you are to boss us around like that? We have a leader and it isn't you."

Jillybean turned her snarl toward him only to have a hand clamp down over her lips. Neil held her, for the moment, in check. "I am the leader here, but that doesn't mean I know everything or that my wisdom supersedes that of others. Jillybean has pointed out a few obvious acts that it would be smart to attend to. We should be thanking her, not arguing with her. Now, Fred, everyone, get moving, like she suggested. I want three hundred ears of corn and thirty beams of wood in the back of these trucks before Brad gets back."

Some of the renegades grumbled at first at the idea of work with the sun beating down, but with nearly sixty people going at the tasks, they doubled what Neil had asked for in half an hour. He went among them encouraging them but also telling them to make sure to keep the new food and water a secret from Brad, if at all possible. He was sure there would be a "fee" involved for picking produce that otherwise would have rotted on the stalks.

Many of the renegades, without being asked, even crossed to the other side of the road to pick the beans from the shrub-like plants. It was guessed that they were soybeans though no one knew for certain. During this, Jillybean stood apart from the rest, alternating between a moody muttering and a blank stare in which she seemed catatonic.

"That is the saddest thing," Deanna said to Grey.

"It'll be better when we get to Colorado," he answered, though he didn't know for sure.

Brad arrived soon after. This time he came in a Dodge pick-up truck, its bed filled with gallon jugs of water. His three scarf-clad women went among them offering the water at outrageous prices, only to be politely refused every time. Having left the renegades to swelter in seeming dire thirst for two hours, they were clearly perplexed that their water was turned down.

"We can make it a while longer without your water," Neil said. "Maybe if you were fair about your prices we could talk. Until then, please point us west, so we can get to Colorado." Brad was far from pleased and, instead of going straight west, they went north, passing a number of the mega-herds being driven along by more of the winged riders. Interestingly, among the thousands of zombies were hundreds of cows, trudging along kicking up a cloud of dust.

"I miss steak," Neil said after his stomach rumbled loud enough for everyone to hear.

"I like hamburgers," Jillybean said. She was leaned well over Neil, resting an elbow on the door, her little nose pressed against the glass. "Ipes used to say ham came from pigs and hamburgers came from cows, which never did make no sense. But I know that milk comes from cows for certain. It's in their unders. I know because I read it in books. I miss milk and cereal, and chocolate milk." She sighed. Neil also sighed, as did Deanna.

"I wonder how much they would charge for a cow," Deanna said, "Probably a ton."

Grey knew it would be an outrageous amount. The very thought was unsettling. "The Azael have grown very powerful. Maybe too powerful. It's one thing to control the passage of the plains, but now they have legions of undead under their dominion. And if that isn't enough, they have herds of cattle and a seemingly endless supply of corn and other crops."

"And yet they try to nickel and dime us at every turn," Neil griped. "It's greedy is what it is."

Jillybean shook her head slowly as if in a dream and then spoke as though she were a ghost with barely any breath and less life: "No, it's human nature. It's mean and nasty and also it's ascared. Brad and them, they're ascared of running out in times of…of…famine. I don't know that word, but it's the word Ipes would've used, only he's dead now and I have a human nature in me. She's angry and afraid of everything. I don't like her. She wants a cow to eat, though she doesn't know how to cook it. She hates everyone, including Brad and his three whores. That's a bad word, I know, but she calls them that."

At the word whore, Deanna went stiff next to Grey and he couldn't help but stiffen as well, knowing what she had done to survive. He was sure it would be a taboo word to the day she died. He wanted to change the subject to something cheery, unfortunately he couldn't find anything to be cheery about. Compared to the Azael, the people of Colorado were very weak and he knew human nature better than Jillybean. Weakness invited attack. Weakness was all the excuse some people needed to perpetuate evil.

Brad took them north for a few hours and then swung them west, so that the sun was blazing right into their faces. Jillybean slept, her face calm for the first time that day. She was pitiful even in sleep. There were raccoon circles under her eyes and she was so pale Grey could see blue veins showing through her skin. At least in sleep she appeared sane.

Eventually, Brad guided them onto a highway where a sign pointed them to a town called *Ringwood Station*. According to the sign they were eight miles out. Seven miles later, with the sun touching the far horizon, they came upon the town's limits. It wasn't delineated by signs or the sudden appearance of buildings to show they had arrived and yet there was an official marker: hanging from a telephone pole were the bodies of eight people. They had been hung by their hands.

Oddly, they hadn't been hung from individual poles, though there were many along the road. They had been strung up in a clump, so that they looked somewhat like

150

fish on a jig string. Even more disgusting was the fact that they weren't dead. They were zombies but judging by the bite marks on them, they hadn't been strung up as zombies. Each new victim had died, jerking and squirming among rotting living corpses that had eaten off of them slowly. It seemed a very hard death.

Brad pulled over with the dangling corpses in full view. Grey started to slow, however Neil pointed for him to go further on. "Not with Jillybean here," he whispered. Grey motored them another hundred yards before pulling over. For some reason, this put Brad in a foul mood.

"You just can't go where you will," he said, leaning out of the driver's side window and yelling over the top of the truck. "The Duke won't put up with it and you saw back there what he does to those who break his laws."

"Thank you, but the warning seems unnecessary," Neil answered. "We're paying customers and we have done nothing that can be construed, by any sane person, as unlawful."

"Who says we're sane?" Brad laughed. "This is a crazy world now, Neil. It would be good for you to come to grips with that."

Jillybean whispered: "I could live here if they're crazy."

Neil wanted to say something to that, but Brad said: "The town's a little further on," and then ducked back into the truck. He spun dirt behind his wheels and sped down the road, where, in the failing light there appeared to be a grey wall between them and a little town. It looked clotted and shifted like a river fouled with the refuse of a million backed toilets. It smelled like that, as well.

It turned out to be another horde of zombies, trudging in an infinite circle around the town. Their feet had worn the dirt into a trough that was already several feet deep. Beside them at hundred yard intervals were more of the riders. Their wings sprouted silver lines that dazzled when the light struck them. They kept the zombies moving and could, at a command, send them washing over any enemy.

Brad stopped the truck convoy well back. "Wait here," he said to Neil in the lead truck. "I have to get permission from the Duke for you to enter the town."

"Duke?" Neil asked in surprise. "I thought you had a king."

"We do. It's one of the ways the Azael has grown so large so quickly. Among the other benefits of joining, the King offers titles to those leaders who command large numbers of men. It's all about vanity, and stroking egos. You'd think American men wouldn't be so quick to jump at the chance of a title, but they are. I'll be back soon." He gave his horn a beep and the winged riders kicked and prodded the zombies back with their spears until there was a hole big enough for the truck to zip through.

The renegades waited in the dusky dark. The first stars were beginning to poke through the veil, when Brad returned, this time in his Camry. The women were no longer with him. Instead, three armed men, looking surly and dangerous sat in the car. "The Duke has agreed to see you, but be warned, he's in a mood. It seems things on our western border aren't nearly as calm as they had been." He said this while giving Grey a significant look as he walked away.

"What's that mean?" Neil asked when Brad left, fading to a dark shape. A second later, he was gone and there was only the sound of him opening his car door with a creak and a thud.

"More tricks no doubt," Grey answered. "Another way to scam us. If there was really open warfare, they wouldn't have said anything. They would've slit our throats in our sleep or drugged us and sold us into slavery."

Jillybean snorted at the idea. "They could try."

Next to him, Deanna gasped and when he looked over, there was a flash of silver. The seven-year-old was holding a knife as long as her forearm and the gleam from it was nothing compared to the wicked look in her eyes.

152

Chapter 15

Sadie Walcott

They crossed through the zombie barrier in silence with everyone huddled down. In the lead truck, the other girl in Jillybean sulked in a silent and dangerous fury. Her knife had been snatched from her by the lightning quick hands of Captain Grey. She rode with a bitter twist to her lips and narrowed blue eyes. In the next truck, Sadie shook on the inside as she listened to the mob of zombies. They were a reminder of what she had done to Lindsey. The dark-haired teen was a killer just the same as Jillybean, but she didn't have the luxury of hiding her sin and evil nature behind the skein of a phantom inside her. No, Sadie had to embrace the fact that she had murdered and not just once.

She knew there had been other ways to get out of the predicaments in which she had found herself in besides pulling that trigger those six times. Every time the sun fell and the others slept, she had gone over the evidence meticulously and her inner jury had always come back with a guilty verdict. She was a criminal. Perhaps an un-convicted criminal but a criminal nonetheless.

She figured the town would be pretty much a repeat of Cape Girardeau. There was evil in the eyes of the winged riders. They were definitely not angels, they looked on the renegades with greed and a hungry lust. Sadie shrank back whenever they trotted near, keeping low so that she couldn't be seen above the sill of the truck's window. On her lap, baby Eve squirmed to see outside. She was curious about the sound and smell of the horses clopping along, but Sadie kept her even lower. There had been too many lies on Brad's lips so far for her to trust him concerning infants or anything at all, really.

Once they were through the barrier of undead, the town was maybe a hundred yards further on. It consisted of a main street where a few old buildings stood: a grey concrete courthouse, some rundown storefronts, a school, a theater whose marquee read: *Ron's House of Ill-repute,* and a McDonald's that no longer possessed a single whole pane of glass. The grounds around it were littered with shards and trash. Running parallel to the center of town were three or four side streets, which were mostly populated by a smattering of houses. Everything was black in the town; not a light shone. There were quiet voices in the dark and every once in a while there would be the flare of a match and they would catch sight of the orange ember of a cigarette.

They drove to the courthouse and pulled up in front. It had once been a stately, though dour building with sturdy columns and flags flying. Now it could only be described as scary. Sadie came down out of the truck and huddled behind the other renegades, holding Eve in such a tight embrace that the baby made a face and tried to push away. She even made a fussy noise, something that was most unlike her.

"Here, let me take her," Deanna said. She seemed to have materialized out of the dark and she was suddenly there, pulling Eve away, although Sadie wanted to keep hold of her and use her as a shield to keep the world at bay. Deanna seemed to feel some sort of relief with the baby in her arms. "That's better. I need a little sanity and Eve is just precious. Yes, you are precious, aren't you?" The baby replied by reaching out and grabbing Deanna's slim nose.

"What do you mean by sanity?" Sadie asked, though she need not have. Everyone knew about Jillybean. The little girl failed at hiding her mental instability but her genius had proved valuable time and again, and that overrode everything as far as the renegades were concerned.

Deanna looked to the first truck where Neil was helping people down from the bed. Jillybean was just a little smudge of a shadow next to the larger one that was Captain Grey. They were holding hands. A spark of jealousy zipped through Sadie. No one held her hand. Her apocalypse mother was dead. Her apocalypse father was too busy shepherding the renegades through a dangerous

154

world. Her love, Nico had been murdered, and her apocalypse sister was crazy and looked as if she wanted to kill her. All she had was Eve, but the baby, in truth, belonged to no one. She was just as happy in Deanna's arms as she was in Sadie's.

"It's *you know who*," Deanna said in a whisper, of course meaning Jillybean. "She's acting, um, worse than before. If that's even possible. It's so damned sad to see what she's going through."

Another spark of jealousy. Sadie was barely treading water in a quagmire of depression and no one cared enough to notice. "Yeah," she said to Deanna. She couldn't muster any more of a response.

Deanna jiggled Eve on her hip as if there was nothing more to say on the subject of Jillybean and she was probably correct in this. No one had time for mental illness anymore. It was a 'first world' problem and they were all living south of the third world now.

In spite of the dark, Brad managed to look impatient as the renegades disembarked from the trucks. He stood with the three men he had brought with him and his sighs were the loudest thing in the night, even louder than the moaning coming from the darkened courthouse. The windows of the building were boarded over and there was some sort of dark material draped over the entrance and just before that were the columns and the chained zombies. There were four heft stone columns, two on either side of the door, and affixed to each by chains was a zombie.

To enter, Sadie saw she would have to pass within inches of the two closest zombies.

"Finally," Brad said when the last of the renegades had climbed down. "Let's get go…"

"Not just yet," Neil Interrupted. "Veronica, Marybeth and Michael, stay with the trucks. Allow no one to touch them."

Brad let out another sigh, adding: "Neil, if we were going to steal the little crap you have left, those three wouldn't be able to stop us. But if that makes you feel good about yourself, have it your way. Everyone else, follow me and stay close. Single file."

"Can you watch Jillybean?" Deanna asked Sadie as Brad started forward. "She doesn't like to be around the baby."

Then don't bring the baby near her, Sadie wanted to say. That would've been rude, something Neil would frown upon. "Sure," Sadie said and went to where Jillybean was standing next to Captain Grey. "Can you come with me?" she asked the little girl. "It's been a long time since I've been able to hang out with you. How long has it been?" It wasn't a good question for either of them. There had been a day or two after Sarah and Nico had been killed when they had sat, listless and brain-fogged in the same truck as Grey drove into Alabama. Since then their lives had been a chaos of kidnappings, explosions and blood.

"It's been a while, I think," Jillybean said as she swept her eyes around, noting Deanna standing off to the side with Eve. She also squinted at the Goth girl and saw the pain in her bearing. "It's hard to tell, though I would say it's been about twenty."

Sadie put an arm around the girl and began to guide her to the back of the line. "I'm sorry but you're a little mixed up. It hasn't been twenty days."

A sly smirk crooked Jillybean's narrow face. "No, that's how many people we've killed between us since we've got to really hangout. Without school and summer break, days don't mean too much anymore. I find it easier to remember the people I've killed. I bet you do too."

The arm thrown around Jillybean's shoulder went altogether stiff. Sadie pulled it back as if she thought the little girl had become suddenly diseased, and in a way, she had. She had a mental disease that was eating her up and making her dangerous. "You don't know what you're talking about," Sadie said. "I haven't killed nearly that many and neither have you. And…and it's not really a proper subject."

"Well you killed those five guys in cold blood." She held up five fingers, splayed, each one distinct, each representing a murder victim. "And you murdered Lindsey. Everyone knows that. They talk about it. They whisper it when you aren't around. They think you're really tough, though I don't know why. You were tough, once. Remember the hand grenade?"

A jolt went through Sadie's thin frame. She had forgotten about the hand grenade. How many people had been in the hallway on the cruise ship when she had tried to kill Cassie? Four? Five? Jillybean looked as though she was reading her thoughts. "When you talk in your sleep, you always apologize five times. It's very stupid and dumb, that's what I think. You shoulda killed them. I think you shoulda killed more of them. They deserved to die."

"I don't care what you think," Sadie hissed, giving the girl a little shove. Jillybean fell back, causing a murmur to stir up in the dark. Crazy or not, the renegades looked to Jillybean for too many things and if it came down to it they would kill for her. They would kill out of fear. They were afraid that they didn't have what it took to survive. They depended on her. They needed her. "Watch her," Sadie said to the renegades nearby. They were dim shapes against a dark background and she couldn't tell one from another, though it hardly mattered to her just then.

Sadie couldn't stand being around any of them. They reminded her of the old people, the people from before the apocalypse. They had done nothing while they had watched their country slowly strangle on itself. If the apocalypse hadn't come along something else would have done them in. She walked down the long line of her fellow travelers, trying not to look into their shadowed faces, and when she came to the last, she just kept walking into the darker shadows of the town.

She found an old diner to lean up against as she waited for the renegades to trickle into the courthouse. The diner was very old world. It came complete with cracked leather booths, a juke box, a long nicked-up bar and a black and white tiled floor that seem coated in a twenty-year layer of grease. It was dingy and even with the dark it looked like it had been abandoned years ago. Sadie wanted to slip into it and spend the night alone. The very idea of the courthouse was galling to her. She was sure there would be just more of the same within its forbidding walls: people hurting other people, people scrambling to take advantage of every word and every situation.

She wasn't in the mood to fight for survival. She wanted to be alone…except she was afraid to be alone. All her life she had glommed onto the nearest person and grew to become like them, much like a chameleon. With her friends in school, she had become Goth. With Jack, at the beginning of the apocalypse, she had become a thief because he was, with Neil and Sarah, she had been a daughter, and a damned good one.

When she was left alone, she was a killer. Experience had taught her that.

She could fit in with the Azael if she wanted, but what kind of life would it be? They gave all the appearance of being little more than cutthroats and thieves. Calling them "opportunists" would be a kindness they didn't likely deserve. Unfortunately, Sadie didn't have much going for her with the renegades, either. Most associated her with her father, the River King and blamed her for their capture. This was never spoken aloud, but she saw it in their eyes and heard it in their whisperings.

This left being alone as her best option, but there was her deadly nature to consider.

"Not tonight," she whispered through gritted teeth. She had dwelt upon her guilt long enough—it wasn't getting her anywhere.

The renegades slowly filed between the zombies at the door and Sadie waited against the diner until there were only the three guards Neil had posted by the trucks left in the night. Reluctantly, she went to the courthouse door and, keeping her arms close to her body, she passed between the zombies. The door was noiseless as it opened. Beyond the door, she found herself in a box of a room the walls of which had been fashioned from burgundy velvet curtains; more than likely liberated from the town theater.

There was an exit of a sort marked by brass lamp stands. There were no bulbs in the lamp stands and the dark of the curtained room was so deep, the brass barely threw off enough color to allow the metal to be judged as brass.

Sadie went to the far curtain but did not stride through; she only cracked the curtain as light streamed across her pale face. The renegades, as if they were taking a tour of the courthouse, were walking in a line and looking all around as though the place was more than just a converted government building. It once had marble floors that gleamed and dark wood walls that glistened with polish. Now, there was no more gleam or polish. The building had been converted into a combination of a warehouse, a strip mall and an apartment complex.

It was very strange to Sadie. Every one of the offices had their doors flung wide and in them, smiling people in multi-hued scarves beckoned:

"Come see. I have cold water, wine and Fig Newtons!"

"I have beer! Real beer! The cans are certified as un-opened!"

"Ammo…get your ammo here. I have all calibers. Guns, too. Everything you need to survive whatever tomorrow brings."

Each room was spilling over with merchandise. Coats, frying pans, tents and bottles of penicillin were stacked alongside rifles and spears and baby powder and everything else one could imagine. What struck Sadie as exceptionally odd was that the offices were barren of all normal office furniture, however each had a mattress or two leaned up against some of the wares; the proprietors slept in the rooms with their merchandise. In the bigger offices that seemed like a fine idea, but the smaller rooms just seemed jumbled.

Brad and Neil, with Grey and Deanna trailing, were at the far head of the line and were just disappearing around a corner when someone grabbed Sadie's wrist in a steel grip. "It's not wise to go about unescorted." A man loomed above her. He was tall and slim and of an unknowable age, neither young nor old and it was impossible to tell to which side he was closer. His skin was brown leather as if he had worked in the fields his entire life, and yet his eyes were a soft blue and unlined. They were the eyes of a librarian and somehow they still managed to be striking.

"I'm not too worried," Sadie said, with a reserve of cool that had come out of nowhere. As always, she had matched her surroundings: the man was dangerous, that was obvious. What wasn't, at least at first, was that she was as well. She had drawn her pistol in the instant her wrist was grabbed and now she had the hard barrel shoved into the man's side.

He grunted in appreciation of the slickness of the move. "So you're nobody's slave, I see."

"Nor will I be. So, if you'll excuse me, I should catch up with the rest of the tour."

His hand sprang open, but he remained very close. Not only did he smell clean, there was a hint of cologne about him; it was alluring. "You should come visit with me," he suggested. "They're not going to say anything of importance. A lot of blah, blah, blah."

"Blah, blah, blah about what?"

The man gave her a cryptic smile. "Do you want the truth or a lie?" he asked. "Lies are free."

Sadie grinned right back. "What? You put a price on the truth? My guess is that your version of the truth isn't worth much if you can change it with a dollar."

He gave her a long look up and down before saying: "You must be young indeed if you think that's a new concept. It's being going on since the dawn of time, though in this instance the truth isn't worth all that much. I'm sure it's common knowledge that there's friction between us and the soldiers in Colorado. 'Growing pains' is what I call them. So, they'll go on a bit about treaties and crap. The Duke is just trying to gain leverage, one way or another. It's the American way."

"Not the America I knew," she replied, stiffly. She liked the attention; however, he was still too close and his smile was just a little beyond friendly. "I was always taught that we were the good guys. Now, if you'll excuse me, I should get back to my friends," she said, realizing, with some amusement, she was sounding like Neil.

"Are you sure you can't stay? I have treats." Next to the open door was a locked filing cabinet. A key appeared in his hand and a second later, he was rattling back the middle drawer. Inside was a dragon's hoard of chocolate bars and candy of all sorts. Sadie had been just about to turn away but the sight stopped her cold. Her stomach let out a lion's growl that had the man chuckling. "You look halfway to being famished. Come, sit for a while. We can talk. I have some wine if you're thirsty, free of charge."

He gestured into the ten by ten office and though she should have been creeped out by the pedophile way he had gone about inviting her in, she wasn't. Her Glock was still in her hand. "Free? I didn't think that was in your vocabulary."

"Normally it's not, however, for you I will make an exception."

She had never had a drink bought for her before and, as the man was handsome and personable, the feeling was exceedingly pleasant. "Ok, I'll have a drink, but I have a couple of uh, rules first." She had wanted to use the word "stipulations," but it wouldn't come to her tongue. "First, I'm not going in there. You are a complete stranger, after all. Second, I want to see the bottle."

"Afraid you'll be drugged? Smart. Let's try a Riesling and see how you like it. Normally, I find them a bit sweet, but I'm hoping you'll find it tasty." He reached over where two bottles of wine sat ready for drinking and hefted the bottle of white as if he could judge its merits by its weight. With a practiced flourish, he spun the bottle so she could read the label; it was altogether meaningless to her since she didn't know one wine from another. It was the cap she was interested in. She took the bottle and inspected it, closely. The seal was intact. She cracked it herself and, before drinking straight from the lip, she gave it a sniff.

Both the scent and the taste reminded her lightly of pears mixed with apricots.

It was as sweet as he had suggested. "My name is Sadie," she said, and handed the bottle to the man.

"Richard," he said. There were no glasses available and, like her, he drank from the bottle. He wasn't shy about it; he tipped the bottle back and drank deeply. After two large swallows, he righted the bottle, grunted and smacked his lips in appreciation. "That's better than I remember."

Sadie accepted the wine back and drank. The bottle was half gone when she allowed Richard a turn. Around them were a few others of the Azael. They kept a discreet distance back and pretended that they weren't interested or jealous that they were drinking. Richard sipped this time, but she didn't notice.

"Where'd you get all this stuff from?" she asked. He seemed to have a bit of everything a person could want.

He gave her the bottle and then made a face at his ramshackle little shop. "You mean my sprawling corporate enterprise? Ha, this is all junk. I used to be something. I mean back before the apocalypse. I had a life, a good one, too. I had a Porsche and a fucking penthouse overlooking the lake." He sighed and his face fell a bit. "I used to be big shit and now I run a Quickie Mart." He laughed at himself and reached for the bottle, but this time she wasn't nearly so quick to hand it over.

"A penthouse?" she asked and chugged. "Sounds nice. Where are you from?"

"Chicago, and you?"

She was about to say New Jersey, but a movement caught her eye. Jillybean was standing within arm's reach of her. Sadie jumped, startled. "I need to talk to you," the little girl said. Her voice was flat and her eyes very dark. It was Eve in there, not Jillybean.

"Well, I don't need to talk to you and I don't want to. I'm having a drink with my friend Richard, here, so if you'll go somewhere else that would be great."

"I said I *need* to talk to you," the little girl repeated with an edge to her voice. She cut her eyes to Richard.

Sadie shook her head. "Sorry, but I don't *need* to talk to *you*, so run along."

The girl glared and hissed at a decibel that could barely be heard by Sadie a foot away: "You are being a fool. Neil sent me to find you before you did something stupid. That might not have been what he said, but I'm sure it's what he was thinking."

At this, the two locked eyes long enough for Richard to clear his throat. They ignored him, continuing their contest of wills. "You're bringing danger on all of us," the little girl finally said. "We can't allow that."

"We? Let me hear that from Jillybean," Sadie replied and again there was a moment that drew out between them. "I'll believe it from her, not from you, so come back when *she's* ready to talk."

With Richard standing silently next to the two girls, they glared fiercely until Eve turned away. She brought a hand up to her fly away brown hair and took a patch of it in a grip and pulled hard enough for her arm to shake. It looked as though she wanted to pull her scalp right off her head. Sadie refused to say a thing to her, hoping that ignoring the self-destructive behavior would limit it.

A second later, Jillybean brought her hand down in front of her face and stared for a moment. She then turned around and when she saw Sadie, she gave a quirky little half-smile. "Where are we?" she asked. "Where are the trucks? Who's that?" She pointed at Richard, who was watching her with sharp eyes.

Sadie didn't trust the girl for a second. She dropped down to one knee and looked into her face. It seemed innocent enough and free of the evil within her, but that could be a ruse of the other girl's. There was only one way to know for certain—Sadie held out a pinky to the little girl: "What's this mean?"

"It means we're sisters," Jillybean said, hooking Sadie's pinky with her own.

Chapter 16

Jillybean/Eve

"Can I have just a second?" Sadie said to Richard, handing him the bottle and then pulling Jillybean to the other side of the hallway. Again, she came down on one knee and huddled her forehead close to Jillybean's. She asked in a whisper: "What's wrong? What sort of danger are we in?"

"Huh?" Jillybean asked. Sadie's words were floating in through her ears and instead of lighting upon her brain so she could grasp their meaning, they seemed just to float out again. Everything about her was nebulous and fleeting. A picture on the wall hung at a crooked angle. It made no sense. She went to reach for it but Sadie pulled her hand down.

"You said I was being foolish. You said I was doing something dangerous. Hey, Jillybean, focus. Look at me. What am I doing that's so bad?"

A frown crossed Jillybean's face as she tried to figure out what Sadie was talking about. The last thing she remembered was being in the wide open with blue above her. It had been hot, the kind of heat that turned people nasty when they were in it for too long. *She* had turned nasty and so full of hate that it made no sense to Jillybean, just like the crooked picture.

Really, nothing made sense to Jillybean, not just then. She remembered the Kansas sky and before that, she remembered finding the water and bathing as Mister Neil dumped cool water over her; that had been nice. But since then, she hadn't been allowed to see out. There had only been that deep darkness and the lines of silver dropping down into the nothing where Jillybean feared to go.

"Maybe if you tell me what you were doing that would help," Jillybean said. "*She* has gone deep and tookded all her memories with her and I don't know what's what."

"I wasn't doing anything," Sadie protested. "All I was doing was…wait, let me catch you up a bit. Brad brought us to some town run by a duke of the Azael. We just got here and all I was doing was talking to this guy and having a drink. Everyone else is in with the Duke. They're probably in more danger than I am." She tapped the Glock in her hip holster, meaningfully.

"Oh, then I don't know why you'd be in danger," Jillybean said. "It's strange, but everything's strange right now. Is it day time? Or night time? I feel hungry and thirsty and I gotta go baffroom, and…whoa look at all this stuff!" Her eyes went suddenly big as, for the first time, she became aware of Richard and his shop. Before, he had been a somewhat faceless adult and his store only a jumble of colors. Now, her mind clicked in. She saw the world in detail.

Richard grinned at the eager look on the child's face. "You two sisters?"

Jillybean nodded vacantly as she noted the odds and ends, the knick-knacks, and the miscellaneous wares. It was everything that people in the *before* took for granted. All of it made her realize she wasn't wearing her backpack. She had no idea where it was. "Have you seen my backpack?" she asked Sadie.

"No. Maybe Neil has it or maybe you left it in the truck." Jillybean frowned at the idea, which had Sadie laughing. "You're like Batman without his utility belt."

"I don't know what that means," Jillybean told her. "I just wish I had it."

Richard put out an arm to usher them into his store. "I'm sure I have everything that you might possibly need." He seemed to anticipate the obvious objection on Jillybean's lips. Before she could utter a word, he said: "Don't worry about money. I offer very generous credit terms and there are other ways you could work off a debt." This he said, giving Sadie a smile.

There was an uncharacteristic pause in Jillybean's mind and then what Richard was suggesting clicked into place. He was suggesting that Sadie become a prostitute! Jillybean reached for Sadie's hand and started pulling her away, saying: "I don't need anything, really."

"Not even candy?" Richard asked, once more rattling back the middle drawer of the filing cabinet and displaying the colorful heap of sweets.

Jillybean stopped in her tracks, her eyes going even wider than they had before. "No...I'm good," she said, weakly, as though the sight of all that candy was draining the willpower out of her. Sadie had her head cranked around, also. She swallowed loudly.

"Ok, if you're sure you don't want any," Richard said, and then, very slowly, closed the drawer. The two sisters watched until the drawer closed with a thump.

The little girl immediately began pulling Sadie away, her free hand going to her forehead where she felt damp as if from fever. "That was a lot of chocolate," she said, her mind still taken up by the sight. She could remember the last time she had chocolate; Ram had given her a *Snickers* bar to coax her into eating her beans. He had gone without even a bite of the chocolate and died three days later. She hadn't thought about that in all the months since it had happened, and now it struck her as having been very self-ish on her part.

"I'm sorry," she mumbled. Inside her, the other girl grew restless and strong. Whenever Jillybean felt weak, or afraid, or just drained of life, she could feel *her* begin to take over.

"You have nothing to be sorry about," Sadie said. "Remember that you are a good person. You're not a mon-ster."

Jillybean shrugged. "Ok, sure." She had never con-sidered herself a bad person. *She*, the other girl inside her, was the bad one.

They passed the remaining office/markets with their heads swiveling at all the merchandise and, despite the pleading of the shopkeepers, they didn't pause to browse at any of them. The temptation was just too great. When they passed the last, Jillybean stopped in her tracks.

"I see it now," she said, turning to look down the hallway. Although no two of the shops were exactly alike, they each had precisely one thing in common. The shops all had two bottles of wine, one red and one white, sitting within arm's reach. "The wine," Jillybean whispered. "They all have the same label."

"What's that mean?" Sadie asked.

Jillybean was slow to answer because she didn't precisely have the answer; she only had guesses. "I suppose it means they all came from the same box. And...and because each of them has only two, I think that means they were given the wine."

"To give to us," Sadie said. With a sudden scared look she began rubbing her belly. "Do you think it's poisoned? Or drugged? I checked the cap and it was on like it was new. And...and I feel ok. I mean I feel a little buzz going but nothing else."

"I think they were just probably trying to get you drunk," Jillybean explained. "That's the most likely. Ipes used to say when you hear hooves you think zebras not horses. That's what means we shouldn't jump on conclusions and get ascared for nothing. They probably want to get you drunk so you'd buy more stuff or talk about your secrets, and that would be dangerous."

Sadie opened her mouth but just then they heard a rumble of angry voices coming from beyond a heavy door. Together they crept in and found themselves in what must have been the largest of the courtrooms. Big though it was, it was bursting at the seams with people. Along with the sixty renegades there were a couple dozen of the Azael, led by a man who sat in the judge's chair.

He was a burly sort with black hair on his arms that matched his beard which was fashioned, via several colorful rubber bands, into a long point. Jillybean thought he looked as though his family line might have crossed with a bear at some point in the not so distant past and, like a bear, he seemed exceptionally cranky.

"These are my lands," he was saying. "I have absolute authority. You cannot go here and there without an escort. You will travel when I say and not a minute before."

"What's going on?" Sadie asked, one of the women from The Island. It was Joslyn and she looked to be hiding in the back of the group.

She put her hand to her mouth to cover the sound of her voice and whispered: "Neil wants to leave first thing in the morning and this duke-guy is saying 'no.' It's getting tense."

Neil had been shaking his head and now he answered: "Duke Menis, you do reign supreme in your lands; however that does not mean there won't be repercussions to your actions on a much larger scale. We have paid for safe passage and, diplomatically speaking, it would be wise for you to allow us to leave at our preferred time. If you think our group is weak, I can assure you it is not, and even if it were, we are traveling under the protection of General Johnston of Colorado. This is Captain James Grey, one of his agents."

Menis waved a dismissive hand in Captain Grey's direction. "Johnston's reach is shorter than you realize. His walls are mighty, but outside of them he is nothing compared to the power of the Azael."

"So you and Brad tell us, however, I don't see evidence of it," Neil answered. He held up a palm and gestured to the armed guards who were outnumbered by the renegades. "I see a small town and a bunch of small town traders. I don't mean to be offensive, but you do not strike fear in us. We have been through hellfire and have been tested in combat. We have..."

He was stopped mid-sentence by Eve who said: "Dada," in a piping voice.

Jillybean glanced around and saw Eve with Deanna, who, like Joslyn, was hiding behind some of the larger men. Duke Menis' face grew wrathful at the interruption, but when he saw Deanna his dark brows shot up and a gleam that was unmistakable, even to a seven year old, grew in his eyes.

"Well, who is this?" he asked. The question could have been put to either the woman or the baby.

"My daughter, Eve," Neil replied. "And this is Deanna."

Menis stroked his beard down to its point and said: "Bring them forward. Don't be shy, step forward. Neil! Why did you not tell me you were traveling with royalty? Surely this is a queen."

Deanna, holding Eve, looked radiant at that moment, like a queen, indeed, thought Jillybean. Her recent bath had brought out the rich gold of her hair, the Kansas sun had bronzed her skin to perfection and there was a simple glow of life in her eyes.

The little girl had noticed a change in Deanna as the days had progressed. Every day since her freedom from The Island, she had grown more and more beautiful, which was the opposite of the other ex-prostitutes.

Veronica, for instance wasn't a natural blonde and now there was a mousy brown stripe down the middle of her head three inches wide. Joslyn was sporting premature grey strips which stood out against her dark hair and accented the crow's feet that were forming around her eyes. The rest of the women looked plain without their makeup and their hair styled, and they were frumpy in the baggy BDUs they had picked up in Fort Campbell.

"I am not a queen," Deanna said. "Nor do I want to be one, but thank you." The pink in her cheeks at being singled out did nothing to distract from her natural beauty; it enhanced it. The effect did a number on the Duke, who leered at her, much to the discomfort of everyone else.

Eventually, Neil cleared his throat. "Excuse me, sir? We were discussing fuel? We need three hundred gallons and, as I said, we would like to leave first thing in the morning."

"And like I said, the answer is no," the Duke replied, forcing his eyes from Deanna. "How do we know you are who you say you are? Anyone can throw on a pair of

BDUs and claim to be someone they're not. And even if this man is from Colorado, how do I know his General will pay what is owed? Do you see my problem, Neil? You are asking me to take unacceptable risks. Judging by what *little* I see in front of me, I can only guess that someone like you was in business back before, so I'm sure you understand."

Neil's scarred face contorted at the jab. "Yes, I understand about risks," he said, dipping his head in a slight nod, "It's elementary, clearly so since you have a grasp of the concept. And I understand that a premium can be charged in such cases where the risk to reward ratio isn't optimum."

The Duke clapped his hands together and then rubbed them vigorously. "A premium, yes. But how much of one? That is the question. You will remain here for three days in which time I will judge you and your group as to your respectability. *If* I find you properly respectful then you will get your fuel—though at a sharp rate of return."

"How sharp?" Neil asked. His voice was low and yet heard by all. As if of one mind, the renegades feared the answer and were dead silent, even Eve.

"Three gallons will get you one," the Duke replied, placing an elbow on the arm of the judge's chair, and stroking his beard. The group let out a collective gasp, which seemed to please him as much as the idea of a two hundred percent interest rate. "You see how your poor attitude has affected our negotiations? You have to know when to give, you have to know when a little sugar sweetens the deal." This last he said while gazing with excessive fondness on Deanna.

"I also know when to walk away from a terrible deal," Neil said, with his jaw set. "We will not pay your fee and we will not wait three days. We will leave now by whatever way is fastest." He turned to walk out of the room and there was a general stiffening of everyone. Each group was heavily armed and on a hair trigger.

The Duke held up a hand and when that didn't stop Neil he snapped his finger and said: "You can stop with the dramatics. You're not going anywhere. It's simply a fact that you're now in too deep. You don't have the fuel to make it out of my lands, which means you'll end up walking and that's a death sentence. You don't have enough water or enough ammo, buuut..." He let the word hang in the air for a few seconds and during that time, Neil's shoulders hunched and the renegades seemed to hold their collective breath as they leaned forward, hopefully—none of them relished the idea of walking the seven hundred or so miles left on their journey to Colorado.

"But, perhaps there is one among you who might be better at negotiations. Perhaps someone who isn't so prickly. Someone who is a tad more fair to look upon." He was staring straight at Deanna.

She took a step back, reflexively holding Eve closer. The baby clung, monkey-like with her legs, while one hand had a strong grip on Deanna's white button-up shirt, pulling the fabric very tight across her full breasts. Her other little hand she had been using to play with Deanna's long, blonde hair, turning it into little curls as she followed the conversation after the fashion of an infant.

"Ok," Deanna said, after time seemed to draw out and everyone was left breathless. "I guess I can negotiate, if it'll help. Uh...first, I think, uh I think that three for one is a bit extreme. I can guarantee we're good for..."

Her words faltered when the Duke made a face as though her words pained him. "I'm sorry, but how about we discuss this in private over dinner?" he suggested. "This really isn't the best venue for negotiations. No offense, Neil, but I tend to get my back up when I'm surrounded by so much hostility."

For the renegades, the conversation was a tennis match. Their chins went back and forth with each sentence, hanging on every word. Now, their eyes swung, not to Neil, but to Captain Grey whose feelings for Deanna were known to everyone. They saw his face go red and his eyes squint up; he looked within a word—a wrong word—of killing someone. That someone being the Duke, along with however many of his men got in his way.

Deanna also looked to him and their eyes locked. She smiled a quick grin of pain and indecision.

Their thought processes were beyond Jillybean— Deanna loved the captain, that was clear as day, and he loved her as well, nothing was more obvious, so what was the dilemma? She should say: *Hell no* and then figure out where to go from there. But that didn't happen. After a few seconds Grey's face lost its anger and he nodded, a little jerk of his head.

Neil had watched both of them with an air of defeat, and absently rubbed his chest as if there was an ache beneath his breastbone. Reluctantly, he said: "Ok, I guess. I mean, if this is ok with all parties involved."

"We weren't looking for your permission, Neil," the Duke said. "We're all adults here."

"I guess it's ok," Deanna said with a last look toward Captain Grey. "As long as it's clear the dinner is simply a way to facilitate negotiations."

The Duke said something that was possibly mean, and Grey reacted in a glowering anger and Neil looked pained or confused, Jillybean didn't know exactly which, because at that moment the other girl inside her exploded in pent up emotion. *She* screamed inside Jillybean's mind: *Whore! Slut! Cunt!* The volume in her mind rocked Jillybean and she fell into Sadie and clutched at her black shirt. Sadie said something but that, too, was lost on the little girl, her mind was being torn in two.

Sadie shook her and her dark eyes were at Jillybean's level, boring in with concern and caring, but concern for what, Jillybean didn't know. It was all she could do to maintain her own presence in her own mind. The other girl was so strong that it was like wrestling with a giant or trying to lift the ocean and, for a moment, their consciousness stood in conflict: Atlas versus the earth, God and the Devil, light against dark—and in each, Jillybean was the loser. Then for some reason, the other girl backed away, and that was confusion as well.

Why didn't she take Jillybean over and run her body? She had won, after all. There was no way Jillybean should have been in charge of her own body, unless…unless the other girl wished it so.

People spoke; some moved in the herky-jerky motion of robots, and others made faces that seemed frozen in time, but these were only a backdrop in Jillybean's experience as understanding struck. There was real danger in the room and it didn't extend from Captain's Grey's jealousy, or Neil's painful decision to give up control, or Deanna's difficult choice to accept, on some level, a renewed prostitution.

The danger was in Jillybean and both she and the other girl knew what it was. *She* couldn't control herself. *She* knew she would say or do something very wrong. At a minimum, *she* would ruin their chances of making it to Colorado and there was the real possibility that she could say something that would have them back in chains.

She hung back on purpose and allowed herself to be buried in the deep black which was such a terror to Jillybean.

"Let's go," Sadie said. "We have to warn everyone not to drink the wine."

The words were slow to penetrate into Jillybean's mind and she blinked at them. Around her the renegades were whispering and pointing as Deanna handed Eve to Neil and walked, with her chin held high, to a side door that was being held open by the Duke. She didn't look back to where Captain Grey stood like a statue of purest rock.

"Yeah, sure," Jillybean said, and allowed her hand to be taken by the older girl. "What just happened?" she asked.

Sadie's lips pursed and her eyes flicked to Grey. "I think we're leaving in the morning." That hadn't really answered Jillybean's question and yet she didn't think any explanation would suffice just then. She was too groggy.

"Out to the trucks," Neil ordered, making a beeline for the door and tugging Grey along with him. Sadie and Jillybean tried to follow after, but there was such a press of people that they were separated and Jillybean couldn't make headway against the crowd. Gradually, she was pushed to the back of the line. Even the guards stepped ahead of her and soon she found herself alone in the empty courtroom.

Alone with her curiosity.

She felt the need to know what had happened and, what was going to happen, and so, unable to stop herself, she turned from the door that led to the shops, and slipped on cat feet to the door through which the Duke had taken Deanna.

Chapter 17

Deanna Russell

She didn't know what to do with her hands. They wanted to tremble and did every time she didn't have them employed in some fashion. The only problem was there wasn't any reason for them to be employed at all. Duke Menis had escorted her to the second floor of the building, down a sweeping hall that was tiled in grey marble, and then showed her into his suite of rooms which had been, at one time, some county bigwig's offices. Despite the electric lights, the room was dark and stern with heavy wood paneling on the walls and a somber maroon carpet.

While he busied over a bottle of wine, Deanna continued to try to figure out what she was going to do with her hands. At first, she hooked her thumbs into the belt loops of her jeans, only that felt too casual. Next, she stuffed them into her pockets, only that was too odd; no one stood around like that unless they were cold, which she was far from.

The Duke turned just as she pulled her hands out of her pockets and, feeling strangely guilty, as though her hands were some sort of secret, she gripped them tightly together. Of course, when he held a glass out to her she had to release them a second later. Now he was sure to see how nervous she was by how badly her hands were shaking. To distract him, she pointed at a picture on the wall and commented: "That's an, uh, interesting picture." It was a portrait of an old white guy with mutton chops and a heavy frown—it wasn't at all interesting.

"You like that? It's yours." He beamed at her, acting as though the gift of an ugly painting that had clearly been hanging on the wall since before the apocalypse, was some sort of great display of generosity on his part.

"Thanks," she said, taking a sip of the red wine. She had never been much of a wine drinker—there was always such a fuss about it: good years, bad years and which vineyards were the best and then there was the etiquette involved and the tannins, whatever they were, and all that hoopla, just to get a nice buzz going. It didn't make much sense to her. She drank Cosmos mainly because they were good and a person would have to try hard to screw it up.

The wine was only ok and already their conversation was stale.

"So, a Duke?" she asked. "How did you get that job?"

"My brothers and I formed the Azael and we decided early on, that we weren't going make the same mistakes as the Founding Fathers by trusting the people with democracy. That was one of those roads paved with good intentions but which led straight to hell. So we set ourselves up as royalty and, I tell you, business is booming. People love it. They'd kill for a chance at being Sir that or Lady this. And who wouldn't want to be a Duchess? The position is still open, by the way."

What? Deanna thought in a mental scream that bugged her eyes slightly. Was he really suggesting marriage? Or was he merely dangling the title in front of her face to see if she would bite? Deanna couldn't think of anything to say and the silence drew out. To cover the awkward moment she brought the wine glass up to her lips again, but then remembered the baby growing inside of her. The glass faltered on her lower lip. She looked into the cup and saw only poison. "Well, uh, that is interesting," was all she could manage to come up with as he was very close and he leered as though every rule of society was his to bend or break as he saw fit.

"I'm glad it interests you," he said, and drank from his glass. He smacked his lips, relishing the wine. "You should be flattered." His right hand stretch out and caressed her shoulder.

Alarm bells went off in her mind and her body stiffened. She had to rein in the panic. *He's just being an exceptionally forward man at this point*, she thought. *Nothing more.*

She slid away from him, went to the curtained window and looked out; there was nothing to see. The bedroom had been lit by electric lights and the night was very dark in comparison. But really, what was there to see? Had her night eyes caught up all she would have seen was a dinky, rundown town. "Duke seems like a grand title for this little town. I don't mean to be offensive but how many people do you rule? I don't think I've seen over sixty people so far."

"A thousand or so," he answered. "Most are out scavenging or protecting our borders. Why don't you get away from there? There isn't much holding the zombies back, just that little trench. If they see you up here, we'll have them flooding through the town in no time." His hands were on her again, gently pulling her back from the window. "So how are we going to take care of these negotiations? I have stuff you need and you have certain things I want. Why don't we come to some sort of agreement for the benefit of our people?" The hand began rubbing her back.

"Yes, I would like that," she said, doing her best not to grimace at his touch. "Two hundred percent is really too much, even as an opening bargaining position. That would be like me asking for free fuel. That would be just stupid, right?"

"I wouldn't call it stupid. Free is an option...well free-ish is an option. You see, Deanna, three hundred gallons of diesel is a drop in the bucket for me. Did you see that tanker truck on the way into town? It's full. I have ten thousand gallons in that truck alone. The tanks beneath the Shell station at the end of the road are full to the fucking brim. And ammo? My last count is a quarter million rounds. The theater is piled high with crates and crates, so yeah, I can afford to hand out a measly three hundred gallons of fuel, if I was in the mood to."

Now the hand stopped rubbing and gently pulled Deanna closer until her pert nose was inches from his banded beard. She couldn't help but lean back; her lower lip started to quiver and she shut her mouth tight, but then her chin started to shake. He grinned down at her. "I could also be an ass if I wanted to. There's no law saying I have to trade a single thing. If I'm displeased, you may find yourself walking out of my realm and I don't think much of your chances of making it. The land is wide open and the stiffs can see for miles and miles."

"We wouldn't want that," Deanna replied with an unconvincing smile. She felt sick to her stomach and it showed. "So how about we compromise at, say, a thirty percent interest rate? That's a number which should be more than acceptable to you."

"And what will induce me to agree?"

She knew what he was asking but she tried to pretend otherwise. "I don't know about inducements, but you are a duke. You are royal and noble and generous." He shook his head, telling her: *Nice try*. "Ok, so flattery won't work," she said. "Will begging? Will it help if I got down on my knees and begged? I'll do it if it means you'll help us."

"Getting down on your knees would be a good start," he said, wearing a wolfish grin. When she continued to look sick, he let out a short laugh, suggesting he'd only been kidding. "Why don't you drink your wine and loosen up. Negotiations should never be a sober undertaking. You get angry then I get angry and then people get hurt. No, it's best to relax." She brought the glass to her lips and took the tiniest sip, though she held the glass there longer, hoping he wouldn't notice that she wasn't really drinking. He was too observant. "Something wrong the wine?"

"No, it's just..." She tried to think up some excuse and none would come to her fear-addled mind. Then she realized there was no need to hide the truth from the Duke. What would he care if she was pregnant? In fact it was her hope that the idea would turn him off from wanting her, sexually. "It's just that I'm pregnant."

His hand came away from her shoulder and he lifted a heavy eyebrow as he looked her up and down. Then he gave a small shrug. "You still look good to me." He advanced and she backed away, her hand landing on the butt of the pistol she had tucked into the waistband of her jeans. "What are you going to do with that? Shoot me? Please."

"I won't be raped," she stated, bluntly.

"And I won't rape you. Look Deanna, there's only one way for you to get what you need to save your people."

There it was. Once again she was being forced to whore herself out, not just to save her own skin, but everyone else's as well. *It'll be just one more time. One more and then we'll be done forever,* she said to herself.

This was countered by another thought: *It won't be one more time. He'll make excuses to keep us. He'll keep fucking me until I'm used up and then he'll fuck over everyone else by over-charging them or, if someone spills about who we are, then we'll be sold back to the Colonel and he will probably be only too delighted to hang us.*

Logic won out over wishful thinking. "No. I'm sorry but I won't do it. I am going to be a mother and I-I, that's not something I can do. I hope you understand. There are some girls among us who will. Should I let them know you're available?" Her voice shook the entire time.

Duke Menis glared. "You understood what I wanted when you came in here, which begs the question: why did you bother? Why did you waste my time?"

Deanna drew herself up to her full height which didn't quite reach the man's chin. He was as tall as Captain Grey, however since he carried a haughty anger in his eyes, he seemed so much more dangerous. Once again her hands betrayed her. They began to twist together in knots as she answered: "I came because you asked and because we need you, however I won't give up my integrity, not even for the life of my unborn child. I don't want her coming into the world the daughter of a whore." She might have been conceived that way, but that didn't mean she had to be born that way.

"Commendable," the Duke said in a way that conveyed that he didn't feel it was commendable in the least. Despite his face being covered in a shaggy growth of beard, or perhaps because of it, he could be very frightening when he glared. It was a harsh enough look that Deanna stepped back from it and unworked her hands long enough to again take her pistol grip under her sweating palm.

He sneered at the move—then grunted—then finally laughed: "Ok, you are a better bargainer than I would have guessed. Take your hand off your gun and I'll go scare us up some dinner. You still want dinner, correct? I have this spindly little guy who somehow lived through all of this. He's so small I could break him with my bare hands but that boy can cook. He can cook whatever you want, but I've already asked for steak. I hope that's ok. I shouldn't make assumptions but I can't help but think that all the vegetarians are dead, if not from the zombies but from starvation. It's not like tofu grows on trees, right?" He laughed at his own joke while she seemed bewildered.

"Steak?" Deanna asked as though the word was foreign.

A big grin from the Duke. "Yes, steak. Besides the gas and the ammo, I also have vast herds of cattle and goat. See? You shouldn't have been so quick to dismiss my overtures."

Deanna was still hung up on the very idea of steak and slowly shook her head. "I hope I wasn't dismissive. I just...Uh, I mean, you wouldn't want a whore as a duchess. I mean...I'm sorry, but I'm a little turned around."

"Here, sit," he showed her to a leather couch. It was soft and cool and helped clear her head. She smiled up at him and then it was his turn to look confused. "You're right. I wouldn't want a whore for a wife, but, uh, how about I go check on dinner."

He left and was gone for so long that she was beginning to think he had forgotten about her. She wandered around the front room of his suite and had to refrain from looking in the desk drawers. Though she really wanted to, she was absolutely certain he would come bursting through the door and catch her red-handed. To kill time she looked at the books on the shelves; all were books on law. She cracked one and amused herself by trying to understand a page opened at random.

The law had to do with easements on private property and was unreadable since it seemed to talk in three directions at once and frequently used words like *heretofore* instead of normal English. It was difficult to come across a single clearly written sentence.

Menis did indeed burst in, his eyes raking over everything, quickly. Deanna jumped only slightly. "Dinner ready, I hope?" she asked. She wanted to eat, beg one more time for the fuel that they needed and then get out of there. In the back of her mind she kept picturing Captain Grey waiting for her, wondering what she was doing. He knew she had been a whore and he had to be thinking the worst.

"Yes, it's on its way up now. What's that you were reading?"

His eyes kept scanning around, looking for things out of place, Deanna assumed. "Just a book on state laws. It's ridiculous and complicated, and a wonder that anyone could do anything back then."

"My way is better," he said. He went to the book, gave it a glance and then reached out his hand for her. Just then there was a knock. Deanna pulled her hand back quickly as a flash of guilt lit up her insides. Although she was expecting dinner, she had a sudden, irrational fear that it was Grey on the other side of the door; she folded her hand primly on her knees. It was the Duke's chef and he was indeed thin. His bones were so prominent, that his face resembled a skull. He grinned that skull face in Deanna's direction.

"Dinner for two," he said, wheeling in a cart upon which were a number of covered dishes. "The steak is perfect and the mashed potatoes are to die for."

Menis pushed him away. "That's enough Willy. I have it from here." On his way out the door, Willy the chef, cast another look at Deanna, his grin still wide and unnerving. "Don't mind him," the Duke said. "He's harmless. I just hope he doesn't die too soon."

"What's wrong with him?" Deanna asked as the Duke pulled her chair back from the table for her. The courtly gesture was odd coming from the bear of a man.

The Duke waived his hand at the door. "Willy's not contagious or anything. He's got anorexia. I know what you're thinking: but he's a dude. Seems they get it too. I never knew. It's sad, but you can't ask for anything better than a skinny chef. You know he hasn't been pawing at your food."

When she was seated, he lifted the covers from the plates to reveal two steak dinners complete with buttered mashed potatoes and corn. There was even a side plate of roasted asparagus. The smell was amazing and she was happy that her stomach didn't start growling again.

"Well, it all looks so good," Deanna said. Out of respect for his position, she waited for the Duke to start before digging in. The steak may have been the best thing she'd ever put in her mouth and she chewed slowly enjoying every bite. As she worked to keep herself from groaning in pleasure she wondered what the other refugees were eating. Their supply of canned goods was dwindling and they had been picking over the least desirable choices for the last two days; soon they'd be down to a hundred cans of lima beans.

While the steak was great, the mashed potatoes were only average. They had a sharp tang to them. "The butter is made from goat's milk," the Duke said as she swallowed her first mouthful wearing something akin to a grimace. "Drown it with pepper and it'll taste pretty good. It's something of an acquired taste."

Deanna tried a bite with pepper and found he was correct. "Will I have to pepper this as well?" she asked indicating a glass of milk next to her plate. Its color wasn't exactly the pure white she was used to.

He laughed and then shrugged. "Sure you can try. It's goat's milk as well. Sorry, but we haven't found a single milking cow. Holsteins I think they're called. I'd give my right arm for a milking cow. Willy does wonders with the goat juice but I sure do miss real butter and ice cream and all of it." He went on speaking for the remainder of the meal as Deanna polished off her plate. She had a strong hankering for seconds, however her belly was so full that it was uncomfortable and she didn't want to squish little Emily.

"I've talked this entire time," the Duke said around a mouthful of steak. "Maybe you should tell me something about yourself so I can eat."

For the next ten minutes, Deanna told about her inconsequential life in Wisconsin and then she began a series of lies concerning her time after the Apocalypse. "Mainly," she said, "it consisted of a series of lucky coincidences. I met up with a few women, uh, around, Chicago and then we met some more in Ohio and that's when we found Neil and..." She was about to add Captain Grey's name, but the Duke's eyes narrowed and she faltered "...And uh, he told us about Colorado."

"Where did you cross the Mississippi?" he asked. His eyes were shrewd and glinting.

"Way to the south. There was this guy who wanted to charge an arm and a leg in Missouri, so we went south and found a boat that was still working."

He drummed his fingers on the table and watched her closely. "Did you see the River King's compound? In Missouri? Do you have any idea of its strength?"

"No. Neil did all the talking."

"Yes, about Neil. How does he end up being in charge and not the soldier? That doesn't make much sense to me."

Deanna tried to give a simple shrug, however it came across as muscle spasm. She was growing ever more nervous at the number of questions he was asking; if she misspoke in any way there would be trouble. "We had an election is all and, at the time, Grey hadn't proved himself to the group and so Neil won."

"But he's since proven himself? How?"

She blinked and her mouth came open, uselessly. It was so hard to think with the Duke staring right into her face looking for her to trip up in the least way.

"He...there...Uh, zombie fighting. He's really good at fighting the zombies."

"I'm sure he is," the Duke said. "Better than Neil, obviously. Which leads me to my next question: Neil has been bitten. Those scars all over his face, they're from zombies. I'd bet my life on it and that must mean he's immune and there's only one place you can get immune and that's in New York. When were you there?"

"I-I wasn't. I-I, they might have been, I don't know, but I've never been to New York, not even in the old days."

His eyes bored deep into hers as he asked: "What about as Sarah? Did you ever go then?"

Her fear disappeared in a blink of confusion. She didn't know anyone named Sarah. Neil's ex-wife might have been named Sarah, but the stories concerning her were taboo, in fact all the renegades were in a similar position. No one talked much about the early days of the Apocalypse; too many good people had done questionable things to survive.

"I never went by that name, sorry."

The Duke looked long into her eyes, before he grunted: "Ok, then." He reached into his pocket and pulled out a reward notice that had been handed out to any number of bounty hunters in New York. She read it and exclaimed in a joking manner: "I'm not thirty-six! And I'm not five foot-four, either." Although the description for Sarah Rivers wasn't very close to matching Deanna, they had Sadie down to a "T", including her name. Thankfully, Sadie had been slow to come into the main courtroom and probably hadn't been seen by the Duke.

"I had to ask. There are rumors about these fugitives. Supposedly, they're exceedingly dangerous. And I can't have..."

A sharp pain struck Deanna low down in her guts and she interrupted him by gasping loudly. "It's probably nothing," she said, at his look of alarm. The pain was already fading and she smiled as brightly as she could to cover

over the grimace that lurked beneath the facade of her pretty face. "Now about that fuel, where were we?"

"You were playing hard to get," he answered. "Have dinner with me tomorrow and I will consider a thirty-five percent interest rate."

Twenty four hours was a long time for the group of renegades to sit on their deadly secrets, especially with only the promise of 'considering' thirty five percent. "Promise me thirty percent and the trucks fueled tomorrow and I say we have a deal."

He stuck out a big paw. She shook it as a new pain cramped her belly. The Duke surprised her by standing and helping her out her chair. "Until tomorrow, then," he said, cutting the dinner shorter than she had expected. She figured that he would try more wine or suggest a walk, or a bath, or something. The most he did was stop her at the door, kiss the back of her hand and look so long into her eyes that she grew uncomfortable.

"Good night," she said, pulling back gently so that once again her hand was in her control. She left him to hurry downstairs, and all she could think about was what Captain Grey was thinking. The word *whore* kept spinning through her mind.

When she reached the main hall on the first floor where all the peddlers ran their shops she was surprised to see that it was filled with the renegades who were all chatting freely.

She took one step into the hall and then doubled over. It felt as though a hot knife had lanced into her gut. Her forehead glistened with sweat and she could feel her pulse hammer in her temples. Something bad was happening to her.

Sadie suddenly appeared out of the crowd. "You ok?" she asked.

"You have to hide," Deanna answered, remembering the reward flyer. For a moment the thought of it overrode the pain, but it was only for the moment. She dropped to her knees and grabbed herself hissing: "Oh my God! My stomach."

"What's wrong? What happened to you?" Sadie asked, coming down to her level, her dark eyes wide with worry.

"I-I don't know, but don't worry about me. The Duke has a reward flyer with your name on it and..." A new pain was followed by a new gasp. Deanna fought through the pain and pushed Sadie away. "The reward is for five thousand. People will kill for that much. So go, get away and hide in the trucks or something."

People were staring now, and through the gaping crowd Neil shoved his way. What he saw made him pause for a second and stare as well. Then he began yelling at the people around him: "Do you mind! Give her some damned privacy. Go on. Look somewhere else, the show's over."

"It's ok," Deanna said. "I can get up." She tried but she was overcome with dizziness. The world began to spin slowly.

"No, stay down and don't move." Neil turned to Sadie and whispered: "Get Captain Grey...no. Forget that. Go get Marybeth Gates, and hurry."

"Why her?" Deanna asked, feeling lightheaded and unsure of herself. As far as Deanna knew Marybeth didn't have any medical skill.

Neil squatted awkwardly in front of her. "You're bleeding," he whispered, shooting his eyes to her pelvis. She looked down at herself and saw that the crotch of her blue jeans was dark with blood. Terror filled her mind to such a degree that she almost didn't catch what Neil said next: "If Grey finds out you've been raped he'll kill everyone here."

"But I wasn't raped," she said. Suddenly her head lolled to the side as if her neck had turned to rubber. "I didn't have sex at all," she said in low mumble, the words feeling like marbles in her mouth. Nothing was making sense just then, however it seemed important for her to get that point out though she couldn't remember why. The world was beginning to dim. She was barely able to add: "This is because of my baby. I must be spotting." It sure seemed like a lot of blood to be simply spotting but since her eyes kept closing and her brain was well past foggy, it was hard to tell.

Neil stared down at her in shock. "You were pregnant?"

She wanted to say: *I am pregnant*, only it came out in a mumble and he didn't seem to hear. The next thing Deanna knew, Marybeth was there, kneeling in front of her, wearing a face full of motherly concern and then she saw Captain Grey sprinting down the hall with his med bag slamming into people.

Deanna wanted to tell him that she hadn't done anything wrong but she slipped away into the deepest sleep of her life and, as she slept, Captain Grey could do nothing except wait helplessly as Deanna's body expelled the tiny person that had been growing inside of her. Emily was dead.

The news of her pregnancy, her now failed pregnancy, was all anyone could talk about and it was generally considered a tragic but natural occurrence right up until Eve was also found dead, swaddled in her blankets.

Chapter 18

Jillybean/Eve

Although Deanna's bleeding ended around midnight she went into a sleep that Captain Grey called a 'coma' and she did not wake up. In a show of generosity, the Duke gave three bags of Lactated Ringers for Grey to administer intravenously. He also had some rooms cleared out in an elementary school just down the street, where the renegades could stay.

Deanna was laid out on a cushioned couch in what had once been the principal's office. Grey never left her side that night except once to use the bathroom and once more when Eve was found dead and even then he refused to leave Deanna unguarded by anyone he didn't trust. He planted Neil in a chair, held him down as though he had glued him there and needed a few moments for the glue to set, and then, growling like a wolf, Grey told him not to move under any circumstances. "Even if the building catches fire, you don't move a damned muscle. Is that understood?"

Sadie spent the sleepless night huddled in a pile of corn in the back of one of the trucks. When the sun rose she peeked out long enough to ask a bustling Neil how Deanna was doing. He only shook his head, gravely. When she asked how he was doing, he only stared outward like a painting of someone sad. He seemed altogether flat and without depth. She hugged him, but wasn't capable of more. Her face was tear-streaked and her hands were without proper nails; she had chewed on her nails and torn at them until the cuticles were bleeding.

Despite the fact that he cried almost constantly, Neil was everywhere, doing anything that would keep him from thinking about Eve and Deanna. He was jittery and easily agitated. His eyes were red as a demon's and his voice was tight and high. As the night progressed, he grew hoarse

188

until he could only grunt and point if he needed something. As leader, there was much to be done. The renegades kept him on his toes. At word of Eve's death, many went into hysterics and babbled or cried in fear, thinking that the Duke had poisoned them somehow. Others vowed revenge and began plotting, but most of them just stood around gossiping and gabbing.

These talkers were the most dangerous as they rarely checked to see if there were ears listening in the dark. Neil was kept from grieving over his daughter or sinking into a depression simply because he lacked the time to even come to grips with another death.

This left Jillybean alone for most of the night. She had 'woken' a little before midnight to find herself standing next to the couch where Deanna was lying motionless. The little girl blinked and looked around, completely confused at her surroundings. Her last memory had been of when she was prowling about the Duke's quarters in the courthouse building. There had been many doors, most of them locked.

She remembered hearing a murmuring which she had followed until she had found the Duke's suite. Slow as a turtle she had eased the door back and seen the Duke and Deanna standing very close, talking. Neither saw her and she listened to the strange conversation until she was struck by something so much more urgent than just their chit-chat—it was the smell of something cooking. Forgetting Deanna and the Duke, Jillybean had scampered along, sly as a fox, dodging the occasional guard or wandering man or woman of the Azael, until she came to the kitchen.

The kitchen had once been a break room with little more than a fridge and a microwave, however the Duke had added an electric stove and, beneath a curtained window, a barbeque grille. In the room was the most interesting man. He was spindly and hunched, seemingly made of bone more than anything else. It was as if his skeleton was too big for his body. He reminded her of a praying mantis, but a conniving one. He had secrets that he mumbled to himself as he cut up potatoes and chopped chives and onion. Sometimes he laughed as high as a girl and then poked at whatever vegetable he was reducing to its basic elements.

Jillybean watched him, hoping that he would step out of the room long enough for her to snag something to eat. That was stealing and she knew it was wrong and yet *the other girl* was demanding it. In her heart, Jillybean knew she would probably have done it anyway without any encouragement from *her*.

Then the Duke came and Jillybean shied back, hiding behind a well-worn couch where there was a village of ancient gum wads next to her head. She tried to keep from touching these as she listened to the Duke. He said things, she was sure. She saw his mouth move and his lips clap together, however the words drew out into a long, slow motion groan and when she would blink her eyes, the lids closed as slowly as the passing of a day …and then she found herself next to Deanna's bed with Captain Grey asking her a question.

"Huh?" she replied, wondering what time it was and where she was.

"I said, can you hand me the stethoscope? It's the thing with the ear-buds right next to your hand." He seemed put out by having to ask twice, but it wasn't her fault since she didn't know where her hands were, let alone what was beside them. She looked down and saw the stethoscope and knew it and its use. She also saw the IV lines and the fluid bag, and the blood pressure cuff and the thermometer and the other medical odds and ends and each she described in her mind and categorized. She could understand these things at least.

She handed over the stethoscope and watched as Grey used it in conjunction with the blood pressure cuff. She saw the needle on the glass face of the cuff moving along as though it were a second hand on a stop watch, but then it jumped and started a hitching descent down to a point where it went smoothly again, going slower and slower.

"90 over 60. Not good," Grey said and Jillybean understood this only to a degree. The first hitch of the needle had occurred at the 90 mark where it began to jerk until it had hit the 60 at which point it had gone smoothly down the rest of the way. What the numbers, 90 and 60 signified beyond 'Not good', she didn't know.

She asked Grey and he answered and the knowledge of blood volume and the various repercussions of too low and too high registered on her memory, however she couldn't have repeated a word.

For some reason Jillybean had a great fear inside her. It ate away her insides and made her tummy ache. At this point, only Deanna was known to be sick. Eve was dying and no one knew. She had been given her bottle by Veronica and had her diaper changed by Joslyn, and had been sung to sleep by Anne Gates, who was well known for her soothing voice, and she had been watched over in the back of the first truck by Marybeth Gates, who was standing guard anyway.

And during this Jillybean was afraid and didn't know why. She stayed with Grey for an hour before Veronica burst in with the news of Eve's death. Veronica looked like she had been stricken with some disease; she was all white and her eyes were these big balls that were wet as stones that had just been pulled from a lily-pad-covered fishing hole and stuck in her sockets.

"Eve is dead!" she cried.

This started the renegades on their various paths of mourning or revenge or just plain yapping. Everyone seemed to be doing something, all save Jillybean who followed along behind Captain Grey after he had set Neil on watch over Deanna. Jillybean was just an afterthought to him. She was just a shadow, and she felt as useless as one. The baby lolled in Marybeth's arms. She was perfect as always except she was white, just so awfully white and she didn't move, even though tears kept falling on her face.

Normally, Eve would have grabbed the tears and inspected them, because everything was so interesting and curious to her. She had always looked on the world and everyone in it as a wonder and an experience to enjoy.

With his mouth clamped down like a vice and his eyes ferocious in anger, Captain Grey took Eve from Marybeth and undressed her and opened her little mouth and looked in, to see her soul, Jillybean supposed. That she was dead made no sense to Jillybean and her own lack of shock over it made even less sense. It was as though she had expected it which was only possible if she had known...

"No," she said. Standing there seeing the baby looking so beautiful and lifeless at the same time, Jillybean felt as though there was something in her throat fighting to come up. It had all the characteristics of a bull frog. It was squirmy and alive and it kicked, demanding to get out and breathe once again, however, it wasn't a bullfrog jumping up her throat, it was only her dinner which had been green beans and three spoonfuls of chicken noodle soup. It all went onto the ground except a little which spattered wetly onto her sneakers.

Someone, she didn't know who, asked if she was ok, but she couldn't answer beyond a croak that was again so much like that of a frog that she wondered again if something was alive within her—something more than *the other girl*, the other *evil girl*, that is. *She* had done *something*. Jillybean knew it, and yet when Grey rounded on her, took her by the shoulders and demanded in a harsh, angry tone that she tell him what she had done, Jillybean lied.

"I didn't do anything."

Anything that she could remember, that is. All she could truthfully remember was the weird Bone-man and the Duke, and the overheard whispered conversation and then everything went black as night as the *other girl* took over. Jillybean told herself that all she knew was the black of her mind and the strange and scary silver lines that went down into the darkness where she was terrified to go because down there was...what? What was down there?

Everything, a voice whispered in her mind. Yes, everything, and everything encompassed far too much for one little girl to handle. Down there was where she kept the mind pictures of how her parents had died and how

Ram had been turned into a disgusting monster and then drownded while chained to the boat that Jillybean had sunk. And down there was the memory of Sarah, blackened and horrible; Sarah had stood in front of her and had taken a bullet meant for Jillybean.

In the cool light of day, she remembered these things sure, however they were passing memories and faint. Down there in the black of her mind, the memories were strong and the pain of them stung and tasted of poison. They were waiting deep down there, waiting for her; waiting to drown her if she ever went to explore.

And memories weren't the only things down there. *Everything* encompassed every fright and fear and tear and scream and horror she had ever experienced. Down there was where every monster that had ever reached for her with their diseased hands, lived. It was where she hid the pain she had caused and the blood she had spilt and the flames she had lit that had roasted living flesh. And down there was where the secret knowledge was kept. Down there was where she kept the knowledge that she was a killer.

She had killed people but hid the fact from herself by stuffing the knowledge deep into the black. Consciously, she barely remembered pulling the trigger of her little gun and killing the first bounty hunter and the same was true with how she had killed Ernest. And she couldn't remember at all the sound of the screams as the ferry boats went up in flames, and the memory of the guard on the barge being blasted into bloody chunks when she had blown it sky-high was simply gone.

But down there the feeling and the noise and the pain were perfectly preserved. It was all there in *Technicolor*, as was the scary, joyous, powerful feeling which had accompanied the killings. And down there was…was…perhaps it was where her memory of killing Eve was laid out all perfectly preserved in the hateful black of her mind.

It was best not to think about 'down there.'

"I didn't do anything," she had repeated, to which Grey had grunted like bull and then turned back to stare at

Eve as if he could see through her white skin and see what had caused her death. Jillybean grew uneasy just in case he could. What was in the depths of Eve's mind? Were there hidden pictures there as well and was one of Jillybean doing something she shouldn't have? A shudder that was hidden by the night wracked the little girl.

I didn't do anything was both the truth and a lie. To Jillybean, the *other girl* was a real, live person, just as Ipes had been a real, live stuffed animal, just as the zombies were real, live monsters that would eat you. The *other girl* had done something, but she had done, whatever it was, using Jillybean's body and for that, the little girl was wracked by guilt.

Like most everyone else, she didn't sleep that night. The only person who did was Deanna and she didn't wake in the morning like a normal person would.

Captain Grey was haggard and bitter by first light. He didn't see evil in Jillybean; he saw it in the Duke. The soldier would curse under his breath and bunch his muscley arms whenever the Duke came in to check on Deanna. To Jillybean, Menis looked genuinely concerned. "You will have to stay until she is better," he insisted.

The morning wore away and Jillybean grew bored and restless. Wracked by an unknown guilt, she had an urgent need to be away from people. She slipped from the school, unseen and walked around the town and saw immediately that something had changed in the town—there were more people, a lot more people than there had been the day before. They were all men and they carried guns. She also saw that the monsters who walked in their endless circle around the town had multiplied. They were now a wide and deep river of odiferous, rotting flesh.

No one else seemed to notice. The renegades were busy. Neil wandered around the school in a daze trying to comfort everyone when it was clear he was the one most in need of comforting. Grey was busy watching over Deanna. This mainly took the form of him holding her hand and staring at her. Sadie was busy hiding in the back of the corn truck, and the rest were bleary-eyed, yawning or busy napping after the long, stressful night.

They napped while the trap closed around them.

"What were the Duke and the Bone-man talking about?" Jillybean asked the air. She stood in an alley down from the old theater with the strange wording on the marquee that she didn't understand. She paused after the question and perked an ear, hoping that the *other girl* would answer. When, after three seconds went by and there was nothing coming as way of an answer, she tried again: "Listen, we're being trapped by the Duke. Can't you see it?"

Again a pause, but the *other girl* refused to speak. She was hiding inside Jillybean. She was hiding from the truth. "You're hiding because they'll know it was you who put Deanna in a coma and it was you who killed Eve."

I am Eve, the *other girl* said inside her mind. *I am the only Eve, now. I am the baby, now. I'm the youngest and the cutest and now everyone will only pay attention to me.*

Was that why she had killed the baby? For attention? "What did you do?" Jillybean asked and a shiver went up her spine as she waited on the answer. The voice of the other girl had changed. She spoke in a higher register and there was an affected lisp to her words as if she were trying to sound younger, which she did, though it didn't make her sound any less evil.

That's for me to know and you to find out.

"Why that is so childish!" Jillybean hissed like an angry tea kettle. "We are seven-years-old! We don't say silly..." She heard the sound of voices coming from around the corner of one of the buildings and a second later there was the sound of glass crunching and the tinny sound of a can being kicked across cement. Quick as a squirrel, Jillybean ducked behind a green dumpster and squatted against a wall that smelled like pee-pee.

"That's up to the Duke, not me. A hundred rounds apiece is all I'm permitted to give you, Brad."

Jillybean peeked around the edge of the dumpster and saw the man who had guided them to their current predicament. He was once again dressed as an angel. His armor shone bright and his wings arched tall and beautiful—they did not match the sneer on his face. "First off, you address as me as 'your lordship' or 'sir'," Brad said as they came into the alley and began walking towards the theater. "I have been made a Baron for this, as you know full well, Jim. And second, I have fifty men coming in tonight and I want them ready to go when this kicks off. You don't want to be messing around in the dark, do you?"

The little girl, who was naturally eaten up with curiosity, crept after them and, thanks to Brad's wings, which were large and rustled loudly, she went unseen and unheard.

"Like I told you before, *your highness,*" Jim said, adding a mock bow in Brad's direction. "You need to talk to the Duke. He only lets me give out so much per person, and if I have to do it at night then I do it at night. We haven't had an incident with the stiffs in weeks besides a stray or two, so stop wetting yourself like a girl. So, do you want yours now or when your men arrive? It really doesn't matter to me."

Brad snapped: "Now, of course. I'm not getting up at three in the morning. That'll be all you."

Jim grunted as they came up to a side door. As Jillybean slunk behind an old car, Jim fished out a set of keys from somewhere among his multi-hued scarf outfit. He chose one among them and opened the side door of the theater. "I love the smell of napalm in the morning," he said with a wide grin and then walked past a curtain hanging just on the other side of the door.

Jillybean didn't know what napalm was but she could smell something with a pungent chemical odor waft from the theater. It was so strong that it made Brad's face squinch. With his eyes at squints he took off the harness that held his wings, leaned them against the side of the building, and then stepped through the door. Rabbit-fast, Jillybean darted from her hiding place and sprinted to the door as it closed. She was twenty feet away but it swung in such a slow, ponderous arc that she was just able to dart inside before it thudded home with a loud metallic thump.

Brad was inches away with only a thick velvet curtain between him and Jillybean. "Is that really napalm I'm smelling?" he asked. "It smells like gas."

"Duh, it's jellied gasoline," Jim said. "Of course it smells like gas. Now, come on. The NATO rounds are all down by the stage."

A stage where plays and musicals could be put on was thirty yards down a sloping aisle. The two of them tromped down to where hundreds of wood crates were stacked to the ceiling. Jim went to the first crate he came to and pried back the lid. He then pulled a smaller box from the crate. This was made of metal and its lid creaked when he opened it. "Here you go," Jim said, handing over five smaller objects. "If I can get a signature?"

There was a rustle of paper, but Jillybean wasn't watching. Like a specter of yellow, she had slunk from behind the curtain and was now crawling on her hands and knees through the theater seating. Why she had followed them through the door, she couldn't tell. She was acting on instinct. *Something* was happening, something that required more men and more bullets. Even to the seven-year-old that something was obvious. They were going to try to capture the renegades and she was going to stop them— somehow. She was afraid, of course, however the unknown guilt eating her up forced her on.

"What's that say?" Jim asked.

Brad growled, "Don't be a dick. That says Baron Crane. My title, remember?"

Jim snorted. "This title business is freaking gay. Me, I'd rather have the money. Think about how much those girls are worth and I'm not just talking about selling them back to the Colonel, either. I mean selling them in New York or even to some of the Azael in North Platte. I'm betting you could get a thousand a head, easy, and all you got for them is a stupid, worthless title. That's funny!"

"A title is better than you think. I am the lord of a town now and I can charge the people there taxes and fees. If the town grows, which it will, I'll be way ahead than if I just turned them over for the money. Hell, I could be a duke someday and you'll still be a lowly store keeper. Now, if you'll excuse me, I have a ton of things to do before tomorrow's little surprise."

His armored boots thudded up the aisle and Jillybean slunk down low, her cheek pressed against the floor, her nose an inch from an ancient Ju-Ju-be the original color of which might have been either red or orange. When the door thunked closed a second time, Jim muttered something that sounded like a curse and there came a grunt and the sound of a heavy box being dropped. Jillybean reached out for the Ju-Ju-be. In the dim light it looked dusty but well preserved like a tiny exhibit from a museum.

Try as she might, it wouldn't budge. It was stuck to the floor as if it had been fused there.

"Fifty men at a hundred a pop is..." Jim paused to calculate. "Five thousand. And there are nine hundred per drum, that's...shit. I hate long division." He went on muttering numbers for some time while Jillybean worked at the Ju-Ju-be. The numbers prevailed over the candy.

Jim counted out five thousand rounds in increments of fifty and then he left, turning off the lights and locking Jillybean in the dark.

Her sudden fear made the other girl stronger and she said: *We should leave too. You can't stop the Azael. There are too many of them and their land is too big. They're not like Yuri and Abraham and the stupid River King. You won't be able to escape them with a few explosions and a quick getaway. They'll follow you and hound you and if you do make it to Colorado they'll get you there.*

"Oh, who cares what you think," Jillybean griped.

Forgetting the Ju-Ju-be, she stood and, by feel alone, she made her way to the door and then ran her hands up and down the wall until she found the switch for the house-lights.

They'll see you. They'll catch you.

"No they won't. Don't you remember all the curtains and the plywood? No light gets out of here, I bet. Now hush so I can figure this out."

198

Something was going to happen 'tomorrow' which meant they had to get away that night, which meant she had to knock together a plan. She had in mind explosions—her mind frequently went to them. "Though I don't want to be so close as that other time," she said, thinking about the time she blew up the barge. Her head had rang for two days after that and her brain had been mushy; she hadn't even been able to figure out Ernest until it was nearly too late.

She went down the aisle and looked at the crates. They were heavy, too heavy for her to even budge, and the words and strings of letters and numbers on the sides didn't make much sense. Only by comparing the opened one to the rest did she come to the conclusion that there were bullets in the mountains of crates.

"Humph," she snorted in anger. Bullets weren't going to do her much good. But napalm might. She turned away from the stage and followed her nose upward to the lobby where the smell of fuel was headache-inducing. She covered her little nose with the collar of her dress and inspected the silvery canisters which were as tall as she was. On each was stenciled the word: Napalm B, and there were warnings and the symbol for fire. She tried to push one of the canisters and found them to be heavier than the crates of bullets.

"Well, shoot," she whispered. Because of their weight, Jillybean discarded the idea of using the canisters. What she need was C4.

She began searching. In the lobby with the napalm were big machine guns with barrels longer than both her legs put together and coiled belts of bullets and piles of green objects she took to be bombs of sorts. She ignored these as they seemed unusable by a little girl. In a room behind the concession stand she found part of what she was looking for: boxes of C4 and blasting caps. However, there weren't any detonators.

"They have to be here somewhere," she said and then spent the next hour going through every room in the theater and pawing through every box. Her search uncovered all sorts of amazing things, but she did not find detonators. She then spent twenty eight minutes staring at the C4 and the blasting cap, trying to figure out some way to use one to blow up the other without a detonator. The twenty eight minutes were as wasted as the hour had been.

She might have had a genius level intellect, however there were canyon-sized holes in her knowledge base. On some level, she knew she needed electricity to work the blasting cap, however electricity fell into the same category as magic. It made things work, but how was beyond her. She had somehow been able to piece together the idea that the potential energy in batteries was the same as electricity, but she didn't know how to get it out of the batteries and into the blasting caps. Of circuits she possessed zero knowledge and of wiring she possessed only fear because even she knew that electricity could "zap" you if you touched open wires.

"I need Captain Grey," she said and then was struck by a pain in her stomach. It was the acid of guilt. She suddenly pictured the Bone-man's lips moving as he talked to the Duke. She had seen his lips form an "M" and she could hear the echo of a word: *mor-something*. They were talking about the poison in Deanna. The answer to fixing her was in Jillybean's head. She just had to trace the lines back to…

Stop! the *other girl* demanded and then shut out the memory so that it was now only a memory of a memory. It was like slamming an iron door on a straw house. Jillybean wobbled on her coltish legs and put a hand to her cheek. It felt as though she had been clubbed on the top of the head; her vision played in front of her as if she were standing on the deck of a boat and the world had turned to fluid and bucked under the effects of an invisible storm.

It was a second before everything turned solid again and she could stand straight. She tried to call up the memory of the Bone-man talking to the Duke but now it was misty and cloudy and distant. She still had the guilt, however. She had done something wrong, or knew something wrong, or she was wrong in some way. Wrong and evil, that was her. She was warped and broken and unlovable, Jillybean was sure of it.

But she was still needed. She had a job to do and a family to help. That meant she had to go to Captain Grey, look him in his eye and ask for his help to make the bombs so she could save the renegades once again, so she could save what was left of her family. Men like the Duke didn't understand love and family. They understood explosions, however, and the bigger the better.

Chapter 19

Captain Grey

As much as Jillybean's world had lost focus and she saw things as large and vague, where nothing seeming to fit with anything else, Grey's vision was narrow as the edge of his dagger. He had spent the two hours that Deanna was with the Duke in a state that was somewhat like his own coma. Things occurred around him, people spoke and walked here and there and generally carried on living, however he had only existed much like a tree might. He stood and the minutes passed in an ageless, timeless fashion.

Then he saw her looking pale, but otherwise unharmed. He could tell by her demeanor that she had remained…pure? It wasn't the right word for a woman who had survived on The Island, however it was the right word for that moment and for that girl. She had refused the Duke, he could see that. She had remained steadfast and true—to herself and to Grey—at the risk of everything else, including her baby.

The others didn't understand. They were weak. They still saw Deanna and all the other women who had been sex slaves as whores, however, Deanna was different. Grey had known it from the very start. She had been prickly at first and that was because she was trying to sort things out, to find her rightful place, to understand what honor meant for her. Unlike the others she had grown and as she had, she'd become so much more than she had ever been. She was no longer simply a creature of beauty, something to be gawked at or worn as arm candy. She was a woman with pride and regal bearing.

Or she had been.

Now she was a soft creature, vulnerable and precious. Grey watched over her constantly and his face was a carven mask of anger. Sorrow wasn't his lot. When Eve had died, he had been furious, not mournful. His first thought had been: who had screwed up? Who had failed in their duty of watching her? Who would pay when he found out the truth of her death?

He was furious, and figured that sorrow would come later, but so far it hadn't.

"It'll be a weight on my soul when I die," he whispered. And that too he would deal with when the time came. When he stood at those pearly gates, he figured he would let it all hang out then. That would be far down the road he hoped, both for himself and Deanna.

Once more, he worked the blood pressure cuff and, once more, he felt pain at the extremely low reading.

"Not so good?" a voice asked from the doorway. It was the Duke, bearish and burly. Grey took a long breath before replying and then found he didn't have any words to answer with; he was simply too angry. He was almost certain the Duke had done something to Deanna, just what, wasn't clear.

The Duke stared down at Deanna, ignoring the soldier as he gnashed his teeth. He then had the temerity to reach out and touch her foot beneath the thin blanket of green wool. Grey contemplated taking that hand off at the wrist. He could have his knife out in a blink and it was sharp as a razor.

"Her blood pressure is fine," Grey finally answered. "A low blood pressure can be expected as she fights off the poisons in her body. If they haven't killed her yet, they won't." This was true of most poisons. The body filtered them through the liver and gradually the person got better...only Deanna wasn't getting better, and strangely, she wasn't getting worse, either. Medically speaking, that wasn't normal. Grey's greatest fear was her dangerously low respiration rate. She took eight meager sips of air every minute.

He had no idea what poison caused that. There could be other possible causes. An infection of the blood could be at the root of her problem. She wouldn't have long if she was septic. He started wondering about the possibility of a blood transfusion. In these primitive conditions it could be as dangerous as doing nothing.

The Duke stared at the woman for a long time before he patted her leg with a familiarity that was well out of bounds, and said: "I will check on you later. Perhaps after dinner? I'll have something set up…I mean sent over."

"That would be great," Grey said, without the least sincerity. There was no way he would eat even a cracker if it came from the Duke. He had given very strict orders for the rest of the renegades concerning the same thing. After the death of Eve, Grey knew they would follow the order.

When the Duke left, Grey turned Deanna's wrist over and checked the time on her watch. She wore a Rolex, silver with diamonds studded around the face. In the old world it would have gone for over thirty grand, now it was virtually worthless except as a gadget that displayed the time. It read 2:31 in the afternoon. That was a bit of a shock. He went to the window, pulled back the curtain, and blinked, shielding his face against the brilliant light.

With the perpetual zombie threat, his first instinct was to hide from the light and yank the curtain back in place, however the light was warming, not just for his skin, but also for his soul. He hauled the couch with Deanna on it over to the window so that the sun fell on her—it accented her pallor and he was still grimacing over it when Neil came in.

The small man stared at the woman, his cruelly disfigured face set in stone. "No change." He said this as a proclamation not a question. "This isn't *her* doing." He meant Jillybean and again it wasn't a question. "This is *his* doing, I know it. But why? Did she refuse his advances? If so, I say good for her."

"Yes." Grey couldn't say more, he lacked the energy. Neil stood for some time and looked as though a cramp had him by his soul—he was sort of hunched in on himself, a gnarled little gnome with the weight of the world on his back.

"We need to leave soon," he said. "It's only a matter of time before someone accidentally lets it slip about who we are." He caught Grey's eye in an even stare. "We need to leave soon...no matter what."

Grey felt a new fury build. *No matter what*, meant either leaving Deanna behind, or taking her with them. In the state she was in both would likely kill her. Grey wanted to slap Neil's face, but there was no way he could. Neil was doing his best. In fact, he was doing a great job as leader, Grey thought, however the work had taken a huge toll on him. The horribly tough decisions he was making almost daily seemed to have sapped the warmth and compassion out of him. He was great but also terribly cold.

Neil stared down at the woman he was sentencing to death for a long, slow minute and then left.

Seconds later, Jillybean tapped softly, a sound that was almost a secret in itself, and then she edged her way in through the partially open door. She had traded out her yellow dress for her pink jeans and a pink short-sleeved shirt. On her back was her Ladybug backpack; it swayed heavily.

Like Neil, she stared at Deanna, and just like he had she seemed to undergo some sort of physical pain at the sight of her. She went green and the dark circles beneath her eyes looked like bruises. She rubbed her chest and then turned her chin slightly, saying in a low voice: "I won't, I promise."

"You won't what?" Grey asked.

Jillybean jumped like someone snuck up on; her eyes twitched with guilt. "Nothing, except I'm just aposed to talk about the bombs and nothing else or *she'll* come back. You know who *she* is, right?"

Grey knew. *She* was the nasty, imbalanced creature which resided in the little girl. Perhaps, *she* was even evil. Perhaps *she* had something to do with Eve's death. That was a hard concept to swallow. Seven-year-old girls were never evil. In the movies, sure, however in real life he had never heard of a little girl such as this committing murder. Even a girl with this many mental issues. But who else could have killed the infant? The truth was that anyone could have, yet Jillybean was the only one with even a hint of a motive. The *she* inside her hated the baby. It was a well-established fact.

Then again, *she* seemed to hate everyone.

Grey didn't know the truth. He, along with everyone else, had been in a state of shock and hadn't really considered all the ramifications of Eve's death, nor had he assigned guilt, though he leaned heavily toward either the Duke or the little girl. Both were dangerous.

"Ok," he said, clearing his throat, "we don't have to talk about anything but the bombs. May I ask what bombs?"

She seemed surprised by the question. "Why, the bombs we gotsta build is all. They should be big and remote-controlled like the last ones and I woulda done it myself only they didn't have detonators and I don't know how to make any. I saw a lightable fuse on a cartoon once and that might work on account of all the napalm they have. Napalm is what means gas-flavored jelly. I don't know about the jelly part but boy, is it stinky."

Her words came shooting out of her causing Grey to struggle to catch up. "I guess by 'they have napalm' you mean the Azael?" She nodded to his question and he continued: "And why do we need bombs?"

Jillybean leaned in close. "Because they plan on getting us and selling us to New York. I heard Mister Brad talk about it with this guy named Jim. Only it's Mister Baron Brad now. Baron is what means like a little duke, I think. Anyways, he knows who we are and bombs are usually the answer to these sorts of things, only like I said they didn't have no detonators. They just have C4 and blasting caps and wire and Napalm in these big steel jugs and they also have bullets, like a million of them...I mean a quarter of a million of them...but that may not be right. I think I dreamed...that..."

She trailed off looking confused.

Grey sat back considering her words and, for the moment, Deanna was forgotten. She was just a long thin bundle under a blanket. "If Brad knows who we are and he knows our past, then why hasn't he done anything about it yet?"

"I don't know if I can answer that on account it's not about bombs and I'm aposed to only...Oh...Ok. She says I can talk about that. I think it's because they don't have enough fighter men, but they're getting more of them now. You can see them outside."

A quick turn of his head confirmed Jillybean's story. Across from the school were a number of small homes that had their doors boarded over and their windows heavily curtained. There were faces in the windows and as soon as they saw Grey looking, they withdrew and the curtains swung back. Up the street was a park and, in the shade of a large maple that sat at the park's edge, were three men standing together, smoking. They kept a steady gaze toward the school and their hands never left their weapons. Grey was sure he had never seen them before.

Jillybean seemed to read his mind. "They're new. There are all sorts of new people. They just come trickling in. They're going to trap us." She stared out the window, her blue eyes unblinking and seeing far away.

He eased Jillybean back from the window and let the curtain fall, dipping the room back into gloom. There was a single kerosene lamp sitting on the desk; next to it was a triangular block of wood. On the front of it read: *Principal Bobby*. Grey flipped it over so the nameplate faced down; he could not comprehend the notion of attending a school where the principal allowed children to call him Bobby; the very notion was repulsive to his character.

"I need you to tell me everything you heard and saw about Brad. Even small details. What he was wearing, where he was going, what he smelled like, anything."

She held nothing back, or so it seemed to Grey. She prattled on, going into an amazing amount of detail. The only time she stumbled was when she recounted the mountain of crates around the stage. "I think it was a quarter of a...mill...yun." She paused again with a faraway look. It lasted only a few seconds and then she went back to talking as if the break hadn't occurred. "I don't even know what that is. I know what a ba-jillion is. That's what means a whole awful lot."

"Who said that about the quarter of a million?"

Her eyes suddenly blazed and a sneer swept her sweet features into an ugly cast. "That's for me to know and you to find out," she said, around the sneer.

"Jillybean!" Grey snapped, forgetting for a moment the woman in the coma next to him.

The little girl blinked herself back to normal...what passed as normal at least. "I can't talk about that. *She* won't let me. *She* won't let me cry, neither. When I think of Eve it hurts but *she* gets mad. *She* says I was born a lonely child and that Eve was never my sister and Ram was never my uncle and Sarah was never my mom, and Neil was never my father. I only get to have *her*." Her expression suggested she didn't like the arrangement very much.

"Ok, ok," Grey said with his hands out, trying to calm the little girl. Her voice was brittle with conflicting emotions; she seemed on the verge of a mental collapse. "Just finish telling me what you saw in the theater." Jillybean spoke for ten more minutes and then came to an abrupt end with her failure at making a bomb. "I don't think a bomb will work this time," Grey told her.

He was in a difficult situation. He wanted to act quickly, before any more of the Duke's men showed up. A simple plan formed in his mind: he would take Neil and William Gates, Ricky and two of his crew of ex-cage-fighters and storm the courthouse. With the element of surprise, they could be in the Duke's chambers within seconds. The major problem with this was that the only proof of any wrong doing on the part of the Duke was based on the word of a seven-year-old and not just any seven-year-old, but one with an obvious mental disorder.

If Grey acted too rashly and without the facts, he could be responsible for starting a war between the Azael and the people of Colorado. Brad had already mentioned that there were tensions between the two groups, however the Duke hadn't said a thing in their initial meeting or at any point in the last half-day.

With storming the courthouse ruled out, Grey didn't know what to do, besides getting the hell out of the town. Leaving was the best way to avoid a battle...but he had Deanna to worry about. Traveling could kill her, especially if they ran out of fluids for her IV. "Son of a bitch," he whispered under his breath. Jillybean's eyes went wide at the curse. He said: "Sorry," to her and added: "Could you go find Neil, please. We need to discuss what you've told me."

"Yes, Mister Captain Grey, Sir." She ran off, leaving Grey to stew. Was Jillybean right? Had someone spilled the beans about who they were? The renegades had been told over and over to keep their lips sealed and they all knew the ramifications of being found out...yet the proof that Jillybean was right sat just outside the window.

Five minutes later, Neil came in looking horrible. He was dead pale and his eyes wouldn't stop leaking tears. He would rub them with his sleeve every few seconds. When Grey told him what Jillybean had said, he went to the window to see for himself. "I suppose you believe her then?" Jillybean had been shut out of the room, the door gently closed in her face with an order by Neil to: *Wait here. Don't go anywhere.*

"Under the circumstances I believe the obvious," Grey said. "We both know that something's going on. Deanna is exhibit A and those men watching us, they're exhibit B. And then there's Eve."

Neil flinched at the name and his mouth set in tight lines. "Eve...aw jeeze, Eve. I don't want to believe it but I don't think her death has anything to do with the Duke." He sighed and looked so deflated that he seemed positively tiny to Grey, his shoulders narrow and hunched. A second sigh escaped him, this one was so long that it seemed to age him ten years. "I-I don't know...I just don't understand Jillybean and I haven't a clue about what to do about her. Banishment out here would mean a death sentence."

It seemed there was no question as to Jillybean's guilt in his mind. Grey had to reluctantly agree. "There's also her mental state to consider. In the old world she wouldn't be considered guilty."

"We don't live in that world anymore, but…but that's something I don't want to think about right now. We have to deal with the Duke, now. We can still use Jillybean. If we fight, we'll still need her."

Grey gave a slight shrug. He had never liked "using" Jillybean in any capacity. From the very start, there had been mental issues with the little girl and to him it was obvious that Eve's death was a direct consequence of "using" Jillybean. "She might have reached the limit of her usefulness," Grey said. "If we're going to get out of this, we'll have to rely on ourselves. And we have to weigh the diplomatic fallout if we use violence in any way. We could be precipitating a war."

Neil looked out of the window a second time, saw the lurking men and drew himself up once again. "I can't worry about diplomacy. I have sixty people to protect and guide. If the Azael prove to be aligned with the slavers of New York, or the Colonel, or the River King then I say we have little to fear diplomatically. They are evil and they promulgate evil. If your General Johnston is as good a person as you say he is, then this is all very cut and dried."

A smirk that was part respect part pain, crossed Grey's face. "You never fail to amaze me, Neil. We're in the middle of Indian country, surrounded by armed enemies, with more coming in every hour. We have a crazy girl outside that door who could blow up this building at any moment. We're on the verge of starting a war and you say this is all cut and dried?"

"You of all people know it is. If there is war over the Duke kidnapping and poisoning innocent travelers then it will be a just war."

He was right. Grey had a duty to see the renegades through to Colorado and if there was fallout he would pay the price. "So we're back in it up to our necks."

"As usual," Neil agreed. There had been a time when he would've had a twinkle in his eye at the prospect of adventure and maybe a little grin to hide his nervousness to go along with it. Now, Neil was stone-cold sober. "So how do we do this? Do we just blast our way out?"

The captain squinted, staring past the wall and picturing the layout of the town; it wasn't promising. They were surrounded by who knew how many men and beyond that was a ring of zombies that could be used both as an offensive weapon and a defensive shield, and beyond that was seven hundred miles of open prairie. The obstacles were daunting and his assets were shady. "We either need a tremendous distraction, or we need to take the Duke hostage."

"Will holding the Duke hostage work?" Neil asked. "Personally, I think it will depend on whether his people love or fear him enough. If they don't care one way or the other if he dies, then we'll be screwed. I think we should go with a distraction. I know you don't want to, uh accept Jillybean's help, but she's extremely resourceful and can be the difference. She has been before."

"And what about her insanity? More battles may deteriorate her mental state to an even greater degree."

Another long sigh escaped Neil before he said: "I hate to say this, but it may be too late for her."

Grey's eyes flashed at this and for just a moment the fury he felt at the Duke was turned on the small man before him, but then the truth of his words sunk home. Grey had hoped to find a refuge for the little girl in Colorado but that looked less and less likely every day. "This is all moot. I'm not exactly an idiot. I can come up with my own plans."

Neil nodded once, his face as grim as it had been since Sarah's death. "Yes, but…" he started to say.

"There is no but," Grey snapped. "I am a West Point trained Army officer."

"And she is a genius at destruction," Neil shot back. "We might be about to start a…a shit storm and there isn't anyone else I'd want to be planning a war with than Jillybean. All I ask is that you listen to her. She might have some good ideas."

This didn't sit well with Grey at all, but at the same time he felt foggy in the brain. His love lay in a coma next to him, his eyes burned from lack of sleep, and his emotions were as quick to come as his logic. He couldn't get past the idea of storming the courthouse and sticking a gun in the Duke's face, in fact he wanted to shove his M4 eight inches down his throat and demand answers. After a deep breath, Grey put out a hand and rested it on Deanna's chest between her breasts. Her heart was there, it thumped gentle and slow. Its rhythm was like a metronome that wanted to set him in a trance. "Fine," he said. "Bring her in."

Right off the bat Jillybean piped up: "So, how are we going to build the bombs?"

The girl's voice was sweet as any seven-year-old girl's had ever been and yet Grey cringed at the question. "Bombs aren't the answer, honey." Though what the answer was he didn't know. He had to escape a compound full of armed men and then escape a ring of zombies, and then he had to traverse seven hundred or so miles of enemy territory. Bombs wouldn't help. He needed fuel and a whole lot of luck.

"Then what is the answer?" she asked in genuine confusion.

That was the question. If he had a trained squad of soldiers, the answer would be a combination of stealthy assassinations on the Azael lurking in the buildings opposite of them, coupled with a lightning fast attack on the men lingering around the school. Once this was accomplished half the squad would lay down a covering fire on the courthouse while the other half commandeered the gas truck at the edge of town. This would be followed up, seconds later with the renegades taking to the five-tons and blasting a hole in the ring of zombies and escaping.

It was a fine plan, except for the fact that he didn't have a single trained man he could trust. Neil was about it, but only because Grey knew he would follow the plan or die trying. None of the other renegades, save maybe Sadie and Deanna, if she had been awake, were even close to being battle ready.

"Um, I don't know just yet," Grey admitted. "I haven't completed a proper recon yet."

"Then you don't know if bombs are the answer or not," Jillybean said. "Even *she* thinks we need bombs."

Grey felt an ugly shiver cascade down his back. It was part fear and part fierce anger. "Maybe we shouldn't go any further until we find out exactly what *she* knows about all of this. I get the feeling that what *she* knows would help us tremendously."

Jillybean dropped her chin. "*She* won't let me know. I think it's cuz *she* was bad."

Neil closed his eyes and they remained closed as if he would strangle the little girl if he had to look at her for one more second. "Jillybean," he said quietly. "The lives of sixty people hang in the balance here. You have to tell us what you know. I promise we won't be mad."

"*She* doesn't care if you get mad," Jillybean said, her voice pitched even lower than his. "*She* doesn't even care about the sixty people."

"Maybe she would if she realized that *she* is one of those sixty whose lives are in danger," Neil replied, finally opening his eyes. Gone completely was the old Neil, the sweet husband, the caring dad, the clumsy nerd. It appeared to Grey that the hard world had finally killed off the old Neil. This Neil was hard and cold and dangerous. "I'll make it a point to ensure that *she* is one of the sixty."

The threat didn't faze the girl. Jillybean grew more sad. "*She* says you're not smart enough."

"Then you have to help us, Jillybean," Grey said, dropping down to her level and taking her scrawny shoulders in his large hands. "You have to find out what she knows. Can you do that? Can you help us out?"

"I don't know how. *She's* too strong."

There were tears in her blue eyes and she appeared so miserable that it just about broke Grey's heart. Even Neil lost some of his edge. "*She* may be stronger but you're smarter and braver, Jillybean," he said. "And you have to do this. If you care about any of us you have to find out what she knows."

Grey said nothing to this dangerous guilt trip. There was a chance that Neil was sending her over the edge permanently, but Grey was silent. He had to weight the sixty lives that were on the line and the possibility of war against the mental state of one poor girl.

"I'll try," she said.

Chapter 20

Jillybean/Eve

The little girl didn't know where to start. She certainly wasn't going to make the attempt with two adults watching her so intently. "I'm going to, uh, go out in the other room if you don't mind," she said to them.

"Sure, but don't try to leave the building," Neil warned. "It could be dangerous for you. We don't know what this Duke fellow is really planning."

It doesn't matter where you go, the other girl said inside her skull. *What's going to happen is that I'll stick you down in the black where you deserve to go and then I'll come back and tell them a big fat fib. What do you think about that?*

Jillybean didn't want to think about that, only she couldn't seem to help it at all. She locked her lips shut and hurried for the door. Once in the front office of the school, she went to one of the desks the secretaries had used and shrank down behind it. In the gloom she asked in a whisper: "What kind of fib?"

Oh, I don't know. Maybe I'll tell them that it was you who killed that stupid baby and not me. I'll be all weepy and pretend to be sorry and then they'll hate you just like they hate me.

The words stunned Jillybean. Not the fib part but the confession of murder. "You killed her? You killed Eve?"

I AM EVE!

The words thundered in Jillybean's head. She put a hand out to the edge of the desk but already she was losing the feeling in her fingertips. *She* was taking over. Jillybean tried to fight it. She tried to use the psychic scream she had used a few days before, however *She* matched it scream for scream and Jillybean's head rang like a bell.

That's not going to work, the other girl said. *Not this time.*

The force of the twin screams caused Jillybean to fall over onto her side on the dusty tile. "What did you do to her?" she asked. She was half in control of her body and half in the strange blackness that would soon bury her. It was a crossover transitional phase and, for just a second, she saw a scene that was part-memory and part hazy horror: *A little girl, who was skin and bones, with knobby knees and hair that hadn't seen the pokey end of a brush in days, stood in the back of a darkened truck.*

In the gloom was a bundle of blankets and on them was an infant. The baby was naked save for a diaper; her arms and legs splayed and flung, her hair was damp with sweat. The back of the truck was hot and windless. The baby was thirsty.

The little girl knelt and placed a bottle between the baby's tiny lips. Instinctually, the infant began sucking, as her eyes rolled like marbles in their sockets; a moment later those eyes flicked open and she pulled back from the bottle. It tasted funny. It wasn't normal. After a pause, the little girl tried again, placing the bottle in the baby's mouth.

"Go on you stupid shit-fart," the little girl crooned in sing-song. She was smiling and the baby knew the smile and trusted the girl. The baby was stupid and the baby died.

Horrified, Jillybean felt the frog-puking sensation begin in the back of her throat, however it was distant and soon wouldn't be a problem. She was slipping away, slipping into the blackness of her mind. The one word question: *Why* was first on her lips but she cast it away. She knew why. The other girl was evil—pain and unhappiness was all she knew.

Instead, Jillybean asked: "What did you...*put in her bottle?* In mid-sentence she slipped away from her body and her question became a lone echo that faded like smoke from a candle.

There was laughter in the darkness, an evil snigger, and then the words: "That's for me to know and you to find out," were spoken in her mind and maybe into the real

216

air up above. Jillybean's essence drifted down into the blackness of her mind where she knew she would be engulfed so completely that she and the black would fuse into one until she ceased to be. In truth, it was a comforting feeling, like dying in your sleep. Whenever *she* took control, Jillybean would slip into the cocoon of darkness where she didn't have to know or think.

It was better than the alternatives: there was *up* where she could both see and feel the hate and the insanity of the other girl, or there was *down* where the memories waited to destroy her completely.

Yes, it was better snugged in the nothingness of in-between...however, Jillybean was supposed to be finding things out. Things that would save Deanna and Neil and the others. She fought the closing blackness. It wasn't a heroic fight by any means. She spazzed in fear, kicking and screaming until she could see the twin lamps of her eyes above and the silver lines descending into the blackness below.

With all her heart she wanted to go to the eyes and see where she was and hear the evil lies the other girl was telling, and yet that would be a waste of time and she didn't think they had all that much time to waste. Still she hesitated. The lies and the evil girl were far preferable to what waited down in the black. She dithered, stuck by fear and a sense of duty.

She knew that if Ipes was still around he would have told her to: *focus and stay on track*. Captain Grey would have said: *be brave*, Neil would have said: *I trust you*. Sadie would have said: *I wish I could go with you and share the adventure*, and Deanna...Deanna couldn't say anything.

That was why Jillybean was here. She was supposed to be finding out what happened to Deanna...but how? Where was she supposed to look, exactly? And what if the other girl didn't know anything?

What if...the memory of the Duke's spindly cook suddenly came to her. Memories pulled up from the subconscious by a normal waking person are never distinct.

They are target focused with everything in the periphery hazy with unimportance.

The memory feed straight from the subconscious is far different.

The spindly cook was a giant and the knife he wielded was longer than any sword. The smell of the onions on the chopping block was sharp, making Jillybean's face warp, while the cook's mumblings were loud as though he were speaking into a bullhorn: *He wants steak at ten o'clock, so he gets steak at ten o'clock. Steak and taters and asparagus and wine. He's going to get fat is what will happen. He will be a fatty-fatso, but not me. No, not me. Never gonna be fat again. No one likes a fatty-fatso.*

Jillybean tried to hide from the monstrous cook and to her surprise, the angle at which she saw the cook, changed; she really was hiding. There was a sofa the size of a van that she slunk behind and there were gum wads as large as pumpkins hanging from the back of it. The gum was strangely swirled like cold magma only on each was a flat space and there were thumb prints bigger than dinner plates on them. The detail was fascinating.

She found herself staring and then came a rumbling beneath her Keds—someone was coming. It was the Duke! He was even bigger than the cook. His head reached almost to the ceiling and the ceiling was high enough to fit a normal house beneath it! *I must have her*, he cried and Jillybean cringed from the booming sound. His face was flushed with a greedy desire.

The pretty one? the cook asked.

Of course, the pretty one. She fascinates me and I don't know why. You have to help me. I need to separate her from the others. I need her alone on a more permanent basis. And...and there is another issue, I need you to take care of. She's pregnant.

The cook didn't bat an eye, though he made a face of disgust as if women with babies coming out of them were physically repulsive. *I have what you need on both counts and one will mask the other,* he said and then went to a drawer and started placing pill bottles on the counter, mut-

218

tering over each one. Finally, he grinned and dug out a handful of blue pills only they were too big for even a lion to swallow.

What is it? the Duke asked.

You don't need to know. The wicked grin on the cook's face made even the Duke look hesitant. The cook only shrugged and scrounged for another bottle. *I'll just crush up a teaspoon of this in her milk or mashed potatoes or something and you'll have this woman for yourself.*

The Duke came closer to look at the pills. *And the pregnancy?*

The blue pills are Day After pills. They'll flush everything right out of her. Five times the recommended dose should do the trick. And the white pills are morphine, enough to knock her out but not enough to kill her and I have more that you can put in some IVs. Unless there's someone with a good deal of medical knowledge they'll think the 'miscarriage' will be the cause of her sudden very deep sleep. Your beauty isn't going anywhere.

Excellent! the Duke cried, clapping his hands together. *Make it happen.*

A second later he had turned on his heel and left. Once again the cook went to mumbling only this time Jillybean didn't listen. Her mind was wrapped around the idea that Deanna was pregnant. That's what meant there was a baby inside her stomach. And the Duke wanted to "end" the pregnancy. That's what meant he wanted to kill the baby.

It was a horrible thought and it was also the last one she had of that memory. The other girl woke up to the possibilities of the baby-killing drugs and *she* swamped Jilly's mind. Jillybean could only watch as a spectator as the cook drugged Deanna's food, covered the dishes and left. Then she saw herself dart forward. The other girl was torn between the left over mashed potatoes and the bottle of pills.

The potatoes won out. She scooped three large spoonfuls into her mouth, groaning lustily with each bite. It was with difficulty that she put the spoon down and grabbed the first bottle—the one that had held the blue pills, only it was empty. With a curse, she put it aside and grabbed the white pills. *How many will kill a big baby*? she had asked aloud. There was a drawer open beside the refrigerator; in it was aluminum foil, gallon-sized ziplock bags and smaller sandwich bags. She grabbed a sandwich bag and poured seven of the morphine pills into it.

Now for a bottle, she said.

"No!" Jillybean screamed, trying to pull away from the memory. Watching, as someone who looked exactly like herself killed a beautiful baby, was too terrible to contemplate. She closed her eyes and beat herself on the side of the head with the flat of her hand until she was dizzy. Slowly, she cracked an eye to find herself in the darkness once again. The memory was gone. A sigh of relief escaped her. The relief lasted only a second. It was very scary in the dark, much scarier than before; something had changed. There were moans coming out of nowhere, and screams that were short and sharp and loud like lightning.

She hurried away from the screams.

Sometimes, she saw the ghosts of people in the dark. They were translucent and looked to be made of collected steam. They would drift past, causing Jillybean to freeze in place with a scream on her lips. And then she began passing doors with little signs next to them, but all the signs were blank. There were lots of these doors; not a one of them was she brave enough to open. They reminded her of something but what exactly she didn't know. And the floor, a dirty white tile, was also familiar.

When she paused to look around, she found herself in the dim hallway of a building. It reminded her of a school and, when she reached the end of the hall, and saw two double doors that shook as something gigantic pounded on them, she knew exactly which school. Jillybean was in the school where she had first discovered Ram tied to a tetherball pole.

Going into Jilly-Mouse mode, she backed away from the door, creeping quieter than any whisper. Behind her the double doors faded into the gloom, however the sound of the hammering fists grew into a thunder of tins drums which built into a crescendo and then stopped. There was a metal on metal *clunk* and then a long *creeeeik*—the doors had opened!

Jillybean didn't look back; she blazed back down the hall with her legs turning strange, dream-like circles. Behind her came the hideous thing that had been trapped in the gym. She ran from it as fast as she could, on and on, for miles it seemed, before she got to the door to the outside. The same orange-backed plastic chair propped it open, however now the gap between the door and the jamb was barely a foot wide and as she climbed on the chair the door started to close on her.

"No!!!" she screeched.

Insane terror—terror like she could never remember back in the real world—threw her into a panic. Kicking, screaming, clawing, she fought her way through the gap and instead of finding herself outside in the school playground, she found herself in a darkened stairwell. There was an eerie white glow like that thrown down by a full moon, but otherwise everything was dim. The stairs went down, disappearing into a frightful, murky soup of shadows.

She had no choice but to follow the stairs down. At first she went tentatively, with her hand on a railing but when the door above was assaulted by the monster chasing her, she began to shuffle down more quickly. She came to a landing seconds later. There was another door and next to the door was a little plaque. It was blank. The door was as horrifying as the monster. There were whispers coming from behind the door...begging whispers. Someone was dying just inches away on the other side of the metal.

Again Jillybean backed away. She continued down the stairs and, again, came to a door. It was identical to the first, only the sound coming from it was different. There was a rushing and a crackling and then screams. An explosion made the metal of the door shudder and heat shimmered at its edges. Jillybean ran.

Down she went, passing door after door, not pausing even for a second to listen at any of them. The darkness grew with each step and so it was she didn't see the obstacle on the stairs until she was right on it and it was too late to stop. Wood barked her knees and she tumbled across the obstacle, landing on the stairs on the other side.

Dazed, but not hurt, she pushed herself up and explored the wooden thing with her hands. In spite of the fact that it was so dark, she knew what it was. It was a desk. In fact it was the very same desk she had hid beneath when she saved Ram from Cassie's guards. She ran her hands over it in the dark, remembering the nicks on the wood, the cool flat top, the hollowed area where she had curled up after she had set her magic marble in motion.

A part of her wanted to curl up and hide once again. She even rested her soft cheek on the cool desk. Then she heard the sound of shoes clicking on the stairs above. It was *the thing* after her again! She fled, but her steps were slowed by a memory: the ferocious giant from the school gym had been naked and yet what she heard now was the patter of shoes like a business man might wear, hitting concrete. The fast heel-to-toe clatter, which sounded oddly familiar, was coming closer and closer to her.

A shudder ran up her body making her muscles go weak. Jillybean forced her feet downward where the pale light gave out and all was black. She began leaping down the stairs, each time trusting that there would be concrete at the bottom. Still the shoes came closer and closer.

Jillybean began blubbering as she tried to go faster. Then the stairs ran out and she found herself in a concrete maze. The floors were white and clean; above were evenly spaced light fixtures. Everything was perfect; everything was evil. She knew where she was: New Eden...except where were the bodies and the fire and the zombies. She had destroyed New Eden with a zombie army, only now there was no sign of the destruction.

That's because you never saw the death you caused, a voice explained. *This is the New Eden in your mind.*

The little girl spun around; there was no one behind her. Only the stairwell was behind her and the tapping shoes as they hurried to get her.

Again she ran. Just as in the real New Eden, there were corridors branching everywhere, however these corridors ended in doors and next to each was a plaque. The sight of them sapped her strength yet she ran, knowing that she would have to go into one eventually. The man with the shoes was relentless. He was closer now and when Jillybean turned down a long hall she was able to look back and see he wasn't a man at all.

He was a monster, one of the zombie-monsters.

A scream burned past the blubbering and rushed out of her throat. Blindly she went for one of the doors. She was out of options. It was either a door to who-knew what or turn and face the monster. The doors seemed less frightening, especially the one closest. It was dark and quiet around the edges, in fact there was a coolness whisping toward her tear-streaked face.

Jillybean grabbed the handle and rushed through, slamming it in the monster's face. It had been a zombie monster and one that, like everything else in this strange world, was familiar, terribly familiar. The closed door stopped him cold. There wasn't a sound coming from it, not a moan or a tap of shoes or any of the awful banging.

The only sound came from behind her. When Jillybean turned she saw that she was in a forest at night and far away there were screams and muffled gunshots. At first she didn't know where she was, or when, for that matter. Then she was aware of movement to her right. It was a dark thing, like one of the monsters. The odor wafting off of it was the sickening smell of burnt hair and charred flesh. It was Sarah.

She was lurching along and behind her, darting through the night forest like a sly mongoose was... "It's me," Jillybean said.

Jillybean stared at herself in amazement and also with longing. Under her arm was Ipes. Oh, how she missed and needed Ipes. She stared at the little toy until a voice had her swinging her head around.

"Drop the gun." A man was in the forest with them—it was the bounty hunter! Even with the dark, Jillybean saw him clear as day. The cold eyes, the steady gun hand, the growth of beard; she was so close she could count the pores on his nose if she wished. She was about to kill him. He didn't know it yet, but he was seconds away from dying...and, so too, was Sarah.

The little girl tried to scream a warning, but not even the sound of her breath could be heard.

"Sarah Rivers," the bounty hunter pronounced in a voice as dry as dirt. "And Jillybean. You got the baby. Very impressive."

"You can't have her!" Sarah hissed.

"I can have anything I want and what I want now is Sadie Walcott. Where is she?"

Jillybean saw it all playing out before her: they'd waste the last precious seconds of their lives going back and forth uselessly talking and then would come the murders. In seconds Jillybean would be staring into the hole in the bounty hunter's skull. There would be a tunnel rimmed with blood, with walls of scorched brain. Before, when it was dark and hard to see, the sight of it had driven her into a catatonic state. What would happen to her now when every horrific detail was blown out of proportion? Would she fall straight into a coma like Deanna was in? If so, what would happen to her when the monster with the tapping shoes found her?

She wasn't going to wait around to find out. Terror had her by the heart, and she fled from the murders. The forest grew wild and thick so that she hadn't gone far when Sarah was murdered. Jillybean stopped as sadness took her breath and crumpled its spiky fist around her heart. She stopped for only a moment. What was coming next was far worse. She was on the verge of murder and she was dreadfully afraid that she would feel the amplified sensation of carnal joy at killing that rat-bastard. That exciting sensation had been there, inside of her and now the entire world was going to know that part of her had enjoyed the feeling of power that had come with the murder.

There had been lust buried in her heart. When she killed she was no longer the helpless little girl who cowered and cried and needed grode-ups to feed her and care for her and keep her safe. She was powerful when she killed, and she secretly liked it.

The first gunshot sounded and Jillybean whined and clawed more desperately at the foliage, practically swimming among the grasping vines and supple branches. IT would happen any moment and the world would know. She was so frantic that when her hand came down on a doorknob, she thought nothing of it and pulled.

She found herself back on the stairs. Above her was the desk squatting like a flat-backed turtle in the dark. It had grown immense; the scarred edge of it was now a cliff rising high above her. Below her were inky shadows. They looked thick and deep, like the ocean on a moonless night. She knew the shadows would engulf her completely, but with no other choices she started down, one step at a time. First her worn Keds slipped beneath the shadows and disappeared and then her bruised-up shins and her knobby knees.

Cautiously she swam her hand in the shadows; they were cool to the touch and otherwise harmless. She went down until the black covered her head and she was blind. Her splayed hands wove patterns in front of her to keep her from running into anything, only there wasn't anything to hit. She went down the stairs, oh so slowly, until she reached a landing and her foot struck something soft but unyielding.

Reaching down she felt around, puzzling out what was on the landing. It was mushy with something hard beneath—it was a face! Jillybean pulled her hand back, afraid that she was feeling one of the monsters, only there was no moan, and no movement of the thing at her feet, and it didn't have the rotten garbage smell of the monsters.

"I should see if whoever it is, is alive," she whispered, trying to talk herself into the action. She didn't really think someone was just sleeping down there in the dark, however, she was desperate to find a friend in this weird world. "Hey. Hey you," she said, giving the body a poke. Silence greeted her. A second time she reached out, this time to give the body a shake because she knew that sometimes a person needed that sort of thing to wake them.

Her hand felt something odd, something soft, meshy, and faintly oily. Careful as always, Jillybean pulled back and then tentatively explored the substance. It was hair! Not her kind of hair but hair from a black person. She had never known many black people—Chris and Amber in school; and Donna, Steve and the fellow with the U shaped afro from back in Philadelphia, and there was Ms Shondra who had become a Believer. That was about it except...

The memory came to her in a snap.

She had been on these very stairs, hiding beneath the desk waiting for the magic marble to drop. There had been two people with Ram—they had been black and one had been a woman. She had fallen...or had she been pushed? Jillybean couldn't remember; she had run at the woman with a black sweater held out and there had been an explosion and a flash of blinding light and then...

"She died," Jillybean whispered. "I didn't know...I didn't mean it." The little girl pulled her hands back and clutched them to her chest. She was kneeling before the body of a woman she had killed. Her fingers were entwined and, had there been light, it would have looked like she was praying over the woman. She held the position for a few seconds until guilt had her scrambling back up the stairs.

"It wasn't my fault." She pleaded with the dark as she ran for the door. At the handle, she paused afraid of what was on the other side: the bounty hunter's murder. That seemed far worse than the accidental death of the poor black lady and Jillybean hesitated, uncertain which way to go. It was then she heard a sound from the bottom of the stairs where everything was black and there wasn't even the pale, silver light of the moon to see by.

At first she thought it was the dead coming back to life to have their revenge on her, only just then she heard the clack of shoes on the stairs. Right away she threw the door open and ran into the forest, only the forest was gone and she was in a large room with cages lining the walls

226

and only a narrow walkway between—this was the River King's jails. The cages were filled with people she didn't recognize. She couldn't recognize them, because they were all faceless. They were blank entities. Unknowns.

"You killed me," the first said to her.

"I-I don't th-think so," she stammered. "I don't know you."

It reached for her through the bars, its long arms ending at blackened fingers. "You killed me," it repeated. "On the ferry boat. There was an explosion and a piece of metal went into my back. It cut my spinal cord and I was paralyzed. I could only watch as the fire came closer. It began to cook me and I could only scream. First my feet and then legs, but the worst, was when my hair caught on fire and my eyes melted."

Again Jillybean could only sputter: "I-I d-din't mean it. I-I was j-just trying t-to help my friend." Slowly she moved away from it. Then, from behind her, the door she had just come through opened with a long dreadful *creeeeak*.

With her face cringing and her eyes popping tears, Jillybean rushed away down the narrow corridor between the cells, holding her arms in to keep them from being grabbed by the grasping hands. She passed a dozen cells on either side and only the last one on the left sat alone and empty.

Behind her was the clacking of the shoes. It came on steadily, without hurry. He would get her, eventually, she knew that, however her eyes were drawn to the cell and she paused in front of it, wondering why it was vacant. In all this crazy world it was the one thing that didn't fit and the spare empty room gave her a sinking feeling in her stomach as she looked into it.

There was something wrong with the cell. It shouldn't have been empty and it had a trappy feel to it. So she ran past it to a real door at the end of the long room.

It had an empty plaque next to it. The knob was gold and when Jillybean reached a shaking hand to it the metal was warm to the point of being hot. "It's the ferry boat on the other side, isn't it?" She could picture the boat roaring in flames, shuddering from explosions and tilting as it began to sink. Would she find Ram on the deck, chained by the neck and grey and yucky as all the monsters were? Or would she see the people she had killed, trapped below the waterline, crying helplessly as the water rose on one hand and the heat cooked them alive like a chicken in an oven on the other.

Horrible visions swept her imagination and yet she still found herself turning the gold knob. As she did, excuses started sprouting in her mind as to why she had sunk the boat—she had a million good reasons, but underlying each was the fact that a part of her wondered what a sinking boat would look like. She'd had a queer desire to light a fire, one that was bigger than any bonfire imaginable. That desire was wholly primal and imprinted into her subconscious as it was in nearly every thinking being yet there was a tremendous sense of guilt that came along with it.

It turned out not to be the ferry in front of her, nor was it the bridge going up in two thunderous explosions, nor was it the barge disappearing in a huge fireball and a concussive aftershock that turned her brain practically inside out. And nor was it the white hot blast from the fuel tank in front of the hangar where a thousand monsters were converging on Mister Neil and Sadie.

The heat of the doorknob made no sense because the door opened onto a quiet Missouri afternoon. Across from her was the rail of a small bridge and there was Ernest and herself looking so tiny compared to him. There in Ernest's left hand was Ipes. Even as she watched he started to simultaneously fling the toy zebra and pull his pistol. Jillybean saw her own face morph into one she hardly recognized. Gone were the fear and the heart-wrenching pain that had played across her small features contorting them in misery. In their place was the anticipation of victory, of blood and of triumph, twerking her features into an expression of unholy glee.

Down in the abysmal world of horror and black, Jillybean slammed the door closed before her other self could pull the trigger and before she could watch Ipes, her truest friend, sail off forever leaving her so alone that a part of her great heart withered into a seed of blackest evil.

Jillybean put her back to the door, her breath coming hard and fast. She was back in the room with the cages and the dead hands reaching through the bars, and the steady clip-clip of the shoes and the coming thing that was only slightly less horrible than the bridge.

He was coming closer and closer, but only his black, patent leather shoes were precise in their details. Shining like there was a light in them, they were as glossy as a new car right off the lot. They were size eleven men's—she knew those shoes and she knew who they belonged to.

Her stomach dropped and she ran for the empty cell. With what was coming it was only just and right that she slammed the gated door, locking the door forever, because she knew that the ultimate judge was now upon her. She backed as far from the bars as she could.

He had come.

"I'm sorry daddy. Don't be mad at me, please, please, please. Forgive me."

Her father, his eyes red with fever and pain, his skin pale but with a tinge of grey, his cologne fading, almost engulfed by the rotten smell, stood at the bars, glaring down at her with a look of ultimate disappointment. "That's not up to me," he said in the raspy voice he used right before he left to die. "I don't forgive."

Chapter 21

Neil Martin

The two men waited in the principal's office, both as silent as the girl between them. Neil found himself staring at Deanna's profile; she had a tall nose. It wasn't big, just simply tall. It was regal in its way. He could imagine her with a queen's crown upon her head and looking down her tall nose at him.

Why did you fail me? She would ask. *Why did you let me die?*

Deanna would be the ninth person to die under his watch. Nico had been the first, then Neil's beloved Sarah —his chest still felt like there was a lump of stone beneath his breastbone whenever he thought of her—then Big Jim had been shot full of holes, Lindsey had been killed by Sadie, Arlene had slit her own throat and then there was Melanie, who Neil had put out of her misery.

Then there was the child Deanna had been carrying. She might have been just a fetus, but she was a human fetus. She had been a baby, a *person* in an early stage of development with a future and a life. She was supposed to bring joy and laughter, and sometimes frustration or tears. She was supposed to live.

Neil had never understood the entire abortion issue. One woman, who wanted the little thing that was growing in her, called it a baby, while another woman, who didn't want the little thing growing in her, called it just a mass of tissue; they both couldn't be correct. Neil knew that the tissue mass was indeed human because, given enough time, it was always a baby.

And now there was Eve—another abortion, this one simply later than most. Somebody didn't 'want' her and so she'd been killed, just like that. His mind was full of static when he thought of Eve. He almost couldn't grasp that she was dead and he was afraid of what he would do when he finally allowed himself to come to grips with the fact.

Deep inside of him there was heavy, stony, uncaring desire for revenge. He wanted to hurt someone. Jillybean's face flashed before his eyes, but he wouldn't hurt her even if she had killed Eve because he considered the little girl to be just as much a victim. No, he wanted to hurt those who had hurt him and those who posed a future threat to him and the whole group. Although there were many who fit that bill, Duke Menis was first on the current list. Captain Grey's idea of holding the man at gunpoint had a certain desirable quality to it; Neil would have the opportunity to spit in the man's eye.

"This is taking too long," Grey said. "Go check on her, will you?"

"Sure." Neil stepped out into the admin area of the school and stared around. Jillybean wasn't in sight. "Aw, jeeze," he whispered, feeling a pain in his gut. With the other girl in her, there was no knowing what sort of mischief she could be up to.

He was hurrying for the hall that led to the main part of the school, when something to his right caught his eye; it was a thin little leg in pink jeans sticking out from behind a desk. "Jillybean," Neil said, sharply. He started towards her but the silence of the room, coupled with the fact that the leg hadn't moved even a hair made him suddenly nervous. An insidious thought wormed its way into his mind: *she's dead, just like Eve and just like Deanne will be, as well*

"Jillybean!" he said, louder, and now his feet scurried forward at a trot.

The little girl was lying on her back with her eyes closed. Someone else might have thought she was only sleeping, Neil knew better. The little girl had survived since the apocalypse by living life as if she were a coiled spring; she would've reacted. "Hey, Jillybean, are you ok?" he asked giving her shoulder a little shake. She didn't move and her eyes remained closed.

Neil felt her face, it was cool and dry. "Come on, Jillybean," he hissed, growing desperate. He tried to find a pulse in her tiny wrist, however he wasn't an expert in anatomy and his fumbling fingers felt only the thin tendons running from her forearm down into her hand. He cursed and then dropped and put his ear to her chest.

Her heart was loud and much faster than he had anticipated. Was a fast heart rate good or bad? Neil didn't know, but Grey would. He scooped up the girl, saddened that she was so light; she should've been a bit of a struggle for the small man to hoist up. However she hadn't been eating well, none of them had in fact.

"Grey!" Neil said as he barged back into the principal's office. "It's Jillybean, she's not responding. I can't get her to wake up."

Neil laid Jillybean on the blue shag and watched as Grey pulled back her eyelids, checked her pulse, listened to her chest with a stethoscope and then took the knuckle of his index finger and gouged at her chest, yelling: "Jillybean! Wake up!"

Then he leaned back from her for a second. Neil thought he was going to give up, but Grey was only just beginning. He opened her mouth and inspected her tongue and gums, going so far as to put his nose almost in her mouth as he sniffed. What he was sniffing for, Neil didn't have a clue.

Next, Grey rolled up her sleeves and traced her veins from her hand to the pit of her arm. He then checked her neck and behind her ears. When that proved void of results, he undressed her and inspected her legs, chest, pelvis, and, much to Neil's embarrassment, a two second visual check of her vagina.

"I don't know what this is," Grey said, as he redressed her. "She hasn't been drugged, at least not with a needle and she hasn't overdosed on anything. She hasn't suffered a blow to the head." He looked back and forth from the tiny girl to the woman he loved, his face growing more and more grim as he did. Finally he asked: "What the hell is going on?"

Strangely, the fact that Jillybean was now comatose had Neil almost in a panic. If *they* could get to her, he felt that no one was safe. "So what do we do?" he asked, hoping to God that Captain Grey had an answer.

Grey stared down at the child for a few more seconds before he shrugged and said: "Monitor her just like we are Deanna. There's not much more we can do for her with the limited supplies we have."

"And the attack?" Neil asked. "Is that still on?"

"It has to be. We're racking up bodies left and right here, Neil." Grey stood, his eyes first on the little girl and then on Deanna. He then went to the window and inched back the curtain. When he turned again to Neil his face was rock hard. "We need to consolidate all of our people in the gym. No one should go anywhere without a buddy and the only place they should be going is to the bathroom. I want Marybeth and her daughter, what's her name? Amanda? Either way, I want those two watching over Deanna and Jillybean. I trust Marybeth."

"I do too, but..." Neil started to say, only Grey held up a finger.

"I wasn't done. Next I want all the men to meet me here when I get back. Wait, not Fred Trigg. That guy's a waste of oxygen. I'll take Joe Gates, instead. He may be young, but he's tough. Of the women I want Sadie, Veronica, Kay, and Connie. They're about the only ones that can hit the broad side of a barn with a gun."

Neil, who could only hit a barn if he was up close to it asked: "What about me?"

Grey snorted. "Of course you, unless you've changed your mind about busting out of here." Neil shook his head and Grey said: "Good. I'm going to do a recon of the area. We are completely in the dark here and if we have any chance of escaping, we'll need to know what the Duke is up to. If I'm not back in two hours, fear the worst." Wearing a grin at Neil's startled expression, the soldier swept out of the room moving with the stealth and grace of a jungle cat.

The smaller man already feared the worst. They were in a lion's den, surrounded by enemies with more coming in every hour and Grey was suggesting a gun battle as the answer to their problems. Neil went to the window and looked out; the Duke's men were still in place, while a fourth person had joined the little group sitting under the oak down the street.

He thought for a moment about Jillybean and her desire to get a hold of some bombs. Did she have a plan, or were explosions just her fallback position for every emergency? With her zonked out there was no way to know. Neil couldn't see how a bomb would help. The Duke's men were too spread out for a single bomb to make any difference. They needed a tank, but all they had was one Rambo-esque super soldier and a bunch of suburban survivors.

Neil gathered the group of renegades in the gym. He sent out two teams to fetch Jillybean and Deanna. When the renegades saw that Jillybean was unconscious as well, a fear-babble commenced. He didn't blame them. It felt as though something evil was in their presence, something stalking them. He had thought it was Jillybean and her alter-ego but with her in the same state as Deanna, Neil had to cast his suspicions elsewhere. The problem was that the renegades were an open book; he could see that they were all quite obviously and truthfully afraid.

The answer to what was stalking them lay elsewhere.

"Quiet down!" Neil said, raising his voice. "First off, we don't know what's…"

Fred Trigg interrupted suddenly, demanding: "Where's Captain Grey. What does he have to say about what's wrong with her."

There was that waste of oxygen that Grey had referred to, Neil thought. "He doesn't know either….and we have a worse problem than Jillybean. It seems that one of you has spilled the beans to the Duke about who we are."

There was an immediate uproar with everyone demanding to know who the culprit was. Neil hissed them into silence and then said: "We don't know and for now, it doesn't matter who talked. We'll figure it out eventually and when we do that person will be dealt with. That said, right now we have to deal with the repercussions. The Duke has been bringing in more men all day and we suspect that he will attack at dawn."

Sadie raised her hand and when Neil gestured to her, she said: "He won't attack, not unless he has to. He'll surround us with enough men that we'll just have to give up without a fight."

"Possibly," Neil acknowledged, "however, we do intend to fight."

Michael Gates also raised his hand. "But we don't have near enough guns or ammo. And there aren't any real fighters among us, except Captain Grey, that is."

Some of the cage fighters who had been rescued from Gunner bristled over this, and yet the truth was, there wasn't a soldier among them. The closest was Ricky who had hunted a few times back before the apocalypse had struck. He was a fair shot with his rifle, but he had no experience when it came to someone shooting back at him.

"Regardless," Neil said. "The plan is to fight our way out. It's our best chance at escape. So, I'm going to need Sadie, Veronica, Kay, and Connie as well as all the men, including you, Joe to come with me." Ten-year-old Joe Gates eyes bugged wide and he stepped back at first, looking like he was about to run away but, quicker than Fred Trigg, he collected himself and marched along with the other members of the Gates family: Michael Gates, his brother William, William's son Cody and his nephew, John who was fifteen but always huddled with the men as if he were indeed part of the men's team.

Altogether, including Joe Gates and the four women, there were twenty-one people in the group. Neil cut it down to twenty. "Oh, sorry Fred. We need you to stay and look after the uh, the, uh, school." Fred huffed a little, however everyone saw the relief in his eyes as he started to turn away. Neil stopped him. "And I need your gun. In fact, round up all the guns, will you?"

"Wait, no," Fred said, planting his fussy hands on his hips. "How am I supposed to defend myself, uh, I mean, the school without a gun?"

Neil's face, scarred as it was, showed complete indifference. "I'm sure you'll figure something out. Maybe sticks? I don't really care. I just want the guns and the ammo for the fighters."

"I'm sorry, but Joe is not a fighter," Michael grumbled, showing his concern by the depth of the creases in his forehead. "He's only ten and I'm sure most of the other women can shoot as well if not better than he can. I don't mean to be a jerk, Joe, but it's true."

"And we aren't fighters either," Veronica said, gesturing to the other women who stood grouped close to each other, all, that is, except for Sadie who stood apart from everyone. The teen had an odd look about her. To Neil, she seemed apathetic as if she figured she would die in the coming battle and that it was ok with her. She was pale and cold, looking like the killer she feared that she had become.

As horrible as the look was, Neil preferred it to how most everyone else appeared: scared shitless.

Neil had to change those looks in a hurry. "All I know is that Captain Grey asked for every one of you especially. Really, you all should be flattered. Bear in mind that he knows your strengths and weakness; he's not going to ask you to do more than you can handle. We need to trust him and we need to trust each other."

Sadie took a step forward and cleared her throat, just as Neil frequently did before making an announcement. "Captain Grey has got us this far," she said. "Him and Neil have brought us through fire and battle and zombie hordes and everything else that God has thrown our way, so you all need to try to relax and follow his instructions."

Relaxing was wishful thinking. The renegades as a group, had yet to be truly tested in a straight up battle, and they all knew they wouldn't get away from the Duke without a hard fight. They were jittery and wore their fear openly. The group sat in the darkening gym, nervously smoking, or pacing or cleaning weapons that were already so clean as to be practically sterile or they checked their ammo that had been re-triple checked more than once.

They were afraid because it was one thing to mow down slow moving zombies, it was another thing altogether to trade shots with an armed enemy. Grey, Neil, and Sadie of course had been in their share of gun battles. Of the rest, only Michael Gates, his brother William, and Connie had been blooded in actual battle, although, in each case, the battles had been brief. Michael and William had fired a few long distance shots at Gunner's men back at the Piggly Wiggly in Warrior, Alabama.

Interestingly, the only one of the group outside of Sadie and Neil with any real experience was Connie Markson. The erstwhile ex-whore had fought side-by-side with Deanna and had more than held her own fighting one of the Colonel's squads from the Island during the battle at the church.

The sun was long set and still there was no sign of Captain Grey. Neil checked his watch again and again. That was his nervous tic. Grey had said he'd be back in two hours and on Neil's thirteenth check of his watch it had been one hour and fifty three minutes. "Jeeze-lou-eeze," he whispered, looking towards the gym doors.

He jumped slightly when he saw a shadow moving toward him. Relief washed over him until he saw that the shadow wasn't big enough to be Grey's. It was Tiffany, one of the women from The Island. In the murk of the gym she glanced around at the "strike team" as Neil had taken to calling them in an effort to instill in them a fighting spirit. The way she eyed the chain-smokers and the pacers, it was clear she wasn't unimpressed with them as a fighting force.

"Hey, I want to let you know that all the women voted and we're not going out to pee unless we have some guns. There are a whole butt-load of zombies walking around this town and a stray might come up here anytime."

Neil understood. No one liked the idea of getting caught, like Melanie had been with her pants around her ankles, but on the other hand, he didn't like the idea of giving up even a single gun. He compromised and pulled out the .25 caliber pistol he had retrieved from Joslyn. "This may be small but a head shot will bring one of them down. Just don't miss."

Tiffany eyed the tiny gun but didn't take it. "You got to be kidding. That thing couldn't kill a badger."

"Wrong," Neil said. "This is the gun that killed Ernest and if a seven-year-old can kill a bounty hunter with it, then you can kill a zombie. It's either this or you take a stick out with you."

"Can we at least have some of the men act as armed escorts?" she asked. "I'd feel better with a bit more protection."

Neil checked his watch a fourteenth time and sighed for the thirtieth. "No, sorry. We need to be here for when Grey gets back." He expected Grey to jump into his plan with both feet and he didn't want to have to run around the school searching for the "strike team" when the captain got back. "You'll be fine, Tiffany. We've cleared the school and all the grounds already. There's nothing near us that will hurt you."

In the dark, Tiffany expressed her dissatisfaction by letting out a long, loud breath. "Fine," was all she said before grabbing the gun and stomping away, her feet thudding in a hollow manner along the gym floor.

"Maybe we should…" Michael Gates started to say.

Neil cut him off: "We'll stay here." His voice was harsh and commanding. "Those were the captain's orders. I'm sorry, but the women can take care of themselves. We have to be ready to go at a moment's notice."

This ended any conversation and the group sat in an uncomfortable silence until Captain Grey suddenly materialized before them a few minutes later. "Everyone here?" he asked Neil.

The smaller man jumped and, if his gun hadn't been set to 'Safe,' he would've shot the gym floor full of holes. "Dang! Yeah, we're here. Jeeze, you scared the crap out of me."

"Uh-huh," Grey said, simply. He took out a small mag-lite, twisted it to the 'on' position, and then stuck it between his teeth. Next, he unrolled a scroll of paper about two feet square which he laid on the wooden floor and set full magazines on each corner. The paper was pure white.

He took the mag-lite from his teeth, blew out wearily, and said: "Alright," and then blinded each of them in turn. When the light struck Neil, he couldn't see anything but the brilliance of the beam and yet he felt himself being judged by the veteran soldier and he tried to stand straighter. Grey's own features were shrouded by the dark. He looked like a figure carved from granite and there was no telling what he was feeling, except Neil knew there wasn't an ounce of fear in the man.

"Alright," Grey said, again, after he had inspected his troops. "Hopefully Neil has filled you in on the situation. If not let me sum up where we are: we're surrounded, the Duke knows who we are and he plans on attacking at some point tomorrow morning. Any questions so far?"

Kay raised a shaking hand. "Are we going to have to fight?"

"Our choices are simple. We can put our fates into the Duke's hands hoping that he will throw away an opportunity to make a ton of money and cement positive relations with two of his most powerful neighbors, or," Grey's voice was deadly serious, "Or we can assume that the thirty five men he's surrounded us with are here to kill us if we try to escape and that, by morning, he'll have enough men to storm the school or starve us until we come out, voluntarily."

"There's thirty five of them?" one of the ex-cage-fighters exclaimed. A fearful whispering started among the crowd around Grey, and after a few seconds it grew in volume.

"Thirty five is too many." In the dark Neil couldn't tell which of them was speaking in the high tone of fear, but it was either Kay or Veronica.

Grey splashed the light in the direction of the group of women and they all shied back from it as though it could hurt them. "I think we need to look at this in a positive manner," he said. "The number of men out there cements the intelligence we received. It means the Duke indeed knows who we are so if any of you have doubts about fighting, you need to think again. Be aware of this: If you are captured, the cage fighters will be sent back to die in the arena and you ladies will either be sent back to the Colonel or be auctioned off to the highest bidder."

"That's positive?" Sadie asked. "I must be missing something."

A grimace flashed across Grey's face as he growled: "Yes, it's very positive. For one, we are forewarned of what's to come and for two, the Duke has foolishly shown his hand well before all of his forces are here. Really, we should be happy it's only thirty five men out there. Thirty five is a number I think we can handle. Any more and I wouldn't like our chances."

"You like our chances now?" Neil asked, incredulously. His stomach had dropped when Grey said: "Thirty five." The renegades were outnumbered and outgunned. They were cornered in a school that was trapped in an encircled town that sat in the middle of a vast land filled with enemies. What was there to like?

"Actually yes," Grey answered, giving Neil a sharp look—a look that said: *Shut up, if you're not going to be helpful.* "Yes, our chances are good. We have surprise on our side and remember, we don't have to actually kill all of them or storm the courthouse in order to win. Our objective is escape. Here, let me show you."

Handing the mag-lite to Neil, he dug in a cargo pocket for a marker and drew a large egg-shaped oval on the white paper. "This is the town, and running right through it is the highway." He drew the road as a line dissecting the oval length wise. He then drew the school and across the street from it the block of houses. He then drew four 'X's, two of them on the street on either side of the school and two more behind the school.

"The 'X's are groups of the Duke's men," Grey explained. "There are five men per group. In addition to

240

them, here in these houses," he pointed up the block, "are about fifteen men. They have us boxed in, but don't panic, we still have the upper hand. All we have to do is neutralize them."

Sadie raised a hand. "How do we do that?"

Grey drew three lines from the school in a curve that went to the back of the houses. "It's simple. The twenty one of us will split into seven teams. Three of the teams, led by myself, will act as an assault force and attack the block of homes from the rear to divert attention from the school. At the same time, the other four teams will take up defensive positions opposite each of the marked sites."

Across from each of the 'X's he drew a little line. "When the shooting starts in the houses, the opposition forces at the marked sites will almost certainly advance and, when they do, they'll run right into our four teams who will be able to take them out, no problem. Keep your shooting under control. If you have a perfect shot, then take it. If not, be conservative with your ammo and keep them pinned down. Are there any questions?"

Michael Gates raised a shy hand. "What happens if they don't move?"

"Let's hope they don't," Grey replied. "If they just sit there, it means they're cowards. Give them a few shots to cement that fear. Ok, so we have everyone shooting, it will be at this point that the people in the school will leave the building and get to the trucks. Everyone with me so far?"

He glanced around and saw only shrugs. "Ok, from the moment the four secondary teams start firing, everyone counts to sixty, at which point they will break contact and run for the trucks. The assault force will count to an additional thirty and, at that point, they will also break off the attack and fall back on the trucks and then we just zip out of town. With any luck, it will be a quick, one-sided battle."

"But..." Neil said. It was all he could think to say. Although Grey had made the plan seem simple, Neil couldn't get past the idea that, in every instance, their teams were going to be fighting against nearly two-to-one odds.

Grey gave him another hard look. "There are no buts. It will be dark. Our enemies will be surprised at every turn. When they lift their heads, we'll blow them away and, when they cower, we'll retreat. They aren't trained soldiers, either. They will act and react from a position of fear. Our job is simple: instill that fear so we can maneuver at will. Now to break you up into teams."

Neil was paired with Sadie and William Gates and given the task of stopping the group of men closest to the courthouse. Because there was only one road into the town that wasn't blocked by a barricade of cars, along with the ring of zombies, they were going to have to head right back through the center of town.

That was just one of the many problems with Grey's plan. Neil waited until the teams were divided before he pulled the soldier aside.

"Don't say it," Grey said, and pushed past. He marched to where Deanna and Jillybean slept on and on. "I'm going to need stretcher teams," he said to himself. In the dark, Grey had never looked more fierce and yet he was as gentle as if he were handling a snowflake when he checked Deanna's pulse and lifted back one of Jillybean's eyelids.

"We need to talk," Neil said. When Grey only grunted, Neil turned to Marybeth. "Can you give us a moment?"

The second she was gone, Grey said: "It's the only plan we have, Neil. I know it's not perfect, but it's all we have other than trying to fortify the school and hope that a tornado comes and wipes everyone out for us. Really, Neil, you should trust me. I considered everything, even holding the Duke hostage. That scenario plays out even worse. He's doubled the men around the courthouse and it looks like there are a bunch of new people inside. Likely they're all armed. We just don't have the ammo for that sort of assault. So we'll go with plan A, and it will work."

Neil wasn't reassured. Far from it. For Grey's plan to work, each of the seven teams had to prevail in their own unsupported fights. A failure of one could leave the unarmed renegades rushing out of the school only to be slaughtered. "How many casualties do you expect?" Neil asked. "I noticed that was something you didn't mention in your briefing."

"Because they were scared enough already," Grey snapped. "It could be zero, or it could be upwards of thirty if one of the trucks gets a tire shot out or if we can't break contact and get bogged down in a real fight." Neil's eyes went so wide that the dark couldn't hide them. "Don't look so surprised, Neil. This is how war goes. It's a messy and dangerous business and I sure as hell wish I could tell you that everything will be alright, but nothing has been right for weeks now. We have one choice other than to surrender and that is to fight our way out. Sorry, but that's the way it is."

Grey stood, gripped Neil's slim shoulder for a second, and then walked back across the gym to where his teams were standing in nervous little groups. Neil wondered how many of them would be dead before midnight. It couldn't be thirty. "Please no," he said, whispering a short prayer. "Please not thirty."

How many would be acceptable? Eight? Maybe eight, but which eight? A long tired breath escaped him. He wouldn't be able to stand even one death. What he needed was another of Jillybean's miracles. The problem was that even if she were awake, what could she possibly come up with in such a short time?

"She'd think of something," he whispered, peering out into the darkened gym to make sure no one was near- by. At first he gently shook her and hissed into her ear: "Jillybean! Jillybean, wake up! I need you." When that didn't work, he shook her roughly and lied: "Jillybean, Ipes needs you. Ipes is here and he needs you." It was de- spicable and he loathed himself, but he didn't stop.

Chapter 22

Jillybean/Eve

"But not all of this was my fault," Jillybean said. It was the weakest argument she had ever laid out to her father and it was no wonder he said nothing but only raised a sweat-rippled brow at her. In the cell next to her was a charred beast of a man who openly scoffed.

"Please," the man said, although how he was able to articulate so well without lips was beyond the little girl. "Are you saying it was someone else who did this to me?" Jillybean could only shake her head in distress; she had no idea who the man was or how he had come to look like that.

"I'm sorry if you were on the ferry, but I was trying…"

He threw what was left of his charred hands in the air and said again: "Please! You can act like you don't know me but you do. Deep down, you do."

Jillybean pulled her eyes from the vision of her father and looked at the burnt ruin of a man. There was nothing left of his face save a single eye, a few broken teeth and twin holes where his nose should've been. It was a horribly disgusting sight yet she forced herself to look beyond the burns. She had no idea who the person was—there had been so many fires, after all, but then she saw his shirt. It was an army camouflage shirt. That was nothing new, however the fact that the shirt was neatly tucked into blue jeans was different.

"You were on the barge," she said, in a whisper, remembering the man who had chased her. She had not only thrown a hand grenade at him, she had set a block of C4 off in the barge's fuel bunker while he was still on board. "You were the guard."

"I wasn't just a guard," he spat. "I was a man. My name was Brian and it wasn't my fault I was on that barge.

244

It was circumstance, only. You didn't need to blow me up. I was just following orders."

Guilt wrapped a hand around her throat and kept her from pleading her case. She turned to her dad; he was half zombie because she hadn't been able to take care of herself. He had gone out scrounging because of her! He had died because of her, too. Then her mommy had died, and that was Jillybean's fault as well. Horrified at what she had caused, she backed to the end of the cell and cried.

"Oh, boo-hoo!" Brian snarled. "If I could get at you, I'd give you something to really cry about."

"I'm sorry, Mister Brian and I'm sorry, Daddy." she wailed.

Brian's arm stretching into the cell seemed to get longer, his finger straining to get her. "Fuck you and fuck your crappy apology."

Deep down she felt she deserved the bad words and the mean face that Brian was giving her. The hate was appropriate, however her Daddy's continued look of disappointment seemed out of place. Shouldn't he be mad as well? Why did he simply wear that look of disappointment she hated seeing on his face?

"Answer that question yourself," he said.

"Huh?" Had she asked that aloud? She didn't think so. "Well, uh, I don't know."

He shook his slowly, rotting head. "Come on. You didn't even try."

Even dead he was trying to get her to think for herself. *He hasn't changed*, she thought to herself, and for that her heart felt a touch of happiness in her misery; she never ever wanted him to change. "Ok, maybe because you were never a mean kinda person and that wouldn't change just cuz you're dead and all."

"That's partially correct. How do you know what I was like at work or how I was that one time I came home with the front bumper of the car all smushed in? Don't you think I was spitting mad then?"

She shrugged her thin shoulders. "Probably, but I never saw it."

"Exactly."

Her downy brows came down. "What do you mean 'exactly'? Are you saying that when you're dead you only act the way I saw you?" He shook his head. "Ok, so do you only act the way you did when I knew you before you were in here?"

The disappointed look vanished and he seemed less like a monster as he smiled. "Yes and that's because..."

The words: 'I don't know' wanted to jump right out of her mouth, but she knew better; he wouldn't tolerate that answer too many more times. She was sure she knew the answer. She knew the answer even though she didn't *think* she knew the answer and she knew this simply because *he knew* that she knew the answer—otherwise he wouldn't have asked the question. That was the way he used to be...and still was, apparently.

"Becaaaaause," she said, drawing out the word, giving herself time to think of a reason why he could only be as she remembered him down in this crazy place. Was it because he was just a memory? That couldn't be right since she had never seen him looking like half a monster before, and she had never seen Brian as a charred and angry, talking corpse. Though it was a safe assumption that anyone blown to bits and then put in a jail cell would be very angry.

Was that it? Was Brian an amalgam of memory and assumption? Rather than answer the rhetorical question she blinked, thinking it was strange that she knew the words amalgam and assumption at all when she couldn't ever remember them being used around her. Her mind pictured Neil; he was always using big words around her and it was likely...

"Stop it," she hissed to herself. She had more important things to think about. Was Brian an amalgam of memory and assumption? If the hypothesis were true, why couldn't she imagine her father as an angry man? She had to assume that he had been mad at times. He had to have been mad the time he smooshed up the car and he had to have been mad when he got bitted...

"Bitten," her father corrected.

Again she looked at him oddly. Had she been speaking out loud or could he read her thoughts? "Doesn't matter," she murmured; she had a thought problem to work out. Why couldn't she picture her father as a bitter and angry man, like Brian? A glance in her Daddy's direction confirmed what she thought she would see: ever so slowly he was losing the grey tint to his skin and his eyes were gradually turning from yellow to white again, just like she remembered, and just like she wanted.

There was the answer: *he's not angry because I prefer to remember him as the nicest man who ever lived*—she thought to herself—yes that was it.

Her father nodded and with a smile asked: "And so what does that tell you about your surroundings?"

"I can control parts of it," she said. When he again raised an eyebrow, she knew it wasn't the full answer. "I can control all of it?"

His face fell and the grey threatened to come back. "I'm afraid not. We are in your subconscious as you might have guessed, but then again we are in *hers* as well." He pointed a finger upwards. Jillybean looked up and saw that the ceiling of the prison had disappeared. Far above were the twin lamps of her eyes; they were impossibly far away.

"How can I be sharing my subconscious with *her*," Jillybean said. The thought was disgusting. Again, her father lifted his eyebrows indicating that she was to figure it out on her own. The little girl slumped in defeat and exhaustion. "Just tell me. I'm tired of thinking."

"Ok, darling, I'll tell you. You share the same subconscious with her because you share the same mind. She's you."

Jillybean stepped back away from her father with suspicion clouding her normally sweet face. What he was saying was a lie. *Eve* was someone else. *She* was evil. *She* was mean and nasty and horrible. There was no way they were the same person and only a liar would say otherwise and as her father wasn't a liar this couldn't be him. "She's not me," Jillybean hissed. "She is a monster who only tookted me over. Like Ipes did that one time."

"He did it more than once," her father said. "And do you know how he could do that?"

Jillybean's eyes began to dart back and forth, looking pretty much everywhere save up at her father's face. Was he suggesting that Ipes had been in her? Was he saying that Ipes wasn't real? "I don't know how he did it," she said stiffly. "He never told me."

"That's because you knew. You knew where his voice came from. It's not like he had lips or a tongue. His words came from you because his thoughts came from you. You created him because you needed him to keep the loneliness at bay, and to drive away your fears. He was in here helping you."

"No," she said, taking a little step back. Just then she couldn't have managed more; her legs felt wobbly beneath her. "No, he was real. He had a body. He-he was a z-zebra." She could picture her old friend, perfectly: his little ears, his big nose, his beady black eyes, and his spiking mane. He had been real, she knew it—*But he was a toy*—a voice spoke in her mind—*before your mommy died he had been just a toy.*

"Yes, you made him up," her daddy said. "He was just a ghost of your subconscious like me and like her." Again, he pointed upwards. Jillybean's chin canted up and her eyes followed the line of his finger. He went on: "A mind that's damaged or subject to incredible stress can do these sorts of things to protect itself. You created Ipes because you needed a way to deal with your fear of being alone. That first bounty hunter started a fissure in your mind and, with every subsequent danger, that fissure grew, until Ipes was thrown away. With Ipes gone, there was nothing left in your mind to protect you so you created *her* in order to deal with the dangers in this world."

"And I made her?" That seemed altogether impossible. Eve was evil in a way that Jillybean could scarcely comprehend.

Her father tilted his head in a manner that suggested he doubted her words. It was an 'Are you sure?' sort of look. "Really? You don't know evil? Look around at these cages." They were filled with her victims. "You know death and you know pain. And you know evil with the intimacy of a lover."

"But not all of this is my fault," Jillybean said stamping her foot. She pointed at the burned corpse of Brian. "That man worked for the River King. He was going to turn me over to him if he caught me. And those people," she pointed over at a group of wretches, some of whom had burns and others were wrinkled in way that suggested they had spent a lot of time submerged beneath the water, while others had holes in them or large chunks missing— they were people who had died when the ferry boats sank. "Those people threw things at Ram and they let him get bitten and they cheered when he turned into a monster. They were the evil ones."

"And them?" her father asked, pointing to a particularly shredded-up group.

"You know who they are," she said fiercely. Their robes gave them away as being Believers. "You know who they are and what they stood for and what they allowed."

"So it was ok to kill them or let them get eaten by monsters?"

Jillybean opened her mouth to denounce them but there was one thing she was certain of: no one deserved the death they had suffered.

Her father smiled in his old kindly fashion. "That is correct," he said, "and that's why you created *her*. My Jillybean isn't a killer and never was. She was supposed to go to the second grade, and have friends, and play the part of the Scarecrow in the school play, and bring home pictures to hang on my walls, and straight-A report cards to go on the refrigerator. My darling, little Jillybean was never supposed to be put in a position to kill or be killed and so you made her."

Realization started to slip in: Jillybean saw Ipes as he really was, simply a toy. His lips never moved and his eyes never blinked. His words were her words, only they had been retrieved from a part of her—*your subconscious*—the voice said. Yes, that part. The part of her she didn't quite understand; the part of her she was in at the moment.

"So why am I here?" she asked. Again, her father gave her 'The look'. She knew the answer. She sighed, a sound that wisped up from her soul. "I made her to deal with the harder things in life and now she's too strong for me to control?"

"Sorry, but yes," he said. "She is you, only she's the part of you that was never ever supposed to happen."

Those were nice words but they soothed her little. "And can I get rid of her like I lost Ipes?" Another of his irritating eyebrow lifts told her she wasn't going to be so lucky. "So how do I stop her? She's stronger than me. I mean, really, really stronger."

"I wish I knew," her daddy replied. "She's stronger than you because she has to be everything you are not. You created her to hurt people, to kill them. You created her to thrive in a world that wasn't made for seven-year-old orphans. She's strong but so are you. You are the original Jillybean. She's only a flawed copy. You must fight her with everything you have or she will kill again."

Thoughts and images flashed in her mind: her hand snapping up a shiny pistol. Ipes flying through the air and her thinking that the toy wasn't important; her life was in danger and she fired the gun with all the compassion the rain showed for the mountain. Another image: the grenade and the block of C4 taped together and thrust down the hole where five-hundred gallons of diesel was stored—yes, the guard would die, but other lives, lives that were more important to her, were on the line…the same line that stretched from the grenade pin to her hand. She was so close when it blew up that she thought her mind had exploded along with the barge.

There were other images, however they came in a blur and she didn't try to understand them. The images came with varying degrees of pain; needles that dug into

250

her flesh searching for the nerves that ran right up into her soul.

"Don't let Eve kill again," her daddy warned. "She'll only get stronger and stronger, until you won't be anything more than a shadow, like me." He said this with a sour, sickly grin. "Every day she's in charge you'll remember me less and less."

"No, I'll never forget you, Daddy."

The grin made a brief comeback. "Down here you'll never forget, but up there…I'll be a distant memory and so will everything I have ever taught you. So, please, fight her."

"I don't know how," she blurted out. His brow came up for a last time. Once more he expected her to have an answer to an impossible question. It was so frustrating! Didn't he know that she was just a little girl and that she was all alone?

It's why he's trying to get you to think for yourself? Again the voice came to her. Wait, did that sound like Ipes? No, that was impossible. Ipes was gone. He had been thrown in the river and his words in her mind had been thrown right out as well. That didn't make sense either, but as her father would only make her figure it out on her own too, she decided not to bring it up. Besides, it was too painful.

All at once, she realized she was running out of time. Mister Neil and Captain Grey needed her. "I can think for myself, Daddy, but right now I need your help. Tell me what to do, please, before it's too late."

"Fight her every step of the way. If she wants to go left, you go right. If she says yes, you say no. Force yourself into her head and then force her to listen to you. She is all emotion. Hate is powerful but so is logic; use your smarts. Trick her if you need to."

"Can I win?" Jillybean asked. The other girl was just so big and wicked that the idea of fighting her was daunting.

Her daddy looked up at the twin lamps. "I don't know," he said. "But you have to try. Now go and don't look back." She was about to ask how she was going to get all the way up there, when her father picked her up and, just like he had when she was a toddler, he tossed her high in the air.

Up and up she soared, yet she wasn't afraid of how high she went; she was trapped in her own mind. She couldn't be hurt from falling, she could only be hurt by *her*.

"Which means that I can hurt her as well," Jillybean said. It was with a feeling akin to eagerness that she missiled straight at the right eye. When she got to it, the eye was the size of a manhole cover. Through it she could see the front office of the school in the late afternoon light.

Not knowing what else to do, Jillybean started to climb into the eye. It immediately clamped shut. "The opposite of shut is open," she said before she grabbed the inner aspect of her own eyelid and pried it open.

"Hey!" the other girl hissed.

Jillybean saw her giant hand come up, palm first and again the light dimmed as the other girl rubbed her eye. It was working! She was making some sort of difference. The other girl was reacting.

On instinct only, Jillybean leapt out of the eye and into the hand. It was the strangest feeling in the world to be a living thing inside her own body. The inside of the hand was filled with long bones that were as tall as she was. The flesh of it was pale and translucent. Jillybean could see out, although everything was blurry.

The first thing she did was pull the hand back from her eye.

The other girl stared at the hand, holding it out at arm's length. "Stop it, Jillybean! This is my body now. I control it."

"Oh yeah?" Jillybean asked. "Then stop this." Jillybean threw the hand at her own throat and began to squeeze as hard as she could. The other girl tried to stop her by using her left hand to peel back the fingers, however the right was her dominant hand. It was too strong and slowly she choked herself into unconsciousness.

Jillybean's world went black. Gone were the long bones of white and the pale flesh. At first, she couldn't see anything but then she was aware of swirling shadows and then, suddenly, *she* was there.

"It's time to end this," *she* hissed. "This is my body and this is my life." Without another word, the other girl launched herself at little Jillybean. *She* was bigger than her daddy and was very strong, but Jillybean was desperate and, buoyed by her daddy's words, she was filled with the will to fight.

Together, they grappled in the dark. They punched and kicked and pulled hair and bit each other and wrestled in the horrible world they had created. As day passed into night and, as Captain Grey went on his recon mission and Neil fretted the hours away, the two girls fought. For Jillybean, the fight had a nightmare quality. No punch or kick seemed to make the least difference, the other girl kept coming and she grew in strength as Jillybean faded.

It felt like days of endless fighting went by until Neil's voice echoed through their subconscious: "Jillybean, I need you." The fear in his voice had the other girl laughing.

With a supreme effort, Jillybean pulled herself from the other girl's grip. "They need me," she said. "And that means you need me. Yeah, it's true. The Duke knows who we are and he is coming to get us."

She laughed again, louder. "I know. Who do you think told Brad?" Jillybean gaped at her and the evil laugh went on and on. When *she* could gasp, she said: "I am going to be Lady Eve. Brad promised me a title. Now, who's the smart one? I just dangled the words: *I can make you rich*, in his ear and now I'm going to be a lady with gowns and servants and horses. I get to have all of that simply by getting rid of Neil and the rest of them. They're going to be sold back to the River King or the Colonel or whoever offers the most money."

In flashes, *she* showed Jillybean the memory of her secret conversation with Brad. It had happened at some point after Deanna had been drugged and before Eve was found dead. The little girl had tracked Brad down to an ugly storage rental facility two blocks behind the court-house. It had been converted into thirty horse stalls and the air was sharp with the stench of manure. The other girl wanted a horse so badly, she would've done anything to get one and a bargain was struck.

The dirty deal shriveled Jillybean's heart, but it did not dim her mind. Brad shook hands on the deal but his face was full of lies. "You're not smart," Jillybean said. "You're a moron. Brad's not going to give you anything. Look at his eyes." The memory was now a shared one and, with Jillybean's attention to detail, the condescending look was clear as day.

"No," *she* hissed. "He...he promised. He said I could have my pick of the horses and the dresses."

"He lied," Jillybean said, feeling not only smug but also stronger. Jillybean had grown while *she* had diminished slightly. The other girl started to shake her head in denial which Jillybean stopped with a question: "If your places were reversed, would you hand over a horse and dresses and a title to a little, defenseless girl, or would you sell her, as well?"

The other girl's hands clenched into fists and shook as her face slowly contorted: twisting, snarling lips, a nose that wrinkled in disgust, and eyes that blazed and grew ferocious in their anger. She was huge again and the power rippled off of her. "That bastard! I'm going to kill him. I'll kill him!"

Dwarfed by the black shadow of the other girl, Jilly-bean stepped back, thinking: *This isn't going as planned.*

"It won't do you any good," Jillybean said. "The Duke is the one you really should have spoken to. Brad is nothing. But either way it's too late. You screwed up and now we're surrounded with no way out. We'll be sold back to the River King, I bet or maybe to Yuri in New York. You know what they'll do to us there, right?"

She knew what would happen and the two of them shivered in unison as very bad pictures flicked into their

254

minds. "You need to do something!" the other girl said. "You're smart. You can get us out of this."

"I can, but that means you'd have to give me total control of our body."

"No way," *She* spat. "You'll hurt us or do something stupid like rescuing all of them. No, you just tell me what to say or do."

Jillybean smiled easily and, without lying, said: "I would rather die."

Chapter 23

Sadie Walcott

In her usual black, Goth clothes, Sadie was able to slip away in the dark from the other members of the strike teams. She wasn't in the mood to be around people, especially as some of them had been openly questioning her place among them; the name Lindsey had been whispered frequently whenever she passed by. Sadie, who couldn't close her eyes without seeing the terrified woman's face as she was being eaten alive, didn't need any reminders of her latest murder.

She went to look for Neil and found him huddled over Jillybean's limp body and whispering: "Ipes needs you."

This seemed unnecessarily cruel and Sadie was just about to admonish him when, Jillybean suddenly stirred. The little girl put her hands out as though she were blind. She felt the things around her: the gym floor, Neil's sweater vest, her own pink shirt. Her hands played on each with great interest.

It was a few seconds before she pulled her head up and asked: "Mister Neil? Is that you? Where's Ipes? Did you say something about him being in trouble?"

"We're all in trouble," he answered. "We need your help...oh! Jeeze, Sadie, you scared the dickens out of me."

Sadie had come ghosting up, her black Converse sneakers not making a sound. Under other circumstances she might have laughed at how high he jumped and the way his fingers wiggled like spiders just under his chin, but there was a battle coming and she was in no mood for laughter.

"You're going too fast with her, Neil. We should find out what happened to her first," Sadie said. He gave her a pained look, suggesting that there wasn't time for that sort of thing.

Jillybean made it a moot point by answering simply: "I strangled myself is all." She started to get to her feet and then saw Deanna lying motionless next to her. "Oh, right," she whispered as a shudder racked her.

Neil saw it, and grabbed her shoulders and stared hard into her face. "You know what happened to her, don't you?"

Jillybean took a shaky breath and nodded, then without warning, she yanked the IV catheter out of Deanna's arm; blood started seeping out of the hole and the little girl pressed her thumb down on it while she jutted her pointy chin at the IV bag. "That's got morphine in it. That's what means a type of poison that knocks her out if she gets too much. But I didn't do it. The Duke gave it to her."

"Morphine? So she'll get better on her own?" Neil asked. When Jillybean nodded, he stood up and grabbed her hand. "Good," was all he said and started leading the little girl away.

Sadie leapt up and pulled him back around. "What about Deanna. We just can't leave her lying here all alone."

Neil glanced down at Deanna with a confused look. "Why not? The morphine is no longer flowing. She'll be better pretty soon. Better than we are going to be if I can't get a new plan cooked up. Grey's plan is...is just wrong. We're not trained soldiers. You know that, Sadie, and you know that if we try his plan too many of us will be killed tonight."

She had no choice except to agree. Grey's plan called for perfect coordination and precision between the seven teams. They would have to fight in the dark and retreat at exactly the right moment for a slaughter not to occur. If any team broke for the trucks too early, it would leave the defenseless renegades open to a withering assault. If teams retreated too late, they would either be left behind or the trucks, crammed with people would be stuck waiting out in the open. If it all came together perfectly it would be a miracle.

At the same time, Sadie didn't care for the way Neil was treating Jillybean. Once again, he was using her as a tool without regard to what sort of psychological damage he could be inflicting on her.

Neil noticed Sadie's indecision and guessed, correctly, what it meant. "We need her to get us all out of here. If we can't get out, nothing else matters because we'll all be...well, you know what will happen."

Before Sadie could answer, Jillybean said in a small voice: "We'll all be dead. I know. Don't worry about me, Sadie. I know what all this means now. And...and I know I'm not like a normal person. The other girl inside me is like Ipes was, except she's real mean and can take me over whenever she wants. That's not going to get better unless I can get all of you out of here. Then maybe she won't hurt people so much."

Sadie heard the fatality in her voice. It matched her feelings exactly. They were two young warriors who had gone too far and had killed too much. They were at the end of their ropes and there was still a thousand foot drop below them.

"Ok," Sadie said. "Let's figure this out together." She held out her pinky. Jillybean didn't smile at it as she might once have done, instead she grimly latched her own tiny pinky onto Sadie's.

"Good," Neil said. "Now let's hurry. Captain Grey won't like a change to his plans if it means involving you, Jillybean. He doesn't think you're strong enough, but I do. I think you're as strong as you need to be."

That sounded like a bunch of hot air to Sadie, though she understood. Neil was practically at the end of his own rope and he was quite willing to sacrifice one life to save sixty, even if that one life was as innocent as Jillybean's...except she wasn't quite so innocent, Sadie had to remind herself.

Neil snuck them out a side door, making sure to avoid the route people were taking to relieve themselves in the back of the school. In a minute the three of them slipped out into the night and, despite the dark, they crouched next to some bushes.

"Are the bad guys still across the street in those houses?" Jillybean asked.

"Yep and there's more of them," Neil said. He told her of Captain Grey's recon mission and then told her about the battle plan. "I'm afraid of the casualties we'll sustain. I think if these were trained soldiers Grey was leading we'd have a chance, but they're just people and too much depends on luck."

Jillybean gave a shrug. "It still might work...except he hasn't taken into account any response by the Duke or by any of the other people in this town. They might join the fight or they might lay in wait like an ambush."

"I'm sure he knows all that, but we don't have enough guns or bullets to add to his plan," Neil said. "Nor do we have enough people who are capable of acting as a screening force. That's why we need you, Jillybean. You talked about a bomb? How would a bomb help us?"

"I would need lots of bombs, but I don't have what I need to 'splode them. Has anyone seen my back pack? It has a ladybug on it."

Sadie had. "It's in the school's office area...are there bombs in it?"

Jillybean was quiet for a few moments. Her body was rigid and eyes locked on some unidentified point in the middle distance. "They're my bombs," she whispered to herself. "So don't even say that. You wouldn't know what to do with them anyway."

Neil gave Sadie a concerned look over the top of the little girl's head. Sadie touched Jillybean on the shoulder. "Are you ok?" she asked.

"Huh? Oh, I mean, yeah. I'm ok it was just *her*. It was nothing. She likes bombs and wants to blow them up but she can't cuz she's not too smart. Anywaaay..." She let the word draw out as she stepped away from the bushes and stared down at the row of houses across from them. She then turned to look up the road towards the courthouse.

After a minute, a grunt escaped her. It was one both Neil and Sadie had heard before.

"What?" Sadie asked. "You have a plan?"

The little girl turned back to them in a slow-motion twirl. "Most of one, I think. I need a few buckets of mud, all the flashlights we can scrounge up, some scissors or a sharp knife, some of that black electrical tape, and someone to talk Mister Captain Grey into giving me a few bombs."

"Bombs?" Neil asked.

She nodded. "Just a few for…chaos. Is that a word? Yes, for chaos. We need lots and lots of chaos."

A nervous chuckle escaped Neil as he dropped down to one knee so he could look into the little girls eyes. "Maybe you should tell me the plan first."

When she explained what had formed in her mind, he laughed, displaying more nerves. Sadie only turned to look out at the town, wondering how many lives would be lost before the sun came up. The number could be well into the hundreds if Jillybean could get her bombs.

Neil tugged her shirt. "You coming? We're going to go talk to Grey."

She followed them inside and stood silently in the shadows as Jillybean smiled up at the gruff soldier. He only glared at Neil until Jillybean explained what she had seen in the Duke's private apartment.

"Morphine," he whispered. "Yeah, that sounds about right." The little girl then began to explain her plan but Grey stopped her. "Was it also morphine that killed Eve?" he asked.

Jillybean jumped a little as if someone had snuck up on her and screamed in her ear. Her lower lip started to shake as she whispered: "Yeah. It-it was morphine, too. In her bottle." Her eyes were wet and the tears began to pool. Those blue orbs were filled with guilt and they silently begged Grey not to ask any more questions concerning the baby's death.

Sadie quickly stepped forward, putting herself between Jillybean and the tall captain. "We understand, honey. Don't we, Mister Captain Grey, Sir?" She caught his eye and he nodded gently.

"Yes, I-I think I understand. Uh, so you have a plan, too? Why am I not surprised?" Have you heard mine yet?"

"Yes," Jillybean answered in a shaky voice. The relief on her face was obvious. "Mister Neil told me and...and it was good, I guess, only it sounds like one of them soldier plans. And those are real good 'cept we don't have any soldiers, you know?"

Grey acknowledged that he did know this and added: "And how does your plan differ?" Jillybean spoke for five minutes. When she had finished he said: "Damn, that is good, but I don't see why we need so many bombs, just one will do the trick. If we move one of the canisters of napalm down among the bullets they'll cook off and it'll be suicide for anyone to go outside. The only problem is how do we get into the theater to set it? I can't pick a lock and if we try to hammer down the door they'll swarm us."

"Oh, that's easy," Jillybean said. "The back door is open. Before I left I stuck a rock in the locking thingy. You know the little hole on the door jamb where one part of the lock goes into the other? With a rock in there it can't lock."

"Seems like you thought of everything except how to remotely detonate the bomb." Grey said. "If we can't do that, we might as well forget that part of it and hope everything else works out."

Jillybean took her newly found pack off her back. She pulled her battery operated car: *Jazzy Blue* from it. "She's remotely controlled with this little thingy. If we hook up the blasting cap to the receiver unit in the car it should work, though I don't know if it will. It's just a guess. And I don't know how, neither."

"Lucky for you, I do," Grey said, taking the car from her. He turned it over a few times but it was obvious to Sadie that he was dwelling on Jillybean's plan rather than actually looking at the car. Finally, he said: "We'll go with your plan, Jillybean. We'll call it *Operation Broken Arrow*.

We'll need to reconfigure the teams into groups of two each and they'll have to be given their new instructions."

"I'll take Jillybean on my team," Sadie said quickly. She loved Neil and would die for him, but he had become so toughened by the constant pain of their journey that she knew he would use Jillybean up if that was what it took to escape. "Someone has to look after her." Jillybean took Sadie by the hand and smiled up at her and Sadie smiled back, though it was with a queer feeling. She was holding the hand of a murderer.

Then again, she was one as well.

Grey gathered the others and, to their immense relief, he told them about the change in plans. "I want everyone ready to go as soon as possible. You will need to be dressed and ready to move out when I say the word." The renegades went right to work while Grey came up to Jillybean and Sadie. "I'll need the remote control," he said, holding out his hand.

"I want to come with you," Jillybean countered. "I want to see how you connect everything."

He shook his head. "No. I'll tell you all about it when we're safely on the plains tomorrow. Right now I need your help here. If you could use your brains to rig up a stretcher for Deanna, that would be great."

Jillybean blew out a big sigh of disappointment when Grey took the remote controller for the car and left. Sadie nudged her. "Come on. We have to get ready and we have to figure out how to make a stretcher."

"That's easy," Jillybean said. She pointed at a small stage that stood at one end of the gym. Where two large flags, the Stars and Stripes and the state flag of Kansas, hung from wooden poles. "You can use them. There's a heavy duty stapler in the office area on the second desk on the right. All you got to do is staple the flags to the poles. I'm going to go with Captain Grey."

"No," Neil said, pulling her back by the ladybug bag. "You will obey orders, young lady, just like the rest of us. If you sneak up on him he might shoot first and ask questions later." When Jillybean hesitated at the idea of being shot out of hand, Neil gave Sadie a quick look that said: *Watch her!*

Sadie understood. There was no telling what Jillybean would do when she wasn't being closely watched. Thankfully, all she did was pout and argue with herself. She also threw her yellow dress over her pink outfit and then shredded it up. Then she slathered herself with mud until she looked like something that had crawled out of a grave. Sadie did the same until she was practically unrecognizable.

The drying mud was itchy and the coming fight made her anxious but the wait wasn't long. Captain Grey came back more quickly than anyone expected. He appeared out of the dark, right next to where Deanna lay on her new stretcher, still in her deep sleep. Kneeling next to her, he bent over her face so that Sadie thought he was going to kiss her, however he was only checking her respirations. "Ten, yes. That's much better."

Already covered in dirt or grime, Grey was ready for action. He went to where his hand-drawn map was laid out on the floor. "Okay, gather round. It's almost *go* time." He began pointing to spots on the map and assigning teams to each. When he was done, he sat back and gazed at each of them in turn. "This is very simple and it's something we've all done before. Are there any questions?"

Despite the fact that the plan played to the strengths of the renegades, which Grey listed ironically, as being a natural inclination to avoid battle and a mouse-like mindset, they were nervous. Kay raised her hand and asked, timidly: "Do we meet back at the trucks fifteen minutes from now or fifteen minutes from when we start? I don't want to be left behind is why I ask."

"And what about us?" Michael asked, indicating his nephew John and himself. "We've got the furthest to go. We're at the other end of town. It's like a mile away. It'll take us fifteen minutes just to get there and another fifteen to get back. We're going to need some sort of signal."

Grey was quiet as he considered this, while next to Sadie, Jillybean dug in her pack. "You could use this," she said, holding up what looked like a gigantic hand gun. "It shoots light up into the sky."

"A flare gun," Grey said, not bothering to question where she had picked it up. Her genius at finding handy items was on par with her genius at blowing things up. "Ok. Here's what we'll do. I will send you out in teams about a minute apart, starting with Michael and John. When you get to your positions do not wait. Start right then. When you see the flare, make it back here as fast as it's safe to do so. We will not leave without each of you."

He stood and pointed at Michael. "Check your flashlight." Michael shone the beam at the floor for a second and, after a nod from Grey, left. Each of them in turn, a minute apart, flicked on their lights and then left. Sadie and Jillybean were last. They had the closest section which was, supposedly, the easiest.

Unlike the other teams who left the gym with beads of sweat blooming on their brows and their eyeballs looking like twin cue-balls in their mud-caked faces, Sadie and Jillybean stepped out into the night as calm and resolute as a pair of veterans. Compared to the idea of fighting their way out, Jillybean's plan was a walk in the park—a very, very dangerous park, but a walk nonetheless.

The pair slunk, low and slow, in the tall grass and crawled past the five Azael men who were sitting on a hill overlooking the south side of the school—they were exactly where Captain Grey said they would be.

Even when they were safely passed the men, Sadie and Jillybean remained only stealthy shadows that went unseen. Ten minutes went by and the moans of the zombies grew louder with each step and, veterans or not, it wasn't easy for the two to purposefully walk towards what could be a horrible death. They steeled themselves and crept forward until the river of zombies, walking in their endless circle, was right there, thirty yards away.

The smell was atrocious, even more so than usual. The zombies' non-stop march around the town had cut a run, two feet deep into the dirt, which was filled with an ugly mud composed of urine and feces. There were close on ten thousand of them and the only thing keeping them going round and round was the pressure of those walking behind and the fact that they lacked the wit to do anything but follow the beast in front.

If they slowed or strayed, for whatever reason, the winged horsemen would prod them back into line with their spears. Not many horsemen were needed to keep their perpetual motion going. The Duke kept his town dark and quiet during the night—there was no reason for the zombies to stray from their infinite path.

Sadie thought the entire idea of the ring of zombies was a stroke of genius. It would take a concerted attack by a few hundred soldiers to break the ring of grey meat and on the flip side, the horsemen could goad the zombies into a mass attack. Yet, there was a flaw in the genius idea that Jillybean had picked up on. The zombies were a double-edged sword if someone had the guts to wield it.

"Ready?" Sadie asked when the closest horsemen had slowly clip-clopped almost out of sight.

Jillybean raised herself up so that she could peer over the tall grass. A deep breath was followed by a quiet: "Yep."

They both had flashlights. With a quick nod from Sadie, they started flashing them at the ring of zombies. The zombies reacted immediately. They surged from the rutted road and came stumbling right at them as fast as they could. In seconds, the arc of the circle in front of them had disintegrated completely.

"Holy crap," Sadie hissed. She would never in her life get used to the idea of *not* sprinting away when a horde of zombies bent on eating her alive, came at her in a run. The sight of them charging gave her a jolt. It was like a re-minder of life. Since she had plugged Lindsey between the eyes, she had been going through the motions of living. This vague semi-life had culminated with Eve lying dead in the gym, wrapped in towels.

The baby had died, and Sadie had cried but it had felt forced. It was like she was only going through the motions of grief, as if she were nothing but a bad actor. She had thought that she didn't care whether she lived or died, but now with the zombies bearing down on her, she knew that she cared. She cared a lot!

"It'll be ok," reassured the seven-year-old, in a low voice. "Just be a monster like I taught you back in New York. Come on." She started walking straight away from the zombies swarming at them. The little girl took on a lurching, stumbling gait that was an exact replica of the beasts coming after.

When Sadie was slow to imitate her, Jillybean angled slightly away and clicked her flashlight a few times over her shoulder. The undead beasts changed course as well, giving Sadie a few seconds to collect herself. The teen went into her own routine: arms out and hanging as though suspended by invisible wires from the clouds above, her legs lurching like she was on the rolling deck of a sailboat in a typhoon, and moaning like she had just puked up a quart of vodka and a basket of bar fries onto the bathroom floor of her mom's house.

She became one of *them*, meaning they ignored her completely and kept going after Jillybean. At first, Sadie thought that this was no big deal, because this was Jillybean, after all. She was letting them get close and closer and...Sadie gasped as she realized that something was wrong. The zombies were no longer fooled and were within feet of attacking the little girl!

Sadie clicked her light on and off and the entire mass of grey beasts, like a formation of bombers, changed direction as one and came on in a great press. Sadie's eyes bugged. They were practically running and, as much as she wanted to run as well, she couldn't. Her cover would be blown; she would be human in their eyes and thus free game.

But to continue to stagger along in her pathetic charade was an invitation to be pulled apart and eaten alive. Closer they came and with an iron will, she kept up her pretense. But still they came straight for her. She decided she would give it a few more steps and then she'd run. It was a hard decision since it would mean leaving Jillybean all alone in the middle of a zombie horde. As well it meant she would open herself up as a target for the zombies coming from every direction. The other teams were doing their jobs and the ring of undead was collapsing in on the center of town—very soon there wouldn't be anywhere to run.

These thoughts had Sadie hyperventilating, turning her into more of a target.

Then Jillybean was angling towards her. She had one arm stuck out as if it was dislocated and hanging askew, while the other was pulled in close to her thin chest. It was in this one that she held her flashlight. She flicked it on, sending the beam outward to strike a tree thirty feet to Sadie's right. For a second, the tree could have been a tall man wearing a cloak with his arms flung out in a dramatic gesture. In a snap the zombies rushed at the tree, their hideous claws scrabbling at the bark. One even launched itself at a jutting limb and latched on with its teeth.

Sadie knew she looked very human as she let out a sigh of relief and let her "zombie" shoulders droop.

Jillybean worked her way to her and grinned. "Like cats with a laser pointer," she whispered. "Next time hold the flashlight close so they can't see it. That's what I forgot. Monsters don't carry things and I was carrying a light. So silly, I know." She was smiling in a familiar mischievous manner when a gunshot cracked the night. It was followed by two more; then came a rattle of what sounded like machine gun fire.

The tree was forgotten by the zombies who moved forward in a wave. Ahead of them were the five men that Sadie and Jillybean had slunk by ten minutes before. They were dressed in their odd scarves and with the multi-hued hoods thrown over their heads they looked like strange clumps of dirty laundry and not like humans at all.

Silently, they scurried away from the onrushing horde. They might not have looked human, but Sadie reasoned they didn't want to risk a chance touch that would leave them exposed and torn apart. They retreated toward the courthouse and the horde followed along as the night began to crackle with more insistent gunfire.

The thousand or so zombies that Sadie and Jillybean had unleashed were nearing the school when one of the horsemen came up at a gallop. He charged right across their front, using the bulk of his animal to stop the forward progress of the zombies.

Sadie and Jillybean were stuck in the stinking crowd. They were jostled from all sides and had to fight to keep from being trampled. Gradually, the horseman started turning the leading elements on a course parallel to the one they had been going.

"Shit," Sadie hissed beneath the moans. She was about to whisper: *What do we do?* when Jillybean glared her into silence. The little girl then began to slip through the throng, angling for the edge. She kept her head down but her eyes up while her elbows jutted to keep the zombies away. When she got to the edge, Sadie thought she was going to slip away, but the girl stayed just behind the zombie in front of her, some tall thing that had been a man at one time.

She stayed in his shadow as the horseman came up with his spear spun around. He was jabbing the blunt end into the zombies to keep them turning back to the shit-stinking road when there was a quick move from Jillybean. Steel flashed in the night and suddenly the horse reared up and screamed like a terrified child. It bucked, and then lashed out with its rear hooves, catching the tall zombie in the chest, sending it bowling backwards.

Jillybean stepped neatly to the side in the nick of time. She stood all alone outside the crowd of zombies, a dangerous thing, but no one noticed. All eyes were on the horse that was whinnying and the rider who had lost his spear and was now trying desperately to cling to the back of his animal.

The horse, with a six inch hunting knife sticking out of its back quarter could not be controlled. It leapt once and bucked a second time with its rear hooves flying, this time in an effort to rid itself of the rider. The man tumbled right over the top of the animal, breaking his silken wings and losing his shining helmet in the process. When he sat up he looked too much like a human.

His scream was as loud as his horse's had been when he was suddenly swarmed.

Sadie moved away from the others and started moaning toward Jillybean. The little girl was not in character. She was staring at the clump. "*She* liked that," Jillybean said in a tiny voice.

"Don't look," Sadie said, turning her away. "Let's get to the truck. That's what the plan is, right?"

Jillybean turned and though her walk wasn't that of a zombie's, her blank stare was. "Yeah, that's the plan. I—I hurt the horse. I wish I didn't have to...but *she* liked it. *She* liked it a lot."

Chapter 24

Neil Martin

At one point, Neil had thought it an honor that Captain Grey had chosen him to be his wingman. That was before the thousands of zombies had come.

"Keep them off of me!" Grey barked. They were both arrayed as the undead in their rags and mud-daubed faces, however neither was acting the part. There was no time. They had been the last of the teams to leave the school. Grey had given Marybeth final orders: "Wait ten minutes and move everyone to the trucks as quietly as possible. Don't let them fight over seating. Split them evenly into three groups and have them hide in the truck beds. And I want you to watch over Deanna personally."

Marybeth had nodded but looked uncertain under the captain's fierce gaze. "You'll be fine," he added, with a smile that was brief and not very comforting.

Now, Neil was wishing he had Marybeth's job. He had thought he was simply going to assist Grey with stealing the fuel truck parked down the street from the courthouse. It sounded easy enough but was proving extremely difficult. The Duke was no fool. Not only had there been a man guarding the truck who had to be overcome, but, of course, the keys were with the Duke and the steering wheel was chained to a ringbolt on the floor of the cab.

"We can shoot it off," Neil said after Grey had slipped up and thumped the guard on the back of the head with the butt of his M4.

Grey rattled the heavy chain and held the near fist-sized Yale padlock for a second. "That usually works best in the movies. In real life it'll take four or five shots and where do you think the ricocheting bullets will go?" He gave a significant glance to the rear of the tanker, where ten-thousand gallons of diesel sat waiting to explode like a bomb.

"Oh," Neil said, disappointed. Stealing the fuel tank had been one of the highlights of Jillybean's 'chaos' plan. It was heart-wrenching and very scary to think they would have to leave it all behind and try to make their escape in trucks which were low on fuel.

For a second, Grey stared at the chain. He then gave it a mighty tug, testing the bolt. When it didn't give and Neil's face fell even more, Grey said: "We're not licked yet. First thing is to get this hot-wired and the next..." That had been when the first gunshot had rang out. It was surprisingly close.

"You think that was Michael?" Neil asked in a whisper.

"Don't know, don't care," Grey said, crawling under the dash. He took out his ka-bar and began prying back the molded plastic. "Keep an eye out and shoot any of the Duke's men if they come sniffing too close."

Neil almost shot Michael. He and his nephew came sprinting out of the dark, their shredded zombie-clothes flapping. "Slow down!" Neil hissed as he lowered his pistol. "Act the part or you're going to get shot. And another thing, stop shooting. Zombies don't shoot guns."

Michael threw a glance over his shoulder where hundreds upon hundreds of zombies were charging. "There was a rider. We didn't have a choice except to shoot." They weren't the only ones shooting. There were shots coming from all around them.

"Just get to the trucks," Neil said. "Leave as soon as everyone is back." Michael left, still in such a panic that he looked more man than monster. Behind him, the zombies closed quickly. Neil slunk low in his seat and then reached out and slowly closed the truck door.

"Don't close that yet," Grey said. "You still have to fire the flare gun."

Neil wanted to argue that everyone had to be running back to the trucks by then, but he knew what Grey would say: *Stick to the plan.* "The zombies will see us," he said instead.

Grey grunted, saying: "They're going to see us anyway." He then turned on his flashlight and griped: "I can't see anything under here."

That had been the beginning of their problem. The zombies saw the flickering light and went bonkers trying to get at the two men. While he still could, Neil rolled down his window and shot the flare into the sky to alert the others to retreat back to the five-tons.

After that they were under siege.

Zombies piled over each other to get at them and soon they were getting close to the height of the door. Neil was starting to roll down the window with his Beretta in hand when Grey's door was flung open and scabby, diseased arms and bodies crammed into the opening. "Keep them off of me," he snapped. "Just don't miss."

Grey was lying on the floor of the cab and was completely exposed to attack. Neil shot over him. From four feet, he couldn't miss and in eight shots he had cleared the door. Right when he lunged forward to close it, his own door opened behind him. Thinking he was slick, he spun on one knee and started blasting in that direction.

"These doors have locks, you know," Grey reminded him.

So much for being slick.

Neil had been traveling in military vehicles for so long that he had completely forgotten about the locks. Embarrassed, he shot twice more to clear his door. As quickly as possible he slammed it shut and locked it. When he turned he saw a zombie was reaching for Captain Grey, his sharp claws already entwined in Grey's brown hair. When Neil had first met the man weeks before, his hair had been creeping over the tips of his ears. Now, his hair was so long that he'd been complaining of being a "hippie" for the last few days.

The zombie had a good grip and started to pull.

"Do something, damn it!" Grey hissed through gritted teeth.

This was a tougher shot since the zombie was reaching up from below and Neil had to aim between the steering wheel and the side of the seat. His arm was strong and his aim surprisingly steady and yet, when the bullet left the Beretta, it clinked off the steering wheel. There was a snap of metal on metal which was followed by a string of curses from Grey.

"What the blazes are you doing?" he cried. "Get closer, damn it!"

"Right," Neil said, realizing he wasn't using his head at all. He crawled along the bench until he was right over the zombie. It hissed at Neil, showing cracked and broken teeth in a black, dank mouth. One bullet blasted out the orbit of its right eye, lodging somewhere in the thing's head. But it did not die. It fell back, still with a grip on Grey's hair.

"Son of a bitch!" Grey said.

Neil shot again, this time blasting a hole in the thing's temple and though it's remaining eye went blank, its hand remained clenched. "It won't die!" Neil cried. He went to shoot it a third time, however the pull of the trigger elicited nothing—it was empty.

Neil fumbled for his remaining clip, dropping it once. Before it clicked in place, the soldier took the razor-sharp knife that he'd been using to splice the wires with and ran it across his hairline. The zombie dropped among the rest and Neil forgot his weapon and reached for the door. Ugly grey hands and fingers got in the way of it closing but he kept slamming the heavy, metal door on them until it finally latched shut. A second later, he slammed the lock down.

"Oh, man. That was close," he said, breathless. "You ok?"

"Yeah," the soldier said, touching his head as though searching for cuts or scratches. "Yeah, I'm good." He sounded relieved.

A grin crossed Neil's face. "Not as good as you think. You look pretty stupid and that's coming from a man in purple crocs."

The soldier felt the ragged edges of his hair and grunted out a laugh of his own. It was short lived. Just then, a zombie crawled up onto the hood of the fuel truck.

It stared hungrily in at Neil just a foot away and then launched itself at the glass, smearing it with a nasty scum.

"Hurry," Neil said to his friend. More of the grey-skinned beasts were tearing their fingernails out trying to get at them. They clawed their way onto the hood and onto the fenders. Soon, all the windows were being subjected to fists slamming into them. "Come on!" Neil said in a whining voice. "What are you doing down there?"

"I don't know," Grey groused. "Something's wrong. I'm not getting any spark on any of these. There's something wrong with the battery…if there's even a battery in this thing. We're going to have to check it out."

His eye caught Neil's. The look was full of meaning.

"We're going to have to go out there, aren't we?" Neil asked.

Grey struggled out from beneath the steering wheel before answering. "It's the only way. There's a latch on both sides of the hood. Here's the plan: we clear our sectors, pop the hood and see what's what."

"What's what?" Neil asked. He tried to smile but, instead, he looked like he might vomit.

"Yes," Grey answered, simply. "Ready? Now!"

Neil wasn't ready at all. Wasn't there supposed to be a moment to collect himself or to check his limited ammo supply, or even to pray? Grey didn't give him that moment. The soldier threw open his door, knocking over the precariously perched zombies. He took two seconds to blast away the undead creatures clinging to the fender and the hood before he snapped the latch up. He then gave Neil an incredulous look from the other side of the glass.

Neil had yet to move.

"Oh, sorry," the smaller man said and then put his shoulder into his door. It gave way about three inches. He had to lift his feet and piston out with his legs in order to bowl the creatures back far enough to allow him to climb out onto the fender. Scabby hands grabbed at his pants and a finger hooked into one of the holes in his crocs. A cry of fear wanted to come bursting out of his throat. All below him was a wriggling, moaning mass of evil and his grip was precarious on the side mirror.

He thought he had reached the maximum of fear, only he had a reserve of cowardice in him that he didn't know he possessed. His right croc was pulled off his foot and he went into a spasm of panic as his ankle was grabbed and his body was stretched. He felt himself being elongated like taffy.

"The latch!" Grey bellowed.

The latch was the farthest thing from Neil's mind. He was only hanging onto the mirror by a few fingers and they were slippery with his sweat. His legs were being pulled into the gaping maws of the undead and he couldn't get the picture of his toes getting chewed off out of his mind.

"Oh God!" he cried as he pointed the gun into the mass of undead. All he saw were leering, hungry faces and a hundred hands reaching out to him. He began firing the Beretta into the crowd, concentrating on the zombies directly beneath him.

He kept firing until he saw a hole suddenly appear in the toe of his remaining croc—he'd shot himself!

"Holy crap!" he screamed. He had shot himself, but where was the pain? The only thing he felt was a sudden coolness and his leg no longer felt weighed down by two-hundred pounds of zombie. He looked at his foot a second time and saw that the croc was gone and that his socked foot was intact save for a split seam at the very tip of his big toe.

He had missed after all! Out of the blue, he suddenly cackled like a mad-man and stuck the hot Beretta into the waist of his BDUs.

"Get the latch, Neil!" Grey yelled again.

With his socked-foot digging to find a grip on anything that would help to secure his position, he said: "Yeah, yeah. I'm getting to it." In that one moment he felt he had finally matured as warrior. It didn't matter that seconds before he had been practically wetting himself; that fear was in the past and was already practically forgotten.

What mattered was that he had collected himself in a heartbeat; his mind had leapt back to the task at hand.

He saw the latch and snapped it up.

Grey heaved back on the hood, exposing the engine. Not knowing what else to do, Neil climbed back into the cab, shooting three of the hardier zombies on the way. When he was safe once more, he cracked his window and yelled over the endless moaning: "What's the problem?"

The soldier was sitting in the engine compartment, hunched over and seemingly oblivious to the hundreds of zombies who were surrounding them. "The battery is disconnected is all. Do me a favor and watch my six while I get this reconnected."

"Sure," Neil answered. Killing zombies from the safety of the locked cab was right up his alley. With the window never more than a few inches down, he fired the Beretta every few seconds at any stiff that got a good hold and threatened to climb up at Grey. He had just fired his sixth shot when the dashboard suddenly lit up. "Oh, hey! We've got lights in here."

Grey turned to the window and grinned. "Clear my door," he said.

The driver's side was swarming with the undead. "No," Neil said. "Just come in my way." Grey nodded to the idea, then, with the dexterity of a monkey, he swung out over the crowd, using the side view mirror like Tarzan uses a vine. In a second he was crawling past Neil and going to work on the wires beneath the dash. Eight more seconds passed and then the engine suddenly coughed into life.

"Hot dog!" he exclaimed, happily. Just then the first of the five-ton trucks chugged up. Everything seemed to be falling into place. "Go! Go!" Grey yelled to them and then stuck the fuel truck into gear.

"Aren't you forgetting something?" Neil asked, pointing at the heavy chain that still hung from the steering wheel.

The truck lurched as Grey struggled to find second gear. "This mother is sticking," he griped. Finally there was a grinding of metal and the ride smoothed. Only then did he glance over at Neil. "No. I haven't forgotten the chain. We'll worry about that when we have time."

"How the hell are you going to drive this thing with a chain on the steering wheel?" Neil asked.

"Very carefully," Grey answered as he heaved the steering wheel as far to the right as possible. The chain was loose enough to allow a ten degree arc either right or left. It meant their turns were going to be great sweeps and it also meant that when Grey had answered: *very carefully*, he'd been lying through his teeth.

The fuel truck swerved far out to the right leaving the streets behind. "There's a tree...that's a tree!" Neil cried, as he planted his feet on the dash, bracing himself against the crash that he was sure was going to happen.

"I see it," Grey said. "I'm not going to hit..." The truck missed the tree trunk by inches but not the very large branches that jutted out from it. The windshield exploded inwards while the side view mirror next to Neil was torn off and the passenger window was punched in. Neil threw himself onto the bench covering his face from the flying glass.

The truck shuddered from the impact but had enough momentum to struggle onwards. Ahead of them on a straight course that lead out of town, the three five-tons trucks filled with the renegades were blasting through the zombies in their way, leaving a trail of mangled bodies.

Neil only gave them a glance, he and Grey had their own problems. In front of the fuel truck was a drainage ditch "Are you going to hit that head on?" Neil asked, grabbing his seat belt. In the dark the ditch was a shadow-line; it could've been two feet deep or eight.

"No, at an angle," Grey answered.

"Oh, good. So, uh, you are going to slow down, at least?"

Grey grinned at Neil and revved the engine louder, but then took his foot off the gas. "Of course. I'm not looking to kill us. You should know me by..." He jerked in surprise. A spark flashed off the hood. It was followed a second later by the crack of rifle fire.

Neil was slow to catch on. "Was that..."

"Yes!" Grey snapped, dropping his foot back onto the gas and up-shifting. "What the hell do they think they're doing? If this thing explodes it can burn down this entire town." He jerked again as something *thocked* into his door. Crouching lower in the driver's seat he dug in his cargo pocket. "This should give them something to think about."

In his hand was the remote controller for *Jazzy Blue*. With his own evil laugh, he turned it on and then pressed one of the controls upward. They both chanced a look back. A few long seconds went by and the quick look turned into a long stare, disrupted at last as another bullet whined off of metal.

Quickly, they both slunk down again. With one hand on the wheel, Grey fiddled with the remote until the next bullet hit the truck. "Check the batteries," he said, tossing Neil the remote. Neil looked at the little black object, saw the red LED light and the panel in the back that slid off with the push of his thumb. It came off easily and he popped out one of the batteries; immediately the LED light dimmed away to nothing.

"It's not the batteries!" Neil said, from his crouched position. He put the remote back together and then examined the controls: there was a stubby joy stick and a trigger-like button under the right handhold—the go-button he suspected. He started working both, however no manner of clicking or swiveling of the joystick helped in any way. The theater, growing smaller and smaller behind them remained disappointingly dark.

"It must be the range," Grey said. "It's a toy; it can't be all that great."

Neil cast a quick look his way and gave a nervous chuckle as he asked: "You aren't going to turn around, are you?" *As if turning was even an option*, he thought but didn't say.

"No way, not with someone shooting at us. We wouldn't make it halfway back before this thing went up.

278

We'll have to think of something else. But first things first." The ditch was coming and Grey kept the wheel as far over as it would go. Although it was picking up speed with every passing second, the truck was like a tortoise in its course change, they were going to strike the ditch at a forty-five degree angle and it was going to be a hell of a thump.

Grey slid his seatbelt on as well and then grinned over at Neil. "Pray for no sparks," he joked. Neil took it to heart and started mumbling out a prayer.

They hit the ditch and, even with his seat belt and his hands and feet braced, Neil flew up off the seat as the truck slammed straight down. A millisecond later the nose of the truck shot skyward, but at an angle that could only be described as catawampus. There was a crash from the left side of the vehicle as the fuel truck landed with its right wheels in the air.

Neil felt the truck pitch to the left and he was able to look down on Captain Grey and he was sure that the truck was going to flop over on its side as a prelude to exploding in a fireball that would flash-cook them both. But then the truck tilted and came crashing down on all six of its wheels. They bucked and shook but the truck remained whole.

"Thank you, God!" Grey yelled and fed the beast of a machine more gas, quickly shifting into third. The other trucks were well ahead and to the right, so the captain took the truck on a slow curve. As an added bonus, they were out of range of whoever had been shooting at them and in two minutes they pulled up behind the last truck.

Neil was out in a heartbeat, rushing forward, his new-found excitement over their escape dying in his soul—someone was screaming in pain. It was a woman and her pain was his pain. He had screwed up again and one of the people in his flock was hurt. Sadie met him with Jillybean tagging along behind and Ricky running up. "Who is it?" Neil asked.

"Marybeth. She was gut shot," Sadie said. "There's blood everywhere."

"I got one, too," Ricky said. "Becca. She took one in the leg. It's bleeding like a mother. Also…Kay didn't make it back to the trucks and the guy she was teamed with didn't know what happened to her. They got separated."

"What about the explosion?" Jillybean asked.

Neil glared at her. "Not now. This is more important."

Grey shook his head. "Actually the explosion is just as important as the wounded, maybe more so. We need to slow the Duke's men down or we'll never get away. Their horsemen will get the zombies under control in a few minutes and then they'll be hard after us. The problem is we're out of range for the remote. I think I should go back and set off the bomb."

Michael Gates had come jogging up. He was ashen-faced at the news of his wife. He grabbed Grey with both of his meaty hands as if the captain was going to go sprinting away right that second. "No. You're the only one who can save Marybeth. You're staying. Send someone else."

"Michael's right," Neil said, jutting his chin out in his best impersonation of manly courage. "I'll go." Whoever went would have to go on foot and the trucks couldn't afford to wait for them to return. It would be a one way trip.

Sadie stopped him. "No. You're the leader and this is a suicide mission. It only makes sense that someone who is, uh, disposable should go and I think that should be me. I'm the fastest runner. It makes sense."

Neil began to shake his head but then Jillybean spoke up in a tone that was like metal on teeth. "I'm going. This is all my fault anyways." She turned suddenly and spoke to a patch of ground to her right. "I know what I'm doing. We can't go back with them. They'll only put us in jail and you don't want that, right?"

"You're not going to jail, Jillybean," Neil said.

Jillybean stood her tallest and blurted out: "I should, I…I killed Eve…I mean the baby. I killed her." This was met with a stony silence as eyes flicked all around. The little girl wasn't done: "And I told Brad about who we were. He promised me a horse if I did. All of this is…is my fault. I should be the one who goes back."

Although Neil had been almost certain that Jillybean had been Eve's killer, the blatant confession was like a mule-kick to the stomach and, on top of that, was the admission of her culpability with regard to their present state of flight. Neil floundered for words, but couldn't find any that made sense. He couldn't possibly send a seven-year-old back to die and yet he couldn't think of anything that made better sense.

They were all dumbfounded. Only Sadie had the moral courage to speak up: "But that wasn't you, Jillybean. That was the other girl."

"So?" Jillybean answered. "Me or her it doesn't matter. She won't ever, ever stop. She'll kill you all and use me to keep her safe. This is the only way. Asides, she wants to see the explosion. She hopes it will be big."

The little group flicked their eyes each to the other, no one coming out with an argument to refute Jillybean. Neil knew it was wrong but, at the same time, sending anyone was wrong. They all deserved life, except for maybe Jillybean. She had murdered. It hurt to even think about it, but if she stayed and they managed to make it to Colorado, what would happen to her? They had banished Clara Gates for less.

Neil knew he had an obligation to protect the innocent and the weak. Jillybean was neither. "Go," he said in a husky voice. "Take the remote and run."

Chapter 25

Sadie Walcott

They watched Jillybean accept the remote as if it were the *Holy Grail* and run away, her shredded yellow dress flapping and her long brown hair streaming. When she was gone, the group of adults toed the pebbles on the road for a few seconds before Neil said: "It's done. Now we have to get moving. I'll drive the fuel truck."

Sadie couldn't seem to stop shaking her head. What they had done was wrong. It was more than wrong, it was evil. They had let the most vulnerable of them go to take the biggest risk. It should've been...

"It should've been me," she whispered, as the little group broke up. Grey ran to the third where Marybeth was still making awful noises, Ricky hurried to the second and Michael to the lead, but only after Neil had pushed him on.

"Marybeth will be fine," he told Michael. "Trust Grey. He's the best chance she has and besides, no one else can drive the truck. So if you want your wife to live, you've got to do your part." Sadie thought this was cold of Neil and yet, once again, it was what had to be done.

Everyone left for their trucks leaving the Goth girl standing there. She didn't know where she belonged. A part of her wanted to run after Jillybean and take the remote back to the Duke and blow his ass to hell. She knew that would certainly mean her death, and probably a bad one at that. At the same time, there was a part of her that just didn't care about anything. That part of her was tired of her life.

"Come on, Sadie!" Neil hissed. The other trucks were beginning to pull away. With a last look at the town, she went to the fuel truck and climbed in. She was about to complain about how Jillybean had been treated, however one look at the interior of the truck left her breathless. There were bullet holes and shards of glass and black blood and tree branches and...a chain on the steering wheel.

Neil ground the gear into first as she stared. "How the hell do you steer?" she asked.

"Not very well," he answered. "Thankfully, I won't have to do much steering for a while." In front of them, the road was straight as an arrow.

Again Sadie looked back. They were two miles away and the town was just a dark, irregular hump in the distance. She watched for ten minutes, waiting for the bomb to blow up. Captain Grey had set it and she was sure that it would light the sky for miles.

But there was nothing.

"Oh, crap," Neil said. Sadie glanced to the front and saw that the other three trucks were turning south on a main road. Neil slowed and turned the wheel as far as the heavy chain would allow. It wasn't far at all and Neil's wide turn sent them into a field of wheat in a long crescent-shaped sweep.

"We need to get this God-forsaken chain off or we'll be caught for certain," Neil griped. "Look around for some tools or something."

The cab was so strewn with debris that it wasn't easy to find anything. "We don't need tools," Sadie said, "We need Jillybean. I bet she could get that chain off in a jiffy."

Neil looked down at the wheel and then took a quick peek under his seat at the ring-bolt. "No. Jillybean couldn't get this off. We need a torch or a saw or something to cut the chain."

"Well there's nothing in here," Sadie replied. Her answer had been short and Neil glanced over at her right before they finally came up on the southern road.

"I'm sorry about Jillybean," he said in a whisper. "I really am, but I'm also sorry about Eve and Marybeth and Becca and Kay. Really, I'm sorry about all of us. Escaping like this in the middle of the night, people shooting, and dying and...and the fact that we might have just started a war; it's all on Jillybean. And you heard her: she can't control it any longer."

Sadie knew all this. She had made her one plea to go back, only she hadn't put much of a fight into it especially after Jillybean had opened her mouth. Now, her soul was swimming in guilt. She faced the broken window, letting the wind whip her short hair back and forth; it also dried her tears.

"Where are we going?" Neil asked, more to himself. The question made Sadie blink. There had been a map in the glove compartment, her hands had shuffled right over it without thinking. Now she grabbed it and, after flicking on the dome light, she saw that it was a map of Kansas. There were a number of red marks and routes traced in highlighter on it.

Sadie poured over the map, losing herself in it. The lines and squiggles, the roads and trails were easier to comprehend, than leaving a little girl to fend for herself. At first the tiny words were bleary but, after running a black sleeve across her eyes she was able to focus

"I know where we are" Sadie said, finally. One of her black-painted nails traced a line on the map. "This is I-77. That town back there was *Ringwood Station*. Here look, I'll steer."

She snugged over to him and held the chained wheel while he squinted. "Oh I see now; here we are, a little over an hour from Wichita. We don't want to go there." They had a rule about avoiding the big cities. The reasons were obvious: there were always thousands of zombies and frequent obstructions in the roads made making any u-turn a perilous undertaking. "Find us a route around the city," he said.

When she had one, he revved up close to the third truck in line and gave it a beep of his horn. When it slowed, Neil passed it and did the same thing until he was leading the pack. Then he drove until he saw a house that was sitting close to the side of the highway. He pulled across from it.

"I got to get this chain off somehow," he explained. "First, let's see how Marybeth is doing."

He jogged down the line of trucks using a weird hopping gait and it was then Sadie saw that he was missing one of his crocs to which she only said: "Huh." She didn't go running after him, instead she climbed atop the cab and then up onto the great metal cylinder of fuel. The liquid inside was still sloshing back and forth in the chamber, making the truck rock gently.

The chemical smell was eye-watering and yet she barely noticed. Her eyes were far away to the north, searching for any break in the night, any glow that would indicate a fire. All around her the horizon was deepest black. What did that mean? Had the bomb been a dud? Had Jillybean been killed before she got close? Had she been captured?

"Would they torture her?" Sadie asked the night.

Below her she saw Neil coming back with a limpy jump every other step. Sadie climbed down before he could see her and ask what she was doing. The fact that there wasn't an explosion meant that Neil's decision had been the wrong one. It meant another death on his shoulders.

"How's Marybeth?" she asked, leaping the final few feet down to the cement.

Neil shook his head and whispered: "She might have been hit in the liver. Grey needs ten minutes to stabilize her and clamp off a bleeder. Will you come with me to that house?"

There was no need to even ask. "Of course."

Together they stepped over an aged, wire fence and made their way along rows of squat shrubs that were ill-tended and growing wild. In the dark, Sadie couldn't place the plants, though it didn't matter. There wasn't time to pick anything.

The farmhouse was a sad little building which had to have been decrepit even before the apocalypse. Its roof was worn and the shutters next to the windows were crooked and missing slats. The door, thin and hollow-cored, had been shouldered in and hung at an angle from a single bent hinge. Weeds jutted up through the peeling porch planks.

Neil went first holding off on using his flashlight until he paused at the door to listen for the telltale moan of zombies. The place was quiet and so he risked light and it was a good thing he did. The floor was littered with glass and broken china as well as the contents of every cabinet and drawer that hadn't been considered valuable by the looters who had come through.

"I'll find you another shoe," Sadie said. "Wait here."

With her own flashlight illuminating the interior of the house she crunched across the faded hardwood floors of a short hallway. To the right was a sitting room. Dust hung in the air and collected on the aging Ethan Allen furniture. There was a body on the floor. Bugs and critters had long ago reduced it to bones and an ugly carpet of hair around a bare skull. There were the remains of a dress shrouding it.

"Hope there was a man in the house," Sadie mumbled. A single sensible black shoe was the only footwear in sight. It seemed even too small for Neil's small feet.

Neil's luck wasn't very good that night. The woman, the late Edith Crenshaw had been a widow who had many years before donated all of her late-husbands clothes to charity. The closest Sadie could find for a fit for Neil was an old and dirty pink slipper.

It is what it is," he said and then shuffled, probably much as the dead Edith used to, out to the garage where he ran his light over a workbench that was not only dusty, but also cobwebbed to such an extent that it was obvious Edith hadn't touched the tools at all since her husband's death.

They took everything that looked like it might have some value: a hammer, two screwdrivers, a hack saw and a ratchet set. Neil also saw an axe and after testing its edge, he slung it on his shoulder and grinned at Sadie.

Neil had never looked worse, she thought. It wasn't just his mismatched and strange footwear, or his torn sweater vest, or the mud and ugly scars on his face, it was in his sky blue eyes where he looked so awful. He no longer had the boyish and naive optimism that Sadie had fallen in love with. What remained was a hard-edged pragmatism that was chilling to see.

Still he tried. "Let's get that chain off. I bet it will be a piece of cake."

It would be if Jillybean was here, Sadie thought to herself. These sort of mechanical obstacles were one of her strong suits. She would've noticed the twenty foot length of chain that Mr. Crenshaw had used to pull stumps out of the ground. Crenshaw's chain was twice the width of the ringbolt holding the fuel truck chain in place. The little girl would've known that the power of the Cummins 240 horse power engine in one of the five tons combined with the strength of Crenshaw's chain could've snapped the bolt off in a second.

Neil put his faith in an old hacksaw and his somewhat undersized arm muscles. When they got back to the fuel truck, he went right at the chain instead of the thinner and stationary ringbolt.

Sadie watched for a moment and then said: "I'm going to check on Marybeth and Becca." As she passed the five ton trucks, she saw the renegades loitering. "Someone should be keeping watch," she said. "Joslyn climb up there and keep watch, will you please."

Joslyn took a look up at the tall truck and smirked. "I'm not going up there."

Sadie rounded on her, filled with a sudden rage. "If you won't climb up there then get your dumb ass out of here." Her hand was on the butt of her Glock and she was within a quarter second of whipping it out and shoving into Joslyn's mouth.

"Who died and made you boss?" Joslyn asked.

These were the wrong words to say to Sadie right at the moment. The gun was out before Joslyn could blink and cracked the woman across the cheek a half-second later. She went down on her back and lay there with her hands up, defensively. Sadie felt a moment of regret but bit it back.

"You want to know who has died? You want me to give you a list of everyone who has died because someone was lazy or stupid or just plain unlucky, or do you want to get your ass up on that truck before someone else dies?"

Joslyn began scrambling to her feet. "Ok...ok, I'll do it. Ok."

Sadie glared until Joslyn was mounting the cab. She then turned to stare at the renegades who had witnessed the incident. With the fire in her dark eyes and the gun still in her hand, no one said a word.

"Good," Sadie said and holstered the weapon and then marched off toward the last truck. Behind her were whispers. She hadn't done anything to cement her position in the group; she didn't really care.

When she got to the rear of the last truck, she went to William Gates and asked in a quiet voice: "How is she doing?"

The usually quiet William, staying true to himself, only shook his head but there was a glint of tears on his cheek that caught in the star light and spoke volumes. Sadie would have to see for herself. She took Jillybean's betrayal as a failure on her part. They had been sisters after all and as the older sister, she should have done more to protect Jillybean.

The back of the truck was peopled to a greater extent than Sadie would've guessed. The entire Gates family, minus William, was huddled around a moaning lump on the floor. The sounds coming from the lump were so low and guttural that it seemed as if they were coming from an animal and not from sweet Marybeth who had never raised her voice as far as Sadie knew.

Becca was there as well. She was a quiet thing and in the month Sadie had known her they hadn't spoken once. She had been one of the fifteen or so women who had been freed from the rape-room in the Piggly-Wiggly. She had been carried to the last truck by her friends and now, they stood around her, hunched by the low ceiling of the five-ton, and wept as though she was on her death bed. Becca fed into the depressing atmosphere and cried with more strength than any.

When Sadie peeked in at Becca's wound, the Goth girl wanted to give her a hardy slap. It was fair to say the wound was probably painful, but it wasn't *that* painful. Captain Grey had to stop what he was doing from time to time and ask her to quiet her "caterwauling" before she attracted every zombie from miles away.

Sadie quickly saw that she was not the only lonely individual: Deanna was lying alone and seemingly forgotten at the very back of the truck. Sadie started to push her way to her, but Grey grabbed her with a freshly bloodied hand.

"Tell Neil I need twenty more minutes," he said, speaking in a low tone directly into her ear. "She'll die if I can't tie off this bleeder."

The request was shocking. Their head start couldn't have been much more than twenty minutes. "I'll-I'll ask him," Sadie said. She turned and paused at the tailgate, again looking northward, this time not searching for an explosion, but looking for the glow of headlights.

The horizon remained dark.

It was small relief. Neil had the same reaction when she told him of Grey's request. He was standing on the step-plate, half in and half out of the cab of the fuel truck, sawing like a madman at the chain when she told him. "What? Twenty minutes?" he exclaimed. He stood up straight and looked eastward with squinting eyes.

"The town is that way," she said, pointing Neil north. "There's no sign of them, yet. I have Joslyn keeping watch."

Slowly, Neil turned his eyes from the north. "Ok, good, thanks. And, uh, tell Grey he's got fifteen minutes and even that's cutting it way too close."

Sadie went back to the last truck in the line, however she didn't say anything about Neil's time frame. It would've been like telling them that Neil had decided Marybeth's life wasn't worth anything. She sat on the tailgate and watched as Grey dug in Marybeth's abdomen while Michael held her hand and their daughter, Anne, pointed a flashlight into the mess.

Fifteen minutes seemed to fly by. A sweating Neil came up a few minutes later; he didn't bother to climb up into the bed. He said to Sadie: "Please tell me they're almost done."

Grey answered for her: "I got two more sutures to go. She'll bleed out if I can't get them placed."

"Fine," Neil said, giving in, "but I want everyone ready to go the second he's done. We have a long night of driving ahead of us and we can't be..."

"No," Grey said, cutting him off. "Marybeth won't live through a long ride. There's no way. Besides, the Duke has a hundred cars that can outrun us; they'll catch us on the open road. The smart thing to do is to find somewhere to hunker down for a few days and let the heat blow over before we make a run for it."

Neil opened his mouth to answer, however just then Joslyn let out a cry: "Headlights! There are headlights coming right at us!"

In a flash, Grey was at the tailgate, barking: "Everyone turn off your flashlights." The lights clicked off and then everyone peered at the headlights coming their way. They looked like very low, twinkling stars to Sadie.

"We have to go right now," Neil said to Grey. They locked eyes for a long, tense minute—on one side was the veteran soldier, the most deadly man in a thousand miles, on the other a small man wearing an old woman's slipper on one foot and a purple croc on the other. They each were headstrong in their beliefs: Neil had the group to look after, while Grey was dead set on protecting and saving the most vulnerable of them.

They stared until it became uncomfortable, but eventually, Grey dropped his gaze and nodded. Then there was a flurry of activity as Neil started yelling: "Get in the trucks! Get in the trucks!"

People scrambled to climb into the closest vehicle. It was mayhem, with one truck over-flowing with people while the last one was only half full. To make matters worse, Michael Gates, began bellowing, demanding that Grey be allowed time to finish saving his wife. When Neil only shook his head, resolutely, Michael went mad and began fighting to get at Neil. There was murder in his eyes. He was so wild that Captain Grey was forced to slap a guillotine chokehold on him.

"Get out of here!" Grey yelled at Neil. "Get the trucks moving; he'll settle down."

Neil disappeared up the line of trucks where tailgates were being slammed shut and engines rumbled. Sadie waited at the last truck until she was sure that Michael wasn't going to be able to get away and then she booked it in high gear up to the fuel truck, arriving just as Neil did.

Neil lost his slipper as he climbed in and had to go back for it. He threw it up into the cab and then followed it up; he ended up driving with a socked foot on the gas which didn't make his ability to operate the weighed down fuel truck any better. The thing lurched and rocked as he fought his way through the gears and all the while the sound of the diesel sloshing behind them was an ever-present reminder that a mistake would roast them both.

But at least the chain had finally been cut away. It made steering the easiest part of that nightmare ride. With the lack of headlights and the intense dark and the desperate need to put more miles between them and the cars racing along in their wake, Neil was taking some serious chances.

They had little choice. The headlights which had started as tiny stars grew larger as the minutes passed.

"So where are we going?" Sadie asked. "If we stay on this road whoever is back there will catch up sooner or later."

"I don't know," Neil said. He seemed so small behind the wheel—the thing was as wide around as a manhole cover and he looked like a child trying to steer a tugboat. "I really don't. And does it matter where we go? All I ever do is lead us into one disaster after another. It makes me wonder why I ever wanted this job to begin with."

Sadie patted him on the arm. "From what I hear you didn't want the job at all. It was simply a choice between you doing it or letting Fred Trigg lead us. We both know he never could have gotten us even this far. You have to realize that's the truth, just like it's the truth you're still doing a great job despite the circumstances we keep finding ourselves in. I trust you and I think Captain Grey trusts you, too."

"And what about Jillybean," he asked. "Do you think she trusts me? Or Marybeth or Becca, or Kay?"

She thought for a moment and then shrugged. "I think they all do in their way. They trust you more than they trust themselves. They're all afraid to speak up. They're all afraid to come up with an idea."

This brought a dry chuckle from Neil. "So you're saying they trust me because they don't have any other choice?"

"Yeah...so which way?" Sadie asked, trying to change the sticky subject. "Those guys back there can't see us. We could pull over somewhere under an overpass or behind a motel or something and they'd drive right by. We have the gas and the food to try to make it straight across country. Or..."

"Or we try to save Marybeth," Neil finished her sentence. "If we did we'd need to find proper facilities for her."

Sadie scratched at the dried mud on her cheek before adding: "And we'll need antibiotics for her and for Becca. We're not going to find that sort of thing out here on the prairie. We'll have to chance a city. Is that what you want to do?" The idea made her queasy. New York, Philadelphia, Washington, Atlanta...all had been death traps.

Neil was quiet for a long time. Without the windshield, the wind blasted them in the face, drying them out. Sadie wanted to take her nails to the mud and peel it away but she waited. If Neil chose the city route she would need that mud if she had any chance of survival.

At last he whispered: "We going to go to Wichita." Under his breath, he added: "God help us."

Chapter 26

Jillybean/Eve

She ran in the night. It felt wrong. Running was what humans did. Every zombie knew that, and boy, were there a lot of zombies! They were going every which way, stirred up by the gun shots and the lights and the trucks and the horsemen.

Still Jillybean ran. She didn't have a choice; she had made a decision—the world was better off without her in it. This little fact she had kept from the other girl inside her. Jillybean had lied about jail. There would be no jail for her. She could cute her way out of it and if that didn't work she knew that given time and a few simple resources, there weren't many jails that could hold her.

The lie had been a trick for the other girl. *Sh*e didn't like jail. *She* couldn't get out of them. *She* wasn't cute at all and *she* wasn't smart. With Jillybean constantly fighting her every thought *she* was scattered brained and couldn't remember who she hated most from one moment to the next. *She* needed Jillybean to do her heavy thinking for her and yet Jillybean had expected more of a fight from her.

She wasn't exactly a stupid girl. *She* was mean and evil but not stupid. But *she* didn't want to go to Colorado where everyone was good and where *she* might go to jail, and really, *she* did want to see the theater with all the bombs and bullets in it, go sky-high.

That was exactly the kind of mayhem *she* liked.

When Jillybean kept running after crossing the little ditch that the monsters had made in their endless tramping, *she* tried to stop Jillybean.

This is close enough, Eve said, with a giggle. *Blow it up*. The desire to see the explosion was so intense that Jillybean's feet began dragging and the remote seemed to rise up to eye level on its own.

"Not...yet," Jillybean panted. She was winded from the three-hundred-yard sprint, but she couldn't stop. There were a slew of monsters in her wake and worse, she saw there were horsemen riding in practiced teams, driving back the other monsters from the courthouse where trucks and cars were being gathered in preparation for the chase. They would be ready in minutes.

Jillybean headed right for them.

Wait, what are you doing? Eve asked. *You don't want to get so close.* Jillybean's feet slowed even more; it was like running through deep water. The other girl began to get agitated. *Stop or I'll take over again and I won't ever let you out.*

"You don't...know how...to work...the bomb," Jilly-bean said. Immediately, she felt her feet spring forward, once again hers to command. She angled toward an approaching horseman who had his spear leveled and was knocking monsters back away from the grassy slope that ran up towards the building. Jillybean didn't have any fear of the man or the horse. Neither was expecting a thinking being to be in front of them.

The monsters came on, slow and stupid; Jillybean was fast. She darted practically under the nose of the horse. It jerked its head and eyed Jillybean with one big, brown orb. In the dark, the rider didn't even see her.

Now will you blow it up? the other girl asked. There was a petulant whine to her voice.

"I've got a better idea," Jillybean answered. "We're going to hold this entire town hostage."

Why? What good does that do us?

"You want to be Lady Eve? That's small potatoes. We could be a princess. Think about that." Jillybean felt a sudden hungry longing and knew that Eve liked the idea very much. "Just don't interfere," Jillybean warned, "or you'll screw this all up."

Silence from within meant that the other girl was fully on board.

As she walked, Jillybean pulled her shredded dress over her head and used it to scrape as much mud off her face as she could. She went unnoticed until she came to the trucks that were filling with men who were armed as if expecting to lay siege to a fortress. They were very large and scary. Most wore scraggly beards and had hair like lion's manes.

They loaded their trucks, oblivious to the little girl until she gathered the courage to step right up next to the tire of one of the trucks. Only then did someone point at her. Another person exclaimed: "It's one of them."

She held the remote up, however it went unremarked upon. Even Brad, who came jogging up to her, didn't seem to notice it. "I'm surprised you stayed," he said. "You aren't too smart."

"Didn't we have a deal?" Jillybean asked.

"I had a deal," Brad said. "You got a lesson in how not to be so gullible."

Eve, hearing that she had been double-crossed straight from Brad's lips, bristled and wanted to explode the bomb right then. "Not yet," Jillybean hissed. She then turned to Brad. "I'm smart enough not to come empty-handed. Captain Grey set a bomb in this town. It's some-where really, really bad for you guys. I'm supposed to 'splode it."

"And what's stopping you?" Brad said. Though some of the men glanced around, nervously, he did not seem concerned in the least. Jillybean suspected that, with the escape of the renegades, his chance at being *Baron* Crane had diminished considerably. He might have even been demoted, but what was below baron, she didn't know.

"I want to renegotiate," Jillybean explained, in a loud enough voice that everyone around them heard. "I want to talk to the Duke or I'll blow the bomb and it'll be on your head, Mister Brad."

Some of the men snorted with laughter. Others looked amazed that the tiny girl was so composed. She was quite literally surrounded, twice over, by enemies and all she had to protect herself was a little black box. To add to her aura, she said: "I think you know that I'll blow the bomb up, Brad. I heard you tell people that I'm crazy. I know what that means. It means I'll blow up the bomb even if you don't think it's smart."

Brad put out his hands and said in a softer tone: "We still have our deal. I was just joking before. I've already talked to the Duke and he said that from here on you're to be Lady Eve. So, if you could just put that thing down we can talk about getting you a tiara."

His lie was pathetic since he had already sneered at her and it didn't help his case that a number of the men nearby were sniggering.

"I know you're lying, Mister Brad and I don't want our old deal anyways. I want a new one and I want something more or there will be trouble for you and for this whole town."

Brad shrugged. "Blow it up then. Let's see what you got." She hesitated and he grinned. "Here's the problem with your little bomb. You're just a one-trick pony. You can't blow up the bomb because you know the Duke will kill you if you do, and you can't just stand there either. You look stupid trying to threaten us with a little hunk of plastic."

He was right on all counts all except her being a one-trick pony. Her ladybug backpack was not only prettier than her old *I'm a Belieber* backpack, it had more compartments as well. There had to be a dozen zippered pocked or meshed-off sections. She kept the things she felt were most handy in the most accessible spots. In a side pocket was a heavy lump.

Switching the remote to her left hand, she reached around with her right, unzipped a pocket and pulled from it a curious item she had picked up at the theater four hours before.

"Is that...Is that a hand grenade?" Brad asked.

"Yeah, it sure is," Jillybean said. "I have more than one trick, though not like a pony. I don't think they can do any sorts of tricks. And this isn't like a magic trick, neither. It's more like...well I don't know, a fireworks show." The rings in all the other hand grenades she had ever exploded had been very tight; she knew there was no way

296

she was going to be able to pull it with the remote in her hand, at least not in the normal way.

She stooped, placed the grenade on the ground and stepped very close to it so that one of her once-white Keds was firmly planted on the ring. With a simple heave of her body upwards, the ring pin came out while she held the spoon on the grenade tightly down with her fingers. Now it was simply a matter of deciding what to blow up.

Blow up Brad, the other girl suggested with sickly eagerness.

"What do you think you're going to do with that grenade?" Brad asked.

She shrugged. "I dunno, 'splode something? That's what it's for." A man tried to slip around behind her using the dark as cover, however she was deeper in the gloom than the others and her night eyes were sharp. "I'm going to blow something up," she said to him. "You should be running away."

The man stopped, measuring the distance between them and sizing up the girl. He clearly didn't think she would use the grenade. "You should stop him Mister Brad," she suggested. "And you should tell those people to get out of that truck." A jut of her chin indicated a black, Ford truck with an extended bed.

Brad looked like he had swallowed something slimy and that it was crawling around in his belly looking for a way out. "Why?" he asked. His eyes kept flicking to the grenade, to her face, and to the truck. His tongue was like that of a serpent's, it flicked out to lick his lips every half-second or so.

Like a pitcher on the mound with a runner on first, Jillybean looked the man, who had been trying to creep behind her, back to where he had started. She then grinned up at Brad, feeling distinctly unlike herself. Here she was with two bombs and part of her—not the evil part that called itself "Eve"—wanted to just light the place up.

She couldn't, however. She had two goals that night: stall the Duke's men long enough for her friends to get away, and to live, free if possible. That meant she had to talk to the Duke and not to Brad, who was only a second rate fellow in the Duke's employment. And he was a liar. Jillybean didn't like liars.

"Why am I going to blow up the truck? Why of course to get the Duke's attention. I have to talk to him about some things that are very important."

"Then start talking," a voice boomed.

Jillybean knew that lion's roar of a voice. She felt like a mouse before the man as he stomped across the pavement toward them. He was in such a towering rage that even the grenade in her hand seemed minuscule before him, as though it would only make a popping sound, and blink a little light and dribble a touch of smoke.

He glared fiercely and her voice escaped out into the night. She opened her mouth but not even a squeak slipped from between her lips. "Well?" the Duke demanded. After a second he glanced at Brad for an explanation.

"She's one of *them*," he said. "She's a bit delusional."

"And is that a real grenade?" the Duke asked.

Brad's insult lit a fire under Jillybean. She thrust the grenade out toward the Duke. "Yes it's real and this is a remote control for another bigger bomb. Captain Grey planted it and it's somewhere special in the town."

The Duke's heavy brows came down pooling shadows where his eyes should've been. Jillybean hadn't seen anything so scary since she had been thrust down into her own mind. The reminder woke the other girl and she took that moment to hiss: *Kill him! Let the spoon go on the grenade, count to three and throw it at him, then run. If they chase you then set off the other bomb.*

"I can't," she whispered. The truth was that killing in cold blood like this wasn't something she could do. It ran contrary to her nature, but not that of the other girl.

Then let me! she demanded. I'll gladly do it. Think about it, we can kill the Duke. He poisoned Deanna, remember? And he tried to capture everyone. He's evil, Jillybean. He's more evil than me. He should die. They all should die. They should burn.

298

Jillybean was shaken by the voice. It was so filled with the hunger of hate that her teeth hurt.

This quick conversation passed in between blinks of an eye and the Duke was only just reacting to the idea that there was a second bomb in the town. He turned again to Brad. "What's this about a bomb? Is she for real?"

Brad paused, letting his shrewd eyes bounce to each of the dominant figures in the night. Jillybean guessed that he was looking for the least advantage. "If I had a guess, I would say that she is not lying. There were reports of someone slinking around the town earlier. The soldier with them seemed capable of planting a bomb."

"And they would leave a little girl to detonate it?" the Duke asked. "That seems very far-fetched."

The logic of this had Brad second guessing himself. Always helpful, Jillybean raised her grenade hand. "No, they weren't going to have me 'splode the bomb, but there was an issue with the range. They were too far away to use the remote and Mister Captain Grey couldn't come back because he was needed for the wounded and Neil was the leader and Sadie was…well, she is my sister, so she couldn't go and so I said I would come back to blow up the bomb on account I had been bad."

Her honesty was enough to convince the Duke. "And so why haven't you exploded the bomb?" he asked. "You've had plenty of opportunity. Have you had a change of heart? Or are you chicken?"

"No, Mister Duke, Sir, I'm not chicken," she replied. "I just didn't think that the 'splosion wouldn't slow you down enough. My guess is that it'll just make you extra mad and then you would go crazy or something. That won't help anyone. Not you and not us."

"You wish to help me?" the Duke asked with a laugh. "Why don't I believe you?"

Jillybean shrugged, innocently. "Maybe because I have a bomb. It's never smart to trust anyone with a bomb, 'cept you can trust me. I don't want to make you mad. I just don't want you to go after my friends."

"That seems unlikely," the Duke said. "They are worth quite a bit to me. There are bounties from all over the place on their heads."

"What the bomb is planted on is worth more, I bet," Jillybean retorted, quickly.

This made the Duke's eyes narrow. A second later he beckoned Brad closer and leaned close to whisper in his ear. Brad grinned at what he heard and then slunk backwards into the night.

"Darn it," Jillybean whispered, guessing that they had figured out the short list of possibilities where the bomb could be planted.

Then blow them up! The other girl cried in an echo that warbled up and down within her mind. *Blow them up, or I will!*

This was no idle threat. Jillybean could feel snake-like tendrils spreading out through her body as the other girl started to exert control. "No," Jillybean whispered. "I'll fight you and you know what will happen. Our muscles will go slack and the grenade will fall. It'll blow us up. You know that will happen, don't you?" Jillybean gave her a mental picture and the tendrils retreated.

With a shake of her head she glanced up at the Duke. He was trying to play it straight, however it was obvious he thought he had Jillybean cornered. There really were only a few places that an experienced soldier like Captain Grey would plant a bomb: the courthouse, the fuel dump and the theater. The Duke's look suggested that he was going to bide his time until he knew that the bomb had been defused.

"You know where the bomb is, don't you?" she asked him. He shrugged, however he didn't have much of a poker face; she knew she was right. "Well, I know you do, so the next question you are asking yourself is: why don't I blow it up now and then throw my grenade?"

He shrugged, however it wasn't with nearly the confidence of the last.

"Because," she continued, "It won't effect the outcome. If there was one thing that Ipes has taught me it's that I should follow each possible course of action to its logical conclusion. That's what he would say if he was here."

The Duke looked nonplussed at this. "Who the hell is Ipes?"

"Oh, he was my zebra. But that doesn't matter right now. I think I have followed every action and every word down their lines and I think I know what will happen. You will wait until Brad returns and then take me prisoner. If you act prior to that, then we will both lose so much more." This was her warning to the Duke that he shouldn't do anything but wait.

He nodded, almost as an equal to the little girl. She knew she was his equal, but only as long as she held the remote. It would be useless in minutes. She'd still have the grenade and with it she would maybe gain a couple of minutes more.

But only as long as you are close enough to actually threaten someone with it, the other girl said.

"You're right," Jillybean said, moving closer to the Duke. When he backed away, eyeing the grenade, she went to the truck that was only a few feet away. When she had come up, men had been heaving boxes of ammo, water, food and extra fuel into the rear. All of it was still in the back. She rested her grenade hand on the tailgate.

"Well, you are something," the Duke said.

This didn't make any sense to the logic-minded girl. If she wasn't something then she would be nothing and that didn't make any sense because she was really real. "I am a girl, Mister Duke, Sir," she told him. "And I am seven now."

"Shame you won't make it to eight years old," he said.

It took her a moment to realize that had been a threat. *Kill him*, the other girl demanded. *Kill him before he kills us. Please. It'll be easy. Just do what I tell you.*

Jillybean hissed: "No!" causing the Duke to raise an eyebrow. He thought she was crazy, a complete whack-adoodle, but she didn't care what he thought. He was a mean, old, bad guy and she thought of him as beneath her.

They stood in a stony silence as the minutes passed. Each minute was a victory for Jillybean. The remains of her family were getting further and further away. Twenty three of these precious minutes ticked by before Brad came jogging up and gave the Duke a quick nod.

"Fun time is over," the Duke said. "We found your bomb and diffused it. Now put the pin back in the grenade or I will have you shot. You have until the count of ten."

The men of the Azael began to retreat to a safe distance, Brad included. Only the Duke held his ground. In his hand was a .44 caliber monster of a pistol and he had it aimed square at Jillybean. It was very disconcerting.

"I-I just n-need to get the pin," she said, pointing at the ground a few feet away. She began to edge toward it, her eyes never leaving the fat bore of the gun.

The Duke shrugged. "Fine, but I'm already up to five...six...seven..." Now, she rushed to where she had left the pin on the ground. She tried to snatch it up, however it fumbled out of her shaking hands to clink back onto the pavement. "Eight...nine..."

Behind her, she heard the hammer of the pistol click back. This only made her fingers go even crazier. They shook badly so that the pin was etching up and down as though she was graphing an earthquake. But worse: the pin was tiny, the hole minuscule and the dark made fitting one into the other as difficult as anything she had ever tried to accomplish in so short a time. The pin just wouldn't go where it needed.

"I got it," she lied right before he said 'Ten'. She stayed hunched over the grenade as she looked back at the Duke. Her smile went squirrelly as she saw that he still had the gun pointed her way. All she could think about was the size of the hole that thing would put in her.

"Then put it on the ground and back away, slowly," the Duke ordered.

"I-I...It is, uh, caught on my shirt." She turned back to the grenade, fearing that it would suddenly squirt out of her fingers. "I'll just be a second...ok, here it goes. Oh jeeze, I got it." The pin scraped the hole and caught the edge. She wiggled it into place and then with shaking hands placed the bomb on the ground.

"Move away from it!" the Duke barked. She crawled a few feet away without looking up at him, yet knowing that the awful big gun was trained on her tiny body. "Now, you are going to tell me where your friends are going or I will kill you."

As that answer was already known, she felt no qualm about blurting out: "Colorado."

"No shit," the Duke snarled. He stepped toward her and a second later she felt the metal bore push into the back of her head. "I want to know which way they went, and you're going to tell me or I'll splatter your brains all over this street."

She wanted to lie, only she didn't know any of the names of the roads they had traveled on and she knew that simply blurting out a random road number would never be believable. She was in such a desperate position that she even turned to the other girl inside her for help.

The other girl had no reply except to rant about the wasted opportunity with hand grenade: *You shoulda killed him. Next time you kill them all!*

There wasn't going to be a next time. The Duke pushed the gun so hard against her head that it seemed as though the gun pushed tears from her eyes. He loomed over her, a monstrous shadow, as he whispered: "I'm going count to three and if you haven't told me what I want to know then I'm going to pull the trigger. What route are they taking? One...two..."

"I-I don't know, Mister Duke, Sir," Jillybean cried. "They never told me which..."

He cut her off by saying: "Three."

Chapter 27

Deanna Russell

Opening her eyes was a tremendous struggle. Seemingly, they weighed many pounds. She had never felt weaker. Her arms and legs were like great flesh logs that were as long as tree trunks. Her fingers felt far away. They were vague and distant.

Her first attempt at opening her eyes was a failure. She could only get her right lid up and even then everything was dark. Three tries was all she had in her before she was overcome by exhaustion. Deanna fell back to sleep.

Hours went by as she slept in a more natural and healing manner. When next she stirred, there was light, the thin grey light that marked early morning. As before, her right eye came open first, then her left. Neither was able to focus.

There were people, mere blobs. She could hear them talking, they had the slow rumbling voices of whales. She saw them move like bouncing clouds. There was something wrong with her.

"Whaf," she said, through numb lips. A hand, long and pale white came up to her face. It was so strange that she found herself staring at it and it was only gradually that it came to resemble a normal hand. It was some time before she realized it was her own hand.

"Das ny han," she whispered. For some reason she was relieved at the realization. She tried to see whether her left hand was still attached to her body as well. It was just like the other except she had even less control; it fell across her face, making her blink and it was some time before she was able to haul her eyelids up again.

An hour had passed between blinks and the grey light had been replaced by a warmer hue. The blobs had turned into humans, though they were fuzzy on the edges. She knew her fingers again; she made weak little fists with them. Even her lips were back to normal.

"I think they're normal at least," she said, touching them with the tips of her fingers. They felt slightly puffy but nothing to worry about. She explored the rest of her face with her fingers, discovering that everything about her was normal again...all except her tongue. That felt fat and dry and tasted horrible, like the bottom of a shoe.

"Uugh," she groaned. Water was needed, badly. She tried to get up, making it to her knees without difficulty, but when she stood it was with all the fine motor control of a newly calved foal. Her legs wobbled and her head began to spin.

In a second, she knew she was going to fall and there wasn't going to be any way to stop it. She didn't even have the mental capacity to break her fall with her arms. The floor came rushing up to knock her teeth out of her head, but it stopped a foot away from her face.

"You're awake!"

Light as a feather, she was lifted and, when her eyes focused on the face in front of her, she saw it was Captain Grey. He was crying fat tear-bulbs.

"What's wrong?" she asked. She thought he was crying because there was something wrong with her—she certainly didn't feel like she was completely alright.

Quickly, he wiped his sleeve across his eyes. Embarrassed, he answered: "Nothing's wrong. I was just, uh, excited. I mean, happy that you're awake, finally. It's been two days."

Missing those two days didn't faze her all that much mainly because she had thought it had been more like two weeks. "So I look ok?" she asked, touching her face again.

"You look great to me," he answered and then looked startled that he had answered in such a forward way. After clearing his throat, he added in a more professional voice: "Outwardly you appear as you always have but I should give you a closer inspection. Stick out your tongue."

Her pale hand snapped up to cover her mouth. There was no way she was going to open her mouth with two day's worth of built up morning breath coating her tongue. "Some water first, please. And can you ask Marybeth if I can borrow her brush. I'm sure my hair is a complete rat's...nest. Hey, what's wrong?"

His face had clouded over and his eyes had darted to the side. Something was wrong and not just with her. Deanna really looked around for the first time since she had awoken. The renegades were in what looked like a very large warehouse. The corrugated metal walls were sixty feet high. There was plenty of room for the five-ton trucks and...and a fuel truck? When did they get a fuel truck?

"Where are we?" she wondered aloud. There hadn't been any warehouses of this size in the Duke's town.

"Wichita," Grey answered.

She was still a little jumbled in the head; she knew Wichita was in Kansas but didn't know where, exactly. And there was another thing bothering her that was more pressing than the fact that they were in Wichita. "What happened to me? And what's wrong with Marybeth? I can tell by your face something bad has happened."

There were bags under the captain's red-rimmed eyes and he was as pale as she had ever seen him. And his hair! It looked as though he had given himself a haircut with a knife. He told her their story and, as he spoke, she slumped further and further until she was as hunched as the letter 'C'.

"Kay is missing? And Jillybean? This is a disaster. And I just can't believe Eve is gone. Eve, I can't..." Her throat threatened to lock up and her eyes wanted to spit tears. She was only barely able to blink them back. "What about Marybeth? Is she going to die?" Deanna asked in a whisper. Marybeth was on a mattress thirty yards away. Her husband, Michael was holding her hand while her eldest daughter, Anne fanned her with a towel.

"The truth?" he asked, just as quietly. "Probably. The bullet just nicked her liver. It bled like nothing I've ever seen and all I can say is that I hope I patched it up right. I'm not a surgeon so I just don't know. And it wasn't just the liver. I had to remove about three feet of her small intestine. There will be complications, that's a guarantee."

"I'm sure you did the best you could," she said.

To this, he only shrugged. "I was just going to go down for a quick nap before I headed out. Both Marybeth and Becca are in need of some serious antibiotics."

"You're needed here," Deanna said. "Someone else should go."

Grey was just about to say something, but he ran a hand through his botched hair and then stopped and patted his head as if he had just remembered that it looked like a wolverine had sharpened its claws on his scalp. Deanna pretended not to notice.

"Uh," he stammered. "There are teams out right now, but it's very dangerous. It's been so hot that the stiffs are lurking indoors and they're acting...I don't know, strange. They're extremely quiet which means our people don't hear them until it's almost too late. We've had a few close calls. Neil thinks the heat is making them sleepy."

"Well, I will go with you when you go out," Deanna said. "I'll keep you safe." She gave him a smile, but it felt odd on her face as though her muscles were still not hers to control.

He grinned at her. "I can't pass up a guarantee of safety from you, but first let me check you out."

Obediently, she stuck out her tongue, followed his finger with just her eyes, allowed him to inspect her ears, nose, throat and beneath her eyelids. He felt along her neck and spine, but for what she didn't know. He checked her reflexes with the knife edge of his hand and then he checked her abdomen.

"A little stiff, but that's to be expected." The remark went right over her head. He sat back on his heels. "You seem no worse for wear, however, I don't think you should go out on any of the scavenging missions. There's no telling if there will be any short term side effects and it would make zero sense to endanger yourself or your team by going into the field too early."

"And I've been carried around for the last two days like a bag of dirty laundry. I feel restless, like I've sat around too much already. So…I'm going and there isn't much you can do about it." She raised an eyebrow to forestall any argument he might have.

He only shrugged as the air seemed to run out of him like a deflated balloon. "Ok, just wait until I've had a few minutes to rest. Don't go anywhere without me. Promise."

She promised and he offered only a small smile before he went to his mattress and slept. His mattress was three feet from hers. He was asleep in seconds, breathing deep and even. She found herself watching him as he slept; she couldn't seem to take her eyes off of him. She studied his features: his strong jaw, shadowed with two days of growth, his nose, thin but with a slight bend to it from a long ago break, his eyebrows, thick and dark. All of this was offset by the strange haircut which gave him a boyish look. It made him look young and less gritty than she had ever known him. She liked it, though she knew he was embarrassed as hell by it.

At some point in her vigil, she fell asleep. She didn't think that was possible since she had already slept for two days, but then she was awake again and blinking in puzzlement, her mind slow to focus. There were voices around her only they were mumbles as though she was hearing them from underwater.

Deanna sat up and the motion seemed to stop the voices; more blinks and her eyes grew more attuned. William Gates stood with his mouth in its usual propped open position. Ricky was there, half listening and half giving Sadie a lecherous eye. Sadie was pretending not to notice.

The Goth girl was in her customary black garb. Unlike Grey, who looked years younger, the Goth girl no longer looked like the teen she was. A decade of worry and fear and sadness had descended upon her. It was a wonder she hadn't gone grey overnight at the loss of Eve. Sadie had been dependent upon the baby to help her deal with her own issues and now that crutch was gone.

308

Normally, she would've turned to Neil, however he had gone through a transformation in the two days that Deanna had slept. There was an obvious wardrobe change, yet the big difference was his eyes. They were still baby blue, but the soft, almost naïve, look she was used to was gone, replaced by something hard and steely. It was a look that left no doubt that, although Neil was a small man and delicately cast, there was a depth and strength to him. Deanna also saw that he possessed a reserve of anger she hadn't known before, and there was a coldness to him that was frightful if seen full on. She caught only a glimpse, but it was enough.

Grey was first to notice that she was awake. He caught her eyes but said nothing. Neil was talking and there was a sharpness to his voice that was as new as his outfit.

"I'm sorry, Grey, but we have to wait until sunset," Neil said in a voice that brooked no argument. "The truck I saw was definitely one of the Duke's. I remember it clear as day. They either know we're here or they're scouting. One way or the other, we can't afford to give away our position no matter what." Grey bristled and Neil's eyes grew colder still. The smaller man wouldn't back down. "No matter what."

The soldier wasn't so easily cowed and he knew Neil's soft spot. "Even if means more deaths?"

Neil was a block of ice. "Yes." Grey set his teeth for a fight but Neil held up a hand. "We have three hours before sunset. Use that time to get your teams up to speed with what they can expect. Three hours won't…" Neil stopped abruptly as he saw that Deanna was awake and watching him. The ice in him thawed in a blink. It was disconcerting. Was she looking at Neil or some strange politician?

"How are you feeling?" he asked, with the warmth of his old self.

"I'm good, thanks. I just feel like so much has happened that it's just…weird. I mean look at you."

Neil glanced down at himself. He was wearing fatigues that he had cut at the wrists so that they wouldn't hang half a foot over his fingertips. A belt cinched the baggy camouflage trousers at his waist. A green bandanna dangled from his neck as though he were one quick move from robbing a bank. The biggest difference in his attire was in his footwear. Gone were the crocs. In their place he wore sturdy Army regulation, jungle boots.

"I guess it was time to give up the sweater vests," he said. "They never served their purpose, anyway." There was enough of the old Neil for him to glow a shade of pink as he admitted: "The truth...I thought they made me look bigger. You know, stronger. That's why I always wore the thick ones. But that doesn't matter anymore, does it?"

No one had an answer for this. Deanna would've disagreed. Projecting strength was even more important now than before the apocalypse. Now, a man needed to provide and protect, while a woman...well, Deanna wasn't sure what a woman's role was in this new undead world. Babies weren't valued in the least and neither was a college degree or her knowledge of books and current events or her smooth, sophisticated banter that had made her a hit at dinner parties.

For a second Deanna found herself floundering, while Neil, this tiny man who was maximizing every talent he possessed, only smiled at her, making her seem smaller than he was.

"No, I guess it doesn't matter anymore," she said, wearing what she felt was a pathetic grin.

Grey saw through it, though he couldn't guess as to the cause—even after a year she still felt lost and grasping at who she should be or what she should be doing with herself. "You ok?" he asked, concerned.

"No...I'm good. It's just Neil in army clothes! What's the world coming to?" She gave a little laugh. The others laughed along with her. For a moment, Sadie dropped the ten years hanging over as she punched Neil on the arm hard enough for him to wince.

"Ok, that's enough," Neil said, rubbing his arm. "You each have your jobs. Let's do them and get out of this in one piece."

310

They nodded, all save Deanna who was sure she didn't have a job, just as she was sure she didn't have a role. Neil left first, then William, and Ricky. Sadie watched them walk away and then sighed as if under a ton of bricks. "See you in a couple of hours," she said and then left. She didn't go far; there was a mattress lying on the ground against the wall. She sat on it with her knees at the height of her chin and dug through her pack.

Grey paused long enough to catch Deanna's eye. There was a moment between them where their connection flared up. As usual it made him uncomfortable and he was quick to make an excuse to leave. "I've got to go check on Becca and Marybeth," he said. "You should get something to eat and scrounge up a weapon if you're coming out with us tonight."

"Sure."

Food was easy—if one liked corn. Two of the renegades, Travis and Veronica, had roasted about a hundred ears; there was plenty to go around. It needed butter, badly, though Deanna wasn't going to complain, she was famished. When the corn was gone she drew two quarts of water from their dwindling supply.

She drank one quart and bathed herself with the other. After that she went to her mattress and decided to wait for Grey to return. She did not wait long. Not because he returned quickly but because, as she sat there in the lowering light, all she could think about was Eve and Jillybean and Kay...and her own baby.

"Emily," she whispered, rubbing her stomach which felt strangely stiff and a little sore. She remembered Grey saying *that's to be expected*. "That's weird," she whispered to herself. "I've never been stiff before. I wonder what..."

She looked down at herself. She had noticed that she was wearing an unfamiliar baggy dress and had assumed that someone had changed her clothes at one point when she was out cold. She looked around for her jeans and then she remembered the blood. There had been blood on her jeans! "Was that a dream?" she asked, feeling her belly, low down.

The last thing she recalled before her drug-induced coma was having dinner with the Duke and then leaving and feeling sick and woozy. Vaguely, she remembered there had been blood on her jeans. It had seemed like a lot.

"Oh no!" Gingerly, she began prodding her stomach; something was definitely different. Something very bad.

Across from her, Sadie stood and slung her pack over one shoulder. She was leaving. Deanna jumped up and ran to her but only took a few steps before Sadie spun with a Glock speeding into her hand.

"It's just me," Deanna said, stopping with the barrel a foot from her nose.

"Sorry," was all Sadie said, before holstering the gun. "You need something?"

Deanna looked around, suddenly embarrassed and shy by what she was about to ask. No one had known she was pregnant—no one except the Duke, that is. "I need to ask you a question about...about the other night. When I, uh, was drugged." Sadie's eyes darted away telling Deanna all she needed to know.

"My baby?" she asked.

Sadie looked confused. "You don't remember? It was the Duke. You should never have told him you were pregnant." Deanna wanted to ask how she knew anything about the conversation, but Sadie cut her off. "Jillybean was in the room that night. She saw almost everything...only it wasn't really Jillybean, if you know what I mean."

Deanna didn't have a clue what she meant. Just like those moments after she had left the Duke, her mind began to swim. Strange images flashed in front of her: the blood, the way everyone whispered and pointed, Neil rushing around, Captain Grey kissing her and whispering: *It'll be alright*.

"But it won't be alright," Deanna said. Her hands clutched the lower part of her abdomen where Emily should have been growing. She was empty, hollow. She was no longer a mother. Her child had been killed before she had a chance to take her first breath. Deanna began to cry. She wept huge, fat tears and a wail of despair began to build within her.

Sadie cut it off. The teen grabbed the taller woman by the shoulders and shook her fiercely. "What the hell do you think you're doing?" she demanded. The angry tone and the hard fingers digging into her arms stifled the wail before it started. "Do you think crying is going to do anyone any good?"

"I...I..."

"The answer is no. Look around you, damn it. Now is not the time to be acting like you're the only one who's lost someone. Marybeth is about to die. Becca is probably going to lose that leg if we don't find antibiotics. Travis had a three month old child who was killed. Neil's parents and his wife and daughter are dead. We've all lost people close to us. You're not the first and you won't be the last, so you can either wallow in pity and bring down the group or you can grow a pair."

Deanna was shocked at the girl's tone but was even more so when Sadie pulled out her Glock again. She turned it to the side and said: "You know what I like about the Glock? There's no safety. There's no dicking around with this baby once you pull it. I suggest you get one and if you find yourself in the same room as the Duke, you put a bullet in his eye."

"I can do that," Deanna said, stiffly. Her face was an angry red and now the tears were purest fury. Sadie was right. Tears for the dead were a waste. The dead deserved loving memories and sweet revenge.

Chapter 28

Captain Grey

In the hour before they left, Grey drilled the twenty seven renegades. They were broken down into nine teams of three, each with their own destination and each with their own objectives.

Some were going to the homes of veterinarians in search of antibiotics, surgical supplies and pain killers, while others were going to strip-malls that had been home to electronic stores. These groups were looking for two-way radios and all the batteries they could carry. Neil's group which included Sadie and Connie had one of the harder jobs. They were going to Town East Square, a mall that was billed as the largest shopping district in Kansas. Again radios and electronic supplies were what they were after.

"I don't get it," Randy said. "You want me to go to a vet's house? Wouldn't it be smarter to go to a normal doctor's office or to a hospital?"

Neil shook his head. "No. All those places were inundated with patients when the virus broke out. They were mad houses and if they had anything left when things calmed down, you can bet the Azael raided them later. Few people remember that vets made house calls, especially out here in farm country."

"I think it's a genius idea," Veronica said.

Normally, Neil would have blushed at the compliment, however he surprised Grey by agreeing instead. "Yes, it is a genius idea, so naturally it wasn't mine. Jillybean thought of it."

"Jillybean," William spat. "Good riddance."

Neil glared at him. "What happened to Marybeth wasn't her fault. If you don't have the wit to blame the Duke, then blame me. Jillybean was the way she was because of me."

"No one's blaming anyone," Grey said, coming between the two men. He stared them both down and then gave the others a once-over. "Veronica, you look too...well you still look like a woman. Stow the cleavage and add more ash to your face. This isn't a beauty contest for zombies." She pouted but without much conviction. Grey guessed that the cleavage had been exposed quite purposefully.

He turned to Deanna, last. She was in a quiet mood and he hoped that it was only the morphine wearing off. "You ok?" he asked. Her eyes were red and there was an angry cast to them. She replied with only a nod.

When everyone had passed inspection, Grey nodded to Neil who clapped his hands to get their attention. "Ok, we all have our maps, our routes planned, and our contingency plans. Remember, if you run into any of the Duke's men you run and hide. You should all be confident enough now to be able to slip into any zombie horde. Now, let's mount up."

Grey's group, consisting of himself, Deanna and Travis, had the most dangerous job. They were going to make an attempt on McConnell Air Force base which was located in the southeast quadrant of the city. The group was low on ammo and they were too lightly armed for any major confrontation with the Duke's men. He could only hope they were going to get as lucky as they had at Fort Campbell.

They took the first truck in line and as soon as he had two of the teams in the back, he rumbled the engine to life. When he heard the other trucks turn over, he flicked his light at the main set of doors where Joe Gates was waiting. Immediately the boy began hauling on the chain and the door slowly began to slide upward.

When there was enough clearance, Grey pulled out of the warehouse. Next to him, as always, was Deanna. She had a red cover over her flash light to minimize its light output. It was enough to see a map by. "Take your third right," she told him.

"You sure you're ok?" Grey asked. "You don't seem yourself."

Her mouth came open and hung there for a few moments before she shook her head. "It's nothing." Her hand stole to her belly. He reached for it and brushed her fingers, lightly. Hers was small and cool, his was rough and scarred.

Travis made a point of looking out the window until Deanna politely pushed Grey's hand away. "Sorry, but it feels like you're jinxing us," she said in a husky voice. "Everything I love dies."

"I understand, but when I get you to Colorado..." he left off and was gratified by her smile. "Ok, no more jinxes. Which turn is it?"

Their first stop was a hundred yards down from a strip mall. The first team, led by William Gates, slid out of the back of the bed and began to shamble to the side of the road. Their zombie technique was perfect.

Grey drove another two miles and stopped just down the street from a mall. Michael Gates, his nephew John and Veronica climbed down. Grey noted that Veronica was only iffy as a zombie, while Michael was little better. Worry for them began to creep up his throat.

"Damn, Michael, you're going too straight," he whispered to himself. "And Veronica, oh my Lord..."

Now it was Deanna's turn to take his hand. "They'll be fine. Trust them."

As he was out of options he had no choice except to follow her advice, He watched them stump away for a few seconds and then he drove through the cluttered streets to his final destination: McConnell Air Force base.

He had never been there before, however it had that same feel to it as all military bases seemed to possess. Even dead as it was there was a quality to the air, as if he was coming home.

They parked in a low-rent neighborhood across from the airstrips and almost immediately ran into trouble. Zombies came piling out from the nearby houses. They were too close to pretend that they were zombies, and

316

there were too many to fight. Grey drove in a big circle around the block and, when he got back to his beginning point, the zombies were far down the street and only just realizing their prey was now behind them.

By the time they reached the truck, Grey, Deanna, and Travis had slipped out of the neighborhood and were limping in the field toward the perimeter fencing. There weren't just holes in the fencing, there were places where it had been ripped out of the ground and twisted as if by a giant.

"Tornado what prolly did this," Travis said.

Grey grunted. He really didn't care what had torn up the fence, he was just happy to have gotten through so easily. He had not relished a mile long 'walk' down to one of the gates; zombie walking wasn't an easy thing to do.

They still had half a mile to go across the tarmac. "Spread out. Deanna in the middle. Travis on the right." Slowly they trudged toward the nearest buildings which grey knew to be airplane hangars. On the way they passed a pair of A10 Thunderbolts. Affectionately known as the Warthog, they were the ugliest planes in the American arsenal. They were also tank killers and right handy when things were tough.

Grey paused next to one, considering the possibility of somehow removing the 30MM rotary cannon in the nose of the plane. It was a fantastic piece of weaponry that fired depleted uranium armor-piercing shells. With it, he could turn one of the five-ton trucks into scrap metal in a few seconds.

"But how would I stabilize it?" he asked himself, slapping the gun with his bare hand. It was a pipe dream under the circumstances. What he really needed were some crew-serviced, heavy machine guns and maybe a few mortars and perhaps a TOW missile system thrown in for fun.

It was not to be. Four hours of searching through the ruins of the base left him nearly empty-handed. It appeared to have been plundered on more than one occasion and even the moldering corpses strewn here and there among the buildings had their pockets turned inside out.

The one item of interest came from a walking corpse that attacked Deanna, who was carrying what she thought was a particularly useful looking piece of equipment to Grey for inspection. The beast, in its camouflage, and under the cover of darkness surprised her by appearing suddenly at her side. She cursed and shoved the 'weapon'—what turned out only to be a water cannon used to clean the planes—at the zombie, fending it off until Grey came up from behind and kicked its legs out from beneath it. He would have used his Ka-bar and sliced its spinal column where the skull sat on the vertebrae, however it was 'wearing' a helmet.

The helmet had slid back and was being held on by the chin strap which was tight across its throat. To kill it, Grey stepped on the thing's head, pinning it to the perfectly flat cement of the hangar floor and punching the Ka-bar into its temple.

"Holy-moly that was close," Deanna said in a frightened whisper.

"Maybe you should keep a better..." Grey stopped in mid-sentence. Something about the zombie had caught his eye. He knelt and turned the thing's head to the side so that the front of the helmet was revealed. "That's what I'm talking about," he said.

Deanna put her hands on her hips and said: "Talking about what? That thing nearly killed me."

"Yeah," Grey answered, though he did so more out of habit. He was too busy pulling a hunk of technology from the zombie's helmet to really pay attention.

"What is it?" Deanna asked, no longer in the strident tones she'd been using.

He grinned, his white teeth glowing in the dim light. "If I'm not mistaken these are AN-20/PSQ enhanced night vision goggles." He dug out his flashlight and, after cupping his hands around it, turned it on and studied the helmet-mounted device. "Oh yes, these are the dash twenties!"

Deanna shrugged. "Meaning what?"

He almost felt like a kid at Christmas. Excitedly, he blurted: "Meaning it's a passive intensification and thermal imaging device! It uses both I2 and long wave infrared sensors. Oh, I hope the batteries haven't started to corrode it."

He began to work the old double A batteries out of the back of the device. As he did, Deanna pointed at what she'd been carrying. "I found that."

Grey swung his flashlight at it. "That sprays water. They probably use it to clean the equipment."

"Oh."

"It's fine," he said quickly. "Keep looking. We're bound to turn up more." It turned out that this was an incorrect statement. All told they found six MREs, all Chicken-ala-King, twenty-three rounds of ammo, the front end of the pressure washer and the AN/PSQ enhanced night vision goggles for which they did not have batteries.

And, they were late! They should've been back at the truck thirty minutes ago, but there had been too many stiffs about to move at anything more than a limp. Discouraged, they set off back across the tarmac which Grey saw had already begun to spring long cracks. In a few places weeds had sprung up and were flourishing. Before the apocalypse the airstrips had been immaculate, every inch of it being examined and cleaned on a daily basis

Now there are weeds, Grey thought to himself. It was depressing to realize that there was precious little remaining of the United States military. It had been, during his entire lifetime, the greatest force for good the world had ever known. With it, any country could've been conquered and subjugated, its people slain wholesale or sold into slavery; its riches plundered.

Only that had never happened. No gold was ever stolen, not one drop of oil misappropriated, no women were ever raped as a matter of policy. And when evil was done by individuals wearing the uniform of the United States, the perpetrators were severely dealt with.

This desire for righteousness was the ideal that Grey had served...and now it was crumbling away just as surely as the tarmac was being split by the power of time and weather.

Breaking his zombie-lurch, Grey knelt down and began pulling the offending weeds. Travis watched with a smirk on his face, however Deanna came down beside Grey and helped. This little gesture had his heart stirring all the more.

"Tell me you plan on smoking all that," Travis said. "I mean, why else are you wasting time with..."

Suddenly a sharp light cut across the night. It was a beam zipping out across the tarmac coming from almost directly in front of them!

Travis stared at it as it slowly swept the field from right to left, heading right for him. Grey jumped up and tackled him, pushing his face down into the tarmac. "No one move," the captain ordered in a hiss, as the light swept over them. They were concealed by the tall grass that bordered the airstrip, but only barely. The light was inches above them.

The light went back and forth for a minute and then they heard voices talking and what was the unmistakable sound of a gun being dropped on the ground. This was followed by a low curse and then a whispered order to: "Shut up!"

With the light pointed away, Grey raised his head and scanned over the tips of the grass. He could see the dim shapes of men squatting just beyond the torn-up fence. There were possibly a dozen of them, spread out in a long line.

"Go back," Grey whispered. He crawled backwards, keeping his head and ass as low to the ground as possible. Deanna tried to replicate the motion but could only scrape herself back, awkward and slow. Travis spun on his belly and low-crawled off the tarmac and into the deeper grass.

Grey led them down a steep grade and into a concrete drainage ditch. From there he lifted himself in a hunched position and scurried as fast as he could along the ditch. It was dry and sandy with little in it save the occasional jumble of bones of some poor long-dead airman.

They had left the men working the searchlight a hundred yards back, when there was a sudden crack of rifle fire. All three threw themselves down on the embankment; Grey was the only one who had his weapon up and pointed outward. His eyes were black but sharp. A single gunshot made no sense unless...

"They're trying to make us give away our position," he told them. "Don't move." He scrambled up the embankment and again raised up just high enough to see only it was too dark to see much of anything in any direction. A breeze shifted in his direction bringing with it the rich smell of lilac and the rumble of a truck's engine.

A second truck engine sounded from the other direction

"Quick!" he ordered. He slid down the incline and then hurried up the other side. They were being hemmed in by the Duke's men—it was the only logical conclusion. A second bit of logic suggested that, since the ditch was the only real hiding spot, it had to be abandoned right away.

He reached back and took Deanna's hand, pulling her up the steep hill. Travis scrambled up on his own. "Oh God! We're fucked," he said in a panic.

"Possibly," Grey replied—what more was there to say? Fear was a waste of time and energy.

The rumbling of one of the trucks stopped a distance away, while a second truck continued for a few hundred yards and then stopped as well. Grey could picture what was being arrayed against them: fifteen men per truck, strung out in a line of a quarter of a mile. They would, in all probability, advance into the field and catch the three renegades in the open as they tried to cross the next airstrip.

By turning north and hurrying down the drainage ditch as he had, Grey had put his little group directly in the center of a trap which was now closing in on them. He bit back a string of curses and tried to focus. Surviving meant understanding his enemy.

What were the Duke's men thinking just then? On the macro level, they would be confident that they had the advantage in numbers. On the micro level each man would be nervous at best and downright scared at worst. These were not trained soldiers. They had never tasted combat save against the mindless, stumbling masses of undead. Being shot at in return was a whole other can of worms.

Because of that they would instinctively clump, leaving gaps in their line through which three very quiet and careful people could slip—if they were lucky. Grey's first job was to maximize that luck.

He risked another look over the top of the grass. A second searchlight had been added to the first. It swept the land north of them, showing Grey more than it showed his adversaries. When the light panned wide, zipping by at the height of the tall grass, it showed an empty field. They weren't advancing yet, meaning he had time to move.

"This way," he said, leading them deeper into the trap. There was a metal culvert ahead where a stretch of concrete jutted toward the fence. The Duke's men would be leery of the culvert. They would crimp in toward it, fearing that it would be the most likely place the renegades would hide. Their line would thin as extra men gravitated toward it; gaps would form approximately fifty yards on either side.

On their bellies they crawled through the grass which seemed to rustle loudly beneath them and yet nothing was louder than Travis' panicked breathing. He was on the verge of hyperventilating and sounded like he had just sprinted a mile. Grey was just turning to tell him to calm down when guns started blasting the night.

All up and down the Duke's lines men fired. Grey wasn't fooled. He had long ago developed an ear for the direction of gunfire and, even though the air hissed inches over their heads with the passage of blazing hot lead, he knew they weren't being targeted; the firing wasn't concentrated.

Travis, who was on the verge of true panic, began to heave himself to his feet, obviously ready to run away. Grey didn't blame him. Three million years of evolution had programmed the flight instinct into him and he was just following his nature. Grey and Deanna had the same instinct, however, Grey's training and superior intelligence superseded the urge, while Deanna was able to overcome it through trust alone.

Her eyes had been on Grey from the moment they had first seen the light zip across the field. In her eyes he saw only trust. She had put herself in his hands, totally. Trust was another evolutionary trait that allowed humans to bond and form cohesive families and communities. Trust mitigated fear and this was why she wasn't freaking out like Travis, who, even as Grey watched, began to climb to his feet, ready to flee like a spooked rabbit.

Grey was faster. He gathered his legs beneath him and, still in a squat, launched himself at Travis, tackling him before he could give away their position. Travis tried to fight Grey but there was no way. The soldier had arms like banded iron and his grip could not be overcome by the spastic energy of pure fright.

"Stop it," Grey said, beneath the last echoes of gun-fire. "They can't see us unless you stand up. Trust me Travis, I've been doing this sort of thing for a long time. Trust me and I'll get you out of here in one piece."

Over the course of the following minute, Travis calmed enough for Grey to push him on. They started to move not a second too soon. The next time Grey peeked his head up, he saw that the Duke's men had started forward. They were moving with all the caution of men un-trained for the task before them and if the night vision goggles in Grey's pack had working batteries, he would've eaten those men alive.

"Quicker," he hissed. They needed to move thirty yards in less than a minute for Grey to feel good about their position. Low-crawling wasn't an easy thing to do under the best of circumstances. Neither Travis nor Dean-na were experienced and, time and again, Grey muttered: "Get your ass down." He knew, from experience, there was a tendency to lift up the longer one crawled. In this case they had about twenty inches of grass as their only cover. "Spread your body out," he advised. "You'll stay lower."

When they had reached a spot that he could only hope would work, they hunkered down with their weapons at the ready, listening with fine-tuned ears to the crunching of grass that marked the enemy coming closer and closer.

Grey took his hand off his M4 to reach out and grip Travis' shoulder, in what he hoped was a reassuring grip. He gave Deanna a rakish smile to let her know that he wasn't worried in the least. In truth, he was pretty sure they were going to die in the next few minutes. The Duke's men had shifted toward the culvert just as he had expected, however someone had barked an order and the line had dressed itself, to a degree, so that the gap between the men was less than twenty yards.

Still, it was a dark night and the three of them were dressed in shredded rags that blended well with their sur-roundings. All they had to do was freeze in place and not breathe like a locomotive chugging up a sharp incline, which was exactly what Travis was doing.

The grip Grey had on Travis' shoulder grew tighter the closer the approaching feet came. They were going to be found out for sure if Travis didn't shut up. Then, Dean-na reached over and put her index finger on Travis' lips. It was like magic. Travis quieted. Even when the star-shad-ow of the man swept across their boots, Travis was like a mouse.

In a minute, the danger was thirty yards away and fading.

Travis let out a long breath. Grey did the same, only when he did it the breath was soundless. Now, all they had to do was keep still another minute before crawling for-ward and slightly to the right. They would lose their five-ton truck and have a long walk back to the warehouse, but given the circumstances it was a small loss.

The minute passed and Grey had just nodded to the others when a whistle blew and a voice began bawling: "Return! You missed them."

324

Even Grey was shocked. They were screwed. Lights were sweeping all around them as if they were being directed by the devil himself. Grey could only wonder who it was after them.

Chapter 29

Jillybean/Eve

Two days earlier:

"...Three," the Duke said, the gun in his hand as steady as if it had been welded to his flesh. Jillybean squinched up her face, ready for the bullet that would end her life. She hoped that the angels with their harps and their little round baby-bellies and their absurd wings would forgive her for all the bad things she had done. Her concept of heaven was ill-formed to say the least but one thing she knew for sure was that bad people didn't go to heaven.

Her mommy would be there and her daddy, too. Jane from down the street was a shoe-in because she was always so nice and Squatty, the old monster who couldn't see straight would be allowed in on account that she had never hurt nobody and it wasn't her fault that she was a monster.

But Mrs. Bennett wouldn't be there; she had been mean even back before. Neither of the two bounty hunters would be allowed, either, because they were bounty hunters and that's what meant they were as bad as anyone. And not Brad, because he had been bad from the beginning, or the Duke, neither. What could be worse than killing a kid?

She was about to find out.

"You are a tough one," the Duke said, with what sounded like admiration in his voice, as he pulled the big gun away. "A gun doesn't scare you. I suppose now-a-days guns aren't nearly as scary as they used to be. Too bad for you, because I know what is scary. Brad! Get some men and clear me a path to the first post."

Jillybean didn't know where the first post was, but anything that was scarier than being shot in the head had to be really, really bad.

As usual, she was right.

Horsemen of the Azael came galloping up and forged a wedge straight through the zombies. In their wake, the Duke strode along, pulling Jillybean by the wrist. The second they had crossed the dirt ditch where the zombies had once trudged, the little girl knew where they were going. They had passed the gruesome marker on the way into town and the swinging kicking bodies, hanging by their stretched hands still haunted a distant part of her mind, down deep in that black she had found herself in earlier.

In desperate fear, she began to pull back on the big paw of the Duke, but it was useless. He was a giant, while she was a tiny thing. Sure enough, their destination was the light pole where eight bodies hung from their hands.

"No, please, no," she begged in tears. Her little body lost all strength at the sight of the zombies with their crazy-long arms and the evil red gleam in their eyes as they stared down at the little girl. He dragged her on, her sneakered feet making parallel streaks in the dirt.

"Tell me where they went," the Duke answered. "By what route and I'll let you go."

That's a lie, the other girl inside of her said.

"Help me," Jillybean pleaded with her. Lies, half-truths, vagaries, and all sorts of deception were *her* strengths. If anyone could squeak their way out of this it was *her*, but it would come at a price. This they both knew. Perhaps the price was heaven.

Jillybean looked up at the monsters, terrified beyond all reason. The Duke would pull her up there by her hands and the monsters would eat her. She would scream and kick all to no use. It would be like a game of bobbing for apples and she would be the apple. They would take chomps out of her and slowly they would whittle her down to the bones.

"You want help?" asked the Duke, "Answer me. What route are your friends taking?"

One of his men came up with a length of rope. The man was young, young enough to see the terror in Jillybean's eyes and understand it. He swallowed hard, bobbing his Adam's apple up and down, yet he said nothing. The rope pinched, and the little girl cringed and cried, though not from the rope. The monsters were grinning down at her. They were grey where they had skin left. Where they didn't they seemed like living skeletons.

The terror that grew in the seven-year-old was too much for her broken mind to handle. She felt a great crack open beneath her feet and then she was falling out of the world. She fell with a whistling that slowly faded as her hearing grew less acute. All sight began to fade as well as she dropped deeper into the dark crevices of her mind.

She thought that she was falling but she was in fact hiding. She hid and there was no left to take over her mind and body except for *her*.

Eve, the other girl...the other twisted girl, grinned triumphantly. Jillybean and all her stupid niceness was only a memory now. She was able to pull her baby blue eyes from the monsters. She stared coldly at the Duke until his brows came down and for just a second he seemed unsure of himself. "I know where they will go," she said. "Untie me and I will tell you."

"No," he said. "Tell me or die. Those are your choices."

"And what happens to me if I do tell you?" Eve asked, still as cool as if they were talking at a picnic bench in a park and the sun was out and there were a hundred screaming and laughing children around them and everything was normal again in the world. "The reason I ask is that I want to see Neil and them die as much as you do."

The Duke's mouth came open. A grunt that was wholly unconnected to thought escaped him. "What the hell?" he asked, confused. Eve grinned up at him from out of Jillybean's eyes; her normally smooth face and soft lips twisted in a sneer.

"I told you she was crazy," Brad said from among the small group of men who had come to be entertained by another death. "She's bi-polar or schizo or something that there isn't a name for."

328

Finally understanding the extent of the girl's insanity, the Duke took a step back as if 'crazy' was catchy. "Crazy? I don't care if she's crazy, I just want to know if she is lying. Will she tell me where they've gone?"

Brad studied the little girl for a moment, before saying: "Yeah. She really does hate them. She'll tell you what she knows, though she might charge a price."

"I do have a price," Eve declared. "Get the jerk-face out of here." She lifted her bound hands to point Brad's way. "He is a liar. He said I would be a Lady, but that wasn't true, I know it. So get him out of here if you want to know anything."

The Duke considered and then waved a hand at Brad in a dainty gesture of dismissal. "We're wasting time, Brad. Go make sure the trucks are fueled and the men properly armed."

"Ha!" Eve cackled as Brad frowned. "See you later ass-butt!"

The Duke rounded on her and there was a magnificent air of anger all about him. "That's enough. Tell me what I want to know or I will string you up right now."

Jillybean wasn't completely gone. She was watching everything, looking out as if she were in a deep well where the walls were sticky wet and black. She wanted to scream: *Don't say anything!* but her courage failed her yet again. Her fear of the rope and the dangling monsters was too great and her words came out as a whisper that barely made it to her own ears.

Eve ignored her completely. *She* was in charge now and she was stronger than ever. "They went south on the same road Brad tookted us here on. Neil isn't very smart or creative. He'd be afraid to get lost to go any other direction."

"They're going back the way they came?" the Duke asked. "How far? What's their final destination?"

She answered with a roll of her eyes and a: "Colorado, duh." She then gazed south, somehow knowing where they were going. She pointed again with her two hands. "They're on that road, only they're not gonna stay on it for long. They'll take a different road to Colorado. But they aren't going to go there tonight. You shooted two of them pretty bad and if I know them, they're going to stop."

"Where?" the Duke demanded. Instead of answering, Eve held up Jillybean's bound hands which had the immediate effect of causing a burst of curses to break from the Duke's mouth. He yanked out a seven-inch hunting knife, but instead of cutting her hands free he held the knife in front of her left eye.

"Where?" he asked again, in a cold-as-death tone.

She glared at him over the tip of the knife. Not for a moment did she fear the knife or the Duke. That was the good thing about being her and not Jillybean. Stupid Jillybean was always full of fear. Sometimes for herself but more often than not she feared for others. It was stupid.

A string of dirty words screamed from the Duke's mouth and echoed in the night. "Where?" he demanded, throwing her down and leaning over her.

The back of her head hurt where it had struck the road and his knee on her stomach made breathing almost impossible. Jillybean would've cried, Eve knew, because she was a weak little nothing. Eve was the tough one. Eve could endure a little pain and a little shouting. She had been made to endure the pain Jillybean couldn't handle.

"Cut me free and I will tell you," she said to the Duke. Their eyes locked and her determination was a force. In a second, he gave up his anger, seeing that it wasn't doing him any good. When her hands were free, he picked her up and set her on her feet with an expectant and somewhat mad look on his face as if he was the one who was really crazy and just seconds from having a cataclysmic meltdown.

"I'll need a map," she told him. "Neil will give in and let Captain Grey try to fix Miss Marybeth only she's gonna die anyways, I know. But he will try and they'll need somewhere safe to stay."

"And you think you know where?"

She almost let out an honest shrug which would've been bad for her. She was full of guesses, many of them likely accurate now that stupid Jillybean wasn't guarding all the good knowledge. Now Eve was the smart one. "Yes, but only when I have a map. And I'll need to come with you, too."

The strange, explosive look on the Duke's face morphed into a look of wariness. "Fine," he told her, "but you'd better come through. And if you even think about escaping, I'll haul you up there by your intestines."

He grabbed her by the back of the neck and roughly propelled her up to the courthouse where the trucks were parked. The Duke's men were all over the place. Some were getting the zombies back into position, while others were getting ready to go into battle. A third group was tending the wounded from the breakout. There were ten casualties all told: four dead, three seriously wounded and who weren't given much of a chance to survive and three who had suffered only flesh wounds.

Brad broke the bad news to the Duke, adding: "We only have fifty-two men ready to go. We can count on another fifty arriving in the next few hours and another hundred over the next few days. If you want me to call up your Barons I will, but..."

"But what?" the Duke snapped. "But what!"

The volcanic anger caused Brad to step back. "But...all I was going to say is that this may not be the best use of your resources. I mean they may be more trouble than they're worth. We've all heard the rumors out of New York and Jack Wallins saw the remains of the River King's bridge, himself. They were the ones who blew it up. These people are dangerous, a little more dangerous than I realized."

"Here's what you're missing, Brad," the Duke said, clapping Brad hard on the back. "I am dangerous, too. Not only do I command armies of the undead, I also have a thousand men I can call up with a snap of my fingers and guess what?" He reached out a long arm and snapped his fingers under Brad's nose.

"Make it happen, Brad," the Duke said. "Send out riders to my barons and tell them I want them here as soon as possible. Those miserable bastards out there have something I want. I aim to get her back."

Brad nodded judiciously before asking: "And your brother, the king? Do we alert him as well?"

"Not yet," the Duke answered. "Let's see if we can take care of this ourselves, first." He looked down at Eve. "You had better come through for your own sake."

Though she smiled up at him, encouragingly, doubt crossed her mind. It was like a whisper of fear only that couldn't be possible since she had no fear. It gave her the chills and a shiver ran up her spine. It made no sense, which meant it wasn't coming from her.

"Stop it right now, Jillybean," she hissed. "You only think you're tough cuz there ain't no monsters around." The Duke gave her an eye, but also a shrug. He didn't care a whit about her. Eve saw the shrug and at first she couldn't understand it, then she felt suddenly brittle as if she were made out of twigs and that anything could break her; her bones would be blown out onto the plains where they would crumble in the first rain.

This thing, this loneliness staggered her. It was a force nearly as strong as fear and it was new to her and it was horrible.

"I said stop it!" she yelled, suddenly, bringing her hand around and striking herself across the face. The blow was loud in her head and sounded like a whip cracking to everyone around her.

The Duke grabbed one of his men. "Watch her. Make sure she doesn't hurt herself. I don't want her damaged. It'll bring down her price."

The man was the same youth who had tied her hands so painfully. Eve wanted to hate him but all she could think about was her "price."

You know what that means, a voice said inside her mind.

"I'm going to be sold."

332

A new, unpleasant sensation struck Eve. It was odd, akin to being seasick. She knew what it meant to be sold as a girl...Jillybean had looked up words that sent a new shiver running across her skin. She took a step away from the youth guarding her.

He put out a long arm and reeled her in. "You want a real slap?" he asked. "Cuz I'll give you one if you even think about running. You got it?"

At this threat, Eve felt the familiar fire that had brought her to the surface. With Jillybean's power of observation, she studied and memorized his features. Then she set him on her list. She would kill him the first chance she got.

"I got it," she said, through gritted teeth, Jillybean was still inside her making noise and bringing up crap that was best left undisturbed, but Eve was still strong. Let that stupid Jillybean mess around in her mind. It made no difference. "I'm still in charge and that's the way it should be."

This she mumbled so quietly no one heard all except for the little girl inside of her who realized she had made a big mistake. The Duke had never intended to string her up. Jillybean had been tricked and now she was alone in the Great Blackness. Her father was gone as were the cages filled with the people she had killed. There were no doors, no nothing. She was alone with no way out.

Eve heard her misery and laughed, though she did so under her breath. She was starting to understand what other people thought of as crazy and she didn't like the word applied to her. She wasn't crazy and she didn't need Jillybean to do her thinking for her anymore.

It made her feel superior.

Stupid was occurring all around her and it was difficult not to point it all out. The Duke's men were mostly young and seemed to rely on guess work to order their lives. Here it was the renegades had been gone for over thirty minutes and they were still not ready to go. The Duke began to scream them into the trucks.

Quite naturally, Eve went to the first truck, a big green army one, and began to climb in as her escort made useless noises of indecision. "I can't very well find your prisoners from in the back of one of these things," she said slowly as if explaining something to a younger child. "It is why I'm here."

"Right," he said, but still didn't look convinced.

A minute later, the Duke climbed up into the driver's seat. Eve was forced to slide up next to him as Brad and her escort, who was named Jimmy, also climbed in.

"You had better be able to find them," the Duke mumbled again, putting the truck into gear. He tapped his horn lightly and then progressed at a slow speed down to where the horsemen were driving the monsters back.

"I can't make any guarantees," Eve answered. "You guys took so long, they could be halfway to..." the name of anywhere suddenly slipped her mind. She couldn't even remember where she was born. It was Jillybean in her head, acting stupid again, trying to make everything difficult.

"...halfway to being gone forever," Eve said.

"Don't remind me," the Duke groused. "Just find them or I will string you up."

The threat washed right over her. She only feared being sold to some weirdo and even that fear was starting to fade. If it came to pass, she'd deal with the weirdo in her own way images of wickedly sharp knives came to mind.

The Duke flipped on his headlights when the last of his trucks had passed the monster barrier and their speed picked up. Eve was quiet, seeing everything in the high beams, taking mental notes: speed, direction, land features, monster patterns. They drove for ten minutes, passing the occasional dirt road. It wasn't until they sped past another, paved road that she saw something out of the ordinary.

In the headlights she saw just a simple monster staggering down the side of the road. It seemed mesmerized by the light and made no move to come off the shoulder to get at them.

"Turn around," she said. "We've gone too far."

"How do you know?" the Duke was quick to ask.

Eve mulled the question: was it easier to say: *Because I know* or was it better to explain the simple manner in which monsters moved? Whether it was toward prey or just in their daily meanderings, monsters acted in a manner consistent with Newton's first law of motion: A monster either remained at rest or continued to move in a straight line unless acted upon by an outside force. Had Neil come through here, the monster would've been in the road and not walking parallel to it.

"Because I know," she said. Though Jillybean liked to explain things so she could teach others, Eve liked the idea of having secret knowledge. It made her important. "Turn around."

"I can't believe I'm taking orders from a fucking kid," the Duke snarled as he slowed and made a three point turn.

He turned at the last intersection and sped south with his lights blazing. Fifteen minutes later Eve saw trash that was not in sync with their surroundings. "Stop!" she ordered. This time the Duke didn't argue and the truck shuddered to a halt. "Get out," she said to the Duke. His only argument was a shake of his head, yet he complied.

The four of them walked back to the trash. Eve squatted on the side of the road, Jillybean's knees jutting out in that frog-like manner of hers. "They were here."

"How can you possibly know that?" the Duke asked. "I get the feeling you're just running us around in circles so that your friends can get away."

The question seemed ridiculous on its face. "How do I know? The real question is: How come you don't? I get the feeling that the little squirrel you call a "brain" must have run out of nuts. Look! Bandages, with fresh blood! It's still wet. Weren't you listening when I told you that two of them were hurt? Lucky for you they're not far."

After that, her instructions were followed to the letter. She tracked the renegades to the city limits of Wichita but soon lost them; there were just too many monsters to make heads or tails of anything.

Brad had the map open on his lap. "They're probably trying to give us the slip in the city. We should skirt around the beltway and position men at each of the main roads heading west."

The Duke glanced at Eve who shook her head, her eyes zipping over the map of the city. "No," she said, quietly. "The only reason they would go into a city is to hide. They're not trying to escape just yet. With that fuel truck they could have just shot straight west in the hope of out running you guys. No, if that had been their plan, they wouldn't have bothered going through a city. It's too dangerous and would slow them down. No, they're hiding, probably to give Captain Grey time to try to fix the wounded."

"Ok," said the Duke. "The question is where? Do you know?"

"How could I know that?" she asked, astounded. "There are ten thousand places to hide in a city that size." Eve suddenly grinned, a wicked grin. "But I do know where they'll go, eventually." She pointed at McConnell Air Force base. "I'd bet their lives on it."

Chapter 30

Neil Martin

The mall was exceedingly dangerous. There were stiffs everywhere, slowly stumbling down the wide halls, crunching glass under their feet and sometimes gazing in through the broken display windows at this store or that.

Neil got a queer feeling when he first saw this. He assumed that it was some sort of deeply ingrained, programmed marketing scheme that had instilled the shopping behavior so deeply that even dead people couldn't help but shop. It was sort of sickening and he was appropriately queasy right up until he looked into the first store and saw someone lurking in the corner.

The 'someone' wasn't grey and nasty with the shredded remains of their last outfit hanging off their walking corpse. No, this someone was slim and pale, dressed smartly in blue jeans, a white shirt and a burgundy half-coat. In a blink, Neil broke cover and out zipped his Beretta.

"Careful, that's a manikin," Sadie whispered. "They bite if you get too close." The third member of their team, Connie snorted but otherwise remained to all appearances, a proper zombie. Neil wanted to reprimand Sadie for talking while in "character" however she had that twinkle in her eyes which was becoming rarer with each passing day.

"That's it? That's all the harassment I get?" he asked, stowing the Beretta back under his garments.

The twinkle grew and even under all of her zombie make-up, her grin was clear and honest. "No harassment, just a question: I couldn't help wondering if she reminds you of one of the inflatable girlfriends you had back in New Jersey?"

Neil grinned back, but only for a second, then Connie whispered a warning: "Stiffs coming, lock it up."

The grins forgotten, the trio went back into their routines and completed their mission in a proper dour mood. The mall really was depressing. What once was open and pretty and full of life was now dark and miserable and full of the dead.

Neil stumbled to a wall-mounted map of the mall, took a mental note of the destinations he had in mind and stomped away with the other two following him ten yards back. The sporting goods store was a bust—it had been ransacked and looted of anything valuable. The first electronics store, although it was in one piece, was also a waste of their time. It held little besides computer games.

Halfway down the length of the mall was the second electronic store, a place called: *Watt an Idea!* Neil rolled his eyes at the sign and slipped in. The place was darker than most and perhaps because of that, the shelves were still full. The only problem was that he couldn't tell what kind of merchandise it was, nor could he risk a light.

"Looks like this is where I come in handy for once," Sadie said, pulling one knee to her chest and stretching out her hamstring. She did the other leg as Connie looked on without understanding.

"I'll take your pack," Neil said. "Try to meet us at the food court in twenty minutes. If not, we'll meet at the truck in thirty-five." Neil wanted to tell her to be careful, but knew the advice would not be heeded and likely would not be needed. He took her pack and squeezed her hand. Then she was back in the large open hall stretching some more in an obviously human manner. She then started skipping away toward an escalator that was frozen in place.

Connie's eyes went even larger. "Is she crazy?"

Neil was already turning away and digging in his pocket for a flashlight. "No, she's just fast." He wanted to watch his daughter tearing up and down the mall, but he couldn't act the part of proud father, he had work to do.

As Connie stared at the gazelle-like speed and grace of Sadie, Neil flicked on his light and then whistled at the full shelves. "Jackpot!" he said. He filled their packs with two-way radios, batteries of every size, and even a remote controlled car that was a sparkling red version of *Jazzy Blue*.

"Turn around," he said to Connie. He unzipped her pack and shoved the car inside and as her back was to him, she didn't see him rub a sleeve across his eyes. The car reminded him that Jillybean's death was his fault. He knew that he had acted for the good of everyone in sending her back—she was dangerous to friend and foe alike—and yet he felt it had been cowardly of him to send her to detonate the bomb.

There hadn't been much fight in him when she had asked to go, there had only been rationalizations.

Neil shrugged off the thought and clawed through the shelves until he found what he was really after: a radio scanner. With it he could be one step ahead of the Duke. With it there was a chance at actually escaping. He actually kissed the box before sticking it in his pack.

"Let's get out of here," he whispered, turning off the flashlight.

They shambled back the way they came with even more care than when they had come in. The mall was like a hornet's nest that had been kicked over. Sadie was not in the food court, but Neil wasn't worried. She had her Glock and would've used it if she had been in trouble.

The two slipped through the broken glass doors in a most unzombie-like manner but went back to lurching and limping until they reached the five-ton. Still no sign of Sadie. Nervous, Connie climbed up onto the roof of the truck and tried to peer through the darkness for the teen. Neil went to work putting batteries in the two-way radio.

When he clicked on the first one and set the frequency he was in for a nice surprise: "*Possum* this is *Meerkat*. Come in *Possum*. *Possum* this is Meerkat."

Neil was quick to respond: *Meerkat* this is Possum I read you Blue. How do you read me?"

"I read you *Ford Explorer*. I am also in contact with *Wombat* and he is a five."

This brought a grin to Neil's face. So far the three teams who had gone out for electronics had succeeded and as each had answered with their designated code word, they were all safe. "Any from news from *Rat*?" This was Grey's codename, something he had lifted an eyebrow at when Neil had assigned it.

"Negative, *Possum*."

Neil checked his watch; it was early still and Grey had a lot of ground to cover at McConnell. Neil had wanted the entire twenty-seven person scouting party to hit the base, however Grey had felt a 'twitch' over the idea and had insisted that only his three-person team should go.

There was still plenty of time before Neil had to worry. "Gather your teams and meet at point Charlie, out."

Neil went to put the two-way on the dash and then nearly jumped out of his skin: Sadie had climbed up into the cab of the truck as noiseless as a passing cloud.

"Scared you?" she asked, in mock- innocence. He should have wrung her neck for frightening him like that, instead he grabbed her hand and squeezed. Grey wasn't the only one with a 'twitch' that night. Neil had a bad feeling; everything was going too easily.

They collected Connie from the roof top and then chugged their way back to where they had dropped off the other two teams. One had come up short in regards to antibiotics but had found an entire pantry of canned goods. They came hustling out of the night draped in grocery bags and grinning from ear to ear. The second team had just one bag, however it rattled with the noise of a thousand pills.

"Excellent!" Neil said with a huge smile on his face. They had found both pain killers and antibiotics. Things were moving along nicely—he didn't like it; nothing ever went this well.

Neil met the second truck at the meeting spot and the good news kept coming: five of the six teams had struck gold in some fashion or another. The bad news: no third truck and no Grey. With a growing anxiety making his insides shake, Neil decided to head toward the Air Force base, picking up the two teams Grey had dropped off along the way.

One had found radios and a six pack of coke in cans that had faded nearly to pink. The other team had found nothing in the vet's home but walking corpses. Still, the mood was high as the teams intermingled and talked about their night. They relaxed, thinking the hard part was over.

Neil fretted, unable to relax with three of his people missing. He stared down the road where he expected to see Grey's five-ton at any moment. Sadie was nervous as well. She hooked the power cord of the radio scanner and started searching. It wasn't long before she started picking up traffic in the form of garbled and static-distorted words.

"That has to be close," Neil said. "Tune it."

It took a delicate touch to find the right frequency and then they heard: "...over here quick! Jack saw something near the airstrip."

"Airstrip? Which one?"

"...the east side. Just like she said. We're moving to contain them now. Get your men over here, on the double."

A long moment went by as both Neil and Sadie stared at the scanner in disbelief. Then Neil was leaping out of the truck, yelling: "Mount up! Mount up! I think they've trapped Grey's team." The reaction of the group: only a slow look from one to another wasn't what he'd been expecting. Why weren't they racing into action?

"You *think* they trapped him?" Ricky asked. "Shouldn't we be sure before we go running off?"

Neil's disbelief was such that his mind took a full second to process this insane request. There were only two ways to deal with this: a calm discussion of the facts and the options open to them or a full-on screaming fit. Neil chose option two. "Either get your ass in that truck or we will fucking leave you right here. Now! Move it everyone. Right. Fucking. Now!"

His wrath was an elemental force and the group scurried before the smallest man in the group. He stood there seething until the last of them was in and the tailgates pulled up. Only then did he dash to the first truck and climb in.

"Nice potty mouth," Sadie said.

He grunted and then pointed to the map that sat between Connie and Sadie. "Get me a route down to McConnell then to the east side of the airstrip...wait, see if there's more than one airstrip."

There were, however, since they were all in a row it was logical for Neil to vector toward the furthest one. He was two hundred yards out, running without lights when gunfire rippled through the night. Next to the window, Connie sucked in a hard breath. Sadie patted her knee as if she were the one who was ten years older. "They're not shooting at us otherwise you'd see what looks like fireflies blinking at you."

Connie grinned, her teeth white in the black of the night. She was the coolest of the ex-whores, other than Deanna, and still her eyes were wide circles of fear.

Neil had to ignore her. His eyes and his mind were on the scene before him. There were three deuce-and-a-halfs on the frontage road bordering the airbase. Grey's five-ton was nowhere to be seen, but Neil knew that didn't mean much. He would've hidden it in the maze of houses east of them. What mattered were the ghostly shadows moving forward in the grass that grew as high as their thighs. Further on, far across the airstrip another four trucks came rushing up, disgorging forty or fifty men along the west side.

The danger was obvious. What wasn't so obvious was the evil mind behind the trap. Jillybean was out there somewhere. Even if Neil hadn't heard the words: *right where she said*, he knew the Duke wasn't smart enough to lay a trap for Captain Grey. It was Jillybean, or, more likely, it was the evil thing that had hid in her all this time growing ever more revolting.

That evil thing was Neil's fault. He had turned to that nasty force time and again, in order to save himself or his friends and by doing so he had allowed it to grow and take roots in the mind of the innocent creature that was Jillybean. Sadie had been right all along. He should never have relied on and burdened Jillybean.

Sadly, now it was time to right that wrong. He would kill the little girl if he could, but that was secondary to saving Grey. He drove the truck further on, looping it around the block so that he had an escape route he hoped wouldn't be under fire. The second he killed the engine he ran to the back to release the tailgate.

"Hurry! Move!" he hissed, trying to get the renegades to move faster. The Duke's men had been advancing into the field and it was only a matter of time before Grey, Deanna, and Travis were trapped, forced to either surrender, run, or try to fight their way out.

Grey wouldn't surrender and he would only run as a last resort. He would fight. It was in his nature. He would kill many of them but he would die in the end and he would be perfectly happy going out in an honorable blaze of gunfire. Grey had never liked the idea of 'using' Jillybean and he had been correct.

Time to right that wrong.

"Gather up," Neil said. No one was nearly as gung-ho as he was, except perhaps Sadie, who was right at his side, checking the load on her Glock. Neil found himself in an unenviable position: he had a battle to plan without the help of Captain Grey or Jillybean. He had no experience or training to guide him and his 'warriors' were afraid of their own shadows. He had to plan for fear.

"Here's what I think we should do," he said, thinking on the fly. He did a quick count: including himself there were twenty four of them. "We will split into two groups. I'll take the first group." here he tapped Sadie on the shoulder and then Connie, who was good under pressure. After that he simple pointed to the next few people in line.

"We will go straight out in a line, staying low, ok? When I say 'go' start shooting. We'll fire for thirty seconds and then we'll retreat. Crawl if you have to. The second group led by Ricky will take up a position on a slant…you know, a diagonal. Stay hidden until the Duke's men come after us and then, you know, light them up."

Ricky nodded slowly as if expecting more. "And then what? You guys run away and leave us in the lurch?"

Neil's mouth came open as his mind went blank. The only thing rattling around in his mind was a whining: *Do I have to think of everything?* "Uh, no, of course not. The first group will set up a second line further back. We'll shoot a few times to draw their fire and then we'll all scoot out of there. That should give Grey enough time to escape."

He looked around, basically hoping someone would come up with a better plan or at least point out the glaring flaws in his, which he was sure held plenty. All he received were shrugs and a lot of scared looks.

"Ok, then that's the plan. Let's go. First group, on me. When we clear these houses keep low and spread out." They crept between the houses, staying close together. When they got to the last of the houses facing the airbase, Neil saw that luck was with them. The spotlights playing over the airstrips and the tall grass, illuminated the Duke's men perfectly.

They were sitting ducks.

"Spread out and pick your targets," Neil hissed. He then grabbed Sadie, who was about to scurry off. She had to feel how badly his hands were shaking but she said nothing. "I'm going to try to get closer to their trucks. If something happens to me, I want you to lead our guys out of here."

Though she was just a shadow in black, Neil could feel her emotion coming off of her in waves. "Don't leave me all alone," she hissed. They were the last of their original post-apocalypse group—the list of the dead between their first meeting in New Jersey and right at that moment was long and sad. Too sad to think about just then.

"I won't," he lied, automatically. "I'm sure I'll be fine. Now Go." He nodded off to their right. She gripped his arm with surprising strength and then left him, slinking low and quiet like a stalking panther. The others followed her.

Alone, Neil slunk to the left. He didn't move with the same grace or silence. He couldn't afford to. He had to get much closer than the rest and he had to get in position before Grey was found.

Sacrificing speed for stealth, he rushed forward, stopping when he heard a single gunshot from the field. Though he wasn't an expert, he could have sworn it came from an M4, the same type of weapon that Grey carried. He was just stopping to try to catch a glimpse of what was happening, when there came a quick *pop, pop, pop* from his right. It was Sadie's Glock!

Just like that, a barrage of gunfire erupted down the line to his right. His team was shooting. Who knew if they had targets in mind or if they were hitting a thing? It didn't matter. Neil threw himself down and began squirming forward as fast as he could. He could see the legs of people just on the other side of the Duke's truck. At first they crouched and then, one after another, they rushed to the nose of the truck, using it as cover from Sadie's fire.

They were in a perfect position to die. Neil was twenty feet directly in front of them, hidden by the night and the tall grass. He didn't even need to jump up. The Beretta came to shoulder height and his finger began squeezing off rounds right into them. *Bam! Bam! Bam! Bam! Bam!*

Two went down screaming. A third twisted as he tried to run; he fell hard against the hood of the truck and held it with two hands as if trying to wrap his arms around it in a hug. His gun clattered to the ground and, out of mercy, Neil didn't waste another bullet on him.

Guns were going off all over the place and there was no way for Neil to know if he was being targeted or not. It almost didn't seem to matter. He had a job to do, a mission. The warrior in him was full of passion for the fight. He leapt up and ran for the truck just as someone darted from behind the hood. Flashes of light blared in his face and the hot zip of lead whistled past him as he threw himself to the side, rolling to his right in the grass.

He came up with his gun trained but, whoever had fired from around the nose of the truck, hadn't dared to come around. Neil wasn't about to go charging at a pre-pared foe, but with time against him, he also couldn't just lie there in the grass. The answer to his dilemma was right in front of him—the deuce-and-a-half, a smaller version of the five-ton, was still a tall vehicle; there was plenty of room for a small man like Neil to crawl under it.

With gun blasts erupting every which way covering the sound of his scraping along the pavement, he had crawled practically to the other side of the truck, when he saw a pair of black boots, the wearer of which was crouching in wait for him at the front of the vehicle. From three feet away, Neil fired his Beretta. There was a scream. A gun fell, forgotten and then there was a heavy thud as a man came down next to it.

It was a large bearded man; it was the Duke.

Neil brought the gun up to point into his face. "Please, don't," the Duke gasped.

The simple plea made Neil hesitate. He wanted to dissect his choices, mull them over, only he had no time. The renegades' gunfire was slacking off. They'd be retreating any second, as he had instructed them and then Neil would be caught alone. He had to decide to take a life right there and then.

He thumbed back the hammer and fired very deliberately into the tire next to the Duke's face. As the truck settled in that direction, he said to the Duke: "Let us go or I will kill you. This is your only warning."

The Duke nodded, but if he had deception in his eyes the pools of shadow hid them. Neil scrambled backward, keeping his gun pointed at the Duke all the while. Once clear of the truck, he leapt up, ready to run, when he spied a small face staring at him from the half-cracked driver's side window.

It was Jillybean. Again a crucial decision presented itself: should he grab her and run? Should he abandon her and get out of Dodge before it was too late for him, too? Should he kill her?

She helped his decision immensely by tossing something out the window at him. It was roundish, more egg shaped than anything and right away he knew what it was. Now there was no time for thinking. His world slowed. With a smile gleaming in the night, Jillybean disappeared from the window; this Neil saw only in his periphery, his focus was on the grenade which seemed to float, mockingly in the air.

How many times had he been in this position in his life? Picked last for backyard baseball because he couldn't catch the easiest popup? How many sets of keys had gone clattering to the ground when tossed innocently his way? How many hand grenades, a second from turning him into human goo had been thrown at him? Just one and he couldn't afford to miss it.

His Beretta went tumbling away as he stretched his fingers, forming a basket that couldn't help but cradle the grenade if it landed neatly, which, of course, it did not. The grenade bounced off the heel of his palm, then off his wrist and the tips of his fingers, as he fumbled lamely for it. With a thunk it landed at his feet.

Was there time to pick it up? Was there time to run? Both answers were the same: no.

Jillybean was too smart for that. This wasn't her first grenade. She knew there was a delay and she would've accounted for it. There was a clunk as the passenger side door was thrown open. The little girl was running, knowing the grenade was on the verge of going up.

Neil found himself frozen between the choices of running or trying to scoop up the grenade—a full second of indecision passed and then he was out of options. He would be too slow to pick it up and too slow to run.

Chapter 31

Deanna Russell

The Duke's men turned on command and came stalking back through the tall grass. Someone yelled: "Shift to your right by five big steps!" The entire line did so, putting one man on a course to walk almost over Travis' legs.

Travis looked over at Grey; his eyes were comically big, but there was nothing funny about what was about to happen. They were going to be discovered for sure and the only question was if they were going to fight and die, or surrender and still, probably die.

Grey had his M4 at the ready position, answering the question.

The man came closer and closer. As he did, the sweat built up on Deanna's palms and her pistol became slippery. She regretted having turned down one of the M16s. Those had a sling. There was no way she could drop one and lose it in the tall grass as she was worried she would do with her handgun. Hell, she didn't even know what kind of gun it was. It was black and heavy and had a magazine that she could slip in and out with a little button on the side.

When she had accepted it, she didn't think she would need more than the pistol. She was going to be with Grey, what more protection would she need?

Another step closer and, almost too late, Deanna saw that she was aiming at the same man as Grey—as if he would miss a target so close. She shifted her weapon toward the next man over, twenty feet away. It was a much iffier shot. The man was little more than a crouching shadow. Even if it were bright out, the shot would be...

Grey's M4 suddenly seemed to explode. It seemed louder than ever, like a bomb. The line of men froze, all except the man who had been shot of course. He just toppled right over. When he thumped into the grass, all hell broke out.

Deanna popped up just at the height of the grass and fired her pistol three times; her target dropped but she had no clue whether she hit him or not. He might have dropped down to hide which seemed like an excellent idea. The entire run of grass was suddenly a maelstrom of gun flashes, bangs, and the deadly whisper of bullets zinging past.

She was crouched but that wasn't good enough for Grey. He came flying over and smashed her into the ground. She could barely breathe with him on top of her. Instead of feeling protected, she was panicked. She needed him off of her so she could run. Running was a very sound idea in her opinion.

From her vantage, the entire world was gunning for them, which made Grey's grin all the more strange.

"It's Neil," he said, his lips tickling her ear.

It's Neil? What the hell did that mean? She was having trouble putting two and two together. Not even when Grey whispered: "Start crawling," did she know what he meant. He pointed back the way they had come and gave her a shove.

Far across the open fields and the airstrips, she could see tiny army trucks and even tinier men jumping off of them. He wanted them to crawl that way? Wasn't their five-ton the opposite direction? And what in God's name did he mean by: *It's Neil?* Neil couldn't be here and, if he was, then why the hell was he shooting up the airstrip? The bullets coming from behind the trucks seemed far more deadly than anything the Duke's men were doing which was, essentially, cowering in place.

Grey pushed her. Reluctantly she started crawling. This time she crawled less like a professional soldier and more like an earth worm. Though her face was scraping the dirt she managed to crawl faster than she expected and in seconds Grey gave a light whistle and pointed to the right.

She turned ninety degrees and as she did a real explosion lit up the night. It looked as if one of the closer trucks on the east side of the strip had just erupted like a volcano. Grey gave her all of one second to blink at the sudden onset of light before he smacked her foot. He mouthed the word: *Go!* She went.

There was a pause as the firing died down and then the Duke's voice could be heard screaming over the dimming violence of the night: "They're getting away!"

Someone, seemingly very close, muttered: "Who the hell cares?"

"Get your ass up!" a new voice demanded.

The line of men stood. There were gaps here and there, but Deanna couldn't believe so many had lived through all that shooting. She was surprised any of them had. But she was also happy—the men were advancing away from her!

Grey crawled up next to her and jerked his head for her to keep going. It was the perfect chance to escape. The Duke's men were moving in a crouch toward the frontage road and had their backs to them. The three, Travis had come along as well, got to their hands and knees and began scurrying faster, moving parallel to the line of men.

Fifty yards into their fast crawl, the night again came alive with the sound of guns. This time it came angled from the side.

"Excellent," Grey said. He jumped to his feet and then helped Deanna up. He didn't stop to watch the show. He jogged in a straight line, keeping the fight on their right. Only when the firing died down again did he change course, this time angling in the direction of where he had left the truck. In Deanna's eyes the course took them dangerously close to the fighting—to her, anything within ten miles was too close.

"They won't be advancing anytime soon," Grey explained, seeing the fear on her face. "They won't want to taste that medicine a third time. Damn, Neil, you really came through this time." His grin stayed in place until they neared the frontage road and heard the roar of engines. "Stop," he hissed. His head was cocked to one side, listening. "Was that two trucks or three?"

Travis, who looked sick, said: "I think it was three."

Grey grabbed Deanna's hand and said: "This way," just as he began to run at an angle. "There's only one smart direction to take to get out of here. Let's hope Neil is smart."

They ran. It seemed useless. The five-tons were slow to start but they were faster than humans—unless, of course, they were being inexpertly driven. Even from a distance they could hear the grind of gears worse than ever. "Sounds like my Neil," Grey laughed. He wasn't winded in the least. However he saw Deanna was flagging and said "I'll stop them."

He kicked it into high gear and left her and Travis huffing. He didn't have to go far. Two five-tons were making uneven progress down the road. The first of them took an alarmingly wide turn just in front of them. Grey ran up next to it and began hammering on the door.

Deanna heard an alarmed: "Where's Neil?"

She was nearly spent as she came up and saw Sadie pointing back the way they had come. "I-I...he-he didn't make it. The explosion I-I think. You should get in. He told me to leave if..." The girl in black couldn't go on. She blubbered as if she was crying out the last of her soul.

Grim-faced Grey looked back the way the trucks had come. He stared for a long time before he began nodding as if coming to grips with the idea that Neil had died. "Travis," he said in a quiet voice. "Drive this truck. Deanna get in with them. We need that third truck if we're going to make it to Colorado. I'm going to get it."

"Not alone, you're not," Deanna found herself saying. It was stupid she knew, but she couldn't leave him. She didn't know if she could ever leave him again. Neil had died alone. It wasn't something she could ever contemplate happening to Grey, not right then. He didn't argue and neither did Travis. He wanted out of there and fairly flew up the side of the truck.

Grey didn't wait for the trucks to leave, he ran between them with Deanna's hand in his. He ran softly, his step making barely a sound. She, on the other hand, ran in a shuffle, her feet so heavy she could barely pick them up.

She never remembered being this far out of shape—then she recalled that it had only been that afternoon she'd been in a coma. It was no wonder that her muscles were quivering with exhaustion.

"Thank God," she whispered, when she saw the five-ton sitting alone in the street just as they had left it. Grey hurried her to the passenger side and began to lift her into the truck when he stopped with her halfway up.

A looming figure had appeared out of the shadows, freezing the captain in place. He'd been caught unable to defend himself. Deanna's gun was in her holster, but she was no quick draw.

There was dead quiet moment before the man said in a deep husky voice: "Captain Grey?"

"Yes," Grey said, slightly shifting his weight. Deanna took that second to tighten her grip on the truck's door. Grey was a blink from making his move. The man was too close for his own good. He was about to find out how fast Grey was—she hoped. She hoped Grey would be the quicker, or they would both be dead.

"Good. I was afraid you had left without me."

"Neil?" Grey asked.

Neil stepped closer. His face was a bloody mess. Dark blood was streaming in multitudes of tiny rivers from a cut somewhere in his hair. "Yes?" he asked, in a somewhat dazed and tired voice.

"We thought..." Grey began and then laughed. "Never mind. Let's get you out of here. You don't look all that good."

Deanna stepped down to help Grey get Neil up into the cab. She knew that they had to be running short on time. The Duke had to have heard the trucks. If he was going to chase after them, it would be in the next few minutes.

The second Neil was in the truck Grey ran around and got in as well. He thumbed the start button, asking: "What the hell happened to you?"

"It was Jillybean," Neil answered after swallowing, with a sticky sound, as though he was scraping old blood from the back of his throat.

"Her," Grey said, angrily. "I knew she was behind this."

Neil shook his head and then nodded. "Yes and no. She threw a hand grenade at me, but...but she hadn't pull the pin. I swear it was the bad girl in her who threw it, so why didn't she pull the pin? She was trying to kill me, I know it. She had that nasty grin of hers...but she hadn't pulled the pin. It makes no sense."

Expertly, Grey threw the truck into first and gunned the engine. They spurted forward and a moment later he was in second gear and gaining speed. "So if there was a pin in the grenade, how come you look like that?"

"Oh, right," Neil said, touching the blood on his face. "Well I threw the grenade at this other truck and uh, and uh, I'm not too sure what happened. I think I got hit by something when I was running away."

As Neil touched his head again, Deanna stole a peek in the side view mirror fearing that she would see the Duke's men in an angry mob chasing after them with guns and torches. The mirror was all together black.

"Anyway, I kinda found myself lying in the grass," Neil said, with much grimacing as he explored his wound. "There was some shooting and yelling and who knows what, so I just staggered over to the trucks, but they left just as I came up. Pretty much all I knew at that point was that I had to get out of there and that this truck had to be nearby, so I went searching for it. That's it. That's my whole story."

"Well it's a damned good story," Deanna told him. "Sadie will be happy to see you. She was a wreck."

He sighed. "I worry about her so much. She's lost everyone. In a way, she's been kicked around like Jillybean. I just don't want her to, you know, lose it."

"Then we'll get her to Colorado," Grey said.

Neil glanced at his watch. "Yeah. We'll go tonight," he said. Grey snapped his head around but Neil only gave him an exaggerated shrug. "Look, the Duke knows we're here in the city. If he hasn't already, he'll throw roadblocks over every way out of here. We'll be trapped and it'll be just a matter of time before he finds us. We're basically out of ammo, our water will be gone by tomorrow and, I'm sorry to say this, but Marybeth doesn't have much of a chance, anyway. We are leaving, with or without you, Grey."

"I say we go," Deanna said. As much as she liked Marybeth, she was desperate to get out of the city. To her, the city felt like the gaping mouth of some tremendous demon and somewhere in the dark sky its teeth were starting to close in on them.

Grey drove in a smoldering silence for a long time. It wasn't until they pulled into the warehouse and saw Sadie cast to the side, alone and weeping, that he nodded his head. "Ok, we'll leave in twenty minutes," he told Neil. "Deanna, help Neil down and see that his orders are carried out. I'm going to go talk to Michael."

"I'm fine," Neil told Deanna. A second later he collapsed in her arms as he tried to get out of the truck. "Just a little woozy," he said. "I think I might need some stitch..." he stopped as Sadie came rushing up.

"You?" she said and then began to blubber and smile at the same time. "Never count out my Neil. Never. That's what I told myself but I didn't believe, but I swear I will from here on out. I swear." They hugged and wept. Deanna backed away, fearing that they were celebrating too soon. The jaws of the demon were closing. The Duke wouldn't let them go so easily. He had Jillybean on his side and she knew too much and she was just too smart, and she was a demon in her own right.

"Ok people!" she yelled. The renegades were casually sitting in groups, talking about the one-sided battle, each boasting about how many of the enemy they had killed. The way they spoke, one would have thought they had routed the Duke instead of fleeing into the night, and that two-hundred dead bodies were stretched out in the tall grass waiting for the crows to come feast, instead of the four or five that was the likely number of dead on the other side.

They quieted only when she screamed: "Hey damn it! We are leaving tonight. In fact, we are leaving right now, before the Duke can get his men in place and trap us. I need you all to gather your stuff, right this moment and load up. You have five minutes to load your gear and five minutes to pee. Now move or you will be left behind."

Fred Trigg opened his mouth but, before he could speak, a gun was pulled on him. Sadie had pushed Neil behind her and drew her Glock in one fluid motion. "Say one word, I dare you to, because I am sick to death of your negativity."

Fred looked around with a hurt expression, but no one wanted to cross Sadie, not when they saw how deadly serious she was.

Deanna wouldn't have been so blunt, but she didn't chastise the teen, since she was just as sick of Fred as anyone. "You have your orders, Fred," she said, with a tongue of ice. "They do not involve running your mouth." Fred snapped his lips closed and left. Deanna turned to Neil and asked: "What do you need to get us out of here?"

"A map," he answered, simply enough.

Deanna found the map and, as Neil studied it, the renegades ran about getting everything together. To one side, Grey spoke quietly to the Gates family. "I've convinced them to come with us," he told Deanna. "Explain to Neil that I'm going to need ten minutes to get Marybeth in the truck."

Though Deanna felt that every minute counted against them, she got Neil's permission to delay their departure. He used the time to assign positions in each of the trucks and to disperse the two-way radios so that each of the four vehicles would be carrying one.

With a minute to spare, the renegades were ready to go. Grey drove the lead five-ton with Deanna by his side. With them were Sadie and Neil. The map was spread on Neil's knees and the scanner was set in front of Sadie, who worked the dial with the delicate fingers of a surgeon.

"Thank God we found those painkillers," Neil said. "This is going to be a bumpy ride." No one knew what he meant until he told Grey to stay off the highways. They trundled directly through the city, driving on neighborhood streets, taking directions from Sadie who used the scanner to steer them away from the Duke's men who were numerous but undisciplined when it came to using their radios.

They crept down alleys and back roads and even when they reached the outskirts of Wichita, they didn't chance the main roads. Neil pointed them across the last main highway north of the city. On the other side of it was a field of overgrown wheat. "Right through there. Keep north and we'll run into a dirt road in a few miles. It should lead to this other road here that runs west a little."

Before the field, there was a ditch—Neil was right about it being bumpy.

"Just one second," Grey said, and then fumbled with the contraption he had taken off the undead airman back at McConnell. He loaded new batteries into the night vision goggles and when he put it across his eyes he grinned; he then showed Deanna the view.

Although the night was extremely dark, the night vision goggles painted everything in shades of green. She could see, sixty yards out, almost as if it were day. Suddenly a grayish figure passed in front of her view. "Is that a...is that a zombie?"

Grey took the goggles back. "Yep. These also register, in laymen's terms, on the infrared scale, meaning these babies can see heat." His excitement was contagious and everyone grinned at the prospect of having an edge over the undead, however the excitement died quickly as they went down into the field.

The ride was slow and choppy. Deanna felt like her teeth were rattling in her head by the time they picked up the dirt road a half hour later. The ride smoothed but because of the frequent zombies, their speed didn't pick up all that much. Many long hours were spent that night driving on dusty back roads, few of which were paved and even fewer of which possessed names; they were just lonely ruts meandering between farms.

They all grew bored and, really, that was a good thing. There was no sign of the Duke. They had slipped the net thrown out for them in such a manner that even Jillybean couldn't find them...or so Deanna hoped.

As the eastern sky began to brighten behind them, Neil found a barn to hole up in for the day. As they had the marvelous and somewhat magical goggles of Captain Grey's, Neil decided it would be safest to travel only at night.

That was a fine idea, except that with the sun beating down on the barn it was blazing hot and with the hundreds of flies buzzing about made sleeping nearly impossible. The one good bit of news was that the water from the farm's well was clean and cool. Everyone had a chance to drink to their heart's content and to bathe.

In the late afternoon, Grey stitched Neil's head and then went to check on Marybeth. She was still alive and she now had antibiotics working in her system—it was the only good thing one could say. She looked dreadful, nearly as grey in the face as a zombie. They loaded her up with extra painkillers for the drive that night.

So far they had progressed a little over a hundred and eighty miles from Wichita. During that night, they spun another three hundred miles under their wheels. Again, as day threatened to undo the night they found a farm with a large enough barn to hide the trucks and to sleep in. That day was a repeat of the one before. The only change was when a herd of zombies went by. There had to be ten thousand of them moaning and kicking up a dust storm.

They were gone by sunset and the renegades, after refueling, were as well. Just after ten that night they saw a sign that buoyed their spirits: *Welcome To Colorful Colorado!*

For the first time in a few days they broke out fresh grins. "Where are the mountains?" Deanna asked, peering out of the window. "Why can't I see them?"

Grey laughed and pointed westward. "We're still on the eastern plains. We have another two hundred or so miles."

In the old days that would've been a run of about three hours. Neil refused to get caught up in the excitement of being so close to their destination and kept them on the rutted and sometimes washed out dirt roads that had never been all that well maintained to begin with.

Still, by dawn they were very close to the looming Rockies. Deanna's spirits soared while next to her, Sadie could only manage a sour smile. "Sarah would've loved to have seen this," she said.

"And Eve," Neil replied.

"And Ram," Sadie said, growing quieter.

"And Jillybean," Neil finished in a whisper.

Neither Neil nor Sadie would say anything after that and it was up to Grey to find a spot to hide the trucks. They had looped far north of Denver where the land was still flat and open. He couldn't find a barn that would fit all four vehicles and had to settle for one that could hide two of them. The other two were parked snugged up close.

Other than the four people in the front of the lead vehicle, no one wanted to stop. "We're an hour away," Fred cried, throwing his hands in the air. "We could be there in time for breakfast." Their food had run out the day before and everyone was hungry.

"No," Neil said, calmly, while next to him, Sadie's hand was on her Glock. "We don't know the state of things. The mountain roads can be blocked with ease. A trap could be set up in minutes. And we aren't an hour away. We will go north to Larimer County, cut west on I-14 and then south to Estes. If all goes well it will be a four hour trip."

Fred, with an eye on Sadie, began to get riled, but Neil put his hands out. "Calm down. I only plan to stay here until noon. That gives us a six-hour rest. Use it wisely. We have no idea what may be in store for us."

The noon departure was set back an hour due to the unexpected arrival of another of the mega herds. It came down out of the north making a collective noise that sounded as though the earth were dying. Deanna watched from an upper window in the barn and shivered at the sight. Grey came and put an arm around her. They stood that way for a while, saying nothing and yet, just like that, the strangeness between them disappeared.

When the herd had wandered south, Neil clapped his hands. "Time for the final lap."

The renegades, including Marybeth who was alive but so pale and skinny that she was closer to a wraith than a person, loaded into the trucks one last time.

The trip to Larimer County was made in no time. I-14 was harder to manage. The road was narrow, at times only a single lane. Frequently they came across the remnants of rock slides and a few times, boulders had to be nudged out of the way by the powerful five-ton trucks. Still the sun was high in the sky when they were finally able to turn south onto a series of mountain roads that were smaller still, practically only paved trails. They were bordered by sheer rock walls on one side and heart-stopping cliffs on the other.

The views were magnificent. The air smelled pure in a way that reminded Deanna of something, but of what she couldn't put into words. "The air smells good," she said.

"What you smell is life," Grey told her. "We don't have too many zombies up here. Down there," he pointed at the plains far to the east, "the land is sickened by the dead walking across its surface. Here, it's just...it's just better."

They wound in and out of the mountains and Deanna, despite the fresh air, feared an attack at any moment. Then they came around a bend and saw below them a beautiful lake and a wide land between great mountains. Everything was green and beautiful and wonderfully calm and quiet.

Deanna didn't need to be told they were looking at Estes Park, Grey's home. Nothing had ever seemed so inviting. She began to cry.

Chapter 32

Jillybean/Eve

The little girl, the innocent one, had her one triumph. For days on end, or so it felt, she had languished in the black depth of her own mind. During this imprisonment it was as though the glue holding the remains of her life together was failing and that at any time she would drift apart and become nothing, like the thin smoke disappearing above a candle.

For the most part there was little to do and less to see, though every once in a while she caught glimpses of things: a monster staring into the headlights of a truck, a stained bandage that she knew had been used to dab the blood away from Marybeth's wound, an air-control tower that somehow she understood to be at a place called McConnell Air Force base, though how she knew this was beyond her.

Those were just glimpses and yet each had been important in some manner unknown to her. Now she saw something that was of such grave importance she stood up and strained to see through the twin lamps of her eyes. There was Neil Martin crawling backward in some tall grass and, closer, she saw a hand grenade being held in small fingers. It was a second before she realized: those were her own fingers!

"Oh no," she whispered, knowing what was about to happen.

"Oh, yes," Eve said, and then cackled like something evil...like a witch.

Eve was going to kill the man who had once given her a very pretty doll for no reason except to make her happy. He was the man who had taught her to catch fish, one of which she had named Chedrick. He was the man who always ate yucky beans so she could have something better, like ravioli. He was the man who tucked her in at night and who made her brush her teeth. He wasn't perfect by any stretch, but he always tried his best.

He was going to die and he didn't deserve it.

The only problem was that Jillybean was powerless to stop his death. Eve owned the body they shared.

"Then why are you still here?" a voice asked. "Wouldn't it be easier on everyone if you just faded away?" It was not the voice of Eve, or her father or Ipes or any of her past victims. It was her own voice. A figure came to Jillybean and she felt a new fear: that of being revealed. She tried to hide in the shadows from the figure. But the figure was all in white and wherever she went, she exposed the flaws in the world.

Jillybean ran. However it wasn't like before, where there were doors and walls, here was only darkness and when the figure came, the darkness departed, leaving the shadow cast down by Jillybean's body the only evil in their presence. Slowly the little girl turned.

It was like looking into a mirror or the silver waters of the clearest lake, only this little girl was glowing.

"You made her," the girl said, pointing upwards. "Just like you created all of this around you. Just like you created me, and before me, you created the specter of your father and before that, you created Ipes."

"No," Jillybean said. "Ipes was real. He had a real body and everything."

The other girl shrugged. "He was as real as I am."

There was silence between them, and yet there was noise as well. The Duke was groaning over his shattered ankle; the guns were barking from all around, and there was someone crying for their mother in the high grass.

"How do I un-create her?" Jillybean asked, also pointing up.

The girl looked sad. "You can't. You can only bury her somewhere deep and hope she never comes back. But know this, she will fight you."

Jillybean already knew that, though in truth she knew all of this. "Why are you here?" she asked.

"Because," the figure said. "You don't trust yourself. You see yourself as only a frightened little girl in a scary world and you know that if your daddy, who was so much smarter and so much bigger than you, could die, then what chance do you have? So in a sense, I am here to show you why *you* are in here. You are here because you are afraid. Remember, S*he* trusts herself completely. *She* has no fear."

Jillybean looked up again and saw the small hand—her own hand—reaching for the grenade's ring. When she looked back, the little girl in white was gone. Jillybean didn't know what to do, she only knew that she couldn't pull that pin. Neil would die and the world would be darker, and a much worse-er place without him in it.

But how to stop it from happening?

The hand reaching for the ring was moving in slow motion and Jillybean squinched up her face in concentration, demanding, on some level for the hand to stop, even though she knew it would mean another confrontation with Eve. Amazingly, the hand stopped. The hand clenched on nothing. It made a fist and did not open again.

Eve didn't seem to notice. Her laughter filled her as she threw the grenade out the window. It was a sad laughter to Jillybean. It was evil and since when did she have evil in her? *Really, when did that happen?* she wanted to know. Had it been all the 'splosions and all the fire that made her head hurt sometimes that had turned her that way?

Jillybean felt the world shift. Eve was moving. She expected the hand grenade to 'splode and she was leaping out of the truck with the ease of a monkey, coming to land next to the Duke. His face was red and sweaty. His left ankle was a bloody mess. He was in pain. Eve sneered at him, hoping he would die.

Jillybean felt sorry for him—his ankle had to hurt real bad.

Eve wanted to run, however Jillybean refused. The Duke needed help. That was so obvious that she didn't need the help of any spectral figure to know it. She concentrated and her feet held firm to the ground as if they

362

had grown roots. Somehow she was gaining control of her own body again!

"But he's the bad guy," Eve hissed.

"Yes, but so are you," Jillybean replied.

"Am not!"

"Then help him." Jillybean knew that good guys helped people. They helped people even if it meant risking their own lives. She had risked her own life to save Ram, more than once. The same was true for Neil and all the renegades. "That means I really am a good guy," she said in awe. She had never before made that connection.

"I am good," Jillybean declared.

"Are not!" Eve hissed. "Remember the bottle?" A new image: Jillybean holding the poisoned bottle to the baby's trusting lips.

Jillybean felt her stomach lurch. "That was you," she said to the evil girl.

The Duke was watching the little girl go back and forth but turned as there was a thunk of something heavy a few feet from him. Jillybean turned as well and saw the grenade she had just thrown at Neil roll under the back of the next truck in line. There was no pin in the grenade, now.

Realization struck Eve and she screamed: "Run!"

Fear rippled up Jillybean's little body and, involuntarily she took two steps before a thought came to her: *What about the Duke?*

Eve hissed like a snake: "Let him die."

Jillybean's first thought was: *That's what a bad guy would say.*

Neil never did think like Eve and neither did Ram or Captain Grey—they were good guys. They did things, often scary things, to help others. They were brave.

"You used to be like that," Eve said, with poisonous breath. "But not anymore." In a flash, Jillybean remembered the stark, raving mad fear that had turned her insides to jelly when she had been on the verge of being hauled up by her hands to be eaten to death by the swinging monsters.

That was when she had lost it. That was when Eve had come back stronger than ever. She cackled again as a wave of goosebumps blistered Jillybean's arms and back. Her feet started to lift—Eve was gaining control again and she was going to run. Her body felt like it was being used as a see-saw. It went back and forth as Jillybean and Eve gained and lost control.

The logic-minded girl considered the see-saw and had a sudden insight: What was the fulcrum of their back and forth battle? What was the pivot that meant control or lack thereof?

An answer came immediately: Fear.

The more afraid Jillybean was, the stronger Eve became. The harder that Jillybean fought against her fear, the weaker Eve grew.

The figure in white had told her to trust herself. "That's what means being brave," Jillybean said and then, in the heat of the moment, she turned and threw herself across the Duke, because that's what Neil and Ram and Captain Grey and Sadie would have done. And it's what Sarah *had* done when the bounty hunter had come to kill Jillybean. She had pushed Jillybean behind her and had died to save the little girl.

The grenade exploded. A quarter-second later the truck's fuel tank went up like a volcano turning night into day and baking Jillybean's back. The concussive force of the twin explosion socked her a millisecond later. It was too much for her already damaged brain. She passed out, but, even as she did, she knew that, for at least that moment, she had won. She had been good and she had been brave.

When she opened her eyes next, she found herself in a strange room. Its walls were made of white sheets and there were beds, the ends of which could be seen jutting from the hanging sheets. A lady sat on the bed next to her. She stared at the floor with dull eyes. One of her hands was chained to the metal headboard. There was a red ring around her wrist where the chain had bit. Her nose was bent and her lips swollen.

Jillybean turned from her and looked to the right. There was another woman in another bed. She too was chained. Jillybean knew her. Her name was Kay. She had been one of the ex-prostitutes who had escaped from the Island. They had never talked all that much. She went to wave at Kay, only her little wrist was snaked by a chain as well and she could only raise it as high as her shoulder.

"You're awake!" Kay whispered.

"Yes," Jillybean answered somewhat dismissively. Being awake was obvious, how to get out of the chain was not. She rattled her chain, testing its strength and then began to examine the metal frame that made up the bed.

"She's awake!" Kay screamed at the top of her lungs, causing Jillybean to nearly jump out of her skin. "Hello, she's awake!"

One of the Azael came hurrying up. It was a woman, dressed in a thousand scarves that rippled as she walked. "Shut the hell up," she cawed. "I can see she's awake."

"Well, the king said he wanted to see her when she woke up," Kay shot back. The lady turned and hurried back the way she had come. When she was out of hearing range, Kay turned to Jillybean. "You got to go along with me. I told them that you were, like, this real special genius but that only I could control you."

Jillybean was still waking up and trying to figure things out. Her head had a painful thump to it and her mouth was dry as a tortoise shell. Eve was still inside of her. Jillybean could sense the other girl in the back of her mind waiting for a chance to get out again and run things, but she was weak now, very weak. Jillybean knew what made her strong: fear. But fear could be controlled and thus Eve could be as well.

The idea of control brought Jillybean around full circle. "You can control me?" she asked. "Why would I need to be controlled?"

"Because they think you're crazy. Please go along with it for my sake. They'll send me back to the Island if you don't. I can't go back, Jillybean. They'll do things to me there. Real bad things. You don't want that, do you?"

"No, of course not."

Kay grinned. It was more creepy than happy. "Then you'll do it? Good...good. Just act nutty until I stroke your head."

Nutty? She wasn't sure how to act nutty. Was that what squirrels did when they ran up and down trees? No other answer presented itself and so she agreed. "Ok, I suppose. Say, where are we?"

"Nebraska," Kay answered, her eyes twitching back and forth. "We just got here yesterday. You've been asleep for two days. They wanted to send me off but I convinced them I could control you. So remember, play along."

Eve grew stronger. Everything Kay had said made Jillybean's fear greater. Asleep for two days; that didn't sound good. Nebraska? As far as she knew Nebraska was on the other side of the planet and as far from safety as the moon.

Her fear ratcheted up when the silk-clad woman returned, accompanied by a soldier wearing the bright armor of the horsemen. The man was tall with blonde hair that ran to his shoulders. He grinned down at Jillybean and the little girl knew him: it was Brad Crane.

"You live a life as odd as your name, Jillybean," he said. She wanted to mention that he had a bird's name, but didn't know if that would sound 'nutty' so, instead, she cheeped once like a chick. He only smirked while Kay nodded in encouragement.

The three marched out of the long room which was peopled only by sad-looking women and furnished with beds that had stained sheets. Jillybean had seen a room like that once before: at the Piggly-Wiggly. Women had been raped in that room.

Yes they had, Eve said in her ear. *Here, it's women and little girls.*

Now a trembling began in the pit of Jillybean's stomach. The three marched through the halls of the building, what once had been a hospital, and then outside into the sun. Before Jillybean could get her bearings, they crossed a street and entered a library.

It was the only library Jillybean had ever seen with armed guards in front. There were more of the shining armor-wearing guards inside. And further on was an open area where a dozen men sat around a great fancy desk of glossed wood. All the men wore the shining armor and all had long beards. Rather like very tall dwarves they were to Jillybean. They were eating and drinking and talking, seemingly all at once.

When one of them saw the three approach, he cleared his throat and the rest fell silent. The largest of the men, a veritable giant in Jillybean's eyes, stood and gazed down at the little girl.

"This is she?" the man asked, glancing to his right where Duke Menis was seated with his bandaged foot propped up.

The Duke said only a single word: "Yep."

"Well then, come in Jillybean," the man said, gesturing her forward. "I am King Augustus. My brother here tells me that you are some sort of genius of destruction. He says that you are a veritable goddess of chaos trapped in a little girl's body."

There was a pause and Jillybean, who had forgotten that she was supposed to be acting 'nutty', answered: "I don't know what that means."

"It means you have a unique ability when it comes to causing ruin. Let me see if I have this right. You were the one who sank the two ferry boats in New York, in spite of the fact that they were being guarded by fifty men?"

Eve was growing gleeful inside of her. Jillybean tried to ignore her as she fidgeted and answered in a small voice: "Yes, Mister King, Sir."

"And you destroyed New Eden with an army of zombies?" She nodded and he grinned. "And you blew up the River King's bridge after escaping from a jail cell, again under the eyes of the guards?" She shrugged and nodded, feeling the weight of the accusations pile on her thin shoulders. "And then you blew his barge sky high and then held his backup bridge hostage?"

"Yes. Mister King, Sir, but not all of that was my fault. Those people were being bad."

"That's not the question here," the King said. "The question is if you did all that, and how?"

Jillybean couldn't lift her eyes from the floor. She nodded a small nod, saying: "I know about bombs and such, at least, a little."

Kay stepped forward quickly and put an arm around Jillybean's shoulders. "She knows more than she's letting on! I would say she is worth a thousand of your men, but only I can control her, so if you want to use her, you need me."

The king moved around the table and stood, towering over Jillybean, who felt she had all the strength of daisy stem compared to him. Inside of her, Eve started to dance and sing: *He gonna eat you, Jillybean. He gonna eat you right up, Jillybean.*

"Is this true?" he asked Jillybean.

Jillybean was just remembering her promise to Kay. She cheeped like a chick again, but she did so with fear-filled eyes.

Next to them Brad shook his head. "It's a bold lie, your highness. The girl is definitely bonkers. She's got a split personality is my guess. Her other 'face' you might call it, hates everyone and everything. She'd help you without an issue. She loves the idea of killing. However, this Jillybean is more of a goody-two-shoes."

"So she really can't be controlled by this woman?" the King asked, gesturing at Kay.

"Oh, no, your Highness. Kay *can* control Jillybean, watch." Without warning, Brad grabbed Kay by the back of the hair and threw her down on the tiled floor. He then slapped her hard across the face so that Kay's chin went skyward and her eyes crossed.

Jillybean was frozen in shock at the sudden violence in front of her and, even as she stood there slack-jawed, Eve started taking control—first her fingers went numb, then her toes.

"Look at me, Jillybean," Brad demanded. "You are going to do what I tell you or Kay gets another slap. Is that clear?" Jillybean nodded. Brad looked to the King. "What would you like her to do?"

King Augustus grinned appreciatively and said: "Nothing for now, Brad. Let's hold her in reserve, just in case."

Duke Menis tapped one of his crutches on the table. "Don't waste such a gift. Keep her nearby—of course keep her chained, she's a dangerous one, but keep her nearby. She's very insightful as I have explained."

"Sound advice," the King said, walking back around the table and seating himself in the place of honor.

Eve was dancing and singing all the more. Jillybean had to stop her before she got out of control. Whatever these people were planning Eve would only make it worse. She was gasoline to their fire. "Whatever you want from me, I won't do it," Jillybean said, gritting her teeth. "I'm not afraid of you. None of you." Though the men chuckled, Eve quit her dancing...only she knew that Jillybean wasn't lying.

"Oh, you may not be afraid, but Kay here is really, really afraid," the Duke said. "When you hear her scream you'll do what we want."

"And what is that?" Jillybean asked, her voice surly and her eyes hard. Jillybean was willing to risk a beating if only to stop Eve.

The King's eyes narrowed at her impolite manner but he answered her regardless. "Quite simply, you'll help us destroy the people of Colorado. They sit astride the only route to the west. I've been looking for an opportunity to start a war and my brother and his foolish desire for a woman has given me just that excuse. All of this... all of your running around the country making an uproar, has turned almost everyone against you and by extension the people of Colorado. I'll have my war in large part thanks to you."

"And you plan on using this girl?" one of the bearded men asked. "We have four thousand men and half a million stiffs. What do we need her for?"

The King grinned like a wolf. "I am sure we don't, brother. I am more than confident that we have the power to destroy our enemies, however," he paused and smiled fondly at Jillybean. "It's nice to know that I have this little monster on my side."

Jillybean shook her head. "I'm not a monster, you are! I'll never be on your side," she hissed. She was a sight to see: this tiny thing with her fists balled and her face splotchy red.

"Really?" the King asked. "Brad, a demonstration if you please."

The little girl pursed her lips, steeling herself for the blow she was sure to come, but Brad turned to Kay and beat her with his closed fists. Kay wailed and screamed in hysterics and begged Jillybean over and over again to do what the King wanted. When Kay's blood was scattered on the tile like rain drops, and her voice became hoarse and her face was battered and ugly, it became too much for the little girl. Jillybean leapt at Brad with her hands clasped and begged: "Please stop. I'll do whatever you want."

Epilogue

Sadie

The girl walked among the fields of the valley, running her fingers over the golden tips of wheat. She then went to where the barley was laid out in perfect rows and breathed in deeply.

Her heart was calm for once.

Sadie had been on the move for so long that the last week of doing absolutely nothing was the very healing she had needed. She had seen too much death, and felt too much pain, so that when they had first come into the valley and the others had danced around in a great big circle hugging each other and crying, Sadie only shook her head and looked around at the surrounding mountains, wondering where the next vile enemy would come from.

She hadn't joined any celebration, nor had she feasted with the General or bothered to meet this officer or that lady. She had slept little, waking constantly to go look out at the heavily mountainous horizon, picturing in her mind, where the next battle would take place. And when she looked into the stern but handsome faces of the soldiers, she did so searchingly, looking to see if one of them was the next villain they would have to fight.

Only gradually had sleep come to her that week and only gradually had she felt a return to normal. She fought it every step of the way because she was convinced that the people of the valley were only living the dream before the nightmare. In her mind, she felt that here was no way this land of peace could last.

Captain Grey had walked her around the battlements, to show her that their walls were tall and strong. There were only three ways into the valley and each was narrow and easily guarded by walls of cement, rolls of concertina wire, deep moats, and men with heavy weapons. Grey pointed out the sniper positions in the rear and the machine gun nests on the concrete walls.

He showed her the artillery and mortars and he could've shown her a nuclear bomb for all the difference it made to her. So far, no wall and no force had ever been enough. The renegades weren't just unlucky or jinxed, they were damned.

But slowly, the serenity of the mountain valley with its picturesque views, its abundant game and large crops had worked its magic on her. Ever so gradually, she felt herself relax. There she was breathing and feeling once again, and only the day before Neil had introduced her to a boy her own age and she hadn't glared at him while keeping her hand on the butt of her Glock.

The other renegades were fitting in and adapting nicely. Fred Trigg was already starting an opposition party to General Johnston. The General was a very friendly and fatherly man who wore his afro buzzed a quarter inch off his scalp; its edges were so perfectly angled that Sadie was sure that a ruler had to be used in the clipping of it.

Due to his seniority, Grey found himself in command of an infantry company. He threw himself into the job and soon his barking voice was ringing throughout the valley as he drilled his men, mercilessly.

Deanna had bloomed like a flower and had to beat the men away with sticks, though when it was found out that Captain Grey had his eye on her, everyone gave way. This same blooming seemed to have occurred among the other women, as well. No one asked about their experiences before coming to the Estes valley. It was considered rude.

Other than Sadie, Neil was the last to allow himself a moment of peace. For the first five days, he had accompanied his apocalypse daughter to the barriers that were set up a few miles outside of the valley at the narrowest points. He would look east in silence and then take Sadie's hand and walk back without saying a word.

The day before, when she had come to collect him for their daily inspection, Neil had said: "I don't think I'll go today. I'm good."

372

Now, there in the warm afternoon sun, it was Sadie's turn to say: "I'm good."

She laughed suddenly, but stopped just as quick, as something caught her eye. Instinctively, she went into a crouch, the steel-like muscles of her legs bunched, ready to dash. There was a crow hopping around in the cornfield thirty yards away. Less like a gazelle and more like a cheetah, Sadie suddenly burst into speed, racing as fast as she could straight at the crow.

Just in time, the black bird looked up from its feast and leapt away, jawing at the sprinting girl in strident tones as it flew away. "You better run!" she cried, as she switched gears, gradually slowing her pace and watching the crow glide away. With interest, and with a touch of sick premonition, she watched the crow fly further and further away.

It flew away to the east where there were quite a few little dashes in the sky. Alarmed and not understanding why, Sadie began running along the curving road that headed down to the barricades. As she ran, the little dashes grew bigger and bigger until she saw that they were crows, hundreds of them, wheeling in a cloud.

Using the pull of gravity, Sadie covered the two miles in the time it normally took to cover one. She ran right up the wall and without asking, started climbing one of the ladders leaning against it.

"What the hell are you doing?" one of the soldiers asked. He seemed amused at Sadie's antics. Every day he had been on guard when she had come down and every day he had stared at her unabashedly. She had noticed but pretended she hadn't.

"You better ring your alarm," Sadie said, climbing down the other side. "Call your re-enforcements, or whatever you have to do to get more men down here right now!" She pointed at the crows; there were so many that they formed an ominous cloud.

She ran down the road, coasting now, not wanting to burn out her legs, knowing she'd have to run back when her fears were confirmed. In minutes, they were. She rounded one of the many bends in the winding road and saw below her a nightmare come true. A titanic horde of zombies was pushing up the narrow road.

From where she stood, huffing air in great gasps, she guessed there were five thousand of them, and those were only the ones in sight. There was no telling how far back they stretched.

As she stood there with dread curdling her stomach, the guard came rushing up. In one hand he held an M4, in the other a radio. "Oh, God!" he said, between breaths.

"Call your general," Sadie told him. "Tell him that war has come to his gates."

The End